David Ferrie opened the door. He wore a mortician's grin.

Saving JFK   *Frontispiece (Page 187)*

time travel twins

SAVING JFK

W. GREEN

ZIPPY BOOKS

VELOCITER · SECURUS · ERUDITIO

Time Travel Twins: SAVING JFK by W. Green
Copyright © 2010, 2022 by William R. Green.
All rights reserved
.
Published by Zippy Books
325-809-805 ZippyBooks.com

Frontispiece Illustration by A.T. Olsen

ISBN-13:
978-0615682792 (Zippy Books)
ISBN-10:
0615682790

This book is dedicated to:

Abraham Bolden

U.S. Secret Service

In Memoriam

John Fitzgerald Kennedy

1917-1963

and

The United States of America

1776-1963

TIME TRAVEL TWINS
By W. Green

Saving JFK
X-ooming FDR 1932
X-ooming FDR 1933
X-ooming FDR 1934
Saving Trump

Zippy Books

"The first step in liquidating a people is to erase its memory. Destroy its books, its culture, its history, Then have somebody write new books, manufacture a new culture, invent a new history. Before long the nation will begin to forget what it is and what it was. The world around it will forget even faster.

...The struggle of man against power is the struggle of memory against forgetting."   -Milan Kundera-

CONTENTS

-Chapter I-

The Time Machine

Zak Newman reached ground zero. His pulse raced. Nervous, excited, surfing a wave of anticipation. Alive in the moment, he loved the feeling. He looked down. His right foot rested on a mottled bronze plaque embedded in the concrete. Gingerly, he used his boot to clear away sticky spider webs laced with dead leaves and bugs: *The Chess Corner. Donated by the University Club of Mystic Heights. 1976. Celebrating America's Bicentennial.* He thought of the "good old days" as he read the engraving. Knee-high weeds overran the people-sized game board, raggedly defining the edges of its paint-peeled, cracked concrete squares. Massive World War II memorial columns supported a classical stone entablature that ringed the game-grid. It was an imposing, almost foreboding enclosure. Standing in the middle of the chessboard, Zak looked about warily and then fixed his gaze downward, imagining his destination directly below—Dr. Currant's secret underground bunker. Was he ready to travel time? Too late now to debate that.

A hot summer breeze brushed his face, whistled through the memorial colonnade, and slid down the cliff edge, stirring the waters below. In the distance, a couple of small sailboats bobbed about in the blue of Smuggler's Cove. His mind drifted. It was a scene from one of the photos in the Mystic Heights Historical Museum. A half-century ago, this place, known then as Mystic Memorial Park, with its scenic view and surrounding woods, was a favorite camping spot for the local residents. But no one camped out anymore, and few people ventured into this now desolate, weather-beaten forest. Across the protective waters rested the quiet town of Mystic Heights. A low, early evening sun raked across the colorful roofs in a shadowy play of light and dark. The gold-capped, faceted cupola roof of Randall Tower, the science building of Cordwell University, and the tallest structure in the town reflected sunlight into his eyes. He gave up his squinted gaze and checked his watch: 19:11. There was no time for second thoughts. He had four minutes to get in position.

Although he had not seen either Emma or Ethan, he knew that each had stood on this same chessboard the previous two half-hours. His thoughts focused on finding his place. "F3—white horse," he muttered to himself. He wished he had arrived a few minutes earlier. He knew he didn't have much time. He had to be on that square in three minutes. He focused on the chessboard. It was difficult to know one side from the other. Decades ago, white and black chess pieces had identified the two sides, but eventually, hungry people stole them for the scrap metal. With thirty seconds to go, Zak took his position on what he hoped was the G1 square. He jumped two squares up and then hopped one square left, positioning his feet to ensure he was in the exact middle of the square as Dr. Currant had stipulated. He checked his watch: twelve seconds to spare. He waited. The *TimeTravelle* was about to transport him to its secret location—thirty feet straight down into A.C. Currant's laboratory. Zak knew using the time machine was the only way to enter the bunker, but he would have preferred the old-fashioned way, a few flights of stairs and a door. No such luck, he thought. Sweat rolled out of his pits and down his sides. He glanced at the bay again. The little boats skimmed the water. Except for the screaming of a gull circling above, all was quiet.

Then he felt movement. He couldn't tell if he was moving. Or maybe the world was moving—it was like riding in a subway tunnel. Images flashed along on either side. A persistent hum coursed through his ears. No panic—no pain—but nausea crawled up his gut. His knees knocked with a rush of fear-released adrenaline. Seconds, minutes, or hours may have passed. He had no real idea. He was lost in time and space. Then the floor came up abruptly and whacked his feet. The impact shook his body. Everything stopped. He ran his hands over his face and rubbed his eyes. He was breathing rapidly. His heart beat in his ears. Then, faintly, as if in the distance, he heard the laughter that grew louder with each new breath. Bright lights clouded his vision. He fought to activate his senses.

"Welcome, time traveler Zak. You have arrived. You look pretty good considering that you just dove through thirty feet of solid granite."

Zak recognized the rich, baritone voice of his friend Ethan. He looked about and smiled sheepishly. "*Echale ganas!*. I made it." He gazed about and found the Twins, Ethan and his sister Emma, along with Jacques Dufour and A.C. Currant, standing in a semi-circle in front of him.

"Have a seat, Zak. Something to drink? I'll bet you need it," said Dufour as he handed him a glass of ice water. Zak sipped. Still frazzled by his recent strange transport, he gazed blankly at his beverage benefactor. Dufour was a wisp of a man who spoke each word clearly, cleanly, and with only a slight hint of an accent. But Zak remembered it had taken the better part of his senior year at Mystic Heights High School to feel comfortable listening to the French-born American history teacher as he attempted to explain the intricacies of *The History* to a class full of semi-comatose, hormone-filled teenagers. "Face it," Zak had spouted off one day in class, "*The History* is boring...it's a religion. All doctrine...no fun, no controversy, no anything. It's like when everyone's parents went to church back at the turn of the century...boring." He held that opinion until about six weeks ago when Dufour asked: "What if we had a time machine and we could travel back into history to witness it?" This one question seemed to ignite the sleeping students in robust discussion, contemplation, and second-guessing of *The History*. Zak and "the Twins," as everyone called them, pushed the topic in and after school, resulting in a series of events leading to their meeting today in Currant's underground lair.

"All right. Everyone's here. Let's move along." Zak slid aside, and Dr. A.C. Currant took control, as usual. He was a tall, straight-backed, thin man with salt and pepper hair. His face was delicate yet handsome, deceptively placid. He wore a wide, white smile that captivated those around him and relaxed their defenses. He was accustomed to having things his way for more than seven decades. Friendly and personable, thought Zak, but always in charge.

"Back to the past. Everyone knows Thomas Arthur Vallee killed the President in Chicago on November 2, 1963." A.C. Currant punched out the words staccato. "Three quick rifle shots...one to the lung, one to the heart, and one to the head, and John F. Kennedy was dead." He placed his gun-barrel-simulating finger on his chest and his temple as he itemized the former President's wounds. "The question is, what do *we do* in 1963? We will only have a maximum of twenty-eight days to complete our mission. After that, the *TimeTravelle* turns into a pumpkin. And when that happens, we will be roadkill on the highway of time...ready to be scooped up by the time-cops. I say we take a quick look at this JFK thing. Have a little fun. Maybe do a little sightseeing. And return home."

"Warren Wright...the great detective." Currant laughed lightly. "I know he's your father, but he works for the government. He's a crippled government-hack now. How valuable can his opinion be?"

Emma Callan-Wright squirmed in her chair in the corner of the gray, concrete-walled laboratory bunker. Unlike her twin, she had straight, raven-black hair, pale skin, delicate features, and an elegant, calming presence. Her green eyes narrowed as she cleared her throat. "That's not a fair assessment of our father, and you know it. He worked for the FBI for eight years and fourteen years as a private investigator...when that kind of position existed. He was the best. He has a wall full of awards and commendations."

As Currant paused to catch his breath, Zak looked at his long-time friend who had remained, throughout Currant's monologue, seated serenely in a lab chair like a leopard in a tree. But even when still, Ethan Callan-Wright's body language spoke of action. His solid face and wavy, sun-streaked hair gave him the look of a well-traveled mariner older than his seventeen years. Zak sensed he was about to pounce. Ethan jumped out of his chair. Expanding to his full commanding height, he glanced at his sister Emma, then at Zak and Jacques Dufour, before returning his eyes to Currant, waiting a moment before speaking. "No disrespect, Doctor, but we've beaten this one into the ground. Emma and I talked to our father. He says there will be enough time to get settled into the time zone and figure out what really happened to JFK...at length. He says we should do an extensive investigation of the crime. And I think Warren Wright's opinion trumps your opinion regarding the feasibility of this whole operation."

A.C. Currant circled the lab. His ever-present crisp, starched, white jacket rustled as he walked about. He looked up at the ceiling as if he was acquiring direction from a higher being. Then he shook his head gently from side to side as he walked up to Emma. She sat poised, waiting for a response. Looking down at her, he maintained a smile as he spoke. "OK. My apologies, Miss Callan-Wright. You are correct. Your father's current bureaucratic berth is not a true reflection of his former skills. The world is changing...generally not for the better...and it isn't easy to retain one's greatness."

"Like you, Professor?" Jacques Dufour stroked his koala bear beard and smiled.

"*Touché*," Currant muttered, then said something unintelligible under his breath before continuing. He walked into the *TimeTravelle*—the intersecting double-arched metal structure that dominated the room. Currant stood under the bridgework and spread out his arms Christ-like. His outreaching fingers waved in the air between him and the downward legs of the metal arches.

He stood on one of the jump blocks, a rubberized, textured platform directly below the center of the arch, and looked at the four people seated before him. His face appeared radiant, almost demonic, in the rainbow-like sparkle-light that beamed off the highly polished surfaces of the massive device. "I invented the *TimeTravelle*." He stretched out the last syllable with great emphasis, lacing the name with a Francophilian tinge, adding unnecessary gravitas. "My humble import may be questioned, but the *TimeTravelle* is the greatest invention in the history of the world." Like words from an old pulpit preacher, his bold proclamation echoed off the concrete walls.

Emma glanced at Ethan and smirked every time Currant squeezed out the words "*TimeTravelle*."

Simultaneous with Currant's pronouncement, Zak Newman spun around on his lab stool. "Hey, Professor, aren't you afraid your shouting will be heard by *MOM*?"

Currant stared at him, his face offering pity on the cognitive limitations of Zak's cranial capacity. "Aren't you afraid your pretty-boy body is going to fly off that spinning stool? Think about it...eighty inches of steel-reinforced concrete walls, floor, and ceiling. Electronically swept every five minutes. Physically accessible only to those who can operate the *TimeTravelle*. Your *MOM* is out there scraping information off toilet room walls. She's digging around in your neighbor's garbage. She's interviewing children on the playground, plying them with candy to get them to reveal their parents' every indiscretion, every wayward thought, every strange delusion. But she cannot penetrate my dreams, my world, my greatness." He leaped off the platform into their conversation circle with surprising grace for a seventy-three-year-old. "We are isolated here. We are in this place only. Well, in this place and in the distant past, when we use the *TimeTravelle* to go to such a place...we are free from the ever-present, super-nosy, busybody, nauseous nanny-state. Feels good, doesn't it? Feels like 1955 again. Sunlight and fresh breezes flapping crisp white linens hung out to dry." He paused for a moment, his eyes rising toward the ceiling as he seemingly connected to a lost moment of his youth. "Screw *MOM!* Let's get on with it."

"So let's take a vote. Who's for going back to 1963?" asked Dufour. "Before you raise your hands… I know this was my idea originally. But remember, I brought it up as a thought-problem in history class. At that time, it was just an idea…a way to explore history…a way to gain a different view of the JFK assassination. Now, thanks to Professor Currant and his remarkable device, we can turn this thought-problem into reality. We can go back and witness history. As you know, these are dangerous waters. Any challenge to *The History* is heresy. It is…"

"We know that, Mr. Dufour," interrupted Ethan. "That's why we need to do it. You're the history man. You know things took a wrong turn beginning with JFK's death in Chicago in 1963. Something happened." Ethan looked out across the room before resuming. "Something changed in the world when they blew his head off. And I don't care what's found in *The History: Our Past,* which I know is a *sacred text.*" He rolled his eyes. "We've got a chance to see what *really* happened. I'm not convinced that this one guy, Thomas Arthur Vallee, just happened to get a job in that warehouse at just the right time. And in just the right place so he could do the nasty. I know about opportunity knocking. I know he was the lone gunman. But let's just assume for a moment that he had help. Maybe the 'how and when' of his quick execution by the cops was just lucky. Maybe, but…"

Zak set his water glass down on a nearby table. "Don't forget all the changes that happened because JFK died. History changed. The Cuban Invasion. The death of Castro. Twenty years of war in Vietnam. The Johnson impeachment, and everything else. We have to go. We owe it to ourselves. Maybe if we find out the truth, the truth will set us free."

Emma Callan-Wright got out of her chair. At five foot nine, she was a full head shorter than her twin brother but physically imposing nevertheless. Zak always said she got the looks—*and* the brains. At this moment, she gave Zak a look of disgust. "I'm surprised at you, Zak. Think about it. We're talking about possibly changing the course of history. If there is a real mystery, maybe it's one we don't want to solve. Changing history is a dangerous business. You might not even be around if we tweak it too much, Mr. Artificial Womb Baby #6297. How do you know what will happen if we go back and snoop around and make changes?"

"I thought you were an adventurer, my lady. Maybe you should get into a wheelchair like your father," said Currant with a smile.

"Don't be obnoxious," she said as she glared back at him.

"Zee vote..." suggested Dufour, in tension, his voice regressing to a natural French accent. "Who 'ez for going?"

The four males raised their hands quickly. Emma looked at each, squishing her lips, then slowly raised her hand and smiled. "Don't worry, I'm in. 1963, here we come. But let's be very careful not to squeeze the goose of time too hard. He might just bite our hand and change everything."

Zak looked at Ethan. He was smiling, too, but to Zak, he had the look of a man who wanted to goose the goose.

A.C. Currant held a clipboard before him and checked the notebook chart. "OK, kids. I've got a to-do list that won't quit. We've really got to study the customs, clothes, clichés, and citizens of Chicago in 1963. We'll need old money. We'll need old technology. We need to train on the *TimeTravelle*. We've got *mucho* work to do."

Ethan ran up the ramp of the *TimeTravelle* device, stood on a jump pad, and spun around, facing his audience. "Will this baby work, Doc?"

Currant smiled with a boyish grin. "Sonny boy...we will have the time of our lives."

"Right. But have you time-traveled with it?"

Currant seemed flustered. "Well. Technically, no. But it has performed perfectly for physical transfer, and the computer runs for time travel have gone like clockwork. No pun intended." Currant chuckled at the sound of his own words. "I'm certain it will work perfectly. After all, I designed it." He smiled broadly and extended his hands, palms up as if to end the discussion.

"So what you're saying is that it's untested, and the four of us are test dummies?"

"Well, I would call us all 'pioneers'...."

Ethan sucked in deeply and then exhaled. "OK, Doc. It's your funeral too."

"Please, Ethan. Skip the melodrama. It will work. And remember, I was alive in '63. The *TimeTravelle* will get us there. I'll keep us from making stupid mistakes. Dufour will stay here and monitor *The History* for any disruptions. You can do your junior detective digging. Your sister can worry, and Zak can eat some of the finest fast food ever cooked in the best greasy spoons in Chicago. This will be fun, my friends. It will be a gas."

LOG of Zak Newman --- June 26, 2028: 22:13

I have been told my handwriting is very legible, as it should be since I have been practicing this skill my entire life. In a way, I am a 21st-century monk. I can make my pen produce writing on paper, which, like the typical monk's efforts in the Middle Ages, can be read only by a small minority of the populace. For me, it is simple to decipher the swirls, dots, and slashes that form the letters, words, and sentences. But for most, such writing looks as quaint as Chinese sinographs—very interesting but meaningless. I can thank my mother (the wonderful surrogate provided by the A.W. beta program) for this skill. She started my longhand career when I was two years old. How she knew what was coming, I'll never know. But she knew, and I was given this unique skill. Thanks to her, I can write a log in private. My thoughts are mine to myself—so long as I successfully keep the log hidden from MOM. She, our government within the government, has, of course, forbidden the recording of these thoughts. It's probably verboten just to think them, but this log is now an unimportant and minor transgression since we have decided to time-travel to the past using A.C. Currant's astounding device. I will never know how he can keep that thing a secret while every written, spoken, or imagined idea of every person in the country is captured, cataloged, copied, and coded. Still, he is a certified genius, or so he says. We'll find out how smart he really is once we begin our voyage across time.

I can't say enough bad things about MOM. She has location-revealing nano-implants delivered into the bloodstreams of unsuspecting children when they are immunized against disease; mind-control devices force-

feeding mental poison to the masses; monitoring cameras and microphones in every inch of public space; police armed with sound detectors able to listen in to "private conversations" from a half-kilometer distance; and sensing devices including X-ray machines in every police cruiser that identify every license number, every occupant, and everything and anything in a person's vehicle.

MOM *is like a nasty, nosy dog with very bad breath— totally invasive, always in your face, everywhere and nowhere, sniffing about without reason—just an annoying pest that will never leave you alone. She always claims to be working in everyone's best interest, but nobody wants her, and nobody likes her—she's a bitch. I've been told that many years ago, people and politicians discussed MOM's limits. Some suggested that a government's role should be to maintain a free flow of ideas and accomplishments by protecting the people from outsiders or insiders who would interfere with the American Dream, as it was then called. But after a while,* MOM *poked her wet nose into everybody's life— according to her, to help "them" because they could not possibly help themselves. She became nosier and nosier, and she kept improving her senses of smell and memory until, like a good coon dog, she could even identify a person with an unwanted idea from her doghouse on the moon. She created IfraGuard, a stoolie program that allowed children to rat on their parents. Eventually, people stopped talking about ideas that* MOM *might not find acceptable. People speculate that within the last few years, she has perfected her ability to read minds at will from a distance just to verify that no one is contemplating doing anything, which would upset her plans. This long- distance mind-reading could be just a wild rumor, but I notice more people humming to themselves as they walk about in public. Maybe they're trying to stifle their thoughts. After all, if you don't have a thought, it can't be read. As A.C. said so boldly—in the safety of his underground bunker: "Screw MOM!" I hope her mind-reading machine isn't focused on me right now. She wouldn't like my misty misgivings about life in America in year 2028—nor my longing to taste the freedoms of the past via the* TimeTravelle *device. Everyone has reasons for going back in time. A.C. wants to prove his genius, and Ethan wants to solve the mystery of JFK's death. I think Emma wants to keep Ethan out of trouble and maybe—just maybe—straighten out this screwed-up world we live in by gently tweaking the past. And for me, MOM has made life thoroughly boring, predictable, and confining. I just want to swim naked in the wild river of time.*

END: 06-26-28

-Chapter II-

Creating a Legend

Ethan's eyes scanned the refrigerator's interior, finally resting upon the jar of natural strawberry preserves that his father had brought home from his recent travels. He loved the *real* rather than the *artificial*. The combination of the preserves over some rough bread and a cup of hot coffee provided him a satisfying breakfast. It was a quiet morning late in June. On this clear day, the low morning sun cut through the kitchen windows and reflected brightly off the crisp white tile floor. He mulled over the texture and taste of his toast as he stared blankly at the small quiet pond and two ducks drifting in the blue water. Tiny birds flitted about the tree branches of the surrounding still misty woods. His mind drifted like those ducks. Even though he was seventeen, his father still provided treats, like the strawberry preserves, as if he were a little boy. Ethan warmed to this thought as he downed the last bite. The motorized stair-chair sounded the arrival of his father, Warren Wright. He assumed it would be at least a couple of hours before Emma made her morning appearance. Since school let out for summer break, she had returned to her natural sleeping mode—late to bed, late to rise. "Morning, Dad," chirped Ethan. "Looks like a good one, doesn't it?"

His father rolled into the kitchen. A skilled operator of the latest *gyromobe* device, he brought the machine to a neat stop in front of the coffee station. Then, he activated the caffeine delivery by pushing his screen icon, a tiger, which immediately yielded one large mug of steaming black coffee. With his first sip, he sighed. "Good stuff. Can't live without it."

"You got me hooked," said Ethan. "Coffee," he sipped, "is every detective's elixir." He smiled. "How are you feeling today, Dad?"

His father retained solid masculine looks, black hair smattered with gray, and one of the few mustaches in the country. His upper body was muscular, but his lower body was a withered wisp. Wright looked up from his cup, "Not bad...not bad at all...better than dead," he muttered, almost to himself. He brushed back his hair with his free hand and shook his head gently from side to side.

Sensing his father's angst, Ethan thought about the terrible night five years ago when the news arrived that the detective had been wounded by a bullet to his lower back. He endured a series of complex surgeries, and only his powerful will to live allowed him to survive what should have been a deathblow. Ironically, the shot that paralyzed him came from an off-duty policeman who just happened by at the moment Warren Wright was about to capture two very desperate criminals. The old cop was trying to help when one of the men pulled a gun. In response, the cop fired several shots. One found its mark in the bad guy, but the other hit the detective. This tragedy appeared to be, at least in the public's view of Warren Wright, only a bump in the road of his spectacular investigative career. But his field investigations were over now. *Gyromobe*-bound, he contented himself with ideation, conceptual thinking, and data analysis for the government's domestic security division. His days of working *out there* were long gone, and, as he often remarked, the days of private super-sleuths were dead and gone too—dead as his limp legs.

"We're leaving in two days," said Ethan.

"Are you ready?"

"Well, thanks to you, we got to use the talent of one of the finest forgers in the country...."

"Retired forger."

"Right. I know Longwell served his time, and I know he was doing us a favor because you asked him to. Anyway, he did a great job on the documents. A ton of research. Take a look at these." Ethan grabbed a portfolio off the kitchen counter and retrieved a passel of documents. He handed them to his father one by one. "Driver's license, library card, Social Security card...."

"Hey, I remember these," his father said with a smile. "These things actually paid off for a while until the government gave up the pretense in 2015. Thankfully your grandmother got a few bucks out of it before it went bust."

"Right. But this will be hot stuff in 1963. Here. Check it out. It's a membership card for Emma...the Frankie Avalon Fan Club. He was a singer."

"Don't remember him. Must have been something, though. Fan club?" Wright shook his head.

"We've got bus passes and school IDs for Emma, Zak, and me. We're using 'Springfield Heights High School'...not 'Mystic Heights'...to conceal our true residence. Longwell created several pieces for Dr. Currant also...Rotary Club. Diner's Club. This is the best, a voter's card. Now that's something I've never seen before. Apparently, people could vote if they had this piece of cardboard."

"Well, at least they thought they were doing something by voting," said his father. "We haven't had an election based on popular vote since 2016. You were just five years old then...a little too young to play the game. After that fiasco of an election, they gave up and instituted the VIP...voter implant project...nobody could vote without the implant. Cut down on the voter fraud. Cut down on the voters too. Anyone with half a brain and enough money to support themselves took a pass. The rest are the electorate. As if it mattered. At least they make it look good every four years. They vote, get their public aid, and nobody tells them who to vote for...the computer sorts through that process."

"That's why I thought this card was so neat," said Ethan. "All the adults had them in 1960. And took them very seriously. They voted, and their votes must have counted. Not like today. I read that Kennedy was a dark horse, but he still got elected."

"Right. That was great until somebody blasted his head off. That's the way they did it in the old days. Wrong guy gets elected, thinks he has the power of the people, and boom...off with his head."

Just then, Emma waltzed into the kitchen barefoot with tussled hair. She wore a red terry robe with her name emblazoned across the back like a professional athlete. "Let me guess...JFK. Right?" she said as she began to dig about in the refrigerator.

"You're up early," said Ethan.

She ignored his comment. "Juice and a banana. 'Breakfast of Champions.'"

Ethan smiled and replied, "Well, I see you have done your 1963 homework."

Warren Wright looked puzzled.

"Wheaties. Everyone ate them for breakfast in 1963," she said. "They don't sell them anymore, of course." She shrugged her shoulders. "Heck, they don't sell much boxed cereal at all now. I guess that ended when the milk supply went south. Too much radioactivity per glass, right, Dad?"

"Right. A flurry of big quakes destroyed one nuclear plant too many. Just another thing. Too bad. I enjoyed a glass of milk and a peanut butter and jelly sandwich when I was young. But you are correct, my little buttercup. Once the cow milk turned into *nuke juice*, that piece of farming history died...along with thousands of people and a whole lot of cows."

"So, Sis, are you ready for the big road trip?"

"Stop that!" she sputtered.

"What?"

"Don't call me Sis."

"Come on, Sis..."

Emma ignored her brother and turned to face her father. "Dad. Make him stop. I mean it."

Warren Wright looked up at Ethan and spoke, his voice lowered, "Ethan. Enough is enough. You two have a rough month ahead of you. You better make amends."

Ethan leaned over and gave Emma a noisy kiss on

the back of her head. "I'm sorry, Si...."

She turned around and glared at him.

"Emma," he said. "No more 'Sis'...at least while we're time-traveling."

She relaxed and smiled. "OK. Truce. *Little brother.*"

Ethan nodded. "Fifteen minutes older, my dear twin."

"Right, and years wiser."

Mr. Wright watched the sibling settlement with apparent amusement. Then Ethan saw him focus his view on the window. He turned back and locked in on Emma first, then Ethan. They both sensed the change in his attitude. Wright refilled his coffee cup and asked the two to follow him. Crossing the dining room, they entered the study in the center of the house. Without any windows and walls paneled in solid oak, Ethan always thought it felt like the inside of a wine barrel. He knew those walls were lined with lead sheets, Kevlar, soundproofing, and electronic neutralizing equipment activated when someone entered the room. It was the only secure, safe, isolated room in the house. In fact, it was purposely constructed as a *safe room.* His father asked him to close the two sequentially operating doors. Swinging in the heavy outer door, then the equally ponderous inner door, Ethan's eyes settled on his father. He knew that look. His father was very concerned about something. "What's up, Dad?"

"I don't want you to speak about time travel. The topic is potentially dangerous. You and I know that the government has unofficially banned using time travel devices. Over the past ten years, they've confiscated and destroyed many machines." He tightened his face. "I saw a *bee* outside our kitchen window."

"A bee?" questioned Emma. "Like a honey bee?"

"No, Emma," said Ethan, "a bee like a government mini-drone." He looked back at his father. "You sure, Dad?"

His father nodded. "Yeah. It was one of those little flying snoop machines. You can never tell what they're up to. Maybe it was just passing by. But it did hover for a few seconds in the window while you two were fussing over Emma's nickname. I'm concerned."

"What," said Emma, "do you think they know that we're going 'back door'?"

Mr. Wright steepled his hands in front of him and tapped his fingers together. "You know—I have resources inside and outside the government. I have no information to speak of. I just know how things work. The government will do anything to put an end to time travel. They're so afraid of upsetting their apple cart of control that they will overcorrect in this area."

"So?" asked Ethan.

"So. Don't raise the topic between yourselves...even in the *privacy* of this house. Don't assume anything. Just be cautious. You'll be on your way in two days, and while you are gone, I'll be watching your files. But you must be careful on your trip. Don't do anything that will change history. They have ways of detecting changes...even relatively small ones. Dr. Currant has assured me that his device is isolated and designed to create the minimum backwash in operation. He doesn't believe anyone has or will detect its use."

"Dad, he told us there wouldn't be any trouble." Emma spoke with authority, but Ethan detected some doubt in her voice.

"I know. I had a long talk with him. I agree. Things will be fine if you walk lightly on the path of time and don't wander into the woods stirring up the animals. Just observe. Aside from Ethan's quest to be at the scene of the JFK crime, you should have a great time living in 1963. For one thing, there won't be any *bees*."

"Just 'honey' and 'bumble'," offered Emma.

"And 'spelling'," said Ethan with a smile.

"R-i-g-h-t," said Warren Wright as he spun the *gyromobe* and rolled over to his desk. "Now I have work to do, and you two must start packing."

The Twins left their father and dashed upstairs. In Emma's room, they spread out the clothes they had purchased at secondhand shops. Emma grabbed an outfit and said, "I'm going to change into this one. You try out one of yours, and I'll meet you in the hall for a fashion show."

Ethan scooped up a pair of chinos, a madras shirt, argyle socks, and a pair of penny loafers and left the room. In a few minutes, they regrouped in front of a large mirror in the stair hallway outside their rooms.

Emma, wearing a white blouse with a Peter Pan collar, a cardigan sweater, a schoolmarm skirt, and white cotton socks with white tennis shoes, viewed herself in the mirror. She held a book tucked under her arm as a prop. "I'm not sure about this look. What do you think?"

"Well, I guess you look like those old yearbook photos. But there's something out of place." He thought for a moment. "Your socks."

Emma feigned offense. "What is wrong with my socks? They look authentic to me."

Ethan chuckled. "They're not rolled down. The '63 kids will nail you on that."

Emma sat on the bench in front of the mirror and adjusted the tops of her socks. "Well, I think this looks stupid. How about now?"

"Stupid or not, that is the look." He studied her, gazing up and down. "Not bad," he said. "You'll have all the lettermen chasing after you when we get to Chicago."

"The lettermen?"

"Jocks, athletes, BMOC."

Emma rolled her eyes and smirked at him. "I know. Big Men on Campus. Well, you look like one of Jerry Lewis's nerdy movie characters. What did they call them then? A dork. Right, you look like a dork." She laughed. "Dork...dork...dork. Ethan is a dork."

Ethan was unperturbed. "You're really getting into the part. You'll make a perfect 1963 teenage girl. Pimples and all."

Playfully, she tossed the book she was holding at his head. He ducked as it flew by and landed harmlessly on the floor. Doing an impromptu tap dance, he commented with a smile, "Pretty quick for a dork. Right, *Sis?*"

Hands on her hips, she glared at him. "Dork!" she trumpeted as she strutted back into her bedroom.

A.C. Currant entered the inner sanctum, Warren Wright's safe room. "Reminds me of my laboratory. Nice and quiet," said Currant. "I guess your employer trusts you quite a bit."

Wright rolled into the room on his *gyromobe* and secured the doors behind him. "They trust me. As they should."

"Where are your two overgrown munchkins?"

Wright smiled. "Upstairs. Trying on their costumes, I would guess. You all set?"

A.C. relaxed into a heavy leather chair and set his feet on an ottoman. "It's a cinch for me. I've got family albums and memories. As a matter of fact, I have some business suits that I wore forty years ago. They still fit. Yes, sir, I've been keeping the old body in shape all these years, just waiting for this opportunity."

Mr. Wright rolled around the large room, nodding his head.

"Nervous, Warren?"

Wright pulled to a stop in front of the physicist. "Sorry, A.C., but I am concerned about the Twins. This trip could be dangerous. Many things could go wrong. Just the concept of operating in the past is problematic, but add to that the whole JFK thing, along with Ethan's aggressive attitude...."

Currant tossed his arms out in a stretch and smiled at the detective. "So if it's so dangerous, why send them?"

Wright rubbed his chin with his thumb. "You'll need their youth, strength, and skills, and I need your help, A.C., Not just to keep Emma and Ethan out of harm's way...but for me. I have a favor to ask. A big one."

"Knew it was coming." He smiled. "What can I do for you?"

"Just a small thing. I want you to play ball."

Currant smirked. "Metaphorically?"

"No. The real thing. At 9:12 a.m. on October 31, 1963, at the northeast corner of Clybourn Avenue and Southport Avenue in Chicago, I just want you to catch a little red ball. Don't worry. It won't be hard hit. Just an easy grounder. Just be there and stop it. I'll give you the exact location, so you won't have to be much of a fielder. Can you do that?"

"Is that it? How about some explanation?"

Wright shook his head. "No. The less you know, the better. But it's important that you complete this assignment. Extremely important." Wright rolled his *gyromobe* around so that he faced Currant squarely. "Agreed?"

"For you, Warren. As a friend. If it makes you happy. I guarantee I will catch the little red ball. Just like Frank Malzone."

"Who?"

"Third baseman. Boston Red Sox. I used to follow the Sox even though I lived in Louisiana. They were my mom's team. Helluva franchise."

"Could he catch a ball?"

"With the best—three Gold Gloves."

"Fine."

"You know," said Currant, "given that we'll be time-travelers, some people might ask me to place a bet on a horse. And then bet the winnings on an unknown hot stock of the future and just have me bring back a stock certificate worth millions. But you..."

Wright smiled. "I don't need the money, but I do want you to catch that ball."

"OK, Sherlock. You got it. Red ball." Currant rose from his chair. "Anything else?"

"Just take care of the Twins and Zak. You are the adult in the group. Right?"

A.C. Currant laughed. "Some might doubt it. But I will watch over your teenage treasures. I'm kind of fond of them myself, you know. Especially that Emma. She's a handful, that one."

"She is. And she has a great head on her. Listen to what she says. And don't mention this *red ball* thing to the kids, OK? This is just between you and me. Man to man."

"My lips are sealed," said Currant, adding a zipper-closing hand movement across his mouth. "Mmmm..." Currant made sounds as if he could no longer speak.

"Right... You're the adult in the group," said Wright, rolling his eyes.

LOG of Zak Newman --- June 28, 2028: 10:37

(Day 1 of Time Travel)

We're somewhere below the war memorial, in the concrete confines of Dr. Currant's timeworks, which he calls "Home," waiting to go "back door," as we say in the time-travel business. "Back door" is fine with me. I have no interest in going "front door," as things can only get worse in the future. I would say we are comfortable but apprehensive. The air in here is fresh and cool. Today there's only a hint of subterranean moisture, and I haven't seen any critters. Currant is fussing with his gear, and the Twins are discussing the future, or should I say the future "past." Jacques Dufour is not with us now. He will remain at his post in the school, ever vigilant, evaluating The History *(MOM's official bible of the past) and the unofficial* Flitter *(opinions, comments, and theories from unidentified rogue electronic sources that can be received by those highly modified and illegal black-market computotronic devices). So, when we return, Professor Dufour can tell us what impact, if any, our little trip in the* TimeTravelle *has had on the world. I hope things will be better for our efforts, but only* time *will tell.*

Dr. Currant spent the first hour explaining some of the basics of life in the early 1960s. He has purchased quite a few rare gold and silver coins and about ten pounds of common gold coins dating back to the beginning of the 20th century. Since he is a registered numismatist, he is allowed to make such a transaction without causing a fuss with MOM. These, he will exchange for dollars once we arrive. We're familiar with the idea of dollars. They're similar in concept to the exos we use today, except they are paper, not electronic. But understanding the smaller coins is a challenge. The pennies, nickels, dimes,

quarters, and half-dollars are what Dr. Currant calls
"pocket change." For my money, carrying these coins
around will only create holes in my pocket. I actually like
our decimal system of today, although very few
transactions involve transferring a part of an exo. A single
exo doesn't buy much, and part of an exo buys even less.
But A.C. assures us that these nickels and dimes will
have some pretty hefty purchasing power in 1963. He's
also bringing some cut diamonds. These, of course, are
synthetic. Today, diamonds are just another commodity,
like wheat or oil, because of the low cost of creating them.
According to Dr. Currant, experts today can't tell the
difference between the real and the synthetic. Synthetic
stones are cheap now, but in 1963 diamonds were very
valuable and only available in their natural state. They're
small, easy-to-carry, concentrated wealth, and they'll be
no problem to sell to the right buyer, says Dr. Currant.

So we have our money and our clothes. I'm dressed as a
"good boy" in 1963 terms. Clean-shaven, no sideburns,
cloth—not leather—jacket, nice shirt with a collar, tan
pants, white socks, and black leather loafer-style shoes.
Ethan and Emma are similarly attired, and Dr. Currant is
wearing what he calls a "business suit." It has a blue
jacket and matching pants of a natural material. At least I
don't have to wear one of those "tie" things. Currant is
wearing a red- and gray-striped one around his neck like
an ornamental noose. I must admit he looks rather
dignified (looks can be deceiving). But I do hope he fools
the people at the coin shop, because we're not going very
far if we can't get some of those old-fashioned dollars. I'm
not really worried, though, because Dr. Currant has a
way with words. I believe he can talk his way in or out of
anything and find a way to make a profit while he is
doing so. Such skills will be useful in Chicago. Thanks to

Mrs. Elliot's English class last year, I can still remember the first few lines from another wordman from a hundred years back in time. Sandburg's Chicago *poem.*

"Hog Butcher for the World, Tool Maker, Stacker of Wheat, Player with Railroads and the Nation's Freight Handler; Stormy, husky, brawling, City of the Big Shoulders: They tell me you are wicked, and I believe them, for I have seen your painted women under the gas lamps luring the farm boys. And they tell me you are crooked, and I answer: Yes, it is true I have seen the gunman kill and go free to kill again."

Sounds like the story of the JFK shooting. Bon voyage. On to the Windy City.

END: 06-28-28

-Chapter III-

Field Trip to the Windy City

Except for the contemporary yellow safety goggles, their garb was all 1960s. The four travelers stepped up onto the circular grated-metal platform. They stood at their assigned places, backs against the slightly slanted cold steel slabs, each located at one of the four quadrants of the perimeter ring of the *TimeTravelle*—Emma east, Ethan west, Dr. Currant south, and Zak north. Four old-fashioned suitcases and one paisley cloth valise were positioned in the center of the circle. There was nothing to do now but stare at each other and wait. Emma and Ethan locked eyes. He could tell his sister was nervous. She wasn't into advanced technology, and the *TimeTravelle* was undoubtedly on the cutting edge. He offered her a comforting smile. She returned a fleeting flash of teeth, but he could tell she was agitated. He looked at Zak. Now there's a guy who's looking forward to this experience. He looked like a five-year-old on his first trip to an amusement park. And Dr. Currant wore his trademark "shit-eating" smile. His eyes roamed the metal structures above as he surveyed his invention, obviously enjoying the moment. Although everyone had used the machine several times to travel from the chessboard in the war memorial to the underground bunker, a voyage of about thirty feet, none had traveled in time. For the past few days, Ethan had mulled over the concept of flying through time to Chicago, Illinois, in October 1963. Just thinking about it was exciting. Finally, something big was happening. Life was taking a turn toward the great unknown. He was confident and mentally prepared. His father had given the Twins their marching orders: take no unnecessary risks, observe, but don't interfere, and keep A.C. Currant focused on the project.

Ethan heard a soft humming sound that seemed to swirl around his head like a swarm of gnats. In seconds the pitch and volume of the sound increased to hornet level. Currant said the time-shift experience would be much different than the space-shift into the bunker.

"It's set to initiate at noon," shouted A.C. Currant, his voice bellowing against the surging whine of the *TimeTravelle* device. "Do not move! Or you may leave some of your body parts behind." He laughed.

Ethan shook his head at Currant's joke and looked at Emma. She looked apprehensive. For the next sixty seconds, the machine was alive. Green, red, and blue laser beams shot in front of the travelers, knifing into the spaces between them. Sounds of liquid chemicals rushed through the network of pipes below them. An annoying cracking sound repeated overhead. In total, it was a furious cacophony. He shouted across the steel circle to his sister, "1963, here we come!" At that moment, he lost sight of her. Time-shift really was different...this was his last thought in 2028. It was as if he was being blown through a tuba of time.

An intense swooshing sound attacked his ears. First, everything went black. The only light was a steadily strengthening white dot in the center of his vision. But as he glanced to his left, then to his right, he saw things, events, and people coming into focus and evaporating just as quickly. The little white dot of light in front exploded into a hot blast of luminosity that temporarily blinded him despite his protective goggles. All went black. For a moment, he thought that he had died. Then he felt something on his face like the gentle warmth of the sun tempered by a light breeze. He opened his eyes, reached up, and removed his goggles. He wasn't dead, but he was transformed in some manner. More than confident now, he felt totally empowered. He looked out past the concrete chessboard and the peristyle marble columns, down the green grass of the hill, beyond the cliff, over the waters of Mystic Bay. The distant bell of Randall Tower called out melodically twelve times, announcing noon on October

29, 1963. Ethan looked about. Like him, the three others were absorbing the transformation process and easing their minds into the past.

Directly across, Emma removed her goggles and shook off the effects of sixty-five years of travel in less than two minutes. "That was something," she said, the words sticking in her throat.

Zak trotted into the circle center. Wearing a big smile, he spun around with his arms extended. He signed three times. "*Hijole*! That was incredible."

Dr. Currant appeared somewhat weak-legged before gathering his senses. He looked around, nodded affirmatively, and laughed aloud. "I told you it would work. The *TimeTravelle* works. I knew it. We made it. Now grab your suitcases, and let's start walking." He glanced at the clock on Randall Tower. "It's 12:06. We've got to get down into the town center quickly. I don't want anyone to associate us with the memorial. We'll keep that secret to ourselves. Let's go. March."

The Twins, Dr. Currant and Zak, each grabbed a suitcase, with Ethan handling the heavy valise. It was a crisp, sunny, late October day in Mystic Heights. As they walked down the hill, Ethan took in the view. A collage of white clapboard buildings jutted above and between the rust-colored late fall foliage, with only the gold-capped Randall Tower providing a marker above the trees. The serrated treetop edge, which met the rich blue waters of the Atlantic, gently undulated in the wind. Memorial Drive, a two-lane gravel road, wound its way down the hill, penetrating the tree line just west of the water. The tall teen led the travelers along the half-mile walk. By the time they reached the heart of Main Street, they were visibly tired. Currant had sought and received several rest breaks on the trek, but now he seemed to gain strength as they ambled along the tree-lined seaside boardwalk. Ethan gazed at the familiar buildings housing shops and offices on the other side of the street. They looked the same yet different because all the occupants had changed from those he knew from 2028. For some, he had no idea what they sold: dry cleaners, 5 & 10, Army-Navy? Emma gave him a look as they passed something called a hosiery store.

"Selling hoses?"

Currant jumped in. "Stockings, my girl. Nylon stockings. You don't have any, do you? We'll have to buy some before we catch our train. You won't be well-dressed or authentic without a pair of nylons."

Emma's eyebrows lifted, and she rolled her eyes. "Whatever you say, Doctor. I hope they don't itch."

"And when we get to Chicago, you have to start teasing your hair," said Currant.

"Teasing?"

"Don't worry, that won't hurt either. It will only make your hair look a little stiffer," said Currant. "Believe me. All the girls were doing it in 1963."

"Anything else?"

"We'll see. It's been quite a while for me. But if something comes up, I'll pass it on," said Currant.

"Don't kill yourself. I'm already feeling weird."

It was just after noon, and the townsfolk were on the move. As pedestrians passed the group, they stared at the time travelers, obviously interested in these newcomers to Mystic Heights.

Currant's memory of an earlier time must have been working because he unerringly directed the group up a side street leading to a small rare coin shop tucked into a two-story building fronted by a stone-paved courtyard. A sign on the glass storefront read: *Rich Coins, Est. 1944.* Ethan was pleased they had arrived at their destination. As he passed the heavy bag filled with coins to Currant, the three teens dropped onto a sidewalk bench. In a short time, they heard the sound of a tiny bell ringing as the coin shop door opened and closed.

Emma, seated in the middle of the two boys, quietly commented, "How quaint...a little bell signals his entry. Strange, isn't it?" she reflected. "It's Mystic Heights, but it's not our Mystic Heights."

Zak nodded and, now using sign language, replied,

"*Very strange.*"

Ethan, who had no trouble understanding the silent message, laughed. "Zak, I know what you mean. Like an old girlfriend who moved out of town and returned one day to reconnect. She looks just like before, maybe a bit older, but she has a whole new group of friends that she talks about incessantly, and her makeup seems different...not in a good way, and you notice that one of her eyes is larger than the other."

Still somewhat dazed from their time-travel experience and tired from their walk, Emma, Ethan and Zak gazed absentmindedly at the world around them. Bulky, ancient, brightly colored automobiles—Plymouths, Oldsmobiles, Packards, and Fords, looking like metallic water buffalos swaying, dipping, and exhaling foul gases—cruised the street before them. An open-topped auto full of teenage boys and girls squealed around a corner. The driver honked his horn, and the girls in the back seat laughed and shouted unintelligibly. On the other side of the street, a red and white striped barber pole rotated in a clear glass tube attached to the shop front. Nearby, a young mother carried a baby wrapped in a small blanket. She trailed behind her young son, who scratched his way noisily along the concrete walk, skating on metal-wheeled contraptions attached to his shoes. Overhead, a piston-engine passenger plane droned on, cutting through a few lazy clouds as it climbed over the bay heading south. "You're right, my friend. This is Mystic Heights, but it's not our town," said Emma.

Suddenly, Dr. Currant popped into their view, smiling broadly. He handed the valise to Ethan. The old scientist was animated as he spoke. "It went very well. I know enough about this town to sound halfway intelligent regarding *recent* events. I told them I was just visiting my nephew and his new bride. Cashing in the coins to buy them a belated wedding gift. No forms to fill out. No identification check. No cameras in the ceiling. Just two older fellows doing business. I know now why I fantasize about these times. Living is easy." He patted the top pocket of his suit coat lightly. "I can't flash it now," he said, "but we have over two thousand dollars American to play with. Let's get a couple of pairs of nylons and hop a train out of town."

The 20th Century Limited blew through a grade crossing at 100 miles an hour. In its wake, a trackside tornado of loose papers, leaves, and dust swirled. Three powerful New York Central diesel locomotives hugged the banks of the Hudson River. They rumbled west into the sunset, pulling a train of rolling stock capped by an elegant, round-backed observation car. Zak Newman stared out the rear window, watching tracks, ties, and telephone poles vanish into the darkening eastern sky. The drumbeat of the wheels and rails locked him into a daze.

"Calling Zak ... are you there?" asked Ethan. Slowly Zak turned back to Emma, Ethan, and A.C. Currant, who sat facing each other on the curved, high-backed, blue and gray banquette. "Join the party."

Zak returned and slid in next to Emma.

"We're lucky," said Emma. "This is a great way to travel. And we've got the observation car almost to ourselves."

"Except for those two young couples," said Currant. He studied them for a moment. "I'll bet they're on a double-honeymoon holiday. Judging from their uniforms, they're soldiers. Maybe they're headed for the Army-Air Force football game. It wouldn't be too early to get into the Windy City, have little fun..." Currant's eyes again darted off to the young couple and back, "see the big city, watch the big game, and head back to the hotel for some relaxation." He looked at Emma for a reaction. He smiled wickedly when she blushed.

A Pullman waiter walked down the aisle carrying a tray full of drinks. The Twins and Zak grabbed their Cokes, and A.C. Currant gathered in his Black Label scotch-on-the rocks tenderly as if it were a baby bird. Currant paid the man, delivered a tip, and said, "Thank you, George." The African-American waiter grimaced, nodded politely, turned, and left.

"How did you know his name?" Emma asked.

"Didn't," said Currant, sipping his drink like it was a sexual experience. "People always called Pullman porters 'George'...after George Pullman, the man who invented the sleeping car. A bit crude...but authentic. Or maybe it's 'authentic redneck.' Anyway...you can bet that waiter believes we are of this world."

"Not nice, Doctor," said Emma. "By the way, remember we should not tell anyone we're from Mystic Heights High School. We don't want them tracking us down. We're from *Springfield* Heights. There are hundreds of 'Springfields' out east."

"You got it," said Currant. Then he pulled a tiny silvery toy car from his coat pocket and tumbled it around in his palm like a worry stone.

"What's that?"

Currant smiled. "My lucky charm. This was a gift from the Benz people. 2017 coupe, an exact but miniature replica."

"You're a little old for toy cars, aren't you, Doctor?"

"Maybe, but I know just the person who would really like this."

"Who's that?"

"A little friend." He had a strange look on his face. He picked up his drink and raised his glass. "Cheers, my friends! Or should I say my delightful field trip students?" He took another sip and smiled broadly. "Ah. I love the old days. Can't get good booze like this anymore. I'm looking forward to the football game. Hot dogs, beer, a rousing college marching band, and pretty blonde cheerleaders. Ah...the pageantry of it all...Soldier Field...100,000 spectators...you can't beat it. That will be fun, don't you think?"

"Well, it wasn't too much fun for JFK. He never made it," said Ethan. "Once they made that slow left turn off the expressway ramp onto Jackson, he was a sitting duck for a sniper."

Currant shook his head. "Always on duty? Take a break. Enjoy the view."

"I'll bet Thomas Vallee was hated by everybody," said Emma, ignoring the inventor's pleas for pleasantries. "And I'll bet they were all happy to see him killed by that cop." She took a sip from her Coke and then looked at the glass. "You know, Dr. Currant, you may be right. Even this Coke tastes better than the stuff we drink today." She paused and then took another sip. "Yep. What do you think, Zak?"

Zak held his glass up in a mock toast and nodded in affirmation.

"Zak. Are you OK...not talking?"

Zak signed, "*Just a short-term problem. I'll become a better listener.*"

"You'll make it, Zakaroo," said Ethan. "I'll fill the verbal void. Let's get back to our boy Vallee. This guy *was* hated by everybody. He did it. But they hated *the way* he did it."

"It was brutal," said Emma.

"You're not kiddin'. First shot missed the target. Killed a little girl. Her mother standing behind her, took the same bullet. But she lived. Two nuns were hit with the next shot...or shots. The cops said it blasted through one nun's habit and blew an ear off the other." He shrugged his shoulders. "That made no sense. They were holding a banner that said 'Catholics for Kennedy.' One at either end...at least three feet apart. How does one bullet fired from the front hit two people three feet apart when they're standing side to side facing the shooter? Unless there was another sniper shooting from the side."

"*The History* says..." Currant interjected.

"Screw *The History*. It's wrong. Everyone agrees Vallee's M1 rifle fired eight shots max without reloading. We've got two nuns, a little girl, her mother, and three bystanders who took bullets. And a street sign ten feet in air with a bullet hole. *And* JFK caught three. That's at least nine or ten—not eight. And maybe some missed shots to boot."

Currant looked at Ethan and shook his head lightly. "This is old ground, my friend. You'll see. You won't be able to prove anything. One way or the other. Lots of bullets. Lots of witnesses. But no consensus. That's typical of these events. Fear and panic and shock and disbelief. But nobody can agree on what happened. *The History* tells the official story. Take my advice. Don't get too wrapped up in your theories. Thomas Arthur Vallee was the lone gunman...and a vicious one at that."

Emma nodded. "It was a vicious crime. First, he shot JFK twice in the chest. One of them went right through his heart, killing him. But Vallee fired again and hit JFK dead center in the forehead. His head just exploded. Brain parts rained down on the crowd. All those schoolchildren watching. It must have been terrible."

"We don't want to see that, do we, Zak?" A.C. looked at the boy and took another sip of his scotch. "Man, this is good stuff."

Zak shook his head.

Currant continued, "We'll stay clear of the action. Some place that's safe. Sadly, JFK's a dead man, and nothing can change that."

Currant's attitude greatly irritated Ethan. He raised his voice. "You're wrong about that. JFK doesn't have to die." The two soldiers and their wives stopped their conversations and took notice of the four time travelers.

The others looked at each other blankly. Then Emma spoke out loudly. "You're right. JFK doesn't have to *fly*. He could take the train to the game."

Currant chimed in. "Just like us. I understand he loves train travel...."

Ethan glanced at the two couples. They seemed to have lost interest now and resumed their own conversations. His sister had pulled his butt out of the fire again. "Thanks, Emma."

She gave him that "*you should be*" look.

A.C. whispered, "That was unwise, Mr. Wright. Please watch yourself in the future."

Ethan nodded, realizing he would watch himself. He

would be more careful with his words. But he would not be stopped. He not only wanted to witness history but desperately wanted to change it. He vowed to himself that he would save JFK.

LOG of Zak Newman --- October 31, 1963: 08:48

(Day 3 of time travel)

We arrived in Chicago after decades of time travel and a
full day of train travel. Today is Halloween. I think we
were lucky because if we had any sartorial miscues, they
didn't arouse suspicion, given the variety of strange
outfits worn by the natives. I see plenty of wax lips and
vampire teeth. We spent the day recovering from our trek
in our new home base—a big, old, majestic hotel. It's in a
good location. Downtown, in the Loop, as they say, and
not far from the assassination site, about six blocks to the
west. We're located on Wabash Avenue in the midst of
the diamond center of the city. Dr. Currant has already
traded in some of our diamond stash for cash. We should
have plenty now. We have two rooms. Unfortunately, I am
sharing one with Dr. Currant. I woke up late this morning,
and he's not in the room. He said he might be out this
morning. Maybe he's getting some coffee. I could use
some.

Since Currant does not understand sign language and I
was not permitted to bring my Voicenator, I am graced
with his nonstop monologues in all waking hours.
Sensing his vibes tells me he cares little about the
Kennedy assassination. He is simply along for the ride.
He really enjoys playing present in the past. Of course, he
is the only one of us who was alive in 1963, and so, in a
way, he is going home—back to his past—while the
Twins and I have entered a new world entirely foreign to
us. No amount of reading, studying, or contemplating
could prepare us for this moment. It is, in fact, wonderful
and awful to walk in the world before one's existence. It
is terribly freeing knowing that you have no responsibility

to this world. You have no future. You are not a part of this world. It's much like taking a trip to another land to which you bring all your anticipation of delight and leave behind (at least temporarily) all your responsibilities. We're here to experience and enjoy. I acknowledge our responsibility to the future to be careful with our words and deeds (even Dr. Currant is very serious about this). Other than that, I see this as a great, exciting, once-in-a-lifetime experience.

For the Twins, it is different. Ethan is here to make an impact on the future. He has a bug up his butt about the assassination. No matter what he says, he would love to be the man who saved JFK. And Emma is here to keep Ethan out of trouble. I hope she succeeds because if we can maintain our cover, we can return another time again to a different place in history. This would be the best use of the technology of our time. Other than that, our modern American technology is only useful to keep others in the world from destroying us or the economy. And this same technology that "protects" us denies us the right to be truly free. Our every movement is watched, cataloged, calculated, and calibrated. This is not a life—it is a life sentence in a zoo called USA. So, I'm happy to be a time traveler back in Chicago on Halloween 1963.

END: 10-31-63

-Chapter IV-

Secret Agendas

A.C. Currant checked his watch: *9:10.* He was alone. He had followed Warren Wright's directions. A short cab ride had brought him to Clybourn and Southport, the northeast corner. He was upset. He should have demanded more information from the detective about "catching the red ball." What the hell? He had no idea why he was standing alone on the street corner, but he was ready for action. He looked around. The streets were filled with rush-hour traffic shortcutting down Clybourn Avenue to get downtown. Currant stood before a small, dingy, white clapboard cottage, one of a few houses stuffed between rows of marginal and vacant stores. He wondered if this was it. Was this the right place? He hoped so, but nothing was happening.

Then somebody popped into view. A cute kid in dirty blue jeans and a frayed yellow T-shirt looked about four years old. A mutt followed him into the front yard— a scruffy black-and-white nondenominational barking, jumping, irritating canine. The dog had something in its mouth. It was red. Was this the ball? Currant watched them. They paid no attention to the visitor from another time. Playfully, the dog laid the ball at the feet of the boy. Then he leaped left and right, encouraging the kid to pick up the ball and throw it. The kid looked at the dog and laughed. "Hey, Sparky. Whatdaya got? Oh. Ya want to play ball. OK."

Just then, the dog spotted something climbing a tree. The squirrel was more interesting than the ball now, and Sparky attacked. He raced to the tree, barking wildly. The squirrel focused on him and chattered retorts from a branch just inches out of the dog's reach.

The boy looked disappointed and abandoned. He

bent over, picked up the red ball, and waved it side to side. He looked at the dog. Nothing. He taunted it again. Nothing. Then he tossed it toward Currant, who stood on the sidewalk inches from the curb. The ball bounced along the grass and then rolled up the slight incline. The dog, still fascinated by the squirrel, paid no attention. The boy ran after the ball, trying to stop it before it rolled onto the sidewalk and into the street. Currant saw it coming. It was a slow grounder. An easy out. He timed his approach and reached down at the ideal moment. It took a last-second funny hop when it hit the edge of the walk, but he was ready. He caught it clean in midair. He smiled. Not bad for a 73-year-old.

"Hey, mister. Give me my ball," said the youngster.

"Sure," said Currant softly. "But you should be careful. Never chase the ball into the street. That would be dangerous. OK?" He handed him the ball. The kid turned and ran away, disappearing into the gangway along the house. The dog followed him. The squirrel remained in the tree, still chattering. Currant checked his watch: 9:12. He looked up. Nothing was happening. A couple of cars faced each other in the nearby intersection in one of those "who has the right of way?" driving situations. The car nearest to Currant let the other one pass. The driver and his passenger, possibly man and wife, waved to the other driver and moved on. Currant shrugged his shoulders and walked back to Clybourn Avenue.

"Mission accomplished. I hope you're happy, Warren Wright," he muttered to himself, not knowing if he really had done anything. But he did catch a little red ball. He shook his head and shrugged his shoulders. A few minutes later, he was in a cab headed back downtown.

Emma, Ethan, and Zak strolled down Wabash Avenue to get some air in the big city, as Ethan suggested after breakfast. Pigeons scuttled about the sidewalk, alternately padding toward the trio and then quickly scurrying away when it appeared they were about to be stepped upon. L trains rumbled on the elevated track system above. Heavy street traffic added to the din.

Emma wore a black leather jacket, black turtleneck sweater, black slacks, and black shoes. She felt comfortable in this outfit. She had previewed images of young people of the time and had decided the dress code of the group called the "Beats" matched her personality— young people who liked art, poetry, and movies. They disliked the rigid structure of 1950s society. She spun around to face her companions. "Wonder why they call them L trains. 'L' for Loop?"

Zak gave the sign for the word "*elevated.*"

"Got it. That makes sense. "Where to, guys?" she asked as she skipped ahead, not waiting for an answer. There was none. She stopped and looked back again.

"Any idea where Dr. Currant is?" asked Ethan.

"Zak said he wasn't in their room when he got up," she replied.

"Zak?"

Zak shrugged his shoulders.

"That's fine," said Ethan. "We don't need him right now. Maybe he's cashing in some of his diamonds. This is the diamond district. Whatever. Listen, I have to make a phone call." He sounded tense.

"Call?" Emma sensed something was up. "Last night, Currant said if he wasn't around this morning, we should just eat breakfast and wait. He'll bust an artery if he finds out you used one of those phone-things. Anyway, you don't know anybody in Chicago. Or anywhere else, for that matter. And you don't even know how to operate a telephone."

"I got a number from a book in our hotel room. I practiced. It's very simple. You just input a sequence of seven numbers by spinning a dial. Then wait. The phone creates a ringing sound on the other person's device. He lifts up his phone, and then you just start talking." He smiled. "It's so easy. Even you could do it, Sis."

"Thanks for the compliment, and don't call me 'Sis.'

Anyway, who are you going to call?"

Ethan ignored her and looked up the street. He spotted a public phone about fifty feet ahead. Before she could say anything, he ran to the phone and dropped a coin into the black box.

"Ethan!" Emma cried out, shouting over the sound of a passing L train. When she and Zak caught up with him, he had just entered the last digit. They could only hear one side of the conversation.

"Secret Service? Let me speak to the agent in charge." Ethan was intense. "Well...that's fine, I'll talk to you. What?...That doesn't matter. Look, there's going to be an attack on the President. He's in danger...Yes. In Chicago."

Emma tugged on Ethan's jacket. She couldn't believe he was doing this. "Stop!" she shouted.

Ethan turned away and pushed his head into the payphone enclosure. "Trust me, I just know. The man's name is Thomas Arthur Vallee. V-A-L-L-E-E." Then another train rolled overhead, making conversation impossible for a moment. "Have you got that?... Right. You must find him and stop him." Ethan hung up and turned to face Emma and Zak.

"You're crazy, Ethan," she said. Her face flushed. "You are crazy." You have just violated the first rule of time travel. You're purposely trying to change history. We are now in *big* trouble."

Ethan looked relieved and excited. His voice was almost high-pitched as he spoke. "We're here to save JFK. If that changes history...so be it. Do you like the history that we live with? Do you like our society? Look around you. Do you see any cameras? Do you see those damn bees? Don't you see people free to make up their own minds? Free to live their lives. Just plain free."

Emma and Zak were dumbfounded.

"Don't worry. I know what I'm doing."

Saying little along the way, they walked back to the hotel and entered the hotel restaurant, where they found A.C. Currant having an animated conversation with a pretty young waitress. He looked up as they approached. "Ah. My young charges have arrived. I must bid you *adieu*, my dear Susan. Until later. Here's a little something for you," he said as he handed her a crisp dollar bill. The young girl's face flushed, and she thanked him before heading to the kitchen. He watched her walk away and turned to face the trio. "Where have you been? Luckily I can keep myself amused. I've been playing ball. You should too. Let's go back to my room and talk about our future." He laughed aloud at the concept.

Emma thought he wouldn't be laughing so hard if he knew about Ethan's telephone call.

Returning to Zak and Currant's luxurious but compact hotel room, the four took seats around a small coffee table. A.C. tossed a couple of Chicago newspapers down—a *Tribune* and a *Chicago's American*. The latter flipped open to expose its lead article. Emma grabbed the newspaper and read the article aloud: "*By Thomas Quinn. JFK is coming for a Football Game. President Kennedy will be attending the Army-Air Force football game to be held this Saturday at Soldier Field. Mayor Daley announced today, 'Our President can expect a gala welcome from the fine citizens of Chicago.' The Mayor indicated that thousands of schoolchildren would line the motorcade route when the president makes his way from the airport through downtown Chicago. 'This will be a special day for Chicago and a special day for the President. We have a wonderful surprise for the President, which I will give him at the game. I know he is a Navy man, so he doesn't have a dog in this hunt, but I'm looking forward to joining him on the 50-yard line and cheering on our brave soldiers and airmen who have chosen to do battle in the finest city in the heartland of America.*" The article stated that Jackie would not join the President on this trip and that more than 500,000 people were expected to line the motorcade route. Included within was a small map, which showed the entire motorcade route from O'Hare Airport to the site of the game. "Check it out," she said.

Zak brushed back his hair with both hands. Then

he signed, *"Nice of them to show the parade route...especially if you're an assassin."*

The article upset Emma. It *was* 1963. This was real. President John Fitzgerald Kennedy—now flesh and blood in her mind—would die in two days. Ethan's phone call to the Secret Service. What was he thinking? Maybe he was right. She wondered if she should tell Dr. Currant. No. Not now. "The map," she said. "It was all there for Vallee. He knew the motorcade would drive up Jackson Boulevard right past the building he worked in. It almost seems predestined."

"Almost?" questioned Ethan. "Seems pre-planned. Was it just bad luck that Vallee worked in that warehouse? A nice clean shot from the roof right at JFK; who just happened to be driving by?" Ethan sighed. "Bad luck, my ass."

A.C. Currant arose and walked to the window. Emma could see the wheels in his mind turning. He looked out the window as he spoke. "He's coming, my friends. What are we going to do? What's our plan? What scheme do you detectives have in mind?"

Ethan cleared his throat before speaking. "We've already begun. I called the Secret Service this morning and warned...."

"You what?" shouted Dr. Currant as he quickly turned to face them.

"I called them," he said, "to tell them about Thomas Vallee. To get them to stop him before he kills JFK."

Currant reddened. "Son, you have really done it now. We're supposed to be here to document history. Not create it. Do you realize the spot you've put us in? We're in danger of being discovered now. And you may have changed history." He clenched his fists and grimaced as if he was experiencing a migraine. "You actually called the Secret Service. Damn. Damn. Damn." He muttered the last three words, each more quietly than the previous. "We are in trouble."

Emma could feel her brother's pain. He did precisely the wrong thing. But that was Ethan. He always leads with his head. Quickly, she spoke. "Well, I think we must do what we came here to do. Let's start acting like detectives and hit the streets. We came here to see for ourselves what really happened back in 1963. Ethan, you don't believe Vallee shot the President. But in our world, somebody did. Our job is to find out who did it. Maybe your little phone call will change history, and maybe it won't."

"What do you mean?" Currant seemed intrigued.

"Well," she continued, "if my brother is right, then Vallee didn't do it, or at least he wasn't alone. Even if the Secret Service checks out Vallee, even if they put him in jail...JFK could still die. We have no idea whether Ethan's call will make any difference. I suggest we visit the assassination site and begin to understand the logistics of the crime. We have to start somewhere. Agreed?"

Dr. Currant concurred, and they quickly left the hotel, waved down a taxi, and made the five-minute ride to the West Loop location.

"Sure you want out here?" asked the cab driver as he looked about. They were parked in the center of the Jackson Boulevard bridge, which spanned the Northwest Expressway.

"This is it," answered Dr. Currant. The Twins and Zak exited onto the sidewalk while A.C. paid the fare and joined them.

Noisy traffic and a cold wind blew through the valley of the newly constructed interstate highway below them. Emma surveyed the scene. Multi-story warehouse structures surrounded the bridge. To the east, on the right side of Jackson Boulevard, about a block ahead, stood an eight-story loft warehouse building—the official "sniper's nest." Thomas Arthur Vallee was employed there as a printer apprentice. It offered a good straight-on shot, particularly from the roof, but she could easily judge that even better gun positions were available in buildings both in front and back of the proposed motorcade route. Better sniper's nests and triangulation too.

The highway below ran north and south with an

entrance ramp in the middle of the bridge and an off-ramp to Jackson Boulevard on the west side. They looked at this ramp, which in their time had become one of the most infamous sites in the world.

In her mind, Emma played back the motion picture she had seen hundreds of times. The motorcade finally arrived from the airport. The lead car and two motorcycle policemen swept up the ramp toward the camera, followed by JFK's midnight-blue Lincoln. Hundreds of waving, shouting people lined the chain-link-fenced area on the far side of the ramp. All were smiling. So was JFK. It was a crisp, bright day. Kennedy sat alone in the back seat of the open-topped limo. As if on a throne, the 43-year-old leader waved to his subjects. The sun glistened off his bronze complexion. He looked radiant. Because of the tight left turn, the car slowed almost to a stop at the top of the ramp and then made a wide turn, heading east on Jackson.

Both sides of the bridge were lined with people three-deep, craning their necks to get a view of the thirty-fifth President of the United States—the first Catholic President—the first Irish President—the man who had finessed his way through the October Cuba crisis the year before—who took the blame for the lack of air cover at the Bay of Pigs—who was loved by millions and hated by many others—the man who was about to die. Halfway across the bridge, about where the time travelers now stood, something happened. A shot was fired.

Most people ignored the noise. There is no evidence Kennedy sensed danger. At the right edge of the film, a bystander, a little blonde-haired girl, her smile frozen in time, held a cardboard sign. She crumpled down into a ball at her mother's feet. The camera jiggled and then refocused on the death car. In the next few seconds, other shots were heard. The crowd panicked, and people rushed in all directions. One man tripped over the bridge railing and tumbled onto the roadway below. He survived, amazingly unhurt, having landed in the bed of a truck carrying discarded cow trimmings. The newspapers called it "The Butcher's Blessing." JFK was not so lucky. He was just butchered.

The film captured the limo coming almost to a stop. With the direction of incoming bullets impossible to determine at that instant, the Secret Service driver didn't know if he was heading into fire or away from it. This indecision created an easy target. The car inched ahead. Kennedy's shoulders were driven sharply backward by some unseen force. His head dropped. Then it sprung forward violently, exploding into a pink mist. A large portion of his cranium disappeared, deposited in a rain-of-brain onto those stunned onlookers too slow or fascinated to run. Immediately after this brief violent bullet storm, the driver recovered and slammed the accelerator down, driving the car forward at high speed. In the movie, it disappeared into the distance like a shrinking, dark, metallic dot—until nothing and no one was visible. Then the camera panned to the shooting victims and those kneeling next to them, screaming for help. It was over.

"Long live the King...the King is dead," muttered Emma to herself.

"What's that?" asked her brother.

"I said, 'The King is dead.'"

"Not yet, sis. Not yet," replied Ethan. His voice offered hope. He looked at his watch, leaned over, and whispered in her ear, "We have less than forty-eight hours. We must act quickly."

LOG of Zak Newman --- October 31, 1963: 12:46

(Day 3 of time travel)

Visiting the Chicago assassination site troubled me greatly. It was a perfect place to commit the "Crime of the Century." The death vehicle crawled around a tight turn surrounded by many buildings with excellent shooting positions—lots of windows for the Secret Service to watch. And watching was all they did. Later, reports showed they didn't check out any of the warehouse buildings in the area. If anything, they were only interested in crowd control. They scanned the people who lined the streets—apparently, with no thought that someone with a well-aimed rifle could strike from a distance. When the shots were fired, they were slow to react. In fact, not one agent did anything to protect the President. He was on his own in the big Lincoln's lonely back seat. By the time one of the agents in the follow-up car reacted and raced toward the car, it was too late.

Anyway, after our little visit to the most famous place in the world, we reconvened over lunch to discuss our next move. We agreed that time was running out. Emma suggested we might visit the Chicago's American *reporter who wrote the article about JFK's visit, a fellow named Thomas Quinn—going straight to a source of information to get information. Everyone thought that would be a good idea. In keeping with our plan, we would pretend to be budding journalism students on a tour of the city seeking mentoring. A.C. Currant could not find fault in this approach. He also suggested that in the interest of saving time, he would visit Thomas Arthur Vallee (we have his address and every other tidbit of info about Vallee courtesy of the FBI assassination summary report). A.C.*

*will take along the special eavesdropping tools we
brought from the future. If necessary, his cover (complete
with phony papers) will be that of a Veteran's
Administration worker checking to see if Vallee is
receiving proper benefits from the government related to
his being wounded in the Korean War. I must say that Dr.
Currant, while still very cautious, seems very interested
in Mr. Vallee. So we have our plan for this afternoon's
detective activities.*

I am feeling somewhat like a deadweight. Without my
Voicenator, *I am el hombre silencioso. Other than the
Twins, no one can understand me. Certainly not Dr.
Currant, who seems compelled to ridicule and brush me
off. The* Voicenator *is a small electronic device worn like a
collar around the Adam's apple that creates and delivers
sounds just like a normal human voice box. The sound
quality is good. A turtleneck sweater hides it from view.
It's actually wonderful for a person like me. While the*
Employ America *program's cloning protocol, as usual,
provided tall, dark, handsome, and smart genes,
something dropped out of the petri dish when they made
me—no vocal cords. A minor problem for the technocrats.
When I was about six years old, they delivered the*
Voicenator. *I learned its operation quickly and began to
rely on it over the sign language I had been taught earlier.
I've been offered later* Voicenator *models—the implant
kind, but I've taken a pass. As you might guess, I'm a bit
gun-shy about the technological solutions offered by the
government. And while my voice got lost, other things
were added to me. I'm very strong. I don't look it, but I
can bench-press 700 pounds. And somehow, they gave
me the ability to read people's emotions. This is
sometimes a blessing and sometimes a curse. People can
be very emotional.*

Well, it's time to go visit our new reporter friend. Later.

END: 10-31-63

-Chapter V-

Cub Reporters

Not far from the assassin's sniper nest and a short walk from their Loop hotel, the Twins and Zak found themselves staring at the stark, gray stone façade of the *Chicago's American* offices. Earlier, Ethan had made another phone call to request permission to stop by the newspaper offices. But the reporter Tom Quinn didn't answer the call. Whoever answered told them to just come by and hung up.

"Well, let's give it a shot," said Ethan, trying to hit an enthusiastic note. "Remember, we're students interested in a career in journalism. We're here to gather the blessings of knowledge from the news gods. Right?"

Zak nodded, and Emma made a face. As they entered the building, they sensed the throbbing sounds and vibration of the printing presses giving birth to today's edition. Two flights of stairs brought them to the paper's newsroom. On opening the door, the three were immediately greeted by an onrush of smoke, smell, and noise. This was an office, nothing like those typical of the year 2028. Worn wood floors, old black metal file cabinets and desks, bare-bulb fluorescent fixtures overhead, with people—almost exclusively men and boys—dashing about, shouting, talking on phones, chewing cigars, scribbling on legal pads, and most intriguing to the Twins and Zak, totally ignoring their presence.

Finally, someone noticed them. "What do you kids want?" They spun around to face a tired-looking bottle-blonde woman sitting in the glare of a tall, dirty window, casually blowing cigarette smoke in their direction. "Well...?" To her left was a small green potted plant, the only semi-pleasant object in sight. She snuffed her cigarette out in its dirt.

Emma spoke. "We're here to see Mr. Quinn. We're students."

The blonde picked a particle of tobacco off her lower lip. Then she cupped her hands to form an improvised megaphone. "Hey, Tom. You got company," she shouted over the noise. Halfway back into the depths of confusion, a sitting man at an ancient typewriter lifted his head and looked at her. "What?" he shouted back.

The woman lazily pointed toward the travelers with a look of total disinterest. In response, the man looked at them and shrugged his shoulders. Then he lowered his head and continued his two-finger typing for a few seconds, finishing his thought. He got up, stretched, and looked at his guests. Emma smiled at him. After rolling his eyes, he pushed toward them through a gaggle of other reporters. A short man, ruddy-faced, with patches of black hair hanging onto the sides of his otherwise bald head, he cleared his throat and coughed noisily as he walked.

Ethan surmised he was about forty, although it was difficult to gauge a person's age at this time. Everyone looked much older. More than slightly overweight, Quinn's suspenders curved around both sides of his gut like the rubber fenders of a tugboat bow. The loose striped tie roped around his prominent neck, dangling limply. A pencil and pen shared space in a yellowed plastic protector lining the pocket of his starched white shirt. His other shirt pocket neatly bulged. Ethan deduced this was the source of his congested lungs and wicked cough—a pack of cigarettes. It seemed to him that everyone was smoking something in 1963. Sometimes the people-generated smell and smoke overwhelmed the time travelers, who were not accustomed to such massive personal pollution. Quinn sized up the boys quickly, spending slightly more time on Emma, who looked striking in her black outfit. "What are you selling?" His voice was gruff but with a tinge of humanity.

"We're not selling anything. We're..." said Ethan.

"Everyone's selling something, kid. It's the nature of

things."

Emma jumped in. "Please, Mr. Quinn. We're students from Springfield Heights High School out east. We're taking a journalism course, and well...."

"And you're here to see the professionals in action." Quinn laughed aloud. "Well, look around. This is our zoo. Anything particular in mind...I do have a couple of things to do this afternoon, kids." He looked over at the blonde for an out, but she was gone. "I don't give guided tours. Sorry." He wrestled the pack of cigarettes from his shirt pocket, tapped one out, popped it between his tight lips, extracted a khaki-colored Zippo from his front pants pockets, and in one deft move, flipped the top, spun the spark wheel, lit the cigarette, closed the lid, and returned the lighter to his pocket.

Fascinated by this display of nimble fingering, Ethan couldn't help but ask, "Were you in the armed services?"

"What?" Quinn paused. "Oh. My lighter. Yeah. Pacific. Marines. The Zippo was a gift from my Uncle Sam. Four years of hard labor. One lighter. Not a good deal. But we saved the world for you kids." He took a deep drag from the unfiltered Lucky. The burst of nicotine seemed to relax him for a moment. "Well, you got eyes, kid. That's a good start in this business. Where did you say you're from?"

"Springfield Heights," answered Emma. "A small college town out east."

"You a budding beatnik or just dressing up for Halloween?"

"I'm sorry? Emma replied, feigning distress.

Quinn laughed again. "Nothin'." He turned to Zak. "What about you, pretty boy? You dying to join the ranks of city reporters?" Zak appeared to rankle a bit with this comment. He shifted his feet, trying to find a place of mental comfort.

"Sorry, Mr. Quinn. Our friend Zak can't talk. But I'm Emma Callan-Wright, and this is my twin brother, Ethan."

Quinn stared at the two. "Twins?" he asked.

"I hate to admit it," answered Emma, "but this is my fraternal twin. Unlike Zak, he talks *too* much."

"OK." The reporter shook his head. "Never heard of a reporter who couldn't talk. Can't shut most of them up. Oh well, it's a new world." His gaze returned to Emma. "Why me?"

She smiled and quickly answered, "We saw that movie *The Front Page,* and we really enjoyed it. That's what got us interested in your newspaper. Scoop after scoop...that's what *Chicago's American* is known for...you people are real reporters. This is where the action is."

Quinn smiled. "Pat O'Brien. My Irish bother. Did a good job in that movie. Talked real fast. Some people say I look like him. But *Front Page* is about the good old days. I guess even now, we've got a reputation for getting stories...no matter what. Say, what's with the Callan-Wright. You born in England or something?"

Ethan smiled back. "Right. Our father is English. Old family name."

Quinn massaged his chin with his free hand. "Come to think of it, I've never met any kids with names like yours. Pretty fancy monikers. We're used to "John" and "Mary" here in the Midwest. Maybe we're old-fashioned. Not like your elite Eastern Establishment. Maybe you should visit the *New York Times.*" Quinn laughed.

Ethan smiled. "If we're going to be reporters, we need all the guidance we can get, Mr. Quinn." He looked around the newsroom. "This is a real newspaper. And Chicago's a real newspaper town. We could use your help."

"OK, shoot. Whatdaya want to know?"

"We saw your article in today's paper about President Kennedy coming to town. We thought it was particularly well written. We were wondering about the map. Whether it's something that you have to get permission to print. I mean from a security angle. Know what I mean?"

The reporter dropped his backside onto the edge of

the desk, exhaled a cloud of smoke, and nodded. "Well, maybe you cubs could get off the bench. You're right. It's an issue, but in this town, we spill the beans on the entire route because Mayor Daley wants a big turnout. He wants them lining the streets. And he don't want 'em guessing, so everyone has the same scorecard. Every news hawk's going to pop in the map. Just good politics."

"But isn't it dangerous?" asked Emma.

Quinn thought for a moment before replying, "It's a dangerous world, little lady."

"But. He's the President," she said.

"Hey, JFK can take care of himself. The Japs couldn't kill him. He's gonna be fine. Don't you worry." He flicked an ash onto the floor and lifted himself off the desk. "Sorry. I have to get back and sling a few words. OK? Nice of you to stop by. Look around if you want."

Ethan looked at the others, then back at Quinn. "Can we have one of your cards?"

"Sure, kid." The reporter dug around behind his cigarette pack and retrieved one. He handed the crumpled business card to Ethan. "Say, you look like you might play a little football yourself. You on the Springfield Knights team?"

"Springfield Heights. And I do," Ethan lied. "We love our football."

"Right. What position? Wait, let me guess. Big guy like you, 6-foot-3, maybe 230. Look like you can run...fullback?"

Ethan paused and glanced at Zak, who knew something about the game. Zak nodded. "Yes. I do fullback."

Quinn gave him a bit of a look.

Sensing a possible *faux pas*, Ethan changed the subject and held the man's card up high, wiggling it in front of his face. "Thanks much for the card. One last thing. Maybe we should mention this, Emma." He looked at her for agreement, then back at Quinn. "Have you heard about a man named Thomas Arthur Vallee?"

The reporter looked puzzled. He paused. "Maybe I've

heard the name, but I don't know where. Why? Who's he? One of your teachers?"

Ethan smiled. "No, he lives here in town. He's a former Marine. We thought you might have heard something about him from the Secret Service or the police."

The reporter moved closer to Ethan and looked up into his face. He lost his fatherly look. "Now, why would I be talking to the Secret Service? They don't do interviews, sonny. And I don't like where you're going. Do you know something I should know? You got something on this fellow Valley?"

"Vallee," said Ethan. "Sounds French. Not like 'Death Valley'—V-A-L-L-E-E."

"So?"

Emma vamped. "Our teacher, Dr. Currant, he knew him in the Korean War. He talked with him today, and he, well...."

"He what?"

"He made some negative comments about the President. Frankly, Mr. Quinn, what he said made us nervous. Maybe not a threat, but Dr. Currant said he seemed very agitated. So we're just telling you. There might be a story here. Vallee lives on the north side...Uptown area. Maybe you want to check into him. We're just kids, but you know. Trying to do our reporter job. Anyway, we have to go. Right, guys?" The others nodded and gave a quick wave to the reporter.

"Right...maybe I will," said Quinn, his words stretching out to become a question. "Say. You have my card. What about you? In case I want to get back to you."

"We're staying at the Plaza House," said Ethan. "We're in town for the game. Emma's going to write an article for *The Shout*. Our school newspaper. You know. JFK loves his football. Loves Chicago. The pageantry, Soldier Field, the gridiron battlefield...like ancient Rome."

"OK. Wish you luck." He looked over at Zak. "You too, Valentino."

Zak appeared puzzled by the comment.

"It's a compliment, Zak," said Emma.

"Got that right, young lady," said Quinn. With a wave of his hand, the reporter turned and headed for his desk.

LOG of Zak Newman --- October 31, 1963:15:23
(Day Day 3 of time travel)

Happily, our little visit to the Chicago's American *offices seemed to go well. Ethan assured us that our only job had been to ask questions and plant ideas. He remains determined to somehow avert the horrible reality that will arrive in less than two days. Emma may be buying into the possibility of saving JFK. However, she's still very concerned about changing history. "How do we know that things will change for the better if somehow we do save JFK?" That's a good question. When we first planned the trip, I thought we could study the event, maybe find holes in the official story, and explore those holes on our return. Instead, with Ethan's recent gambit, we may alter history. For all we know, Humpty Dumpty may be lying cracked and broken at the base of the wall of history, or for the moment, he may still be teetering back and forth, buffeted by the winds of time that we have stirred. Time will tell.*

Dr. Currant volunteered to scout out Vallee's place. I think he jumped on that idea to keep Ethan from getting near Vallee. Too dangerous for Ethan and too dangerous for history. Currant is a very strange individual. Charismatic and very smart. His invention, the TimeTravelle, *is a story in itself. Initially, the site up on the hill overlooking Smuggler's Cove was a secret underground air raid shelter built by the City of Mystic Heights at the same time as the World War II memorial above it. The hideout was stocked with food and water. It had a separate ventilation system, a direct underground electrical hook-up to the grid, a large backup generator, and state-of-the-art post-war electronic devices to communicate with the outside world—that is if there was anyone left alive on the planet. It was built at the beginning of the Cold War with the Soviets. Fear of atomic attack was in the air. People thought bombs would be raining down at any moment. Air raid drills in elementary schools had students ducking under their desks and covering their heads to save them from nuclear destruction.*

Dr. Currant told us that the air-raid shelter was really not intended for the use of all the town people but instead was only for the mayor and other "special" people lucky enough to be invited. Very few knew of its existence. Everyone thought the underground construction was just part of the War Memorial above. In time, the Cold War fears quieted, and the embarrassing shelter was sealed and forgotten. Many years later, a young physics student at Cordwell University named A.C. Currant took a summer job helping to build the concrete chessboard in the middle of the War Memorial. On his own, secretly, he discovered the sealed bomb shelter below. Time passed, and as head of the physics department, he secured government grants, which enabled him to develop the theories and practices that perfected time travel. Ultimately, the entire program was taken over by the military, and his involvement ended—above ground, that is. But over the next decade, he secretly occupied the underground bunker and constructed his own machine— the TimeTravelle, and we are its first official users. I keep asking myself, why us? I think the answer lies in Currant's relationship with Mr. Wright. He always seems to disparage the Twin's father, but there's some kind of odd connection between them. Otherwise, I can't explain why Mr. Wright would have his only children and me venture into time and danger with this weird wizard of Mystic Heights.   END: 10-31-63

-Chapter VI-

Meeting the Assassin

A.C. Currant had no trouble locating the aging Northside apartment building that provided shelter for Thomas Arthur Vallee. Small studio apartments created from the leftovers of a defunct hotel furnished minimal domiciles for the residents. Currant suspected more comfortable and expensive accommodations were not a priority for Vallee. From his research, he knew the 30-year-old man was somewhat down on his luck. As an apprentice printer working in the "assassin's lair" building on Jackson Boulevard, he made just enough money to survive. But this was not his only source of income. Sometime in his second tour of military duty, he had been classified as an extreme paranoid schizophrenic, and therefore he received disability funding from the Veteran's Administration. A high school dropout, he was a loner who lied about his age to join the Marines. He had been wounded in a mortar attack in the war and was at one time billeted at a U-2 base in Japan. He had a gun collection and no shortage of ammo. Someone reported he made threatening comments about President Kennedy before the assassination. In short, there was no doubt that he was the man who shot JFK—a "lone nut" with a grudge and a gun. After he killed the President, police killed him in a quick, one-sided gun battle—case closed. He would have been an American hero if he had died from his encounter with a mortar shell in the Korean War. But as it happened, he became the most hated man in the country.

Currant's cab had dropped him off at the diner across the street from Vallee's place. After a quick cup of coffee and a view of the building and its surroundings, he was confident that the area was clear. As he crossed the street, he carried a recently purchased hard black briefcase. He looked official. He entered the building, climbed the wooden stairs to the second floor, and knocked on the ex-Marine's door. There was no answer. He waited a minute and then placed a phony Veteran's Administration business card in the doorjamb. On it, he had written the note: *See me about your payments.* It was early evening, and he anticipated Vallee would return home from work shortly. He was not disappointed. Back on the street, he saw a man approaching in a car. Vallee's car was a surprise. It was a 1962 Ford Falcon. Currant remembered this car—one of the first compact cars. Almost new, it bespoke of someone on his way up in the world. It didn't fit with the rest of the picture.

The physicist dropped his head as he neared the car, pretending he hadn't seen Vallee pull up. But when he glanced over to Vallee, the man was eyeing him and the dark blue suit he wore. Maybe Vallee tagged him as a cop. He stopped walking. "Are you, by any chance Thomas Vallee?"

"I am," said the man.

He wore a gray tradesman shirt under his lightweight jacket. He was of medium height and medium build, and his somewhat receding blond-brown hairline defined a typical Chicago face. Not a mean look, thought Currant, maybe tortured, but not mean. "I'm John Reynard, Mr. Vallee. I'm with the Veteran's Administration. Stopped by your place. No one answered, so I left my card. It's good that I ran into you. It will save us both some time."

Vallee looked wary. He appeared to be debating what his next words might be. He made a humming sound while he thought for a moment before speaking. "Something wrong? I'm getting my checks."

A.C. looked up and down the street and then at Vallee. "Can we discuss this in your apartment?"

He nodded, and the two made their way into the building and up the stairs. Vallee grabbed the card out of the doorjamb, scanned it quickly, and stuffed it into his pants pocket. They entered the apartment. It was a box and nothing more—a Murphy bed in the wall, one sofa, one chair, an old round-screen television, a phone, a closet, a bath, and a Pullman kitchen. The one bare window over-looked an alley view of utility poles and wires. Vallee removed his jacket and tossed it on the sofa. He offered the beat-up bentwood chair to Currant while he sat on the couch.

They faced each other, and neither spoke. Currant feigned a cough, then another, and sounded somewhat distressed as he asked for a drink of water. When Vallee got up, Currant removed a small button-like device from his pocket and carefully and unobtrusively attached it under the bottom of his chair.

"Thank you. Dry throat. Part of getting older." He sipped the water. "Much better now...Vallee. That's French, right?" asked Currant. "I'm part French also."

No reaction

Currant pushed on. "Well, let me get down to business. I know it's getting late, and no doubt you've had a long day." He pulled out a small notepad and fountain pen from his coat pocket. He looked hard into Vallee's eyes. "We're checking on people. I read that you took a hit in Korea. Later, after your discharge, you got into a bad auto accident. Is that right?"

Vallee nodded.

"Nice car, by the way. Had it long?"

Vallee twisted his body as he digested this question. "It belongs to a friend of mine. On loan until I get on my feet financially."

"I see. Well, that explains it. Now the records show that your war wounds alone were not enough to secure a complete disability rating for you. Is that correct?"

Vallee now crossed his legs and brushed back his hair. He exhaled a sigh, which sounded almost painful to Currant. "I wasn't able to complete my time. The accident slowed me down, and the mortar shell. I got a Purple Heart, you know."

"Yes, yes. That, we know." A.C. looked around the

room. "You live alone?"

The man nodded.

"How about friends. You must have some. Like the person who loaned you the car. Do you have many friends?"

This seemed to agitate Vallee. He got up and paced the room, now talking in mumbled bites. "Right. I have a few friends. Look. I'm a Vet. I was wounded."

"You're a printer now...apprentice. What did you do before that?"

Vallee's eyes narrowed. He cleared his throat, emitting that humming sound again. "Is there a problem, Mr. Reynard? Am I...should I not be on the disabled list. Is that what you are thinking? Well, forget it. I didn't ask for it. They gave it to me. And I'm taking it. I need everything I can get. Times are tough. Somebody who does somethin' good for his country always gets the shaft. And the pretty boy politicians suck up all the money. I don't need you government guys looking up my rear. It's clean. I'm clean. I love this country. I..."

"You keep a weapon?"

Vallee glared.

"Just asking. You know, with your record of instability, you could be a danger to yourself. I'll bet you still have your service weapon."

"If I did, Mr. Reynard, I wouldn't tell you, would I?" By this time, he had raised his voice far above the mumbles. He looked out the window talking away from Currant. "I told you I have friends. My friends will tell you that I'm an OK guy. I got friends in *your* world too. I'm not totally alona dependable guy, even with my troubles. As far as I know, I can work. I can get my government money. It's all good. Isn't that right?" He sniffled and extracted a rumpled handkerchief from his pants pocket. He snorted into the rag. "I need that money," he said softly.

Obviously, Vallee was upset. Currant noticed the beginnings of tears in the corners of his otherwise expressionless eyes. He arose from his chair. "Sorry to upset you, Mr. Vallee, but you know we must check up on good patriots like you. Some are not so patriotic. But you, I can tell, are a man of integrity."

Vallee had quieted down. "I am a good citizen. I am. You check on me, and you'll find out."

Currant packed his pen and pad away and offered his outstretched hand, which Vallee accepted. "I may be back again." He turned and exited, leaving the assassin standing in the doorway. Once outside, he quickly walked away from the building. Vallee had not followed him down the stairs, and the apartment had no street-facing windows. He crossed the street and returned to the diner, confident he had not been seen.

"Hello, friend," greeted the hash slinger across the counter, "another cup of java?"

"Yep. You make a mean cup, my friend." Currant paid the man and took a window seat facing Vallee's building. He sipped, listened, and waited. Hidden in his right ear was a small radio receiver earbud. Currant sipped and waited. About a half-cup of coffee later, he heard the old rotary wall phone being dialed. He knew his recording equipment was the most sophisticated non-military device available in 2028, but still, he wondered if he would be able to hear both sides of the conversation. No matter how the phone was positioned, the device he had hidden under the chair in the apartment was supposed to detect, interpret and transmit any sound vibrations emanating from the phone's earpiece or Vallee's jawbone. In fact, it worked perfectly.

A.C. cupped his hand over his listening ear. He heard the sound of a phone ringing, then a low, firm, and modulated voice. *"Who's this?"*

"Six," replied Vallee. *"Something happened."*

"Go on."

"I had a visit tonight from a guy named Reynard who says he's from the Veteran's Administration. He was asking a lot of questions. Checkin' up on my disability pay. So he says."

"Doesn't sound right," the voice became more intense. *"Did you get a phone number, address,*

whatever?"

Vallee stumbled. *"I got a card. Wait. A minute."* Currant could hear him digging in his pocket. *"The card just has his name: John Reynard. Veteran's Administration. No address. No phone. But when he left, he said I was OK."*

"What else did he say?"

"Nothing much. He was in and out pretty quick. But he asked about weapons. I didn't tell him anything. I think he thought I might commit suicide or something."

"Did he say he was coming back?"

"No. I don't think he will."

"Alright. You were smart to call. This guy sounds bogus. But we'll check it out. If you see him again, call me and keep him busy for a while. Tell him you have to call your landlord and then just say: 'I put the rent check in the mail,' and hang up. You detain him, and I'll send someone over. We'll take care of it."

"Got it."

"You ready for the 'big event?"

Vallee stammered, and he emitted his little nervous humming sound. *"Ready."*

"Make sure you make that purchase we talked about before we meet."

"Right. Three hundred. There's a Sears store just down the street. I'll pick them up on my way in. We're meeting at 11:30 Saturday...right?"

"In the parking lot behind the building. Don't come early. Don't come late. 11:30. I'll have the banner for you. It's a big one, but you can handle it. 'JFK FREE CUBA.' Big, bold letters. You like that. Correct?"

"I do," said Vallee.

"You're going to be part of history, my friend. Things will be put on the right track once we embarrass that Commie-lover. Correct?"

"I'll do my part. It's time. I'll see you then."

"Good. Remember. Call me if you see that Reynard character again."

There was a click that ended the call. Currant

listened for a few more minutes but heard nothing of interest. In the background, Vallee clicked on the television—*Ozzie and Harriet* time. Pots and pan sounds—Vallee was making dinner. A.C. decided to give it up. He focused again on the diner. The place was filled with workers ending their day. The counterman shouted orders to the grille man. Burgers sizzled. The air was filled with the tantalizing aroma of fresh-cut French fries bubbling in animal fat. The milkshake beaters buzzed in the background. A.C. was tempted to indulge himself with an authentic 60's fast-food meal but decided to minimize his presence instead. He got up and set the empty mug on the counter.

The counterman glanced at him. "Thanks. Come again."

Currant gave him a nod, but it went unnoticed.

LOG of Zak Newman --- October 31, 1963: 18:07

(Day 3 of time travel)

We're waiting for A.C. Currant to return from his meeting with the assassin, Thomas Arthur Vallee. I like to write Vallee's name just like The History *does it—John Wilkes Booth, James Earl Ray, Mark David Chapman (long live John Lennon), Louis Madman Mortay. This last fellow really didn't have the middle name 'Madman,' but it was a name given to him by the public. Madman Mortay— another "lone nut"—put the frosting on the cake of the 'Great Fiasco'—the 2016 presidential election, by rolling an Army-issue hand grenade between the feet of the newly elected President Swindell as he walked along the Inaugural path of victory in Washington. About two weeks later, Swindell died footless and fanny free. With him died another part of America. This act, on top of years of documented vote fraud, starting in 2000 and 2004, and vast voter apathy, effectively ended the national election process in America. The seat of government was quickly moved to the Groom Lake area of Nevada. A whole new isolated, hardened Capitol complex arose, or should I say, sunk into grounds surrounding the former Area 51. Except for certain diplomatic meetings held in one of the underground structures of Denver's airport, all the executive functions of the national government are now maintained in what has become known as the 'Mother Bunker.' Unknown to the public, there is no longer a single chief executive but a committee of directors selected from the 'best and brightest" corporate and financial entities in the country. And every six years, they, in turn, choose an executive team of three people to run things. Each one is in charge of a branch of the government—*

executive, legislative, and judicial. Of course, the judges still exist, as do the senators and Congress people, but they have no real power and are of little consequence. These shameless shills delight in the close proximity of "New Washington," to Las Vegas—devouring the Sin Capital's non-stop gambling, sex, and corruption. Everything simplified.

The smoke and mirrors of the old system have been removed. Few citizens find fault with this hybrid corporate-socialist-totalitarian system. The weak and poor survive. The rich thrive. And the power-hungry enjoy omnipotence. Almost everyone agrees that the old system wasn't working—or, as some cynics would say, the reality of the old system became too obvious and that fiction could not be maintained. Whatever. In a way, many look upon Madman Mortay as some kind of accidental hero for putting an end to the painful pretense. But happily, local politics still exist, and the activities of those fools provide great amusement for all. What the heck—some are even honest and hard-working. So I would say, on the whole, that democracy, on the local level, still exists. Chicago in 1963—Mayor Daley and local politics are alive and well. He controls the City Council of Chicago like a great Machiavellian maestro, making beautiful political music for the dancing pleasure of the good people of the City of Chicago. In that sense, nothing has changed in the past 65 years. But maybe something will change if we can alter events in the Windy City. Tonight, our little troika—Emma, Ethan, and I await the Currant news report. Hopefully, he has found something to help us turn the tide of events and save JFK.

END: 10-31-63

-Chapter VII-

Friend or Foe

At this time of the day, the City Room of *Chicago's American* was a dark, dense forest of round tree-like columns supporting a concrete canopy above. A single desk lamp illuminated a corner of this petrified forest casting its harsh yellow light upon the pockmarked, bristled face of Tom Quinn. He sat silently, alone, staring at his typewriter. A cup of old coffee stood idle on his desk, and a half-smoked cigarette smoldered lazily in a green glass ashtray. The presses were quiet now, and his thoughts recapped his day—he covered a police press conference about slowing the growth rate of homicide—he wrote a phone follow-up story on the gallows that stand ready, should the 1920s escaped cop-killer, Terrible Tommy O'Connor ever be recaptured—updated a story about JFK's upcoming football game visit and motorcade through the city—and he handled a half-dozen other unmemorable tasks.

He checked his watch: *7:12.* He glanced at the photo of his wife and two kids in front of him. He knew his kids wanted him home to see their Halloween costumes. It was time to type *"30"* on the blank sheet in his typewriter and end his workday, his habit since his days as a cub reporter at the *Daily News*. He leaned back in his chair and used his thumbs to stretch out and pop his suspenders. "Enough," he said softly to himself. He tossed his pencil, punched in the last characters on his Remington, snuffed out his cigarette, and switched off his desk lamp. It was a *"30,"* he thought to himself...the end of a long day. He'd get a beer, burger, and fries at the spoon down the street and head home. Chicago could live without him until tomorrow.

But as he arose, his thoughts drifted to the three

students who had visited him earlier. He dumped back down into the chair, flipped on the light again, and popped a Lucky into his mouth—lighting it, dragging deep, and exhaling the smoke—he created a cloud of questions. Who were these kids, really? His gut told him something was fishy about them—somehow strange—the good-looking kid who couldn't talk, the football player with enormous feet who didn't really seem to understand the game, and his sister, the tall beatnik gal. He remembered her feet also. They were too big. She should have been a size six. Thinking back, she had to be a ten at least. He wondered about their feet and their comment regarding this guy Vallee...Thomas Arthur Vallee. Like he was some kind of playwright. He picked up the phone and dialed a number by memory. It took a couple of drags from his cigarette before he was connected.

"Detective Kowalski."

"Tom Quinn. How's it hanging?"

"Ready for action, Tom. As always. In the holster...but I'm ready to draw my weapon whenever necessary."

Quinn chuckled. "I'll warn all the girls here." He heard a laugh-cough on the other end. "Anyway. I want to bounce something off of you. We had some kids come in here today. In town from somewhere out East...so they say. Cub reporters for their school newspaper."

"Le' me guess. They wanted the big-time reporter Tom Quinn to show 'em the ropes."

"Maybe, but something bugged me after they left. They were asking about a guy named Thomas Vallee. They called him 'Thomas Arthur Vallee.' Said a teacher friend of theirs had talked with this Vallee, and he had some bad things to say about the President."

"Well, that's no crime, Tom. For Crisakes, people are always blowin' off steam."

"Right. Right. But they also said they called the Secret Service. I guess to warn them about this guy."

"Secret Service?"

"Yeah. To me, that's weird. I don't even talk to

them." Quinn inhaled again. Smoke billowed out of his mouth as he continued. "You know JFK is coming into town on Saturday...."

"We know. There's a buzz in the department."

"Anything outside the norm?"

"Well. Strange that you should bring it up." He paused.

"Kowalski?"

"I'm here. Just thinkin'... I'll tell you this. Something is going on."

"What?"

"Can't say just yet, but I'd say something is buggin' somebody. We had a briefing today. Big push about the safety of the President. Vigilance. No BS. Do your job. Et-cet-ra. I dunno, but somehow this time is different than before. Much more heat."

"Is that it?" asked Quinn.

"That's all I can say. You know the Secret Service...they want to run everything. They want us to stay out of the way. Call me back tomorrow. Maybe I'll have something else. Say, what else about these kid reporters?"

"They said they were staying at the Plaza House."

"Right. Anything else?"

Quinn slid his chair closer to his desk. He thought for a moment. "Big feet."

"What.

"Never mind. I'll call you tomorrow. Thanks." He hung up the phone and stared at it blankly. The little hairs on the back of his neck perked up. Something's up, he thought. He was energized. The burger could wait. He searched his desk drawer and pulled out a yellowed dog-eared card. He verified it—*Special Agent Carl Smith. FBI Chicago.* He dialed the number. It was late. He doubted Smith would answer, but he did on the second ring. "Carl...Tom Quinn over at the *American*."

"Busy now, Tom."

"Busy? It's after seven. I didn't think you Feds worked at night."

"Just spending your tax dollars, my friend. What's up?"

Quinn related the cub reporter story again, and Smith, on the other end, grunted in acknowledgment at each segment of the tale. Quinn could tell he was interested.

"What about it? Anything going on with this visit? Anything you can tell me?" Smith was silent. Quinn waited.

"Tell you what. Buy me dinner at that burger joint by you, and we'll talk. Fifteen minutes?"

"You got it. See you there. It'll be a quick one. Got to see my kids dressed up for Halloween." Quinn hung up. He made a face, thinking, "there's shit in the air. I can smell it".

After he visited the assassin, A.C. Currant called the hotel and left a message for his young friends to meet him at a nearby restaurant located on the Chicago River. Currant sat near a window with a water view. He sipped his scotch, letting the chemicals work to relieve the built-up tension of the day. One rarely gets to interview a presidential assassin, especially before the deed is done. He watched a bright red fireboat bearing the name "Joseph Medill" as it cut through green waters on its way to its berth upriver. Currant remembered other riverboats he had watched for hours as a youth in New Orleans. He thought about the opportunity to return to his childhood home in Louisiana. He had to do it. He had to go home and make things right. There might never be another chance. His musings were disrupted when the Twins, Zak, and the waiter appeared before him. The other time travelers quickly sat down, and when the waiter left, they unleashed their questions.

"So what happened? You met him. Was he frightening?" asked Emma excitedly.

A.C. tilted his glass again, savoring the historical moment before answering. He smiled. "Well, my little chickadees, I have met one of the most infamous men of the Twentieth century."

"And…" said Ethan.

Current screwed up his face. "And, I must say it was a disappointment. Mr. Vallee appears to be a very nice young man. A bit disturbed possibly, but all and all, I think he was more frightened of me than I was of him."

"Was he threatening?" asked Emma.

Just then, the waiter returned. They placed their orders, with Emma translating Zak's sign language. The old waiter was patient while the silent decision process transpired. She directed him to bring Zak a Monte Cristo sandwich. When the man left, Emma said Zak didn't know anything about the sandwich, but he liked the book. Zak smiled broadly at Emma's disclosure while the others laughed.

Currant dived into the conversation again. "Threats?" he paused. "No, there was no mention of JFK. There were no threats. He was mostly concerned about keeping his disability pay."

"Did you try to draw him out?" asked Ethan.

"You bet. I even asked him if he had a gun at home. He was very cool about it. I would guess there are guns in the apartment. He was upset while I was there. Maybe even to the point of tears, as far as I could tell. But to be honest, he didn't appear dangerous."

"*Programmed assassin?*" asked Zak, hand gesturing below table height to avoid drawing the attention of the nearby patrons. Emma tossed the question to Currant.

"Who knows? That might explain his attitude. But somehow, I actually took a liking to the young man. Maybe he was a bit pitiful, but he was not what I expected."

"Great," said Ethan. "Less than 48 hours to go, and we're taking sides with the designated killer. Are you saying there was nothing suspicious going on?"

"Lower your voice, please…" cautioned Currant as he looked around the restaurant. No one appeared to be paying attention. "I didn't say that. As a matter of fact, I recorded a phone call he made to someone not five minutes after my departure. I'll play it for you at the hotel. It's interesting. Our friend was really concerned about me. And whoever he contacted knew him as 'Six.'"

"That's something big, Doctor," said Emma. "Sounds like a spy code or something."

"I thought so too. And the party on the other side talked to our friend about the *'big event'* that would happen on Saturday. He also said something about giving Vallee a banner."

"Banner? There's nothing about a banner in *The History*," said Emma.

"I think they plan to hang a banner somewhere that says 'JFK FREE CUBA.' Maybe on a bridge over the expressway when he passes. Or maybe from a building window. I don't know. They didn't say. But Mr. X is going to give it to Mr. V. on Saturday morning.

"Hey, this may not be a giant conspiracy, but two people are plotting something. Sounds like they're going to show up JFK," said Ethan. "Definitely a conspiracy. Nothing like this in *The History*. They say he was simply a crazed murderer." Ethan leaned into the table and quietly posed his next question to Currant. "Who's the guy on the other end?"

"I don't know. His name never came up. He never hinted as to his position or person. The only thing I know is that they are planning to meet Saturday at 11:30 in the morning. In the parking lot. Behind the building. That's where Vallee was shot to death, according to *The History*. Also, he is supposed to bring 'three hundred' of something on the day the 'big event' takes place."

Emma spurted, "We know about the 'big event.' We have seen the 'big event.' We must stop it."

Currant again cautioned them to stay calm. "I have his phone number on the recording. It's very clear. We just have to count the clicks."

"Did you call?"

"Not yet. We must be careful," he said in a soft voice. "The man on Vallee's phone said he was going to 'check me out.' If somehow he identifies me, I'm afraid we may all be in danger." He took a big sip of his scotch. "Dangerous people. Killers. We're not just correcting history now. We may be caught in the middle of a conspiracy to kill the most important man in the United States."

Zak flashed a sign that the waiter was returning with their food. For the rest of their time at the restaurant, they simply enjoyed their meals without further mention of the "big event." Zak silently announced that the Monte Cristo was a better sandwich than the book.

When they arrived back at their hotel, they were greeted at the front desk by the hotelman, who recognized them immediately and quickly commented. "Dr. Currant. You had a caller, but I told him you were out."

Currant was startled. "Someone called for me? Asked for me by name?"

The man behind the counter answered in a steady but somewhat apprehensive voice. "Well, not exactly. He gave me your physical description and talked about your young people. You know, the 'junior reporters.'" He looked over to the Twins and Zak. "So I knew it was you."

"What did he want?"

"Of course, I do not know, sir. But he said he would soon be in touch with you. I hope everything is alright...."

"No problem. What did this man look like?"

The man behind the counter thought for a moment. "Square jaw. Big smile. Dark hair. Black framed glasses. Not too tall."

A.C. glanced over at his friends, trying not to reveal his concern. This was not good. "No problem. Thanks for the information," he told the hotelman. "Goodnight."

Few words were exchanged on the way to A.C. and Zak's room. Once there, they played the Vallee recording several times. It was clearly a threat to embarrass JFK, if nothing else. By bedtime, A.C. knew that no one had been fooled by his casual attitude. No doubt Zak picked up his nervous vibes and told the Twins. It was tough to sell a convincing poker face knowing Zak's ESP abilities.

LOG of Zak Newman --- November 1, 1963: 06:26

(Day 4 of time travel)

Early to rise today—writing this in bed. The first light of the day is brushing up against our window. Chicago's people and machines are beginning to rustle and bump in the streets below. I can't sleep anymore—too much excitement. On the other hand, Dr. Currant appears to be unruffled. He's in the bed next to me, sleeping like a baby—a very noisy baby—a snoring baby. But I think he had trouble falling asleep. I sense he was more disturbed than he admitted last night after he heard about the inquiring visitor. This guy knows about our hotel and our cover story. What brings him to us? Possibly he's a mysterious friend of "Mr. Six"—or maybe Ethan's telephone call to the Secret Service brought him out—or maybe it's just our presence here in 1963. As much as we think we blend into the temporal background, it's just as possible, even with all our precautions and plans, we stand out like aliens from another planet. I sense people we meet have an uneasiness about us. It's probably a feeling that doesn't come to them directly but gnaws at their thought patterns like termites attacking wood, creating a mental void, and quietly saying something strange.

Those kids from out East and their professor chaperon are different— this is what I sense at times. Mr. Quinn, the reporter, for sure felt this. Of course, he is trained to detect inconsistencies. He spotted something about us that didn't register correctly. Something in our dress, our demeanor, the way we talk. I can't say—but Quinn's not buying us. He has what they would call 'street smarts' in the 1960s. And at the moment, the whispers of those thoughts may be creeping into his subconscious. Just a little checking by a trained reporter like Quinn would poke big holes in our "cub reporter" cover story. I have mentioned these vibrations to my friends. We've agreed to be careful when dealing with Quinn.

It is also possible last night's visitor is not from this moment. He could be a time-cop from 2028. I hope not. This would be much worse than someone from 1963. I don't think we've done anything yet to change the course of history, but I'm no expert on time travel. Nor do I know the detection capabilities of MOM. Dr. Currant said they're able to sense changes in the electrical matrix. But these short-lived electrical field disruptions are a fleeting precursor of time tampering—not likely to provide evidence of 'who' and 'where'—only indicating a 'when' possibility. We can only hope he is correct in his assumption. He is a genius—a little weird but smart. So I'll assume he is right. We need not fear the future unless we change the past. That could happen. I have the feeling—only a feeling—that Ethan's dream of saving JFK will come true. I am good with feelings— I was built that way.

Time is not on our side, however. Today is November 1, 1963. According to The History, *tomorrow at 12:03 pm, John Fitzgerald Kennedy will be shot and killed by Thomas Arthur Vallee. Feelings aside, I believe also that history is a systematic amassing of the destinies of millions of people. Everyone has his destiny. Each member of our time travel team has a destiny, as does JFK. We shall all soon confront our destinies.*

END: 11-01-63

-Chapter VIII-

The Brothers

The time travelers found a comfortable restaurant
not far from their hotel. A.C. had instructed Zak to walk
about a hundred paces behind to ensure no one followed
them. No one did. They sat in a booth clad in red vinyl
and trimmed in chrome. Hot coffee steamed in heavy
china mugs. Tiny clear-plastic tumblers were filled with
fresh pulpy orange juice. An array of egg dishes that
would bring tears to the eyes of any chicken was spread
before them on the Formica-topped table. As she set down
a platter of sausage and bacon, the waitress asked if they
needed anything else. Sure, thought Ethan, she had to be
kidding. They could never eat like this back in the future.
Meals that were delightfully tasty, incredibly large, and
non-synthetic. The people of 1963 really enjoyed their
food.

The time travelers dug into the breakfast.
Somewhere a radio played. Ethan's mind drifted while he
ate. Bob Dylan's nasal voice pushed out the *"The answer,
my friend, is blowin' in the wind. The answer is blowin' in
the wind."* Ethan wondered about the answer. His quest
for the truth about the JFK murder made him seek
answers that would change his world. Now, he sat almost
transfixed by the words of the song *Blowin' in the Wind.*
Why was one man's death so important to him? Millions
had died in scores of confrontations over the past couple
of centuries. Even Jack's brothers, Bobby and Ted,
showed little interest in playing detective after their
sibling's death. Undoubtedly many were better people
than JFK. The attractive leader's weaknesses for pretty
women and life in the fast lane had been extensively
documented, even in *The History.* It was almost as if the
controllers of the facts had focused on JFK's fondness for

the flesh as a justification for his violent death, with *The History* almost implying that he deserved it. *"How many deaths will it take till he knows? That too many people have died?"* Dylan continued to wail.

Ethan? Are you here? Emma asked. Her bright eyes danced as she tapped him on the shoulder.

He snapped out of his daze and replied, "You knock yourself out on old movies, and I get lost in old songs."

A.C. Currant looked around as if to find the source of the music. "I always thought Dylan needed singing lessons. Good ideas...bad execution. Well, let's get down to business. Time is running out."

Sitting next to him, Zak nodded in affirmation.

Currant dug vigorously into his omelet and tore into a piece of hot buttered rye toast. He talked while he chewed, which brought a frown to Emma's face. "We need to break up into teams for efficiency." He swallowed. "You two can work on the phone number. Maybe check back with your reporter friend, Quinn. And Zak and I will hang around Mr. V's place. I have a feeling things will start popping there soon."

Ethan smiled at Dr. Currant. "Emma and I are way ahead of you, Doc. We figured out the phone number, and she already called it."

"And...?" A.C. stopped eating and focused on Emma.

"And," said Emma, "the number belongs to the Cook County Sheriff's Department. Special Investigations Unit."

"Any idea who Vallee called?"

"No. But I did ask the operator who was in charge. Richard Cain. He's the head of the SIU, as they call it. But I didn't ask for him."

Ethan nodded. His sister was sharp. No point in arousing anyone's attention. Her call could have been from anyone seeking information. "Good work, Emma. You played the role of a routine caller perfectly." Her face lit up with Ethan's compliment. "Anyway, this is *important* news. Do you remember who shot our Mr. V friend?"

Zak signed quickly, and Emma translated, "A sheriff."

"Right, Zak," said Ethan. "An off-duty sheriff who just happened to be in the area. After Vallee had done the evil deed, he left his rifle on the roof. He made his exit down the back stairs of the printer building. Headed for his car parked out back. And..."

"And he showed a revolver and was gunned down by a Cook County sheriff. His name, as every school kid knows, was John G. Milner. The man who killed JFK's killer," Emma rebounded.

"Right. A bit strange that Milner just happened to be in the right place at the right time to eliminate the assassin. No escape, chase, and capture. No news interviews with the killer. No trial."

Currant sipped his coffee in silence. "Hmm..." he muttered. "Maybe he's the one who spoke with Mr. V. Maybe he met with Vallee at 11:30, just like they discussed in the call. Maybe Vallee went up to the roof. But instead of unrolling his anti-Castro banner, maybe Vallee decided to kill the President. And he opened up with his M1."

"Milner knocked off Vallee. Someone else was there. A Chicago cop, right?" asked Ethan.

"It was a Chicago cop," said Emma. "He's the man who heard Vallee's dying words: 'Long live Fidel.' That's what I read in The History. That's what he said. That's what fired up the American public. Remember."

Ethan shook his head. "Yep. That was it. According to the book, the people demanded blood. And they got it. We crashed the beaches at seven different locations and freed Cuba. Months later, the official report said Vallee was a *lone nut*. Not a Castro supporter. But by that time, it was too late. The Big C, his brother, and his henchmen were killed during the invasion."

Currant agreed. "Right. The good old U.S.A. cleaned out the Communists. Captured thousands of Russians. Sent them back to Moscow. Destroyed hidden missile installations aimed at the U.S. And Cuba became a tourist paradise. Sandy beaches, palm trees, hotels, gambling."

Zak signed: "All because one cop heard those famous dying words from Vallee."

"And his name is lost to history..." said Ethan.

Emma smiled and spoke softly, "Not quite, my dear brother. Don't laugh at my movie fetish. Stanley Kowalski. *Streetcar Named Desire.* Marlon Brando. Vivien Leigh."

"What?"

"Kowalski. He's the Chicago cop that heard Vallee's magic words."

"Stanley Kowalski?" asked Ethan.

"Don't know about the Stanley part. But you can bank on 'Kowalski.' The dying words that launched a thousand ships."

"Ain't she something," said Dr. Currant. "What a memory."

"*And very pretty,*" said Zak silently with a smile.

No one translated. Emma turned red. Ethan laughed. And Currant looked bewildered.

Tom Quinn seemed pleased to get their telephone call. Ethan began to ask questions about Richard Cain, but Quinn cut him short and suggested they stop by his office for a visit. Earlier, Ethan had reviewed all the Chicago newspapers—the *Tribune* and *Sun-Times* in the morning and the *American* and *Daily News* in the afternoon. He was impressed. News coverage in the Chicago press was extensive and detailed. All four papers covered the upcoming Kennedy visit, each identifying the motorcade route. Kennedy was a Navy man, so he would be an impartial guest. He planned to sit on the Army side of Soldier Field for the first half of the game and the Air Force side for the second half. There was little mention in the papers about Cuba. Such news had died down after the October crisis in 1962. The little island, 90 miles off the coast of Florida, sat quietly, now almost unnoticed by the press. Vietnam was making the news, though. The U.S.-backed puppet government run by the Diem brothers was losing its grip on the country. Over the past few months, headlines and news coverage spoke of Buddhist dissenters, protest marches, and monks igniting themselves in flames in public places. Life in Vietnam in early November 1963 was volatile and dangerous. Of course, Ethan knew from reading *The History* that the public would have deaths of leaders in two countries to contemplate in tomorrow's newspapers— JFK and the Diem brothers.

The Diems, however, would suffer a fate similar to the little town of Peshtigo, Wisconsin, in terms of historical reference. Peshtigo caught fire the same day as the Great Chicago Fire in 1871. The Wisconsin fire would later be recorded as the most deadly of any fire in the history of the United States, but the Great Chicago Fire always overshadowed the event. So it was with the Diem brothers, thought Ethan. Their deaths by assassins as part of a military coup, occurring just a few hours before the murder of JFK, fell into the cracks of history, appearing on a single page in the epic history book of the Vietnam War. Had JFK stayed in Washington that day, if nothing else, to show respect for his fallen Vietnamese allies, he would have survived. But he chose to attend the Chicago football game and died.

When they arrived at the newspaper offices, the presses for the afternoon edition began to rumble ominously. Quinn met them at the top of the stairs and escorted them to a conference room. They sat at a modest oak conference table that wore the visible badge of years of journalistic hard labor—dents, scratches, and cigarette burns blended into a patina of dirt and grease. It told a story of late-night meetings, deadline parties, and leaking cartons of Chinese take-out. Ethan looked at Quinn. He wore a different face today without a condescending attitude. This time he was all business.

"So what's this about Richard Cain?" asked Quinn as he lit another cigarette. Emma winced when he accidentally blew smoke in her direction. "Sorry, young lady."

"Emma," she said.

"Right. Emma. What's your interest in Cain?"

"We believe he or someone in his office is, involved with Thomas Arthur Vallee," she uttered quickly.

"Ah. Mr. Vallee again," muttered Quinn. He got up and walked around the small room, huffing and puffing like a steam train. "You seem fixated on that man. How does this involve him?"

"Vallee was talking with Cain or someone from his office yesterday about something which may happen tomorrow," said Ethan. "They talked about something called the 'big event.' Remember...Vallee was bad-mouthing President Kennedy. Tomorrow Kennedy is arriving in Chicago and...."

"And what?" asked Quinn. He stopped pacing and sat down across from the Twins.

"And we...we want to know if this fellow Cain has any issues that might concern the safety of the President," said Emma.

Quinn's face reddened. "You should talk to the Secret Service. I'm just a reporter."

"We tried," she said. "We called them. But we can't get too involved." She stumbled. "We're...after all...we're just some concerned kids. But you are a distinguished reporter for this fine newspaper. You would certainly be able to get their attention."

Quinn smiled. "Flattery will get you everywhere, Emma. Now you're learning the business." He stubbed out his cigarette into a white ceramic ashtray with a hand-painted hula dancer growing out the back of it.

"Nice dish," said Ethan, almost exposing his inability to say the name of a common 1963 object.

"What? Oh yeah. She's a cutie. Brought her back from the Pacific. She's a survivor." He laughed. "So you want to know about Richard Cain? Well, I can tell you a few things. Cain was a Chicago cop for a number of years. I've met him. Our most notable reporter Jack Montana uses him as a reliable source. He helped put a crooked judge in jail."

"Sounds like he's ok then," said Ethan.

Quinn grimaced. "Well, not quite. He did get a fair amount of good publicity when that happened, and he moved up in rank on the force. But...he was a bit 'hinky' in his police work. Lot's of accusations that he misused his office. People said he stole money. Said he roughed up a few people."

"Sounds like a cop to me," said Ethan.

"You've got a point. Anyway..." Quinn continued his chain smoking. "Anyway. Things got a little hot for him. He left the force after doing some outside work for a politician here in town. He got caught installing some illegal cameras to spy on one of Daley's people...not good. They made him resign from the force, and he went private."

"Private detective?" Emma asked.

"I don't know. I guess so. I heard he was doing work for the Feds. Then I heard he went to Mexico. Then, he was deported from Mexico."

"Busy guy," said Ethan.

"You might say that. As I said, he's at least a little 'hinky.'"

"What's 'hinky'?" asked Emma.

"You know. Not kosher. A little bent."

"Bent like crooked?" she asked.

"Possibly. There are rumors that he's tight with the 'boys'...the 'Outfit.'" Quinn looked at Emma, who was obviously tripping on his words. "Mobsters. Organized criminals. Now I'm not saying that's the case. Cuz' that wouldn't be smart for one thing. But I've heard rumors. Anyway, now he's legit again. He got that job with the State's Attorney office as an investigator. And now he's the boss man with Ogilvie."

"Who's Ogilvie?"

"He is...my lady...the Sheriff in this town. And Cain is his right-hand man."

"Is Ogilvie a little 'hinky'?" asked Ethan.

Quinn laughed lightly. "Far be it from me to know about him. He's a lawyer. Drove a tank in my war. Worked in the organized crime division of the Attorney General. He's on his way up, my friends. And Cain is his buddy. If I were you, I would be careful not to make him nervous."

Ethan fidgeted in his chair. "So that's clear. What does Cain look like?"

"He...wait... I'll show you." Quinn got up, returned to his desk, and retrieved something from his files, a news photo. They studied the picture. It showed two Chicago policemen exiting a building. "He's the one on the right," said Quinn.

Ethan looked at the man. Square jaw. Solid looking. Not tall. "Does he ever wear glasses?" he asked.

Quinn thought. "Yeah. I think he does now. I saw him at a press conference about a month ago. With the peepers."

"Black-framed?" asked Ethan.

Quinn nodded. "Right. Like Jack Benny wears. Or like Ogilvie, for that matter. Did you see him?" Quinn looked concerned.

"Not really. But he might have stopped by our hotel last night to see us," answered Ethan somewhat tentatively. "We're not worried, though." Ethan looked at Emma. She looked worried.

"You should be," said Quinn.

LOG of Zak Newman --- November 1, 1963: 9:32

(Day 4 of time travel)

Since Dr. Currant does not understand sign language, we can't have a conversation. So, as we ride, I scribble in my journal. Now, I'm also eating another five-cent candy bar—called a 'Seven Up'—seven different flavor bites in one bar—all for a nickel. I can't get over how cheap they are. We're traveling north on Lake Shore Drive, heading for Vallee's apartment. A.C. is busy talking shop with our cab driver—World Series baseball—surprisingly, Dr. Currant seems to be a baseball buff. Somehow, he knows that the Dodgers beat the Yankees in a four-game sweep. Somebody named Cofax really did well, or so it would seem from their enthusiastic banter.

We've been in 1963 Chicago just a short time, but already I am more relaxed than ever. Things are different here. People think, act and move about without concern for what they say or do. Sure they're generally polite and well-behaved, but they also exude the essence of freedom. They're happy with life. There's a built-in logic to their existence that's missing in our 2028 lives. They work together to accomplish the goal of getting through the day, the week, the year, and the rest of their lives with a clear measure of pride and sensibility. It's obvious they have no fears of doing or saying the 'wrong thing.' How I envy them.

Normal street conversation includes the weather, sports, and politics—talk filled with prejudice, titillation, scandal, and personal philosophies. It seems like everyone has at least one opinion that they are happy to share regularly. All this is quite a contrast to our lives in 2028. In most circumstances, all conversation is monitored by MOM's *watching, listening, and mind-sucking devices. Just thinking the wrong thought can result in an electronic brain massage from* MOM. *She doesn't appreciate independent thinking—not conducive to a well-managed society.*

Most of our people in 2028 live in tightly-contained, highly-populated, 'clean-water' cities like Detroit, with its 15 million people, or Chicago, for that matter, with its 22 million. There are no suburbs or exurbs. Our cities are almost like the walled towns of medieval times, except the walls are electronic now. People don't venture out of the town. That would be dangerous. This point is reinforced by constant media coverage of those who attempt to leave. They are usually found dead and sometimes dismembered by the gangs of 'evildoers' who roam the countryside. Our big cities may be boring, but they are safe and virtually crime-free. Of course, people do disappear on occasion. We assume MOM *removes these folks because they are not good citizens.*

There are people outside the big cities other than criminals—like the people of our hometown. Mystic Heights is not large. Maybe 50,000 people. It's an isolated college town. Such places exist as almost monastic enclaves for the researchers and for the intellectual elite who learn and teach—trade schools for MOM's *busybody brigade. The Twins and I are supposed to join 'the team' in two years. But I doubt that.*

Also, a small number of people maintain the food and industrial processes located outside the big cities. Natural food production is efficient. Government-owned robotic machines handle the growing, harvesting, and distribution of grain, corn, and soybeans. Asian Carp and other fast-growing commodity fish are collected in programmed mass kills in the Great Lakes. Algae harvesting, oil shale mining, and the Gulf of Mexico oil bonanza has finally eliminated the Mid-East domination of the world's energy. This production technology runs by itself, with very few people involved. It's mostly machines working with other machines—connected to pipelines— connected to cities. People do travel about, but few can afford it. Such travel is always by secured air transport. Trains only haul freight. Automobiles are tiny and built for in-city transit only, and all-electric with limited range. You couldn't escape the city if you wanted to. Petroleum-powered ground vehicles in cities were phased out completely in the early 20's. Walking, electric bicycles, scooters, and micro-cars are the transportation modes of 2028. Not like this big, yellow gasoline sucker, I'm riding in now. STOP—we are here.

END: 11-01-63

-Chapter IX-

A Crowded Rendezvous

Currant directed the cab driver to slowly drive past Vallee's apartment and continue down the street. Vallee was not in sight. Nobody suspicious appeared in the area. A trip around the block placed them in front of the diner. They entered the eatery and purchased a couple cups of coffee and donuts, and sat in the same booth that Currant used the night before. It offered a clear view of Vallee's building. A.C. looked around the diner. A few people sat at the counter, indifferent to the time travelers. He looked back at Zak.

"Hear anything?" asked Currant.

Zak shook his head from side to side quickly.

"OK, well, let's just sit here for a while and wait. I don't hear anything, either. Maybe he's out." A.C. positioned the listening device earpiece he wore to make sure he was getting a signal. Momentarily plugging his other ear with his finger enabled him to hear the hum of the refrigerator cooling Vallee's beer in the apartment across the street. "It's working."

Zak nodded and pulled out a comic book that he had purchased at the hotel. He thumbed through the pages slowly. Currant observed the young man focused on the ads for novelties—phony beer and foaming sugar tablets, bird whistles, and disappearing ball tricks—just like he did when he was young. Zak was lost in his reading as they chewed through the donuts over the next ten minutes. Currant ordered replacements and another round of coffee. He made a couple of trips from the counter to the booth delivering their order and sat again.

Currant whispered, "We'll wait a few more minutes and then go somewhere else. I don't want to appear to be killing time."

Then he did something that he knew would get Zak's attention. He pulled out a pack of Tarrington cigarettes and proceeded to light one. Inhaling the smoke into his lungs, he fought back the urge to cough, and seconds later, he battled a more severe feeling of nausea. That's enough, he thought. No inhaling...just pretend to smoke for effect. He glanced at Zak through the smoke cloud. He was chuckling. But Currant was not amused. He was intent on fitting in with the other diners who, when not eating, were smoking. This was what men did in 1963, he thought, and damn it, he was going to look like one of them even if he turned green.

Donuts eaten and cigarettes smoked, they went outside and sat on a bus stop bench. This location, a few feet from the arterial street, was upfront but inconspicuous. Just then, Currant noticed a large, dark gray Chevy making a left turn onto the adjacent side street. It parked almost directly in front of the entrance to Vallee's building. Two burly men dressed in business suits exited the car and hurriedly crossed the street. A.C. glanced back at them. They could be cops, he thought. He leaned over to Zak, "We've got company. I don't think Vallee is in. Listen up." Currant listened intently, trying to block out the nearby sounds of traffic. Thirty seconds passed. He thought he could hear footsteps. Then there was a sound of knocking at Vallee's door. More seconds passed with no answer. The bug was working perfectly. He could hear someone inserting keys into the lock, then the sound of a door opening and closing. He looked over to Zak for confirmation. Zak nodded.

"*Not exactly the Taj Mahal.*" Currant detected an East coast accent in that voice. Maybe New Jersey, he thought.

"*Let's get to it,*" said another voice. Midwestern twang thought Currant. He could hear someone opening and closing cabinet doors and drawers.

"*You know, this could be a lot of nothing, Sam.*"

"*Could be. But things are happening. We got those two skinny Latins locked up. We got an FBI flash about teams of shooters. We got tips on this guy 'Vallee' up the wazoo."* He paused. *"Something's going on."*

"Yeah. And we got one day to find out what," said the Ed voice.

The sound of another door opening and Currant thought something may have hit the floor.

"Shit."

"What?"

"Look at this." Currant heard a low whistle.

"Jesus."

"Well, what do we have here?" asked the Ed voice. Seconds passed. *"Check it out. But don't touch."*

"Someone's ready for the next war—M1 Sniper," quipped the Sam voice.

"And a carbine."

"And six boxes of ammo."

"Close it up, and let's get out of here."

"Right."

A.C. looked over to Zak, who made a face. If Currant had to guess, he would say his young friend was upset. They heard the men leaving the apartment. A.C. looked over his shoulder. Soon, the two men exited the building and quickly returned to their car. They did a three-point turn and headed back toward the time travelers. As they passed, the driver glanced at them, his gaze lingering. Just then, a green and white city bus pulled up. A.C. got up quickly, and Zak followed as he got onto the bus. Standing before the bus driver, they looked out the windshield. The cops made a right turn and headed east.

"Fares..." said the bus driver talking at the windshield.

Currant and Zak looked at him. The bus pulled out into the traffic lane. Currant looked back at the diner. A short, dark-skinned, dark-haired man wearing a short black leather jacket popped out of the building and stared at him. There was quick eye contact between them.

"Fares," said the driver dryly.

Currant and Zak looked at each other with vacant stares. A.C. couldn't even guess the amount of the fare.

He looked about the bus. Passengers studied them. He waved a dollar in front of the driver, who grabbed it without looking, called out the next stop, clicked out four quarters from his changer, and handed them to Currant. Taking a shot, he tossed two quarters into the fare box, and they moved on. The driver appeared unconcerned, and Currant flicked his head back at Zak as if to say, 'get going.' They cautiously walked to the back of the moving bus and took the last seat. The other passengers seemed to take no particular interest in them. "I think we're OK," said the older man. "At least we're heading in the right direction, but I think we should get off at the next big street and get a cab."

Zak raised his eyebrows and shrugged his shoulders.

They rode for a few minutes and then exited the bus with a crowd of other passengers heading into the L station.

Currant scoped out the area. Traffic was heavy, but no cabs waited. Then a big, light blue Ford passed. He noticed the driver was the man he had seen leaving the diner. Again the two made eye contact. This time the contact unnerved Currant. He searched again for a cab and was relieved to find one waiting at the stoplight. Quickly, they were on their way back downtown. As they headed toward the lake, A.C. looked out the rear window. Then he turned and whispered to Zak. "I saw a guy...when we got on the bus. He came out of the diner. He had a look about him. Like he was checking us out."

Zak ran his finger across his throat in a slicing motion.

"Right." Currant leaned back in his seat. "He drove by when we stopped to get the cab and looked right at us. I don't see him now. Maybe it's nothing. I hope not."

The cab made a turn onto Lake Shore Drive, and A.C. relaxed. Maybe he was being too cautious. Sometimes one can breathe life into a thought pattern and give it meaning it doesn't deserve. One man. Two locations. Eye contact. You're nervous. You're frightening the kid. Relax.

"You fellows from out of town?" The cabbie viewed them in his rear view mirror.

Currant took a better look: a black man, about fifty and large. He wore a thick, matted pullover sweater that had adapted to his shape like nubby body paint. The collar of his shirt was worn but clean. His big hands gripped the steering wheel delicately. He was at one with his vehicle and his passengers.

"Right. How did you guess?" asked A.C.

The driver smiled. "Lot of rubber neckin'. Nothin' wrong with it. I see you checkin' out the sights."

"I guess we are. First time back in a while."

"How long?"

A.C. thought. He was going to say about fifty years, but then he thought again. "It's been a few years."

"Where ya' all from?"

"East coast. Small town called Springfield Heights. Just here for a visit. I'm a school teacher, and I'm taking a few of my students on a field trip to visit the big city."

"Good for you," said the driver. "Enjoy it while ya' can." He laughed.

They cruised along in the right lane. To his left, Lake Michigan was a dark blue backdrop for the parkway trees, and on his right small boats huddled in Diversey Harbor, one of the many enclaves that dotted the lakefront.

"Say..." said the driver. "You fellows know the President's comin' to town tomorrow. Big football game at Soldier Field. You could see the motorcade...HEY!" he shouted.

A.C. looked up quickly. What was happening?

The cab driver focused on the scene in his side mirror. "Shit!" he said.

Currant sensed something was coming, but he couldn't react. He didn't move.

The cabby turned his head forward. He moaned like a cat in heat.

Currant's eyes filtered a time-lapse image of reality.

A random glint of sunlight reflected off a sailboat mast; he squinted, and his vision returned. The cab driver's fat fingers squeezed hard on the wheel. Neatly clipped nails with a big gold, onyx ring, the little black hairs stood tall on his whitening knuckles. Currant blinked. Out of his eye, he saw a flash of blue metal outside—a car rushed at them—collision next. He froze. The other vehicle filled the window, and he saw the driver—the same guy—dark, mean, and demonic. "Hang on!" Currant shouted as he braced for the inevitable.

The contact was swift and effective. The right front fender of the attacker smashed violently into the cab. Without seatbelts, Zak, A.C., and the driver bounced around viciously. Currant focused on what lay ahead. Out of control, the cab swung sharply to the right, jumping a low curb, and onto the grass headed for the lagoon. It smashed through bushes and small trees. The driver jammed on the brakes. Barely slowing, the cab skidded at high speed across the lawn. A boy riding a bicycle popped into view. Wide-eyed and about to be run down, he reacted to the careening cab, twisted the handlebars, and drove his bike into the ground. He flew off. Seconds later, the cab struck the bike and blasted it skyward—a fleeting glance at the boy's fear-filled face. Currant knew they were going into the drink. He braced his hands on the seat back in front. Impact—the car hit the steel railing—swatted it down flat —a sickening sound of metal scraping metal—their heads hit the roof—Currant's body took off—they were airborne. A railing part smashed the windshield.

A split second later, the cab hit the water and flipped over. It sank. A cold flood poured into open windows. Zak and Currant were now upside down in the back seat, their heads jammed onto the roof. A.C. was stunned. He felt nothing but icy wetness closing in. In a panic, he breathed in the liquid—his lungs burned. He struggled and fought to remain conscious. In absolute silence, the water-filled metal coffin rocked gently on the bottom. Fifteen feet of Lake Michigan crushed down. Time expanded—every second an hour. Death was certain. Currant's world shrank into darkness. Then he felt Zak's powerful grasp turning his body right side up. He reached for Zak as his friend's outstretched fingers grabbed onto his belt.

Zak pulled him along. The door was caught on the muddy bottom, immovable. Zak reached back and grabbed A.C.'s wrist. The young man's mighty grip pulled him through and out the window. Again Currant grabbed Zak's belt. Conjoined, they shot to the surface. A.C. popped out of the water, sucking air and coughing painfully. Zak's face was inches from his. In a fog, Currant watched Zak take a deep breath, turn his body, and dive. Dimly A.C. heard someone shouting. He looked up, straining to find the source. Finally, two men on the deck of a powerboat came into focus.

"Grab it!" One shouted as he tossed a rope.

The rope swatted Currant in the face, momentarily stunning him. Somehow he caught it and hung on. They dragged him toward the boat. A small platform projected off the stern. One man jumped down and took hold of him. The other joined in. Together they flopped him over onto the platform. He lay in great pain, sputtering, coughing, and choking. Fluid bubbled out of his mouth.

Just then, Zak broke the surface, gasping for air. He held the cab driver's head above the water. The man was breathing. Zak was smiling. Currant could only lift his head long enough to look and understand the situation. Then relieved but totally exhausted, he let it go, and it banged hard on the deck. The blue car and the driver's face jumped into his mind—a killer, he thought. Someone wanted them out of the way permanently. He took a deep, painful breath, coughed again, and smiled. He was alive.

LOG of Zak Newman --- November 1, 1963: 13:20

(Day 4 of time travel)

Now we know we have dangerous foes. Someone tried to kill the doctor and me. They failed, but it wasn't for lack of trying. Now, we're back at the hotel. A.C. is still shaken by the whole near-death experience. It certainly was a reality check. Neither of us was hurt badly, but the cab driver was rushed to the hospital by ambulance. His arm is probably broken, but I think he'll be OK. Also, I think Dr. Currant is worried about the police. He's afraid of exposure. They asked a lot of questions, but A.C. explained that I couldn't talk (there are times when this is good), and he was so flustered that the cops just let us go after getting our local address.

Dr. Currant is back in the water—the tub. As soon as we returned to our room, he popped down one of his little single-serving bottles of scotch and jumped into a hot bath. I think he was still in shock. Me. I'm OK. I cleaned up, changed clothes, and I'm back in action.

So who was the mean little man in the blue car? Our best guess is that he is a friend of Vallee—maybe somehow connected to Richard Cain. The Twins updated us on their conversations with Tom Quinn, the reporter, and we're thinking this whole thing could extend to 'The Outfit' as they're known here in Chicago—organized criminals. Organized enough that they identified two very unassuming guys just sitting at the bus stop as troublemakers—who needed to be eliminated. We must have looked like bi-generational criminologists. But I'm jumping ahead. We really don't know anything except that someone tried to kill us. And, of course, we know The

History *says that Vallee will kill JFK tomorrow—unless something happens.*

I'm guessing those two guys who broke into Vallee's apartment were cops or some variety of Feds. But why didn't they grab all the guns and the ammo? And why didn't they stick around to grab Vallee? Maybe they've already got him. They could easily find out where he works and arrest him. But for what? Just because some mystery man, my buddy Ethan, calls the Secret Service and says Vallee is a bad guy. And the guns? This town, and this country for that matter, is an armed camp. There are guns everywhere. Today's newspaper has a local sporting goods firm named Klein advertising war surplus rifles for less than $15. I have no idea how may exos that equates to, but it sounds pretty cheap—less than the price of one night in this hotel—rifles, handguns, and probably even war surplus hand-grenades are everywhere. It's the Wild Mid-West here in Chicago in 1963. Mobsters, crooked cops, good cops, and law-abiding citizens—they've all got guns.

But you can't tell the players without a scorecard, and the only guideline we have is The History, *which I'm sorry to say is woefully inadequate to describe the reality of these times. Unfortunately, it reads like a resort guidebook. Everything is clean and neat, and fun. Even the bad guys in history are simple cardboard characters—easy to understand with basic motives like revenge, hatred, greed, lust for power, or that old favorite—insanity. And with few exceptions, like the World War II Nazis, the Mafia, and the money-grubbing businessmen of the late 19th century, the folks that do the dirty deeds in the official history always seem to be acting on their own. Never in a conspiracy. Never planning or cooperating together—just an assemblage of nutty people, over time, doing nutty, greedy, or malicious things that often lead to significant historical events.*

If you believe The History, *everything is pretty much an accident of person, time, and place. Of course, anyone with full faculties could never buy that. They know how they operate on a daily basis—constantly working together, scheming, and planning in an attempt to get ahead. Is it possible to believe that this conspiracy to create change is not being done by rich and powerful people on all levels? I don't think so. The big-money boys are in secure, powerful positions tied together by governmental, corporate, fraternal, and familial networks developed over decades, lifetimes, and even centuries. But it makes for easy reading in* The History *and allows for few questions and even fewer real answers. The real truth is that the U.S. is like a cancer patient in denial. Corruption has spread throughout the system. It is never publicly recognized because it is too horrible to even contemplate.*

END: 11-01-63

-Chapter X-

The Reporter Reports

The four time travelers sat in their hotel lobby, an ornate turn-of-the-century decorative masterpiece

"Less than 22 hours remain before JFK dies," said Emma. "Where do we stand?"

Currant looked about the grand space vacantly.

"Doctor? Are you with us?" Emma was getting impatient. Their leader seemed dazed. She suspected he was still feeling the effects of his near drowning.

A.C. Currant snapped his head back and mumbled, "Sorry...I was just thinking. Zak and I are lucky to be sitting here. Forget about saving JFK. We may need to save ourselves. We're in an alien world. We may think we're part of it, but we're not. We're just visitors. We're not police. We're not officials. We're not part of this society. And if we're eliminated, we won't be missed. At least not by anyone in this world."

Ethan stirred. "What do you mean? Do you want to go back? Are you afraid?"

Currant focused on his charges one by one. His voice was hushed. "Me? No. I'm an old gray goose with nothing to lose. But I fear that I have brought the three of you to a perilous place. You've got your entire lives ahead of you..."

Emma stopped his monologue. "Forget those thoughts, Doctor. 'Tomorrow is promised to no one.' Not even JFK."

"Clint Eastwood," said Ethan. "Right?"

"Pretty sharp, brother. *Absolute Power*...good movie. Anyway, you get the point. We knew what we were getting into. Our father thought it important that we do this, and so did we. What say you, fellow crime-stoppers?" She looked at Zak and Ethan.

Zak signed. "*I'm in.*"

"Zak's in. Emma's in. I'm in," said Ethan. "We're all in this together, Doctor."

Currant sipped from his coffee before speaking. "But we must be careful. Obviously, we're being watched. And we're not just dealing with a "lone nut." This morning's little swimming exercise means others are involved. They're deadly serious, and they won't tolerate any disruption of their plans." He smiled. "I just want to bring you people back in one piece. Dangerous business. If not for Zak, I'd still be at the bottom of the lake. Thanks, Zak." He raised his coffee cup as a toast to the young man.

Zak smiled weakly and nodded.

Emma looked at her friend and laughed. "Hey, Doctor. Cut it out. You're embarrassing the poor boy". Then she dropped the smile. "If you ask me, I think we're here to make *our* world a better place. We know that something happened to America in November 1963, which changed the future for the worse. Look around you. This world isn't perfect, but it's very different than ours. People here inhale the fresh air of freedom. They walk, talk and think without fear of alienating *MOM*. They don't regularly rat out each other to the federal government. They seem to have high hopes for a better future. They're not burned out, running scared, or afraid of their own shadows. They are part of a growth process. They're players in the game of life. They have a future. I'm not sure we can say that about our world in 2028."

"Right," said Ethan. "Maybe there can be a better future. If we only find a way to nudge the dice."

Emma looked at Currant. He seemed to be brightening. He was always a bit strange but never without energy. The car crash had sapped the life out of him. But that life appeared to be coming back.

"Dr. Currant..." Their eyes met, and Emma saw his concern. "Don't worry about us. Focus on our challenge. OK?"

Currant straightened, taking time to reply. They

waited. He cleared his throat and spoke. "Let's do it. We're in this far. Let's save JFK, and the future."

"To the future." Emma raised her Coke bottle.

They clicked bottles and coffee cup and proclaimed in unison…"To the future…"

On their way to the offices of *The American*, the time travelers waltzed their way through crowds of downtown shoppers and workers. They said little as they walked, and Emma's thoughts drifted. Earlier today, when Zak and Currant were fighting for their lives, she answered a call from Tom Quinn. He told her he had important news that he was willing to share if they would reciprocate and tell everything that they knew. Trying to sound like an actual reporter, she said she knew how the reporting business worked. She promised information. They set a time to meet this afternoon. She looked at her watch.

"My watch has stopped. Anyone know the time?"

Zak pointed to an electronic sign hanging off the corner of a nearby bank building…'*3:14*'.

"I hope Quinn is still there. Let's hurry. We're running late."

They walked rapidly for another ten minutes dodging cars and people. By the time they reached the newspaper building, Currant was tired. Emma noticed he had a slight limp now. No doubt an outcome of the accident. Standing in front, they waited, giving the older man time to catch his breath.

"OK. I'm good now," said Currant.

A few minutes later, Quinn greeted them at the top of the stairs. "Saw you coming from the window. Follow me," he said, directing them to another office down the corridor. He unlocked the door. The black painted letters on the frosted glass read '*Private.*'

Entering, Emma took in the space. The single room with blind-slatted windows overlooking the river was furnished with over-stuffed black leather sofas and chairs surrounding a heavy wood coffee table. An attractive oriental carpet lay upon the travertine-tiled floor.

"Close the door," Quinn directed. Zak closed it. "And flip the lock," Quinn grimaced, "I don't want any interruptions."

Tom Quinn opened a wall cabinet. "You want a drink, Dr. Currant?"

Currant looked at him quizzically. "You know who I am?"

"Two plus two," said Quinn. "I take good notes. Drink?"

"Scotch. Johnnie Walker Black. If you have it."

"No sweat, Doc. We've got everything here. This is our decompression chamber, and good booze is the best medicine for overwork and underpay." Quinn poured drinks for Currant and himself and soft drinks for the others. Then he flopped down into the big chair in front of the window.

Emma noticed he had given himself the control position in the room with the sunlight behind him. He could clearly read their faces while their view of him, and any of his telltale facial expressions, would be limited by the window's glare. "So, who goes first?" she asked innocently.

Tom Quinn swizzled the cubes in his drink. He unzipped his Zippo and lit a Lucky. Sunlight shot through the windows highlighting the smoke swirling about his head. "You do," he said with a restrained gruffness. "Tell me what's happening."

Currant jumped in. "Mr. Quinn. We haven't had the opportunity to talk before. But my students have spoken highly of you."

Quinn laughed. "I'll bet."

"Anyway, I have...I should say *we* have been busy looking into this fellow Thomas Vallee since we arrived. We were concerned he might do something to back up his opinions about the President."

"And how did you come to know his opinions, Doctor?"

Currant wiggled about the slippery leather sofa switching one leg over the other. "I'm afraid we can't tell you that—but it came to us with the greatest authority."

Quinn nodded. "And have you done any recreational swimming during your visit?"

Currant rolled his eyes. Speaking slowly, he said: "I see you are a man who can connect the dots, Mr. Quinn."

"Dot connection is my business Doc. So what about the dunking? My sources say that a cab with two passengers, who coincidently are staying at your hotel, went into the drink in Diversey Harbor this morning. And according to the driver, an unknown person forced them off the road intentionally. The cab driver and a distinguished-looking man were saved by a strong, handsome young man. That would be you, Zak?"

Zak gave a small smile and lifted his glass in acknowledgment.

"So, I'm thinking these dots connect to more dots. Like maybe Richard Cain. Maybe JFK. Maybe your Mr. Vallee?"

"I wish I knew for sure, Mr. Quinn. I can tell you that I visited Vallee last night. And this morning, Zak and I spent some time outside his apartment. Someone was watching us too."

"Let me guess. The guy that ran you off the road."

Currant nodded.

Quinn set his drink carefully on a cork coaster. "Well, that's quite a tale. A fish tale with a fishy ending." He chuckled. "So let's get this straight. You and your students are here in Chicago to discover the city and meet the press to enlighten you about the journalism business. And...then you decide to dig into one of the biggest stories this town has ever seen because you heard somehow that Mr. Vallee doesn't like the President's politics. Then, you do a little poking around, and you almost get killed." The reporter sucked on his cigarette and blew out the smoke like a steam locomotive whistle. He gazed at all of them slowly, one at a time. "Is that it?"

They nodded.

"Well, I'm not buying it."

The travelers remained quiet.

Quinn continued. I made a few calls to your hometown. Good old Springfield Heights. By the way, did you know there are dozens of Springfield towns out East? There are lots of high schools, all with student newspapers. But nobody seems to know about any extra-curricular student travel to Chicago. Of course, I couldn't confirm your registration at the school. But I could check on Dr. Currant. Not employed as a teacher or anything else at any high school. Had someone check the local phone directories too. No Currant. No Callan-Wright. Most likely no Zak 'Valentino' either." He sucked on the Lucky again and blew out his next question. "So, who are you?"

This question seemed to stun the time travelers. Currant looked at the Twins and Zak and then back at Quinn. "Mr. Quinn. You may never really know who we are. I am indeed an advisor to these charming students. We are from the East Coast. You may not be able to verify that, but it is true. But you are correct in your assumption that we are not here in Chicago to learn the journalism business."

Quinn smiled. Emma thought to herself...you think you know something Tom Quinn, but you know nothing.

"That's good. I never bought that line. So what are you up to?"

Currant measured his words, "We're here because history is being made. You are part of that history. John Kennedy is coming to Chicago tomorrow, and there are forces in place that wish to remove him. We cannot tell you our sources. As a newspaperman, I'm sure you appreciate that. Just as you cannot reveal your sources. But that is why we're here. We sought your help because you know the territory and the players. Thomas Arthur Vallee is a serious threat. We have tried to warn the Secret Service. Maybe they're taking an interest...maybe not. But I can tell you if something is not done, you may have a front-row seat for one of the worst events in the history of this country."

"So you're not going to tell me your sources, but you

want my help. Why not just go to the police?"

Currant chuckled. "Think about it. You don't like our story. They won't either. They might toss us in jail. Same thing with the Federal police. Or, for that matter, half the cops may be dirty. This town isn't exactly squeaky clean...."

Emma interjected. "Mr. Quinn. It's important that you take this seriously. You're a good reporter. I have to believe you've checked with *your* sources. Right?"

Quinn nodded. "You're story checks out. I don't know about this Vallee guy, but I know there is a big story here, and I want it."

"Now we're getting someplace," said Emma. "So what do you know?"

Quinn leaned back in his chair. "First, this is strictly *confidential*." He paused to read their eyes. "My sources with the Feds tell me there are four professional assassins in town armed with sniper rifles. Two of these guys are now in police custody. The whereabouts of the other two are unknown."

"What?" said Ethan. "Are you talking about Vallee?"

"No," said Quinn. "I am not. I'm saying that there is a team of killers in town who intend to shoot JFK as he comes in on the Northwest Expressway. Maybe from an overpass. The FBI got a tip from one of their informants. Somebody named 'Lee.' And they passed it on to the Secret Service here in Chicago."

"How did they catch the two guys?" asked Ethan.

"Mostly luck. All four guys took rooms in a place up North. The landlady spotted the long guns and called the cops. The cops called the Feds and grabbed two of them this morning. From what I know, those two are not talking at all. And nobody has seen the other two shooters. My sources aren't talking to me anymore. There's a blanket over this whole thing now. And nobody I know knows anything about your buddy Vallee."

"We can tell you all about Vallee," said Emma.

With their almost encyclopedic knowledge of the JFK crime, they spent the next half-hour reviewing

Vallee's entire life from the beginning. Emma detailed his service in the Marines, his severe injuries leading to disability, his mental instability, his tour of duty in Japan, and the fact that he has two rifles and plenty of ammunition in his apartment. A.C. tossed in that he drove a 1962 white Ford Falcon. Emma finished with the fact that somehow he had succeeded in getting a job as a printer in a warehouse building, which overlooked tomorrow's motorcade route. "JFK will drive right by his building on Jackson Boulevard." Emma spared *The History's* version of events.

Quinn listened carefully, obviously enthralled with the amount of information the time travelers were providing, and then he asked one question. "And why is this Vallee, the honorably discharged Marine with two tours of duty, about to kill JFK?"

Ethan answered quickly. "Because he's a *lone nut.*" He chuckled.

"Oh. I see," said Quinn, "that explains everything. A *lone nut.* You're joking, of course. How do you know he has weapons?"

"Because we saw a couple of men...they must be cops or Secret Service...enter his apartment today," said Currant. "They searched it, and we overheard them say Vallee has the weapons."

"If that's true, then why aren't they arresting him?" Ethan interjected hotly. "The guy's going to shoot JFK."

Currant was about to respond, but Quinn interrupted him. "Settle down, big boy. Let's say they have no idea where the remaining two hit men are located. They have two guys in custody, but they're not talking. Maybe the Feds figure Vallee will lead them to the shooters on the loose. The mouse will lead them to the cheese. I have to believe they are holding off for a good reason."

"That might make sense. Or maybe it's something else," said Ethan.

"What's that?" asked Quinn.

"Maybe Vallee has a job to do. Maybe someone

wants to set him up for a fall. I don't buy the
lone nut theory" said Ethan.

"Well," said Currant, "there's nothing we can do
about it. We're certainly not going to call the Secret
Service again. Thanks to you, Ethan, they've been
notified. If they don't do something by tomorrow morning,
we may have to."

"Now you're talking, Doctor," said Ethan.

Quinn spoke up. "Well, junior reporters. This is a
big... *a huge* story. And we're going to all work together to
get to the bottom of it. Right?"

They all agreed.

"But we're reporters. Not newsmakers. Let's get the
facts. If someone is going to get hurt, and we can do
something...we will. But otherwise, in a professional
manner as reporters. You know. I got to live in this town
after you and JFK are long gone."

"Right?"

Again they agreed.

"OK. Let's get going." Quinn looked at his watch.
"We've got about nineteen hours before he arrives. Let's
break it down. Players...Vallee, Cain, Secret Service, CPD,
FBI, four hitmen, my contacts, your contacts. Anything
else?"

"We're running out of time. We have to do
something," said Ethan.

"I said we have about nineteen hours. Let's think
clearly and use them wisely. OK?" said Quinn.

Emma thought his response to Ethan was just like
something their father would say. She then remembered
something evident to them but not to Quinn. "We know
where," said Emma.

For the first time, Quinn looked surprised. "You
know where it's going down?"

"Yes. Left turn at the top of the off-ramp from the
expressway onto Jackson Boulevard. On the bridge.
Shots may be fired from the building where Vallee works."

"You sure?" asked Quinn.

"100%," Emma said flatly.

"What else do you junior detectives have going?"

They all looked at each other. Ethan spoke. "We've got a recording of Vallee on the phone talking to somebody at the Sheriff's department...Special Investigations. Could be Richard Cain."

"Recording," said Quinn. "You got a warrant for that? You know that's not legal. Where did you get it?"

Ethan shrugged his shoulders in a plea. "Sources," he said.

"OK. But I want to hear it. I know Cain's voice." Quinn looked at his watch again. "Alright. Here's the plan of attack."

Emma sensed he was now in his element. She was impressed by how quickly he digested the information and then took control. For the next ten minutes, Quinn, the ex-Marine, barked out marching orders. When he was done, they synchronized their watches like commandos on a mission, ready for action.

"One more thing." Tom Quinn looked at Emma. "You're a pretty girl, Emma, and a smart cookie too. But I need to know. What's your shoe size?"

Emma blushed. "What?"

"Your shoe size."

She shrugged her shoulders and answered, "Eleven. But that's not a question a gentleman would ask a lady."

Quinn laughed. He downed the dregs of his drink and stood up. Whoever said I was a gentleman?"

LOG of Zak Newman --- November 1, 1963: 17:17

(Day 4 of time travel)

I'm the little piggy that stayed home. Since I can't talk to anyone, I've been sent back to the hotel to think. Quinn will set up a meeting with Richard Cain, but he first wants to listen to the voice recording taken at Vallee's apartment. He thinks he can judge if the voice on the other side is Cain's. Quinn also wants to meet with the American's ace reporter, Jack Montana, who apparently has close ties to Cain. The Twins and Quinn agree that maybe if Cain's role is exposed (whatever that is), it can be turned in our favor.

The Twins are busy trying to make a copy of the "wiretap" recording, as Quinn called it. Fortunately, the recording of Vallee talking to someone at the Sheriff's Department is of excellent quality, captured by some of the finest technology available in the year 2028. Unfortunately, it can only be played back on one of the combo earbuds in our possession. Obviously, showing anyone such a device would raise more questions than any time traveler from 2028 would like to answer. We're trying to blend in. This was supposed to be a low-key historical fact-finding expedition. So much for that pipe dream. Now we're trying to stop the assassination. We've uncovered a plot. Possibly we're battling the plotters. They have tried to kill us once. And there's still plenty of time for us to get into trouble.

Watching television on the hotel's 17" black and white receiver has been interesting. In addition to lots of puppet-filled kiddie shows, old movies, and inane situation comedies, I can watch history in the making as shown on

*local news broadcasts. JFK's scheduled visit here
tomorrow is big news. In a live interview, Mayor Daley
said that tomorrow would be "a great day for the fine
people of the City of Chicago." School children interviewed
promised to give the President a most joyful Chicago
welcome. And the big question that had everyone
wondering was which football team would the President
be cheering to victory?*

*Obviously, there was no mention of four or five gunmen
roaming the city, laying in wait to kill the President.
Newsreel footage of JFK was shown from one of his press
conferences. In the close-ups, I can see now why this man
had such a cult following and why he caused so many
people to dislike him. For one, he doesn't look like a
politician. Mayor Daley looks like a politician—kind of
rumpled, oratorical-challenged, beanbag-wearing the face
of a neighborhood butcher instead of a big city mayor. On
the other hand, Kennedy looks like a film star of the
period. Sun-tanned face, sculpted features, and a sharp
dresser, he is—very good looking; highly articulate,
young, humorous, and intelligent. Lots of power, money,
and a beautiful wife. What's not to like or hate? I can
attest to the issue of being too good-looking. I was
designed to be handsome. But the simple configuration of
my skin and bones causes more problems than benefits.
Guys don't like me because I'm the embodiment of
competition as far as girls are concerned. In effect,
they're jealous. Girls are often put off because they view
me as just a pretty boy—or a boy-toy—a man with good
looks but without brains. I know this is just a stereotype,
but it ends up being taken as fact. In that sense, I
understand one of the burdens that JFK carried. I don't
think even his detractors would suggest he is brainless.
But they would find him too pretty. They would be*

jealous. They would be concerned that his popularity would carry him through another election, giving him more power. And after that election, his brother, the Attorney General Bobby Kennedy, could take a couple of turns at the wheel. And then, who knows, even brother Edward, or Teddy as they call him, could have a shot at it. Speaking of shots. It's never going to happen if "shots ring out" tomorrow. The Kennedy's quest for White House control will be over tomorrow morning. Maybe. We'll see.

END: 11-01-63

-Chapter XI-

Technological Trouble

Like Quinn, Jack Montana was a World War II vet. They were both reporters at the same newspaper, *Chicago's American*, but that was where the similarities ended. Montana was an award-winning star reporter who wrote a daily byline column. He was well-known by almost everyone in the city. He rubbed shoulders with politicians, celebrities, sports figures, mobsters, and other newsmakers. A few years back, he joined the American after a successful stint with a competing afternoon paper. Even Quinn, who had more seniority than Montana, gave in to Montana's star power. But, he was never sure about Jack Montana's relationship with Richard Cain. Everyone knew that Cain should be considered a bit suspect. Everyone in the know knew he was the Outfit's man in the Sheriff's office. He was dedicated to ensuring the control of vice and rackets in the city. He used his office to snuff out competition for his masters and to deflect any attempt to arrest any of his friends. As he was about to meet with Montana, Tom Quinn thought about this idea that "everyone knew." What did that mean? It meant that all such suppositions were totally off-the-record, unreported, and not common knowledge—outside of those in the underworld and those who chronicled their wormy dealings like him. From Jack Montana's viewpoint, he used Richard Cain as a source of inside information. And Richard Cain used him as a publicity tool. It was a marriage made in Chicago—"the city that works." It was late. All the tool-and-die makers, plumbers, painters, school teachers, and businessmen were at home eating dinner, looking forward to a night nestled in front of the television. But Montana was still working, and so was Quinn.

Quinn poked his head through the door. "Jack. Need your help. Got a minute?" Without waiting for an answer, he entered Montana's office and closed the door behind him. Montana looked up from his typewriter.

"Tomorrow's column?"

"Right. No rest for the wicked. Busy. Busy. What can I do for you, Tom?"

Quinn ignored Montana's impatience, sat down, crossed one leg over the other, and lit a cigarette. "It's about this JFK visit."

Montana waved his hand in the air. "More publicity for the Mayor and JFK. Political visit. I'm not too interested in that, Tom."

"It's more than that. It's about Richard Cain. "

Montana's blasé Ivy-league look swung quickly from a half-smile to a frown. Quinn knew he hated to talk about Cain. Defending his relationship with the kinky cop was not high on Montana's list of fun activities. Quinn brought him up to date on everything. Montana was unaware that two potential assassins were in police custody and two others were on the loose. He didn't know about Thomas Arthur Vallee—in short, he knew nothing.

Montana now leaned forward, hanging on Quinn's every word. "Assassins...damn. You should have come to me sooner, Tom. This is hot stuff. You could use my help." His voice was a mixture of mock displeasure and subtle salesmanship.

This fish is on the hook, thought Quinn.

"Jack, I'd like to share your byline column on this one in addition to my own stories. OK?"

"No problem," said Montana. "One column shared out of hundreds is a small price to pay for collegial cooperation."

BS thought Quinn. But who cares? "Right. We're all on the same team."

"Who knows about this?"

Quinn thought for a moment. "I got the hit men story from my contact at the Bureau. And I talked to one of our finest, but he didn't have any details."

"Kowalski?"

"Yes."

"Don't trust him," said Montana.

"Why?"

"I hear he has his fingers everywhere. Loose lips too. Anyway, what does Cain have to do with this?"

"Some people I know recorded a call from someone from the Sheriff's Office setting up a meeting with this guy Vallee...11:30 a.m. Saturday, behind the building Vallee works at on Jackson."

"So?"

"So they're talking about dropping some banners or something like that. Some kind of anti-Castro jingo to hang out a window when JFK gets off the expressway and heads into the Loop."

"Sounds relatively harmless. A bit impolite, but harmless," said Montana.

"I agree. But this guy Vallee is known to dislike JFK's policies. He has two rifles and thousands of rounds of ammo. And the building he works in is located right on the motorcade route. It's an easy shot down the street. He's an ex-Marine, so you know he's a good shot."

"*Semper fi...*" Montana nodded. "You think Cain is the person on the phone?"

"Could be. I haven't heard the recording."

"Can we get it?"

Quinn rubbed his chin. "It's coming. If it is Cain, I'd like to confront him with it tonight. Can you make that happen?"

Montana looked at his watch. "It's getting late. But I'll try him at his office. I may have to buy him dinner if he's there, and he's an expensive date. I'll give him a call." Montana dialed, and Quinn waited expectantly. He wondered about the Twins and Currant. They should have come back with the recording by now.

Emma, Ethan, and Currant retrieved the earbud device at the hotel and left Zak behind. They walked quickly to State Street and then south toward a seedier section of the Loop. On their earlier exploration, Ethan spotted a game arcade, which he remembered as having a recording machine. He looked around—dubious-looking stores, strip tease joints, and run-down bars. They found the "Empress Emporium" in the middle of the block and entered. The place matched its neighbors in dilapidation. As they entered, the few die-hard dregs of society playing pinball games didn't bother to look up. Ethan spotted the recording device. It looked like a phone booth. Its curved front canopy had the words: *Automatic Recording Studio* written boldly, and the side read: *Make Your Own Record - Only 35 Cents.* Another sign read: *Like Talking on the Phone—But a Thousand Times More Thrilling!*

No one was in the booth, so they opened the door and looked inside. A black phone handset hung neatly on the wall. Below was a coin slot.

Emma and Ethan put their heads into the booth, but Currant nuzzled them aside so he could see the recording device. "This is it?"

"This is it," answered Ethan. "Unless you have a better technology source. I think they use magnetized plastic tapes to record now, but the town is shut down. We couldn't find another recording machine even if we were willing to pay the price. This one's 35 cents. What a bargain."

"There's no free lunch when it comes to technology," said Currant.

"Well, let's do it," said Emma impatiently. "We promised Mr. Quinn we'd be back soon with the recording."

"Doctor, you better handle this. You're the science expert." Ethan backed away from the machine. "You have enough change?"

Currant dug out some coins from his pockets and fingered them in his hand. "I've got three quarters, three nickels, and a dime. Let me in." A.C. entered the box and closed the doors while the Twins stood sentry outside. A rock and roll tune played loudly in the background. Currant studied the instruction sheet for a good minute.

Then he opened the doors and shoved his head out. "Let's do a test. I want to check out the voice quality. Come on in here."

"All of us?" asked Emma.

Currant nodded.

They squeezed in. It was already hot in the booth. Currant sucked in his stomach, loaded a dime and a quarter into the slide device, and pushed it inward. The coins dropped, and a whirring sound was emitted from the machine. A red light came on. Currant grabbed the phone off the hook and began talking.

"This is Doctor A.C. Currant speaking from the south Loop area of Chicago in 1963..." He rambled on about the heat, the recording booth, and the archaic technology. "And I am here with Emma and Ethan Callan-Wright, who will speak to you now." He handed the phone to Emma.

She stammered, "This is Emma. This is our third day on this trip. We are having a good time. The weather is not too bad for November..." a yellow signal light appeared, indicating less than 30 seconds remained.

Ethan grabbed the phone: "This is Ethan Callan-Wright...time traveler, explorer, and truth-seeker. We traveled here from the year 2028 using Doctor Currant's *TimeTravelle*. We're here to make history and to save JFK. Tonight we will force the plotters to give up their plot. We'll make them ...."

There was a clunk, and a blue light came on. The 90-second recording time was over. Ethan handed the phone to A.C. as a playback of their recording began. Currant listened intently. He frowned and then reset the phone on the wall. In a few seconds, a record slid silently into a slot below. Ethan pulled it out. It was a bright red disk, which read: *VOICE-O-GRAPH—Caution Inflammable!*

"Well?" asked Ethan.

Currant looked flustered. "Please give me air."

The Twins moved out of the box, leaving the old man with his machine.

"Thank you," he said. "Well, it's over-modulated, weak-volumed, and scratchy."

"But will it work?"

"Do we have a choice? Hang on to this." He handed Ethan the test record. "Do me a favor. Close the doors and see if you can get someone to turn down the sound system."

They closed the doors. Emma sought help, and Ethan watched Currant through the window as he removed the earbud device and held it about an inch away from the microphone. A.C. Currant reloaded the machine and went through the drill. Ethan couldn't hear anything, but things appeared to be proceeding smoothly. Midway, he noticed the rock and roll music was quieter. Emma solved that problem. Currant finished recording and listened to the replay. He grabbed the second record as it popped out and worked his way out of the booth. Ethan saw that record mailing envelopes were being sold. He bought two for a nickel a piece. The recording session was over.

Outside, they walked toward the newspaper offices. Ethan queried A.C. Currant, "How was it? Can you hear the voices?"

"Let me put it this way. It's embarrassing. I don't put much faith in this."

Back at the *American*, introductions were made using the student reporter cover for the time travelers. Emma thought Montana was very gracious and handsome.

"So where is it?" asked Quinn. "We've got to get a move on."

Ethan pulled out the two envelopes containing the disks. Emma could tell he was flustered. He didn't know which one was the Vallee conversation. He shrugged his shoulders and gave one to Quinn.

"What the hell is this? Did you guys cut a record?"

"That's all we have," said Emma. "Do you have a machine to play it? She looked at Jack Montana. He had the look of a man seeing his Pulitzer Prize fading away.

Quinn gathered them all together, and they went into a room filled with ancient electronic equipment—radios, wire and tape recorders, and a portable phonograph. He set up the machine quickly, placed the disk, and set it into action. Emma was ready to pounce on the device if he had chosen the wrong disk. It played. "*This is A. C. Currant speaking from....*"

Ethan rushed to the machine and stopped it. He pulled out one disk and inserted the other.

"Sorry," he said. "That was a test."

The second disk played. The quality was not very good, but as Emma said later: "What did you expect for 35 cents?" When it finished. Emma looked around the room. Montana was rolling his eyes at Quinn, Currant was mumbling something about the equipment, and Ethan was focused on Montana.

"So, was that Cain?" Ethan looked at the two reporters.

"Could be...or it could be any one of thousands of people."

"But those words were spoken from the Sheriff's Office. Did it sound like him?"

"Maybe...what do you think, Tom?"

"Maybe," he said slowly. "I still say we have to confront him."

Montana checked his watch and then spoke. "Look. I have to go, but Dick Cain will be in his office for the next thirty minutes or so if you want to run this by him. I wish you luck. My only advice to you is don't push him. Treat him with respect. He is the Head of the Special Investigations Unit. He's a sharp guy. I'm sure he will be helpful. You better go along, Tom."

"OK, Jack. I'll handle this. Thanks for your help setting it up."

"No problem. Give him my best." Montana headed back to his office.

"I don't trust that man," Emma heard Quinn mutter to himself, along with some kind of unintelligible expletive.

"What?"

Quinn shook his head. "Sounded like someone talking in a can. Let's go."

LOG of Zak Newman --- November 1, 1963: 19:26

(Day 4 of time travel)

I'm still sitting in the hotel room, waiting for the team to return. I actually ordered a burger and fries through room service. A first time for everything. I'm enjoying this animal delight as I write. Of course, I took special measures to accomplish this simple task. I wrote a note about my nutritional needs and hand-delivered it to the man at the main desk. He took care of the rest. Charged it to the room. A.C. will love that. At least I won't starve tonight. I've heard nothing from anyone. But as requested by my friends, I have been thinking.

Having the benefit of hearing the Vallee/Sheriff's Department phone conversation and Quinn's info about the captured hitmen, I'm thinking Ethan is right. Vallee is being set up. He's not part of the shooting—except to be a patsy—someone left behind to take the heat. He's been asked by someone to unleash a giant banner on the building—JFK FREE CUBA. Vallee doesn't like Kennedy. He wants some kind of military intervention in Cuba, so he goes along with the plan. But then he's double-crossed. They don't drop banners. Instead, others shoot JFK right in front of the building where Vallee works. When all the action occurs, Valle's on the roof holding a rolled-up banner—ready to unfurl. He hears the shots— sees the turmoil below—panics, heads downstairs, exits the rear door, and is gunned down by our boys Milner and Kowalski, who are part of the conspiracy. Kowalski provides the dying words to link Castro to the crime, and it's a done deal. JFK dead. Lone-nut assassin dead— case closed. The public screams for Castro to be eliminated. It's a nasty conspiracy, complete with a patsy fall guy.

Or, on the other hand, maybe Vallee is a "lone nut" *of sorts. He doesn't know about the other shooters, but independently, and quite coincidentally, he decides the whole* Free Cuba *banner scenario is not enough—it's time for real action. So instead of bringing a banner to the building, he takes his M1 and plenty of ammo and starts shooting. To his surprise, other gunmen are shooting. Milner and Kowalski show up. Let's assume they were only part of a conspiracy to drop the banners—nothing about shooting the President. Maybe they were supposed to help him get away after the banner episode.*

But then everything goes haywire. They get wind of the shooting and decide they would rather have the glory of shooting the Presidential assassin than the embarrassment of being known as the fools who sent an unbalanced ex-Marine with a gun collection—a certified schizophrenic receiving government disability payments— to the roof of a building placing the President of the United States into the line of fire. Heck, they might even go to jail or, worse, as accessories. So they get rid of Vallee—shoot him dead—case closed. An attempted political statement gone bad but immediately self-corrected by two Johnny-on-the-Spot cops: Milner and Kowalski. Of course, this scenario calls for the improbable coincidence that two independent sets of assassins (Vallee and the hitmen) arrive on the same day and place for the killing. Seems extremely unlikely to me. I really don't think Vallee knew anything about the planned assassination. He was set up.

So where does all this thinking lead to? Most likely, everyone took the easy way out. Whatever the motivations of Kowalski and Milner, their story would be the same. They happened on the scene and killed the

*killer. Later, investigators might buy the "lone nut" story
and look no further. Or they might discover the "banners-
gone-wild" plot, but find that tale a messy snake pit of
loose ends, wired connections, and powerful people—all
wrapped around a sympathetic story of taking back Cuba
from the Communists. Those heading follow-up
investigations would find the truth compromised by
expediency, the facts compromised by misleading police
follow-up and political cover-ups everywhere. My best
guess is that months after the crime and the taking of
Cuba, the higher-up conspirators sold the investigative
commission as follows—forget other shooters—Vallee did
it—call him a "lone nut"—"The King is Dead—Long Live
the King." Don't embarrass the new President, the Secret
Service, the FBI, the CIA, the Chicago Police, the Sheriff's
Department, Mayor Daley, and the brave Cuban refugees
who helped take Cuba back. So they didn't. President
Johnson, the military, the CIA, the Havana casino-owning
mobsters, the Cuban rebels, the Cuban dynasties, the
U.S. plantation owners in Cuba, whoever Kennedy
pissed-off while he was in office, the Republicans and a
host of others were happy. Everyone was happy except
the Kennedy family, a few die-hard "lone nut"
disbelievers, all the people who voted for Kennedy, and
the ghost of Thomas Arthur Vallee. For all we know,
Vallee may have uncovered the plot, threatened to expose
it, and was eliminated. In which case, he was a hero.
Lots of possibilities and the time travelers are now in the
mix. So who knows what will happen now.*

*I finished my burger and fries, and I'm done thinking for
the evening. I can't wait to find out how the Cain meeting
went. But no matter what, I have the feeling that the
weather tonight for the kids from Mystic Heights will be
dark, cold, and foggy. Maybe that's why detectives*

always wear trench coats. Hey, maybe I should get one and one of those Sherlock Holmes hats. I could be Zak Newman—The Silent Detective. *I do miss my* Voicenator. *I want to talk again.*

END: 11-01-63

-Chapter XII-

Is Cain Able?

Currant, Ethan, and Emma squeezed into the cab's back seat while Quinn rode shotgun for the ten-minute ride across the Loop to Cain's office. Smoke from the reporter's cigarette drifted backward. Emma coughed loudly and complained. Turning in his seat, Quinn stared back at her, made a face, and then rolled down the window and flipped the half-smoked Lucky out, trading nicotine for peace of mind. Currant announced he rather liked the smell of burning tobacco, and he pulled out his pack of cigarettes for laughs. She was not amused. Ethan also endured some discomfort. Like a broken marionette, his lanky body was shoehorned into the back seat. The ancient and heavy portable phonograph rested on his lap, and each bump and bounce painfully reminded him of the tenuous nature of the evidence. He wondered whether Cain would hear the recording and admit to the Vallee phone call. It was more likely that he would simply kick them out. Ethan sensed the tension in the stuffy confines of the checkered cab. JFK's life was on the line. The taxi moved on. The teenage crusaders, the old scientist, and the veteran reporter coursed through the crisp Chicago November night, aware their success or failure with Cain might decide his fate and that of America.

The night shift guard greeted them on arrival and walked them to Richard Cain's office. Quinn entered first, followed by the travelers.

"Tom Quinn. Working late, I see," said Cain. He stood behind a heavy oak desk as he greeted the party. Mid-thirties, well proportioned, not tall, Cain wore those dark-rimmed glasses that Quinn mentioned. Ethan thought he looked very confident.

"The city that never sleeps..." said Quinn. "Thanks

for seeing us on short notice."

The reporter introduced the time travelers. The office was a minefield of manila folders and clipped files piled everywhere. Quinn and Currant sat in the only two chairs available while Ethan and Emma stood behind. Cain smiled comfortably at the assembled group of amateur crime stoppers. He looked at the portable record player. "Going to a sock hop?"

Quinn chuckled. "No, it's part of our investigation into a fellow named Thomas Vallee. As Jack informed you, we think this guy Vallee is a possible threat to the President."

"Sounds like Secret Service territory to me," replied Cain. "Why bring me into it?"

Currant interrupted. "I don't know your title Mr. Cain...Chief Inspector?"

Cain smiled. "For you, Dr. Currant...call me Dick."

A.C. nodded. "Dick...serious business here. We need your help. We have a recording of a phone conversation between Thomas Vallee and someone in your office. We'd like you to identify the voice."

Cain looked serious. "A wiretap. I thought you people were high schoolers. But let's disregard the legal issues for a moment." He leaned back in his chair. " Play it."

Quinn got up and offered a cigarette to Cain, who declined. The reporter set up the machine. A cigarette hung from his lower lip with a long ash dangling threatening to fall onto the record. He flipped the switch, and the record player spun through 90 seconds of barely intelligible dialogue. Ethan knew they were holding a pitifully low hand in this poker game as he listened. Cain hadn't changed his indifferent expression while listening. Nor did he appear threatened by the recording.

"That's it? Well, don't give up your day job, Dr. Currant." Cain laughed. "You'll never make it in the wiretapping business trying to sell a nasty-scratchy recording like this. I know that world pretty well. But I don't mean to disparage you or your team of junior reporters. However, let's assume you're correct and the call was made to this office. First, the voice quality is terrible. It sounds like someone is talking about setting up a meeting at 11:30. Then something about a 'big event.'" Cain shrugged his shoulders, "I couldn't recognize the voice."

Ethan straightened up to his full height and jumped in. "We think the voice was yours, Mr. Cain."

Cain didn't flinch. "This whole thing is loaded with issues. If it was me, I'd have it tossed out of court. There are laws about this kind of activity. Even though, as a lawman, I don't always agree with these legal technicalities, I'm forced to abide by them. You might think about that too. But the fact is, all we can say for sure is that it is a man speaking to another man."

"What about voice prints? We could have this analyzed."

Cain smiled. "You've been reading too many *Dick Tracy* comic books, son. Can't be done in real life.

"Dick," said Quinn, "you must know the flap about town now. The JFK visit."

"I'm not here for decoration, Tom. I've heard. But it's not my party."

"Do you know Thomas Vallee?" asked Currant.

Cain tossed out a weak smile. "Am I on trial here? I know lots of people. And usually, I ask the questions."

"Did you stop by our hotel last night? We had a report of someone that fits your description asking questions about us."

Cain leaned back in his chair and looked at Quinn. "I'll take that smoke, Tom." Quinn tossed him his pack, and Cain appeared to calm himself in the process of extracting and lighting the cigarette. He inhaled deeply and then turned his head to the side and exhaled. He glanced at his watch. "It's getting late. Where are we going with this?"

A.C. Currant straightened up. "Mr. Cain. We think we've done some good work here. I think you know it, and you know Mr. Vallee. I think that you've been watching us. Maybe you had something to do with our cab being run off the road yesterday. I think you may be the voice on the disk. It's possible you may have been planning this 'big event' with Vallee."

"Enough," said Cain. A new face appeared—his smile turned to a scowl. He squared his shoulders and thrust out his jaw. His eyes narrowed and focused on Currant. "Who do you think you are talking to? I'm afraid you kids are out of your league, and your school teacher here is whistling Dixie. You know, I could have you all run in on charges if I wanted to. But I don't want to make a mess of your little field trip or give you high school kids a rap sheet. You should be more careful, Currant. This is Chicago...not Springfield Heights, and I'm the sheriff in this town. Or close enough to make your life miserable. Take your silly red record and get out." He stood as if to close the meeting.

"Dick. Wait a second...." Quinn sputtered.

With a wave of his hand, he dismissed them.

"Mr. Cain," said Emma from the back of the room. Her voice was quiet and composed.

Cain looked at her coldly.

"Mr. Cain, I know we have barged into your town and into your business. And I know we are only schoolchildren to you. But please have a seat and listen to me for a minute. OK?"

Cain accepted her suggestion and slowly repositioned himself into the chair. "All right, Miss Emma," said Cain in a composed voice. "I'm always willing to listen to a lady. Especially a pretty one. Go ahead."

Emma moved closer. Sliding by Currant and Quinn, she pushed a few file folders to the side to clear a space and then half-sat on the credenza. Cain turned his chair to face her. Ethan could see that he was taking a reading of the young woman. He also knew that of all the people in the room, Emma was a match for Cain. She was smart—captain of the debate team at good old Mystic Heights High. And unlike Currant, who was a genius but lacked diplomatic skills, she was very tactful.

"Let's look at the facts," said Emma turning her head slightly to lock onto Cain's eyes. "JFK is coming tomorrow. Vallee's workplace on Jackson Boulevard puts him directly on the motorcade route. We know two paramilitary shooters in custody and two others armed with high-powered rifles are hiding somewhere in the city. Vallee talked to somebody in this building. I accept that it wasn't you. But because of your position, you are tied to this whole thing nevertheless. And what is the 'big event'?"

"You tell me," said Cain flatly.

"From what we understand, it could just be a way of embarrassing the President. Frustrated people making a political statement. People using the occasion to force JFK into action in Cuba. That sounds harmless enough. Almost like freedom of speech. But these two hit men...whoever and wherever. They are dangerous," she rolled the last comment out very slowly and clearly. "It certainly sounds serious to me. Do you agree?"

Cain appeared to reflect before answering. He exhaled a blast of cigarette smoke aimed away from Emma in Currant's direction. "You know I'll put my faith in the system to take care of them. The Secret Service is pretty sharp," said Cain.

Emma nodded and then leaned in toward the desk. "I agree, but why take a chance? The cat is out of the bag concerning Vallee. You know, and we know the police and the Feds are watching him. For some reason, they've not yet arrested him. Even though they know, he's a prime candidate for danger. The 'big event' runs the risk of becoming the 'big fiasco.' If these shooters are even able to fire one shot, there will be a full investigation. Ultimately, Vallee will talk. Rightly or wrongly, this office may be connected to the attempt. People will take sides. They'll be looking for somebody to blame. And you will bear the brunt. You are in charge. As you say, you're the sheriff in this town." Her face took on a look of honest intensity.

"So?"

"So," she said calmly. "I don't think you want to have to explain anything. You know what they say 'never complain, never explain.' I think there is an opportunity of a lifetime here for a courageous, bright man like you."

Ethan watched Cain react to her words. The cop was visibly mellowing out. Ethan marveled at how big men could always be tamed by a sweet-talking woman. He had no idea where she was going with this story, but he had faith in Emma.

"Someone has to make the call here," she said, looking directly into Cain's eyes. "Obviously, no one in authority wants to admit the situation is dangerous for JFK here in Chicago. But somebody has to. And you'd have to agree this is an awful time to make a bold political statement about Cuba. It's a mess. But one that only you can straighten out...and profit from... if you move quickly."

Cain rested his elbows on the arms of his chair and nested his chin into the intertwined knuckles of both hands. "How so?"

Emma moved closer to Cain and sat on the corner of his desk as if they were the only two people in the room.

"Call it in. Contact your boss, Mr. Ogilvie, now. Tell him what's happening. Tell him he can be a hero if he calls Mayor Daley and explains the situation. As much as Daley wants the parades and the hoopla, he does not want anything to happen to his golden boy...especially in Chicago. Daley *must* call JFK and tell him not to come to Chicago tomorrow."

Cain thought for a moment. His face relaxed, and he smiled. He reached over and held Emma's hand in his. "You know, young lady. That's not a half-bad idea. It's the old *lemonade from lemons.* Fact is...if they don't locate those two shooters...someone *will* have to call it into Washington. And this fellow Vallee may concoct some strange stories if they arrest him. We don't need any bad publicity here either, even if there is nothing to it." He released her hand and leaned back in the chair. "I'll take that recording as evidence. Now, I want you to leave so I can get to work."

Ethan couldn't believe it. He burst out, "So you're going to call it off?"

"Yes. I'm going to do just what she said. If the mayor doesn't call, I'll have my boss Ogilvie call. And if he won't call, then I will. Makes good sense considering all the facts. And someone should benefit. Why not the good Mayor, the Sheriff, and me? Good politics also."

"Good for JFK, too," said Ethan.

Cain rubbed his chin with his right hand. "Correct...he's a lucky man." He stood again and shook everyone's hand. "Success in school. Stop back and see me in a few years. I have big plans, and those people that help me will be rewarded. Stick with Dick."

The time travelers and Quinn were about to leave.

"The record please," said Cain.

Currant handed it to him.

"Thanks, Doctor. No hard feelings. Teachers are important too."

Currant looked at him and said, "We can all learn something new, Mr. Cain."

"You are correct, my friend. I seem to always learn by mistake," said Cain. "That's the story of my life."

LOG of Zak Newman --- November 2, 1963: 08:10

(Day 5 of time travel)

*Well today is the day—*The History *says JFK will be killed in a few hours. According to Ethan and Currant, Emma made a great pitch to Cain last night. My three friends think her logic will sway him. Cain will ask Ogilvie to ask Daley to ask JFK to cancel his visit. We can hope—and that's all.*

I've been listening to the radio news about Vietnam. "FLASH—the Diem brothers committed suicide during a military coup." Right. Of course, in a few days, the world will find out that story is bogus. In reality, the two political puppets absorbed multiple gunshot and knife wounds—execution style—a cold-blooded assassination. So it is with the news. Often the first accounts are wrong with the later versions corrected, or the first accounts are right with the later reports corrected. It really depends on who has been killed and who can control the facts. In this case, the military junta could control the story until the photos of the bloodied brothers' bodies, hands tied behind their backs, reached America. Dressed in priest robes, stowed in the back of a military vehicle trussed up like sheep to be shorn, the Diems had their reign terminated abruptly. So much for the suicide story.

Right now, this Saturday morning, JFK and his advisors are deciding what to do with Vietnam. Even considering the importance of the Diem deaths, The History *has JFK heading off to Chicago to watch a football game. A decision to stay in Washington and strategize would have saved his life, but then he would have to disappoint one of his great political supporters, Mayor Daley. The radio*

reports that Kennedy's advisors are planning to set up a
control room under the stands of Soldier Field so he can
have immediate access to breaking news about Vietnam.
The flitter of 2028 claims that JFK blamed the deaths of
the Diem brothers on the CIA Poor JFK. He just kept
shaking that CIA tree—first the Bay of Pigs and now the
Diem assassinations. I hope today he's at least working
with the military/industrial people. Otherwise, he's
looking like that big egg teetering on the wall.
Bureaucracies, like the CIA and Hoover's FBI, seem to live
long beyond the politicians that create them. A president
can only serve eight years—unless he creates a family
political dynasty. Even then, he probably should make
nice-nice. It's like rock versus wind and water—who
wins? Ask the sand my friend—ask the sand. But I
digress.

We're waiting for news today about JFK. I believe we did
everything we could to take him out of harm's way while
concealing our status as time travelers. I hope we were
successful on both accounts. The President is due to
arrive in about three hours. So far, we have heard nothing
about a cancellation of the visit. Don't come, JFK. It's one
thing to read about great tragedy and another to
experience it in the flesh. For someone with my
hypersensitive psychic abilities, it will be tough to absorb
the mass depression, rage, and hysteria that will be
released by this event. Unchecked emotion will rain down
on my head like a summer hailstorm on greenhouse
glass.

A.C. Currant is in the bathtub again. I can hear him
singing and splashing around. He says taking a hot bath
good for his muscles and bones. I think the last few days
have been a little rough for a man his age. And, of course,

the cab ride to the bottom of the lagoon didn't help. He is amazing. Go-go-go—he's been working day and night. I should give him a bubble bath and toss a rubber ducky into his tub. Toys seem to amuse him. Like the little Mercedes Benz he always has with him. He seems like a guy who's never really grown up—he's just a big kid.

I guess I don't have much to say in this entry. We're just waiting. Soon, we'll join the Twins in their room and watch the television news together. A.C. says room service breakfast is in order. I say, let's eat early. Later, we may not have the stomach for eating. On the other hand, we might be reveling in our success and partying all day long. Let's hope for the latter, but if not, we'll have to deal with the other painful possibility.

END: 11-02-63

-Chapter XIII-

Long Live the King

A notice flashed on the television screen: *THIS IS A BULLETIN FROM NBC NEWS*, followed by the image of a reporter standing in front of the White House with a large handheld microphone:

"*White House Press Secretary Pierre Salinger has just announced that the President's scheduled trip to Chicago today has been canceled. As an indication of the immediacy and spontaneity of this decision, a plane full of reporters, who would have covered JFK's trip, is already in the air on its way to Chicago. Mr. Salinger says quote— 'The continuing crisis in Vietnam will keep the President in Washington. Therefore the President is not going to the football game' —end quote. In Chicago, thousands of people who intended to catch a glimpse of JFK as his motorcade passed through the city's streets, will be disappointed. But obviously, this official business related to the Vietnam situation takes precedence. This is Sander Vanocur, NBC News reporting from the Capitol*".

Ethan switched off the television. For a few seconds, no one—not Currant, not Emma—nor Ethan said anything. Zak sat on a sofa and just smiled.

Finally, Currant spoke, "Well, we did it. The tragedy has been averted. My hat's off to you, Emma. Your speech to Cain must have worked. This whole Vietnam thing is a convenient excuse...but whatever."

"Three cheers for us," said Ethan. "We nudged the past just enough to get a different result. But one which is totally plausible."

Emma got up and hugged A.C. Currant, who seemed to be embarrassed by this show of affection. "Dr. Currant. We owe it all to the *TimeTravelle* and you."

Currant smiled and did a mock bow before his

subjects while Zak waved his arms about, trying to get everyone's attention. Finally, Emma looked over and translated.

"Zak says: 'What about *The History*? We just changed it."

"This will be noticed," said Currant slowly. "They may send someone out." Currant ran his hands through his hair before continuing. "Who knows what effect this will have on subsequent events. Back in 2028, there is a new past starting today. Millions of decision trees are branching out in different directions. *MOM* will not be pleased."

Ethan parried with his own comment, "Who cares? Someone needed to shake up the world. We know *The History* lied about what happened to JFK. For all we know, the entire *History* could be filled with lies. Truth has consequences. We can deal with it." He looked around at his sister and friends. They were quiet.

Zak absorbed the emotions and brainwaves in the air—Ethan was happy with the result, Emma calculated the effects, and Currant was concerned about repercussions. Zak, if he thought about himself, he would have to admit; he was pleased to move on. He really wanted to check out the rest of 1963.

Tom Quinn had a strange feeling after leaving the time travelers last night. He felt like a thousand-pound weight had been lifted from his shoulders. He didn't exactly know why, but he suspected it was because he had a rare glimpse into the inner workings of the planet. He thought it was all hit or miss, things bumping into each other in the night. Planet Earth was filled with people who thought they were in control or were convinced that others, for certain, were controlling their lives. But in fact, the world was an action-reaction contraption. People try their best to make things happen, but even when they know just about everything, even when they are certain their horse is a sure thing, even when the race is fixed in their favor, they had better hold on to their wallet, their rosary, or their crotch, because things happen. The real power some folks have is the power to rewrite history in their favor, the power to make the best of what happens. And the more money, assets, connections, and entrenched power one has, the more likely they will be able to revise the past to fit the desired future. People are short on memories and long on fear. Do what it takes. Make it work. That's how Chicago has survived and grown over the years, he thought. That's how the United States has survived and grown.

The present is only molding clay for a future sculpture created by the Union of Historical Interpretation— governments, industry, financiers, bureaucracies, legal systems, politicians, good old boys, and religious groups. Newspaper reporters are not part of that group. They report what they see. And they see what they are supposed to see. That thousand-pound weight was something he carried with him during the war and afterward when he returned to everyday life. Until last night, he thought he was responsible, in some way, for the world. Not true. I'll work on my family and myself, he thought; let the world take care of itself. I don't have enough power, money, or lifetimes to manage the interpretation of the past to my benefit. Who could guess what Cain would do? But if we depend on people like that to make the world work in our favor, we are in trouble."

Book-ending this most recent philosophical revelation, he received the JFK cancellation announcement over the newswire Teletype about a half-hour ago. He decided to call Kowalski again to see what, if anything, was happening. Maybe they caught the team of hitmen. He asked the blonde to bring him a cup of coffee. He sipped the hot brew as he dialed up and connected with the Chicago cop.

"Busy day, Quinn. Don't have much time."

"What's up?"

"Well, you bowled a strike with your guy Vallee. A couple of the boys who were tailing him made a traffic stop on him earlier this morning. They saw a blade on his front seat. Gave them 'probable' to search his car. Found three hundred rounds of ammunition in the trunk. They think he was on his way to work when they caught him. Of course, makes no difference now. He'd have no target. You heard...right?"

"Yeah. Trip canceled. I caught the news. What else?"

"Well, this was before the news came in from Washington. They had Vallee here for about a half-hour. Roastin' and toastin'. I heard him whinin' like a baby in there. They got him to *agree* to let them visit his apartment. They went in. Grabbed his weapons and a ton of ammo. He's in a holding cell now."

Quinn thought for a moment. "Pete. Is there anybody there at his apartment now? Can you get me into his place for few minutes?"

The voice on the other side hesitated. "I dunno, Tom. Everything's really hot."

"Pete. You owe me. Anyway...there's no secret here. I helped put you guys in this deal, didn't I? I just want to capture the scene for posterity. I'll be in and out in five minutes. OK?"

"OK. But we're even after this. Meet me there at eleven sharp. I'll give you five minutes. No photos and no one else. Just you."

"Thanks," said Quinn. "You're on."

Quinn met Kowalski at Vallee's apartment at the appointed time. There were no other cops around. Kowalski had secured a key from the janitor. He stayed in the entry vestibule and handed Quinn the key. Exactly five minutes later, Quinn returned the key.

"Find what you want?" Kowalski asked.

"Yep. I got what I needed."

"Good. Because you'll never print this story. I guarantee it."

"What are you saying? This is one big story."

Kowalski smiled. "The Mayor's gonna' deep-six this entire event. So save your memories. This never happened."

Quinn shook his head. "And to think I wasted my 'Get Out of Jail' card for nothing.

"Too bad for you. We're even now. Keep the lid on your typewriter. You'll get a call today. Sorry, my friend."

"That's OK," said Quinn, his eyes twinkling, "I have a football game to attend this afternoon."

A.C. had made the request, and somehow Quinn had secured five 50-yard line seats at Soldier Field for the Army-Air Force game. Zak, Emma, Ethan, Currant, and Tom Quinn sat in that order overlooking the green gridiron below. Marching bands made musical crop circles. Cheerleaders raised the crowd's anticipation of action. Everyone sang the national anthem. Then the game began. If Kennedy had made the game, he could have handled the coin toss to the crowd's delight. But that was all forgotten now. Thousands of cadets and Chicagoans were here to enjoy the fall classic. Currant loved the pageantry of it all. In his mind, nothing had changed. This game in 1963 no doubt looked and felt like a college game from the 1920s. It was as timeless as the old Catholic Latin Mass. Football offered something solid, unchanging, and memorable to connect the passing years of one's life. This was like a hot bath in nostalgia for the aging inventor.

"Thanks, Tom," said Currant over the crowd's noise. A chilly lake breeze blew across his face, tempered by a peek-a-boo sun. An Army running back gained twelve yards, and the military contingent surrounding them went nuts. "This means a lot to all of us. Particularly me. I lived my early life down South, and you know how we Southerners love our college ball."

Quinn took a bite from his hot dog. "This is the life, Doc." He didn't really understand Currant's comment because it was drowned out by the spectator noise. But then, he turned to face A.C. and almost shouted into his ear. "I got that gizmo you wanted." He reached into his pocket and handed a small metallic disk to Currant.

Currant pocketed it discretely. "Thanks. That's a load off my mind."

"What is it?

Currant didn't want to deceive the man who had been such a help to them. He suspected Quinn knew something was different with Currant and his friends, but he had maintained silence about their unusual behavior. He guessed that reporters were something like doctors and lawyers. Certain things remained confidential. So he decided to toss him a bone. "It's something I invented. A listening device."

"That little thing is what you used to capture the Vallee conversation?"

"Right," answered A.C. "Small but powerful. It's the way of the future, my friend. The way of the future."

"Speaking of the future. What's on your schedule now that the excitement is over?"

A.C. looked over to the Twins and Zak, who were very engrossed in the game. "I think my students will spend the next week enjoying Chicago and seeing the sights. I'm going to leave them on their own. Later I'm going home to my childhood home."

"Where's that?"

"New Orleans. Well, really, Covington, Louisiana. The most beautiful place in the world. I'm most excited about revisiting my old hometown."

"You know what they say?" Said Quinn.

A.C. sipped from a paper cup of beer, "What's that?"

"You can never go home again...."

"We'll see," said Currant. "We'll see. Anyway, what do *they* know?"

"You're right about that, my friend." Quinn lifted his cup to toast. "To going home again. Enjoy the past."

Joell Costas entered the year 1963 at Chanute Air Force Base in Rantoul, Illinois, a hinterland place located about 130 miles south of Chicago. This arrival location for Costas served his purposes well. In 1963 the base was being used for nuclear warhead missile silo training. It was an essential and well-guarded military installation. In 1993 it was officially closed. Condemned areas left over from its previous incarnation were encapsulated. The southeast corner of the base, the Heritage Lake area, a dumping ground for toxic materials, was also the perfect choice for a time travel nexus. It was, in 2028, off-limits to everyone but *The Authority*, and in 1963 it was off-limits to everyone but the poison dumpers. Coincidentally, the base was the training and birthplace of the Tuskegee Airmen, who achieved fame in World War II as African-American fighter pilots. Costas had a good number of African-American relatives, but this fact was of little interest to him.

As he boldly walked out of this desolate part of the base and into the town of Rantoul, he contemplated the job ahead. In 2028 parlance, he was a 'fixer.' *The Authority* used him when necessary to intercept rogue time travelers. The system automatically detected when JFK did not die on November 2, 1963. It was an unusual case because, typically, the system detects more modest anomalies before they become a significant time/change event.

Nevertheless, it was his job to clean up the problem. He was a veteran of this type of work and enjoyed it. Sometimes it was a challenge for a black man to go back in time to make the necessary corrections because of societal limitations. This was particularly true in America before 1960. But in other ways, in the right situations, being a black man made him invisible—an excellent attribute for a time-detective such as Costas.

He was here in the Middle West of America on November 7, 1963, to locate the unauthorized time jumpers who 'saved JFK' and bring them back before they caused any more significant disruptions.

He caught a Greyhound Bus in Rantoul and headed north.

O.A. LOG TTA2028-1

INVESTIGATOR: Joell Costas

DATE: November 8, 1963 (July 9, 2028)

PROJECT: JFK-11.02.63

ASSIGNMENT: Determine the location and identity of
the person or persons who participated in the alteration
of *The History* as related the *historical* death of President
John F. Kennedy (JFK) in Chicago, Illinois, on November
2, 1963. Take whatever actions necessary to ensure that
there will be no subsequent interference with the
resultant new JFK-related events as now described in
The History. Executive Action, if necessary, has been
authorized.

DISCUSSION: Arrived yesterday, 11.07.63 (local time),
at LZ 5462-008 at approximately 22:22 CT. My arrival
was unnoticed. I proceeded to the nearby town of
Rantoul and took a public bus to Chicago. I am staying
at a local hotel in the near west Loop area.

On November 2, 1963, United States President John
Fitzgerald Kennedy was assassinated. However, because
of a time/event alteration created by unknown time
traveler(s), he is now alive in this time. The effects of
this fact were immediate and substantial and determined
to be not in the best interests of *The Authority.*
However, subsequent events shortly thereafter favorably
resolved the disruptive time anomaly, thus preserving
the overall integrity of *The History.* While there has been
considerable internal debate about whether action is
required at this time, it was determined that there was a
real risk that *The History* might be compromised again.
Although the directive forces in place should overwhelm
any additional attempts to alter events. This is the first

time that *The History* has been affected with such an impact. While there have been minor changes to events due to the use of time travel technology in the past, up to this point exclusively by rogue agents of *The Authority*, those changes either self-corrected or resulted in consequences that were acceptable to *The Authority*. In fact, only a small number of such disruptions to the past were made. In every case, *The Office of Anomalies* successfully tracked down the perpetrators and eliminated them in the past or returned them to the present for processing.

I requested I be given absolute discretion concerning the deposition of those persons causing the time anomaly. While I have this power, I am aware other officers may be placed into position if deemed required by *The Authority*. If so, I will not know until I am contacted by those parties to coordinate our efforts and to assure that no one inadvertently triggers a time alteration. Obviously, the more time travelers operating in the past, including *The Authority*, the greater the likelihood of time disturbance. Again, it can be stated for the record that I am, until officially relieved or made unavailable, in charge of this case.

TRANSMITTED VIA CODED TIME JUSTIFIER AT 10:26 CT 07/09/28.

-Chapter XIV-

There's No Place Like Home

The Panama Limited's matched set of horns moaned like trumpets in a New Orleans Dixieland dirge as the orange and yellow train snaked south through the heartland of America. Up close, the bellowing beast grabbed the attention of every hired hand and villager in its path. Yet seen from afar, it blended into the vast, tranquil graveyards of tawny crushed cornstalks as if one with nature, a golden serpent sinuously coursing through farms and fields in the fading light of the late autumn sun.

The time travelers sat facing each other amidst a party car full of vacationers. Five days had passed since JFK had been saved. As Emma gazed aimlessly out the wide horizontal window, she smiled gently and rubbed her eyes with the back of her hand. Her brother, sitting directly across from her, saw her face brighten.

"What's the joke, Emma," he said.

Dr. Currant joined in, "What?"

Zak wore an expectant look.

"OK," she said. "I just thought that we made such a difference. We...the four of us...the Four Musketeers. We did it. We saved his life."

"Darn right. Just like I said. Ethan smiled, but that smile dropped off when he turned his head to face Currant. "What?...what is it?"

Dr. Currant eyed the Twins and Zak. "Work's not over, folks. That's all I can say. Quinn is headed to Florida. He'll be our eyes and ears. If we're lucky...it's all over. If not. We're not...and JFK's not. What I'm saying is we don't know. Right?"

The others nodded.

"So," continued Currant, "let's get to work." He

reached into his pocket, pulled out four earbud devices, and passed them around. Nonchalantly as possible, they each placed them into their ears. Emma looked around, but none of the other reveling passengers seemed interested in their group. Dr. Currant pulled out the little disk Quinn had retrieved from Vallee's apartment. He used his thumbnail to depress a micro-switch at the recording device's edge. The earbuds were activated. "This is the first time for me, so let's go through it," said Currant as he fast-forwarded the unit past the initial conversation between Vallee and Cain. Then through hours of nothing but refrigerator sounds, television shows, and Vallee snoring. Then past the dialogue between the two men who broke into Vallee's apartment and found the guns the day before the "big event."

He listened for a while, then backed it up and stopped the recording. "I think this must be Saturday morning, November 2nd, just after his arrest. Listen. It sounds like two men and Vallee." Everyone listened more intently. The wheels of the train clicked out a rhythmic background. The voices of their partying fellow travelers seemed to fall quiet as the time travelers focused on the recording.

"OK. Tommy boy. You and I will sit while Larry checks out your pad." The recording was clear. Even the sounds of doors opening and closing could be heard in the background.

Very shortly, another voice is heard. *"So what have we here? Thinkin' of startin' another war, Tom? This is pretty heavy weaponry for plinkin' rats in the alley."*

A long silence passed before Vallee spoke. *"I...I worked as an instructor. It's part of the work I did. You know. I worked with the government. That's why I have these."*

"That's Vallee," Currant mouthed the words quietly for the others listening.

"So he's a government man, John. How 'bout that?"

"I'm impressed," replied the other. *"Look, Tom, we don't give a shit about your Korean War record. But we are*

very concerned about the here and now. About you mouthing off about JFK. You've got guns and ammo. You don't like Kennedy, and he's coming to town today."

"Wait...I'm not talking about Korea. I'm talking about now. I've been working for the government to train soldiers to setup, to clean, to shoot. You know. To handle these weapons. In New York. But that job's over. That's it. Nothing else."

"What soldiers?"

Silence again. *"I'll be in trouble if I tell you."*

"You're already in a shit load of trouble, my friend. If you got something to say, you better say it."

"Cubans—to fight Castro."

"Cubans. Right. And who ya' workin' for?

"I told you. The government."

"Army, Navy, Internal Revenue?"

"I'm not sure. They don't really tell you. But that's why I had the weapons. OK?"

There was a long pause.

"All right, Tommy boy. Let's get you back to the station. Then we'll work it all out. We'll check out your story, and if it makes sense, you'll be fine. But if you're bullshitting us, we're not going to like it. Got it?"

"No bull. You'll see...."

" Let's get going, Larry. Leave the arsenal here for the time being. I'll get someone here to keep an eye on things. Until we check out Mr. Vallee's story."

When the sound of the door being shut was heard, Emma spoke. "Well, that's something," she said. "I wonder if he's telling the truth about working for the government?"

"I wouldn't doubt it," said Currant. "I think Vallee is just a pawn in this game."

"Right," said Ethan. "But whose game is it?"

"That, my friend is the question of the century," replied Currant. "I'll wash through the rest of this recording tonight and see if anything else is pertinent."

Emma looked at Currant, "Doctor."

"Yes..." said Currant.

"Now that we're almost in New Orleans, can you tell us why we're going there?"

Currant smiled, "Because you and Ethan and Zak got what you wanted. Now it's time for me. Anyway, the *TimeTravelle* is my invention. Without it, we wouldn't be here. So that's why."

"He's got a point, Emma," said Ethan.

"That may be so. But why New Orleans?"

Currant crossed his legs and leaned back, locking his hands behind his head. He smiled. "Actually, I'll be visiting a little town just north of New Orleans, taking care of some old business. While I do that, you three will have the opportunity to meet the locals and see what life in the Deep South is like. These are interesting times."

Emma glanced at Zak. He smirked and signed to her: "Maybe he's going to check out an old high school girlfriend."

"What's that?" inquired Currant suspecting he was the subject of a silent discussion.

"Um," she paused. "Zak says 'he's dying for some gumbo.'"

"I'll bet. Man after my own heart," said Currant.

After a full day's travel, the train pulled into the New Orleans Union Passenger Terminal. The footfalls and voices of hundreds of rushing travelers bounced off the terrazzo floor, overlapping and echoing into a solid wall of background sound. The team walked quickly toward the taxi area. Once outside the terminal, they were hit by blazing sunlight and a wall of humidity subdued only by the moderate temperature.

"Little sticky. But a lot nicer than Chicago," Ethan proclaimed to the group.

"Just how I remember it," said Currant. "Like you're always wearing a cheap wool suit soaked in sweat." Taking charge, he swiftly pushed his way to the front of the confused crowd and hailed a cab. "Let's go," he shouted. They piled into the super-sized 1960 Pontiac, and a ten-minute ride brought them to the front of the

French Quarter hotel. It was too early to get into their rooms. They decided to have something to eat at a nearby restaurant.

Across the dining table, Emma surveyed the faces of his fellow travelers. Ethan looked like a caged tiger attacking his food lustily. Zak savored his gumbo, working it down patiently. And Dr. Currant was now a man in his element. He looked relaxed and somehow younger. The authentic smells and sounds of his boyhood home seemed to have transported him back to a more peaceful past. He smiled.

"Somewhere. Very close to this place. At this moment. I am, or should I say the 'little me' is near here."

"Are you excited?" Emma asked.

"Yes," said Currant. "I feel like I'm eight again."

"What about us?" Zak asked, and Emma translated.

"You're on your own for a few hours. I've got some legwork to do. I'll be back later tonight. We'll have some fun for a few days and return to work on Monday morning. Anyway, I may have a good follow-up lead. I know a man who might have trained Cuban rebels in this arena. Just like our friend Vallee did in New York."

"This thing's not over, is it?"

A.C. sighed, then replied. "Maybe not, Emma. I'll know more when I talk to Quinn again."

The mention of Quinn's name reminded her that the deadly game continued. JFK was still a hunted man. And rather than being the Four Musketeers, the time travelers were more like four blind mice. They no longer had superior knowledge. They had no extraordinary powers. They were just three young people and an old man traveling in the unknown and uncharted past. At least in Chicago, they had the potential to delicately unravel the fabric of time, quietly massaging known events. Now they were operating in the dark. They had no idea what was going to happen next. They only knew for sure that they must protect their secret identities.

Therein lay the most danger for them. *MOM* would be outraged by the Chicago outcome and be in the hunt.

They had saved JFK. Now they only had a few days left to help keep him alive. She hoped the President's awareness of the Chicago assassination team would force him into a protective shell avoiding open-car motorcades and glad-handing campaigning in crowds. However, successful politicians don't hide from the public or from assassins; they must press the flesh, kiss babies, and make speeches no matter the risks. "We're lost in time now, aren't we?" said Emma. "The only way we could know the future now is to return to 2028. Maybe we should do that."

"No. Sorry, Emma," said Currant. "This is it. The more we use the equipment, the greater the odds they will track us down. Especially now. I'm sure we're on *MOM*'s most-wanted list. We have one chance to make things better, and this is it. Anyway, I have a feeling we are in the right place at the right time."

Currant departed after lunch, and the Twins and Zak toured the town and then, at Emma's request, went to see a movie. But it was Zak's turn to pick, and his choice was *The Nutty Professor*. This was in honor of their 'nutty Prof'—A.C. Currant. Ethan secretly knew that his sister would love this choice. All her French friends were still trying to live down France's mid-century fascination with Jerry Lewis. She would be the only movie buff in the year 2028 that had ever seen it in the year of its release, the only one to monitor the reactions of the intended audience, and the only one to know if people really laughed at Lewis. Was he a comic genius? Or was he only funny to a 1960s Frenchman? A notch in her gun, he thought. She'll be one up on all her other friends in her "Flick Chicks" movie-watching club. The girl loved her movies. Sitting in the darkened New Orleans theater, they laughed aloud at the Jekyll & Hyde story. The Frenchmen were on target, thought Ethan. Lewis was brilliant and funny. And his nerdy Julius Kelp Jekyll character bore a striking resemblance to Dr. Currant. His other persona, Buddy Love, looked a lot like Currant after a few Johnnie

Walker scotches, debonair with a touch of debauchery. A.C. was right. We're on our own. It was fun becoming engrossed again in the comedy, a good respite from the rigors of detective work.

Joell Costas knew this might be his last chance to fix things. His time was running out. He was in the twilight of a great career. Even though his personal light was dimming, he remained the consummate professional. He wanted to handle this case on his own. Before he left for the year 1963, the talk of sending others to assist rankled him. He always worked alone, got his man, and didn't need help—no matter what. He looked around his shabby, cheap hotel room in the west Loop. It wasn't pleasant. But it was a "no questions asked" residence, a base of operations that would attract no attention to him or his mission. It was his job to find the time travelers. He had no idea who they were or how many. He knew their presence would betray them eventually. Anomalies, those things that didn't fit, and natural errors could trip them up. But Chicago 1963 was a big, sprawling mass of humans, all blindly unaware of the intrigue and deception in the air. JFK was still alive, thought Costas, but not for long. He would die, as *The History* stated. He would be a great martyr slain by a mentally unbalanced assassin. Nothing historically unusual about that. It was his job to make sure that nobody tinkered with the facts.

A stiff, cold November breeze sifted through a cracked window that offered a dirty, patchwork view of the tops of downtown buildings. Costas ignored "reality" and concentrated on the "map." He sat quietly on a beat-up wooden chair facing a small table. A yellow legal pad and a couple of weeks of old newspapers lay in front of him. The point of his pen rested lazily at the top line of the ruled paper waiting for direction. He knew Chicago was a done deal, and he assumed the time travelers would think the same. For the moment, JFK was saved. Possibly they could return to the future and have the new history revealed, then make adjustments and again attempt to save JFK, but the massive use of electrical energy might be spotted. The *Office of Anomalies* was on full alert. Traveling in time again would significantly increase their risk of being caught. He guessed they would not take such a risk.

He scanned the newspapers, looking for something, anything out of the ordinary, something to provide a lead. Finally, he hit on a small article in the *Daily News* from November 1st. The headline read: *Cab Takes a Dive into Lagoon.* A taxicab with two passengers and the driver, Ralph Buford, had crashed through a barrier on Lake Shore Drive and sunk to the bottom of a lagoon harbor. Something seemed wrong with this one. The passengers were unidentified, and the incident occurred a few miles from Thomas Arthur Vallee's apartment. It happened the day before JFK was scheduled to die. The article stated it was the first time in history that a cab had gone into the lake. Highly unusual, thought Costas, and a start. Costas left the hotel and walked back into the Loop. He wanted to talk to the cabbie.

Buford was easy to find. At least for lunch, he hung out with all the other cab drivers in a little Greek restaurant sandwiched between two old loft buildings. The roof of the one-story eatery exhaled a cloud of greasy kitchen exhaust that slid down the storefront and filled the sidewalk air below with the pleasant odors of burning sheep and pigs. However, the tasty animal aromas only rankled Costas. He had lost his appetite months ago. Now such smells quickly brought him to the edge of nausea. He ducked into the joint, ordered seltzer water, gulped down half a glass, and then quietly belched. He surveyed the dining area and spotted his man. The big black man, his arm in a shiny white plaster cast, stood out like a tethered advertising balloon.

"Mr. Buford?"

The man looked up from his meal, "Who's askin'?"

"Name's Art Lucas. Federal Life and Casualty." Costas handed him a card. "I'm following up on that little bump-up you had on North Lake Shore Drive a couple of weeks back." He sat down opposite the cab driver.

Buford checked out the card. "Hmm...insurance investigator...anything in it for me?" He lifted his heavily wrapped arm as a demonstration of need.

"Just might be," said Costas. "Things like this go that way often enough."

"Well, as you can see, brother, I got busted up. Of course, I'm lucky to be here at all."

"Bad?"

"Bad enough. Damn car rammed into us. Sent us into the pond. Right to the bottom. Shit. I thought I was a goner."

"So the other car went out of control?"

Buford laughed. "Oh no. That sonabitch was in control. He wanted us to take a dive."

"Why?"

"Dunno' man...say where you from? Not from here, are ya?"

Costas smiled. "You have a good ear. Harlem. New York."

"Thought as much. Anyway, the only thing I can think of is that they were after my fare."

"Who's that?"

"Older guy with a teenage boy. Kid never talked. Older guy was a gabber. They were from out of town. Said he was a teacher, I think. Out east some place. Visitors like you. But I owe the kid." Buford kept eating his lunch. His frozen arm hindered normal hand-to-mouth movement. His burger made it in, but not without a struggle. A spot of mayo hung on his jowl. Costas spotted it and pointed to his own cheek. Buford looked puzzled and continued eating.

Costas moved on. 'How's that?"

The cabbie swallowed a mouthful before answering. "Saved my life. Strongest sonagun I ever met. Didn't look like much. Pretty boy. But jeezz...he had to be Atlas to get me out. I was drown'n. Trapped underwater. But the kid swam down. Opened the damn door and got me out. I don't know how, but he did it. All I got was this busted wing."

"Lucky for you, man. Names?"

"No names. No nothing. By the time I came back to the livin', they was gone, and I woke up in the back of a meat wagon. Too bad, I owe the kid." Buford's napkin finally caught up with the mayo.

Costas nodded, another successful intervention and a little less tension in his world. The stray mayo was a meaningless little anomaly, but it had annoyed him. His stars were aligned again, and he continued. "You know there's no record of these two guys. Funny, isn't it?"

"Not that funny. I don't card 'em on the way in. I just drive 'em where their goin'."

"Gotcha. But you know their destination, right?"

"That I do, brother...Plaza House."

"Where did you pick them up?" Just then, Costas grimaced. He bent over slightly and groaned. The pain was intense.

Buford looked at him sympathetically. "What's the matter with you, man? You got problems?"

Costas recomposed himself. Stay professional, stay focused, he thought to himself. Ignore it. "Stomach. Something I ate. Biting me back. No big deal." Beads of sweat welled up on his forehead.

"You sure, man? You lookin' mighty white for a black man."

"I'm fine. Thanks." Costas forced the words out of his mouth. They came like meat through a grinder, slowly dribbling hunks squeezed through his clenched teeth. "So what about it? Where did they flag down your hack?"

"Up north. Near the L tracks at Wilson."

"What did these guys look like?" The pain in his gut subsided.

Ralph Buford rubbed the top of his head with his good hand. His big black mitt slowly rippled over the bumps and valleys. "Older one...maybe five-ten...six feet. Dark hair. Looked like late-forties. Young one was a good six feet. Black hair. All slicked back. Not much muscle for a kid so strong. Good lookin' kid, though. Like a pitcher show actor. Ya know what I mean? I don't know. Honkies. All look the same to me." He laughed loudly and looked around the room. He looked back at Costas. "Say I didn't mean to offend nobody."

Costas assumed the driver was talking about white people. He jumped back in. "Don't bother me none. Things seem pretty quiet here in Chicago. Every day is getting a bit rougher out East where I live."

"Shit. Don't let it fool ya. This town will blow up soon enough. Colored folk is gettin' tired climbin' the same shit pile every day." He shook his head and made a face. "The youngin's startin' to carry now. Right out in the open. People gettin' high but feelin' real low. How 'bout you? New York gettin' itchy?"

"Not that bad yet."

"Well, you're lucky. Got yourself a good inside job workin' for the man." Buford pushed out his lips and nodded slowly. "Just help a brother and get me some green. OK? I'm busted up, and I have a hellava time drivin'. You try drivin' with one arm sometime. It ain't easy. Anyway, I need a rest. Send some'n my way."

Costas stood. "Do my best, Ralph. Thanks for the info." He walked away knowing he had lied all over the man, and he was sorry, but not for long.

LOG of Zak Newman --- November 10, 1963: 22:58

(Day 13 of time travel)

Back again. Big gap in the log. Let me talk about this town. New Orleans—in 2028— is Energy City, USA. It's an active, thriving international metropolis. The biggest oil reserves in the world are under the Gulf of Mexico. And the nearby bayous and backwaters provide the largest and most productive algae energy farms in the country. But in 1963, the Crescent City is just a sleepy little southern town filled with slow-walkers, slow-talkers, and slow-thinkers. Maybe I'm a bit harsh. It's a good place to relax and take a breather.

I guess we did well in Chicago. The MAN—JFK is alive. And I guess it could be the result of our little visit. That's exciting and frightening at the same time. Exciting to change history—hopefully for the better—frightening because MOM doesn't want anyone messing with the past, present, or future, for that matter. She loves control. So now, we time travelers speculate about our fate. Are we targets? Hope not. Everyone back in our time should have a new perspective now. President John F. Kennedy—Mr. JFK—is not dead. He's doing whatever he intended to do before the Chicago trip. I'm not really certain what that is, but I would guess that it involves campaigning. Seems like that's all these presidents do. Campaign to get in office—then hustle to get reelected— then if you win, help your buddies get elected—then retire after two terms and—what? Put your brother Bobby in office?

Well, whatever. It worked for these folks in 1963. They apparently liked the system, however flawed it was. At least they had the ability to make a difference or believe that they could make a difference. The voting system here in pre-Post Democratic America is somewhat oblique—one vote means nothing in itself—a block of popular votes may mean your guy wins your state. That's good. Then a group of people called electrons or electors or something like that has the final say in the whole thing. Get a majority of those guys to vote for your guy, and he wins. This is like trying to have sex wearing a full-body wetsuit—"I think I had an orgasm—didn't I? Was it good for you?" But the people must have enjoyed the process. Millions took it very seriously. I suppose that part is better than our current system. The President here is the big boss-man. Not everyone is going to like the guy, but he's in charge, and after the election, life goes on.

Although their system is different, it may be no better or worse than the one in 2028. Even though they voted their legislators and political leaders into office, it seems like 'the fix' was always in. And nobody questioned the selection process for those Supreme Court Justices back in '63. The elite handpicked them just like we now select the entire national government for the Mother Bunker suite. All in all, I think we've just given up any pretense in 2028. We're a more honest, controlled flock now (are you listening, MOM?). Of course, nobody can exercise the right to have vote sex or, even slightly, seditious or suggestive political sex talk in 2028—unless you want to have your proverbial political penis nipped off. It's a good way to get a free trip to the nearest mind massage seminary—to get one of those "rewire jobs."

Did I mention I am on my fourth Mimosa? I think the combination of that Jerry Lewis movie we saw a couple of days ago on top of all this rich food is getting to me. I feel like a Po' boy. My pants are stuffed with crawfish and smoked sausage covered in mayo. Eat me. Po'boys are very rich. That's funny. Sorry for digressing again.

OK. Back to business. Emma and Ethan are tucked in their beds. A.C. Currant is out like a light. I can tell by the intensity of his snores. I'd swear he's pushing a hundred decibels. I get a sense he has some pretty nasty dreams lately. He's disturbed about something. And me, I am the Night Owl of N'owlins. Who? Who? Zak Who? God bless you.

I give up.

END: 11-10-63

-Chapter XV-

Cite' Masque

Currant never explained where he had gone the day of their arrival. Very secretive, thought Emma. He has another agenda. The combination of her intuition and Zak's special mental abilities convinced her that saving JFK was only part of the reason for their visit to New Orleans. Something else was happening with the good doctor, but she didn't know what, when, or where. Like a rogue card shark in a typical RKO western, A.C. Currant liked to play his cards close to his chest. She fantasized about buying him one of those ten-gallon hats and a vest so he could better look the part. But then she decided this was a bad idea. Currant was so eccentric he might just wear such an outfit to publicly embarrass her. He does that quite well without a costume.

Last night, he gave them a peek at his cards. He promised a meeting with some New Orleans players into the Cuban rebel scene. Kind of a Cajun version of Vallee, training rebel recruits to fight Castro on Cuban soil. He laid out the histories of these people who might be the New Orleans equivalent of Cain and friends. A.C believed that Cain had direct involvement with anti-Castro Cubans in addition to his mobster and government connections. The time travelers were beginning to see a pattern emerging—Cuba, anti-Castro rebels, mobsters, corrupt government officials, with JFK a target of all their frustrations and hatred. At A.C.'s suggestion, they decided on a plan to confront the New Orleans contingent of potential plotters. It began with her walking from the hotel to the nearby rebel headquarters. She had no idea how Currant knew about these people. Of course, this was his turf, and he seemed confident about his sources. By now, she no longer had doubts that Cowboy Currant had many cards up his sleeve. She only hoped no bad guys would push over the card table, call him a cheat, and shoot him.

As she walked along Canal Street, she thought about today's big assignment. A.C. Currant had set forth a plan of attack for the young time travelers based on information only he possessed. And from Emma's viewpoint, it was a plan that only made sense to Currant. It involved Zak, Ethan, and her in a scheme to capture the hearts and minds of some pretty strange people. Currant explained that his offbeat plan would defuse the situation. If they approached the plotters head-on, they might be in danger.

For this reason, they would need to sharpen their acting skills. They were supposed to be journalism students on leave from high school learning their craft on the road. Such was the story, thought Emma, the same tale they employed in Chicago, but this time it would be done with a flourish appropriate to the location. New Orleans in 1963 was a red-blooded human gumbo, an ethnic mixture of the Old South, whites, blacks, and combinations. French-speaking, Caribbean-Hispanics, and Indians blended into a Catholic-voodoo belief sauce spiced with hot jazz and sexual kumquats of all sizes and shapes. It was a small but intense city, steaming with raw energy at the bottom of Lake Pontchartrain, full of societal combustibles threatening to burst into flames at any moment. Anti-Castro Cubans, right-wing extremists, violent mobsters, crooked politicians, and a slowly awakening population of disenfranchised blacks were ready to explode.

Emma thought about Currant's scheme and smiled. He wanted them to perform in a building at 531 Lafayette, which housed the offices of Guy Banister, a private detective and retired FBI Special Agent. Currant let out that Tom Quinn, the reporter, had known Banister when he was the head of the Chicago office of the FBI in the mid-Fifties. The aging former cop had also been the Assistant Superintendent of the New Orleans Police

Department. Apparently, Quinn's information led Currant to focus on this man and this building in New Orleans. But Emma sensed that Currant was not giving them the complete story. His tale had Banister's building being used as a headquarters for anti-Castro activities. And he mentioned a person named David Ferrie. Later, Zak revealed that Dr. Currant's emotional intensity rose to boil-over status when he talked about this man Ferrie, a significant person in Currant's world of feelings. Emma had no idea why Zak would get such an emotional read, but she trusted his take 100%. Zak was the master intuitive, and A.C. was the great director. He set the wacky week into motion.

The corner of Lafayette and Camp provided the setting for the ungainly three-story stone and stucco conglomeration that wore two addresses: 531 Lafayette Street and 544 Camp Street. The entry on Lafayette beckoned Emma, but Currant had told her the Camp Street side of the building formerly provided offices for a Cuban rebel organization. A lot of action for a small building, she thought. Emma walked up the stairs alone, armed only with her memorized script. By the time she reached the offices of the Banister Detective Agency, she was sweating. New Orleans, even in mid-November, was hot and muggy. She eased open the door and peered into the Southern Sherlock's headquarters. Not much, she thought—disorganized, disjointed, and dilapidated like most of the other 1963 offices she had visited, but this one had an added feature—it reeked of mold, cigars, cheap perfume, and spent booze. One whiff, blindfolded, first guess, would be a saloon. On the other side of the door, a smiling good-looking older woman greeted her.

"Hello, Sweetie," she said in the ever-present drawl that was no longer a novelty to Emma. "What can we do for you?"

"Hello," said Emma catching her breath. She brushed down the flaring sides of the new mint green dress she purchased just for this occasion. "I'm sorry. It's a healthy walk up those stairs."

"Three times a day for me, Honey. Do tell."

Emma glanced at the little sign on the top of the woman's desk, *Delphine Roberts*. "Once is enough for me, Miz Roberts. My name is Emma Callan-Wright, and I am here to make an appointment with Mr. Banister."

"On what business. If I may ask, Miss Wright?"

"Certainly," said Emma in a rising voice. "I—I should say we received Mr. Banister's name from an old friend of his from Chicago. Mr. Thomas Quinn. As part of our educational tour of America, it was our pleasure to meet with Mr. Quinn, who is a fine reporter for *Chicago's American*."

Delphine Roberts offered a side chair to Emma. She accepted the invitation and slid into it with a rustle of satin and crinoline. "I must say you are a sweet little treasure."

Emma felt herself blushing for real. "Thank you."

"Now, who is 'we'?"

"I'm sorry...."

"You said that 'we' received Mr. Banister's name."

"Oh, yes. We are journalism students from Springfield Heights out East. My brother Ethan. Our school mate Zak Newman. And our teacher, Doctor Currant. It's our summer break, but we are on a special tour across the country to understand the reality of the newspaper business. Mr. Quinn was most helpful in that regard."

"Very nice," said Roberts sweetly. "And how can we be helpful?"

"We would like to present a gift to Mr. Banister from our school. A plaque commemorating his life's work."

Roberts flushed. "Oh. My. That is wonderful. And he is a man so deserving."

"That is what we thought too. Can I make an appointment? We're leaving by the end of the week. So...do you think he possibly might have some time?"

The woman looked through a folder on the desk. After a few moments of study, she spoke. "Mr. Banister is out of town until Wednesday. Could you make an appointment for Thursday at, say...four?"

Emma beamed. "Oh yes. That would be fine. Will that work with Mr. Banister?"

"I'm sure he would be delighted."

Carefully Emma pulled a cardboard-framed photo from her purse. It was one of the documents they had created before they left Mystic Heights. The original was a yearbook photo from the 1962 class of a nearby high school they found in a second-hand shop. After some photo work to switch out heads by Emma, who was most proficient with such equipment, the new photo showed the Twins and Zak hard at work in the high school print shop. The title note read: "Girl Reporter Prepares for Her New Career in Journalism." It was autographed by all three.

"Please. Take this as a welcoming gift from our school," said Emma as she handed the photo to the woman.

It was Delphine's turn to beam. Emma expressed her thanks and left a card from her hotel with a phone number just in case. Then she excused herself and exited stage left, down the stairwell, and out the door. Hitting the hot but fresher air, she breathed in deeply and smiled. So far, so good, she thought.

The next day Emma reappeared at the detective's office. She knew Banister would not have returned, and she played her part as directed by Dr. Currant. She told Roberts she was in the neighborhood and had a thought. "Wouldn't it be better if the award presentation could be made with a few of Mr. Banister's friends in attendance? It would be so much more special." Roberts agreed. She would see what she could do.

The time travelers spent the remainder of Tuesday and all of Wednesday sightseeing. They ventured across the lake after talking with some locals about possible rebel training grounds. One of Currant's new bar buddies had told him about such a camp in a small town north of New Orleans. However, their visit was uneventful. They found some people aware of military activity, but everything had been shut down last June. Emma was disappointed because she saw the logical connection between rebel training here in New Orleans and Thomas Arthur Vallee's training in New York. This lead ended nowhere.

Returning to New Orleans after the day trip, they were reminded of the grittiness of the town. It seemed like they had stepped back two hundred years rather than just sixty-five. All saloons and whorehouses, declared Ethan. Emma defended it. New Orleans operated at a slow, deliberate pace geared to the weather, no doubt, but it seemed peaceful. However, even with all the historical acclimation provided by Professor Dufour before the trip, she was dismayed by the blatant racial discrimination. Separation of the races, in some cases, was easily facilitated by the display of "whites only" or "colored only" signs, which popped up everywhere. The white population was saved from the frightening possibility of drinking from a water fountain previously tapped by a black person or pissing in the same urinal, not to mention the elaborate techniques used to achieve total separation in schools, churches, and public transit. It was called "separate but equal" in those days. And since the atmosphere was always genteel—' Yes ma'am'—' No sir'— it was hard to believe that this lazy, hazy environment had anything to do with a new JFK assassination attempt. But Currant seemed confident it did. While he did not share everything he heard from Tom Quinn, she gathered enough to know something big was happening in this town. It had an always-present but never clearly visible nastiness. A Deep South hot mist of misdirection and deceit obscured all but the obvious.

Late Wednesday, Emma called Banister's office and spoke again with the secretary Roberts. Emma expressed her excitement. "Had Mr. Banister seen the photo? Yes?...great. And would we have an audience of his friends for the presentation?"

Roberts broke off and told her to hold the phone.

She came back and said she had spoken with Mr.
Banister. Yes, he would try to have a couple of colleagues
in for their visit.

"Who might that be?"

"Mr. Martin and Mr. Ferrie may be here."

"Wonderful," said Emma, and she closed with an
appropriately lavish thought. "I am overwhelmed by your
kindness and acknowledgment of this moment's
importance to us." She chuckled, realizing she was
getting into the flow of the Big Easy.

Late Thursday afternoon, the Twins and Zak arrived
at the Banister Detective Agency a few minutes early.
Banister's secretary greeted them at the door. She was
most effusive, bubbling over with excitement. The three
young visitors wore new outfits for the affair. Zak came
dressed in a pale green suit. Emma totally approved of his
choice. She also admired Ethan's light blue pinstriped
seersucker suit that made him look much older and very
handsome. No ties—too hot and muggy. Nicely detailed
light green and blue cotton shirts and well-shined shoes
completed the look. And Emma came at those gathered
with the full sartorial charge. Her outfit was a neat-fitting,
black-and-white lace sundress with large bands of white
lace at the hem and white piping across the top. White
gloves and a matching gaucho hat completed her look.

As they were leaving their hotel, Currant declared
their costumes stunning. Emma's earlier look into the
mirror told her she looked pretty damn hot. Such was the
pleasant view laid out for the three men who straggled
into the waiting area from an adjacent office. Delphine
introduced Mr. Martin, Mr. Ferrie, and Mr. Banister.
Under normal circumstances, Emma might have laughed
aloud. Martin looked like a dumpy dogcatcher. Ferrie
appeared totally weird with his phony red hair and grease
pencil eyebrows. And Banister came off as worn and aged
while exhibiting only a hint of what might have been a
distinguished look at some much earlier date. But smiles
abounded from both lines of people.

"I want to thank you for the photo, young lady. You three look like hard-working reporters," said Banister in a voice that had been pickled rough by a lifetime of drinking.

"Our pleasure, Mr. Banister. Oh. This is so exciting," gushed Emma.

"Well, you have come by way of Chicago to see us. Tom Quinn sent you. That was very kind of him. It's been quite a while since we swapped tall tales," said Banister. "What kind of lies has he been telling you?"

"Just that you were the head of the FBI in Chicago and that you helped put an end to Dillinger," answered Ethan.

"I was there. But that was a long time ago."

"And you are a formidable Commie-hunter," said Emma.

Martin broke in. "Damn right...sorry young lady. But that he is. About time someone gave him credit."

Ferrie walked up to Ethan and Zak. He looked at Zak like a hungry dog contemplating fresh meat. "Well, young fellow. What do you have to say about the Great Guy Banister?"

"Oh. I'm sorry," said Emma. "We forgot to mention. Zak is mute. He cannot speak. We use sign language to communicate. It works very well."

Ferrie smiled. "No matter. Talking is overrated. He reached up and patted Zak on the back lightly. "Isn't that right young man?"

Banister frowned slightly, and his eyes sent a quick message to Ferrie. After a long pause, he returned his focus to the others. "So what do you have planned for this occasion, young people?"

Delphine Roberts, ever sociable, interrupted this line of thinking and suggested they have something to drink. She brought out a pitcher of lemonade and poured out a round for all.

Emma announced they would be making the presentation shortly. She was expecting their teacher, Doctor Currant, to arrive any minute. For the next ten minutes, it was all lemonade and small talk. Then, as if on cue, Ethan distributed more gifts—yellow wallet I.D. cards, which made Banister, Roberts, Ferrie, and Martin each "Honorary Senior Reporters" for the Springfield Shout, their imaginary school newspaper.

Then A.C. Currant arrived—big smile—hair slicked back—white suit—pale pink starched shirt—white shoes—all topped with white Panama hat. Emma was impressed. He looked like the male lead in a Tennessee Williams movie—vintage 'N'awlins.' A.C. carried a package with him. He offered his personal elaborate and gracious introduction to the secretary and somewhat less formal greetings to the three men. He paused for a moment as he fronted Ferrie, taking a look too long at the weird one, thought Emma.

"Well, thankfully, I made it," announced Currant. "For I have the presentation package." He handed a large envelope to Emma.

She opened it and revealed a wooden plaque with an engraved brass plate. "I will read the inscription," she said with great solemnity. "The Students and Faculty of Springfield Heights High School Acknowledge and Salute the Honorable William Guy Banister, A Great American, for his Many Accomplishments, National and Local, in Law Enforcement and the Preservation of the Security of the United States of America." She handed the plaque to the burly detective. She wasn't sure, but there might have been a little glassing of his eyes. This is working, she thought.

"William," he said. "Where did you get that?"

Emma smiled and nodded toward Delphine.

Banister returned the smile and sidled up to his secretary, whispering something in her ear. Then he commented to all: "Well, I am flattered and thankful for this great honor. To be honest, I'm at the age when I don't get as many accolades as I would like to receive. This is one of the best. Thank you, Zak, Ethan, Dr. Currant, and Emma." He singled the girl detective out for a two-handed shake. In one last grand effort, the time travelers announced they would like to sing a song to celebrate the occasion. Everyone, except Zak, joined in for a chorus of *God Bless America*. It was a great ending to this portion of the show.

The celebration was over. There was some talk about the evening ahead. Emma and Ethan casually said that they were going to attend a concert in the park. Currant made a point to say that he was available for the evening. He wondered if the three men and Delphine Roberts could join him for dinner and a drink, his treat. Roberts declined. But once Banister nodded in affirmation, the other three agreed it was *traybone*. Gazing in Zak's direction, Ferrie wondered aloud if the young man could join them. Zak looked at Dr. Currant and appeared to seek his approval.

"Of course, Zak can come along. Right, Zak? Just so long as he doesn't drink anything alcoholic. He is only seventeen," he said, setting the hook into Ferrie.

"He doesn't look a day younger than eighteen." Ferrie smiled like a crazed clown.

O.A. LOG TTA2028-2

INVESTIGATOR: Joell Costas

DATE: November 14, 1963 (July 15, 2028)

PROJECT: JFK-11.02.63

PROGRESS REPORT: I assumed the roles of a City of Chicago Building Inspector and an Insurance Investigator, which allowed me relatively easy access to investigative opportunities.

Interview with Landlord LOWELL NELSON — Janitor of the building in which VALLEE lives, Lowell NELSON, stated that on or about November 6, 1963, he confronted Thomas VALLEE about the continuing police presence in the building and in VALLEE's apartment. VALLEE stated to him that he was taken into custody by police for questioning in the early part of November. NELSON stated that VALLEE contended it was a case of mistaken identity. I examined the apartment (supposedly checking for code violations) during the day when VALLEE was at work. I discovered several firearms and a stock of ammunition. NELSON stated he would demand that VALLEE remove them from the apartment. In addition to the police presence, NELSON stated he saw a middle-aged man and a teenage boy before VALLEE was arrested. These two may have been watching the apartment from a bus stop location across the street. At that same time (most likely the morning of November 1, 1963), NELSON saw two men enter and leave VALLEE's apartment. They appeared to be police detectives, according to NELSON.

Interview with Cab Driver RALPH BUFORD—A news item in the local newspaper described an accident involving a cab driver and two passengers on the morning of

November 1, 1963, in a location not far from VALLEE's apartment. I located the driver. He stated his two passengers were a male 17/18 years old, and a middle-aged man, both white. The older one said he was a teacher. The younger one never spoke but was remembered as having a striking appearance. Apparently, another car forced their cab off a roadway and then drove into a lakefront harbor. The cab driver says the younger passenger saved his life. There is no mention of the identity of the two passengers in the police report, which the cab driver provided. However, the description given by BUFORD matches that of the two people provided by VALLEE's landlord.

Interview with Office Assistant MARJORIE KOSTIK—I checked with all the newspaper offices in the city regarding the taxicab story. No additional information was provided. However, at the newsroom of the *Chicago's American*, a daily newspaper, I interviewed KOSTIK. She remembered that sometime in the last days of October 1963, three young people: a girl about 17 and two boys about the same age or slightly older, visited the office. They met with THOMAS QUINN, a reporter, for about 20 minutes. Later QUINN told her they were journalism students. She remembered one of the two boys was "a real looker," in her words, and the other was very tall. She thought the tall boy and the girl might be twins. She also said she could not be sure but that the same persons may have returned several days later and had a meeting with QUINN in a private conference room. According to KOSTIK, QUINN left for Florida this morning (11-14-63) to cover President John F. Kennedy on tour.

Checking local downtown hotels, I could not locate anyone matching the description of the parties listed above. While posing as an insurance investigator, hotel workers interviewed would not discuss these matters with me. However, one bellhop at the Plaza House hotel, ROBERT NETTLES, recalls three young people (two teenage boys and a girl with an older man) as guests in the hotel in late October and early November. He has not seen them since that time. His best estimate of their date of departure was November 7 or 8, 1963. The hotel guest records were not accessible.

It is possible the four people identified above could be suspects, but I do not believe they are in Chicago now. If they reconnected with the future, they would be aware of the new history. Considering this, I will complete my work here and proceed to Dallas, Texas. I will make contact with the *Office* upon arrival.

TRANSMITTED VIA CODED TIME JUSTIFIER AT 16:09 CT 07/15/28.

-Chapter XVI-

Boys Night Out

This is my lucky night, thought Zak—dining with four old guys in New Orleans. Fortunately, he was only there to look, listen with all his senses and learn. A.C. Currant appeared to be delighted with the situation. At a round table in Mancuso's Restaurant on the ground floor of the Lafayette Street building, Currant was positioned between Banister and Martin, and Zak sat next to Ferrie. Ferrie was interested in Zak even though Zak couldn't return the conversation. At times the clown man would totally disengage from the main chat and talk only to Zak, which was particularly unnerving. One didn't have to be psychic to sense a creepy quality in every word he uttered. Obviously, he was taken by Zak's good looks and very pleased with the one-sided conversation.

A hot 90-proof odor of accumulated sweat hung in the air and mingled with Banister's non-stop cigar smoke as the restaurant, now crowded with regular Friday night patrons, moved from hungry diners to sloppy drinkers. Zak amused himself by watching the attentive and saucy waitress wearing a tight-fitting halter top that revealed as much as it concealed. It appeared to Zak that Banister was a regular customer, and he was afforded special treatment by the wait staff and management. The redhead laid down another tray of drinks at the table. Banister slipped her a silver dollar with one hand, and his other hand playfully grabbed her left butt cheek. She giggled and danced away, seemingly amused but not concerned.

Zak was the only one at the table who was not drinking anything of substance. Given this, he had a ringside seat on reality. Clouded minds ruled the night in an alcohol-soaked conversational mishmash. Loud talk to make a point, words slurred, and faces pushed close together. All this, Zak surmised, to increase the possibility of cogent communication between old drinking buddies. But he was saddled with a close-up view of Ferrie's face, a most distasteful and frightening vision. Zak looked away. Currant and Jack Martin were engaged in a tight bout of banter about World War II. Martin was a frail knot of a man, aged and hollowed out by a lifetime backwash of booze. He and Currant swapped war stories. Zak knew A.C.'s stories were fabricated, and his best guess was that Martin's were equally fictitious.

"I put in my time," said Martin for everyone at the table to hear. "Served my country well. Not like some people I know who spent the war years chasing altar boys."

With this comment, Ferrie dropped his conversation with Zak and focused on Martin. "Jack, you are, as usual, full of feces. If anyone at this table deserves to be recognized for their service to the country, I'm sure it would be Dr. Currant, Guy Banister, or me. Only in your vivid imagination would someone ever find a patriotic act on your part. Of course, I'm not counting all your services and fraudulent roles as a government agent, Army colonel, priest, or doctor."

"Right, Dave. You're a smooth-talker. But I've been around. I know how things work. Just because you want to be a man of the cloth doesn't mean you're an angel." Martin grabbed his drink and downed the last of it.

"I've given blood for my country, Jack. How about you?

"Gentlemen. We are the guests of the good Doctor. Let's keep our conversation relatively civilized." Banister released a hearty laugh followed by a short coughing fit.

Currant appeared to be upset by this aggressive talk, although Zak knew he was not. "That's all right, Guy. I'm used to boys being boys. But all evening, I've been overhearing some of Dave's conversations with Zak, and I'm very impressed. I know you've been involved with patriotic causes, but I didn't know you've been helping to build a team to go after that Communist bastard Castro."

Everyone looked at Guy Banister. At first, he didn't respond. Then he spoke slowly and quietly as if he was letting them in on a secret. The words carefully exited his mouth. "You know, Doctor, we do our work here without fanfare and mostly without the support of people who should be providing support. But I can tell you this, we are very strongly committed to working with those who oppose the capture of any free country by Communists...particularly Cuba. Hell, it's 90 miles from our home. We would have to be fools not to do something."

"Somebody has to," said Ferrie.

Currant nodded. "I heard...I should say...it seems everyone knows...they closed the rebel training camps on the other side of the lake this summer. The *government*...what's that all about?"

"That's what we'd like to know, Doc," said Ferrie. "By the way, they're not rebels. Castro led the rebellion *against* the people of Cuba. Those guys are freedom fighters."

"Right," agreed Currant.

"Some of us have been busting our rears to get some kind of positive movement on this Cuba problem. You can rest assured there are good people in the government who are taking this thing seriously. Not everyone is like that shithead Bobby Kennedy and his brother. There are real patriots out there. People you can trust."

"I take it you don't trust this administration?" Currant looked straight into Ferrie's coal-black eyes.

Zak watched the men's faces. There was no disguising their political positions. Martin's lips curled. Ferrie's eyes narrowed. And Banister flushed. Zak knew A.C. had raised a boil. The young man's special emotional meter ran over the top as he sat there and sensed what they were feeling. These men must hate the Kennedys.

"That would be an understatement, Dr. Currant," said Banister. "Kennedy should be impeached for his actions...or should I say lack of actions...at the Bay of Pigs. And his follow-up give-away to Castro last year."

"We lost a lot of good men in '61. Friends died on the beaches because of that contemptuous Harvard-hack. Good men," said, Ferrie.

Currant raised his glass. "A toast to fallen friends...."

They all raised their glasses. With the uplift of Banister's arm, Zak noticed a large, black pistol resting ominously in a holster beneath his jacket. This is the Wild West, thought Zak. They completed the toast. The three New Orleans men were seemingly deep in thought. Zak and Currant said nothing as if not to interrupt a possible poignant moment.

Then Martin lifted his head and spoke quite abruptly. "Three cheers for Oswald the Rabbit. May he pop out of his hole and fire the shot heard round the world." Zak sensed an emotional vacuum waiting to be filled. It was filled immediately with a mixture of raw emotions. Martin, who obviously had sucked up one too many drinks, looked over to Banister with fear in his eyes. Whatever he was talking about was really hot stuff. Zak had no idea what this 'Oswald Rabbit' signified, but it was something immense to these men. Banister released vibrations of anger. Martin poured out overwhelming fear. However, reading Ferrie, he sensed something else, not fear or anger, but genuine concern and compassion. But for what or who?

"Jack..." The one stretched-out word from Banister slithered over to Martin, carrying an immense quantity of menace. The mood at the table changed very quickly from a somber reflection to one of fear.

"Sorry, Guy," said Martin lowering his gaze in the face of the intensity of Banister's look.

"I'm sorry too. I'm not following this, fellows," said Currant.

"Just a little in-joke," replied Banister. "But it is impolite for Jack to tell the punch line only to people who don't know the setup."

"What is the setup, Guy?"

Banister thought for a moment before replying.

"You remember the cartoon character Oswald, the Rabbit?"

Currant thought about it. "Little before my time, Guy. But I do. He looked like Mickey Mouse with long ears.

"That's right. "Disney's first creation. A real moneymaker too. But Old Walt gave him up after he lost the rights to him. So we got Mickey Mouse. But while Oswald was around, he was quite a comedy hit in the '20s. Not to embarrass you, Zak, but Oswald Rabbit was known for his ability to produce other rabbits. If you know what I mean...."

Zak nodded in acknowledgment smiling weakly.

"Right, you get it. In the cartoons, he would constantly be graced with visits from the stork, providing new bunnies just like him. Well, you might say he...you know...like a bunny. Anyway, let's just say old Oswald knew how to replicate. So that little character has become a symbol to many around here. We're not making rabbits, but we are giving birth to our own bunny warriors, and I'm hoping they will be hopping into Cuba soon if you know what I mean."

"Ah ha," said Currant. "Bunny hopping all the way to Cuba."

"You got it, Doctor. That's our dream. That's what we work for. Right, boys?"

"I'll drink to that," said Martin, obviously relieved. "A toast to Oswald, the fornicating rabbit. Sorry, Zak. To all the Oswalds..."

They toasted once again. The evening continued without anything as intensive as the Oswald revelation. Banister eventually suggested they head out to cruise Bourbon Street with the drinks on him. But Currant demurred, citing the need for the youngster Zak to get his beauty sleep. The last words of the playwright/director, Doctor Currant, were to wish them all a good evening. With tears in his eyes, he gave a final toast, a plea to have "God Bless America." The weeklong pageant ended with an over-exuberant round of handshakes, backslaps, and thanks.

It was almost midnight when Zak and A.C. reached the hotel. Ethan and Emma awaited them in the lobby. They all went up to a rooftop patio, which provided some breathing room and privacy. Sitting poolside, they relaxed and took in the gentle breeze that rippled the watery reflection of the moonlight. Currant brought them up to date, providing a blow-by-blow recap of the evening out with the "Three Stooges" of New Orleans.

"I'm sure Zak had a great time. He had Ferrie all to himself. Sorry about that, Zak. But we needed you there. What did you think about that Oswald the Rabbit story? Was that something?"

Zak fired back in sign language. *"I felt tremendous fear, anticipation, and anxiety in the air during that brief discussion. Oswald is very important"*. He read Banister's cover-up story about Walt Disney and the multiplying rabbits as an out-and-out lie. He also told them about Ferrie's strange, almost protective emotional reaction to the Oswald incident. Lastly, he detected a mix of highly caustic negative emotions whenever Kennedy's name came into the conversation.

"As I thought. Thanks, Zak." Currant looked at the three teens. "This could be a big lead. I would like you to visit the local reference centers...libraries, newspaper morgues, whatever. See if you can find any stories about anything or a person named Oswald related to anything Cuban."

Emma gave him a mock salute. "Aye, aye. Commander."

Currant continued the thought. "Dismissed..." He added, "By the way...great acting job today for our friends. I really think his highness, The Banister, enjoyed our tribute."

LOG of Zak Newman --- November 15, 1963: 00:36

(Day 18 of time travel)

We met some interesting people. They're right out of a Dickens novel. That such people even exist in 1963 is amazing to me. So much life in their veins—they buzz around like hostile hornets on a mission to kill. They hate JFK. They love their comrades in arms. They're violent. Idealistic. They're dangerous. What are they seeking? Do they really have the power they exhibit, or are they puppets dangling from the lifelines of their unknown masters? I guess the big question is whether their obsession with JFK—their obvious desire to see him eliminated—will lead to any action. Or are they just blowing off political steam? In the end, Ferrie tried hard to convince me they were harmless by wallpapering over their words as bullshit banter, but I doubt it. I read that this is very real to them. Are they grown men playing war or bit players in the history of the world? It doesn't make a difference; they believe what they are doing is critical for their survival and the survival of the United States. For decades, people thought one "lone nut" named Thomas Arthur Vallee did the unspeakable. That solid belief was written in stone and sold on every corner. So I would guess it's possible another group of nuts could be doing their nutty thing—intent on killing the President. Of course, in the end, Vallee proved to be a patsy with a "lone nut" legend. Maybe these boys are a little further up the conspiratorial food chain, but they also have great legends that can be retold in many ways as the situation demands. Those that create The History *are skilled wordsmiths trained in the art of deception.*

The hard-drinking Banister—former FBI special agent, right-winger, and take-no-prisoners leader—is a man desperately seeking a heart attack—intense, angry, and unforgiving. Ferrie—is The Good, the Bad, and the Ugly *(Emma's description). Jack Martin—is furtive, fumbling, and apparently motivated to screw people at all times. Speaking of—Banister's overly dedicated secretary will go down with the good ship* Banister. *And then there is this Oswald character. We don't know what or who this is, but the vibrations were way off the emotional Richter scale. There's something there.*

Ethan is very agitated. He's now convinced that there will be another attempt on JFK. After stopping the one in Chicago, he is now a man possessed. Emma is more sanguine. Not that she does not care, but I think she realizes that we time travelers are not really the repair crew for the broken promises of history. And A.C. Currant—he seems really detached lately. Sure he scripted and directed the past week's New Orleans charade party, but something about him tells me that the whole JFK aspect of our visit here plays a distant second to his personal historical issues. Just my reading —but it is very intense. Much like Banister, Currant is battling his own demons. I have never seen him like this before. He has that little toy car that he is constantly massaging in his fingers like a worry bead. From day one, he has had that commemorative trinket with him. I notice when he unconsciously handles it, a certain calmness lays over him as if it was a magical mojo. There is something special about it. Of that, I am certain.

END: 11-15-63

-Chapter XVII-

The Other Brothers

Currant peered out the cab window and let the passing view wash over him. Covington, Louisiana, twenty-six miles north of New Orleans across Lake Pontchartrain, his boyhood home of 6,754 citizens felt both familiar and strange. Everything was exactly as he remembered it, yet not. His memories were warm, fuzzy, and plastic, but the reality was cool, hard-edged, and rigid. Not unpleasant, but much different as viewed through his 73-year-old eyes. A Sinclair gas station featuring its green dinosaur logo looking back over his shoulder reminded Currant he was doing the same thing, looking back into the time of his youth, staring the past in the face.

He begged the gods of time to allow him to make a difference. He wanted to forever alter the Currant family album starting today, November 16, 1963. JFK was important to the Twins and Zak, the history of America, and the people who shot him, his wife, and kids, but Currant's half-brother, Patrick Brennan, was vitally important to A.C. and his parents. The scientist felt like that dinosaur, old and obsolete but looking backward with hope. The cab crossed some railroad tracks, and a distant memory of his brother Patrick bounced around in his head.

Patrick's death mask appeared before him. Sixteen years old, cold, pale, fresh, and angular. He was eight years older than A.C., and he was in a coffin. He killed himself in the middle of the night in the garage. Going nowhere, he drove to his death in dad's '56 Ford on March 9, 1964. He left behind his troubles which no doubt seemed overwhelming at the time and his family. That morning his mother found him, his lips cherry red. She was devastated. It took weeks for her to stop crying. A.C. remembered her sitting on Patrick's bed, sobbing quietly in the dark years later. He left her alone. He was only a young boy then, but he knew she was broken along with Dad. Patrick was the shining light beaming toward the future: intelligent, ambitious, and fearless. But he was also sensitive and caring.

Currant also remembered the day their cat Harriet died. A car had run over the yellow tabby. She loved to just sit in the middle of the road and think, or whatever cats do when they just sit and stare deeply into the night. That night Patrick found A.C. standing in the street next to the squashed feline. He shoveled the remains off the pavement and escorted his little brother into their backyard for the burial services. It was all formal and proper. Patrick dug a grave, gently placed the pussycat parts into the ground, said a small prayer, and sent her on her way to kitty heaven. He hugged A.C. and assured him they would all reunite sometime in the future. He was right.

Currant asked the cab driver to stop about two blocks from the house. He would walk the rest of the way. Large trees arched over the street and provided cozy cover and bright sun sifted through the leafy green ceiling, creating a patch-quilt of sunbeams on the sidewalk. His thoughts drifted. At this moment, he was a man between two times—two epochs seemingly so far apart, yet separated only by 65 years of ongoing progress and change—enough change to destroy any connection to Currant's boyhood past. Nothing in 2028 was the same as this. This is the peace of peace—the sweet, soft, silk-covered cushion of a time lost—a time of innocence, hope, and positive expectation. He looked about and let it all in—the tidy, little bungalows—bright, two-tone automobiles parked in driveways—dads washing their cars—a few kids playing baseball in a vacant lot. He walked along slowly in a daze, pausing briefly when a big black dog casually approached him, sniffed his crotch for signs of life, and, finding none, wandered away. Tree branches above rustled in the breeze, while the hypnotic sounds of push lawn mowers, out for a final season trim, created an almost musical background.

Then he saw her in the distance. His mother was on the other side of white picket backyard fencing, standing on a slight rise in the land, her wicker laundry basket at her feet, expertly pinning bed sheets onto the clothesline. They flapped in the light wind waiting for their wetness to be sucked out by the sun. Currant remembered the smell of clean, dry sheets fresh off the clothesline and onto his bed. That fragrance was his last thought before falling fast asleep, oblivious to the world's problems, bone tired from playing, and always anticipating the next day's adventures. His mother was raven-haired and quite beautiful, he thought. He had never viewed her as a woman, but now as she stretched to hang the wash, wearing a bright blue blouse and well-fitting blue jeans, he saw that she was a real woman of considerable attraction. The thoughts confused him. Quickly, he tightened his thinking. He stood about fifteen feet away, alone on the sidewalk, a man in his mid-seventies who, because of advances in healthcare, nutrition, and diet, appeared to be in his late forties by 1963 standards. She turned his way and spotted him. He was, at once, unable to come to his thoughts. He was stunned by the moment. A yellow cat ran up to him. He looked down at it as it rubbed his leg.

"She doesn't usually take to strangers, mister. I guess you're lucky...if you like cats." Her voice had a pleasant Southern softness but still betrayed her East Coast roots.

His mother smiled, a flight of sunlight caught her face, and she appeared like an angel to Currant. He picked up the cat and looked back at his mother. The last time he saw her, she was dead. By then, his brother and father were also dead. He was stunned to be this close to her again, but he resisted his emotions. He held the cat tenderly, lovingly, a willing surrogate accepting his love and attention.

"Hello, Harriet," he whispered softly into her ear. The cat purred. He looked back at his mother. "Beautiful day isn't it," he said dumbly. She didn't seem to mind.

"I am impressed, sir. You have a way with animals."

"I do like cats," he said. He walked onto the grass, up the rise, close to her but separated by the white pickets. He let the cat down gently, and it skittered over the fence and back into the yard, soon studying a nested bird in a nearby tree.

"I'm sorry. Do I know you?"

"How do you do?" he said quietly. "My name is Crawford. I used to live here many years ago. I've come back to revisit my old neighborhood...a trip down memory lane, if you will. In fact, I lived in this house when I was a child. So you must forgive me if I appear attached." Tears welled up in his eyes until they could no longer be contained, and they slid down his cheeks just enough to be noticed by the woman. He pulled out a handkerchief from his coat pocket and touched up his face quickly. "Sorry," he said. "I'm afraid I am a bit taken by the moment."

She ignored the wash basket and came up to him, looking directly into his eyes. "My name is Mary...Mary Currant. Funny, I feel as if I know you. When did you live here?"

A.C. stumbled on his words. He focused on her beautiful, soft brown eyes. "About twenty-five years ago. It's been a long time. I must say you have made it quite attractive."

"Thanks. My husband and I try hard to make it the best we can."

Then Currant heard a noise behind him. He turned and saw two boys on a red Cushman motor scooter. He recognized them. Patrick was driving, and he, the little tow-headed Arthur C. Currant, sat on the seat in front, nestled between his brother's arms. The machine drove into the driveway and stopped. In almost one motion, the two boys jumped off. The older one locked in the kickstand while the little one ran ahead through the gate into the yard. He raced to his mother and hugged her. The old A.C. was astounded by himself. What a beautiful little guy—blue jeans, striped polo shirt, white socks, and downright ratty, brown leather shoes. He held a rolled-up comic book in his hand. If he only knew how valuable that twelve-cent comic would be sixty-five years later, thought Currant. Then he realized how ridiculous that thought was. Little A.C. cared nothing about investments but loved the stories about mad scientists, robots, and gadgets.

"This is Mr. Crawford, A.C.," she said casually. " He lived here many years ago."

The young A.C. studied the older. "Hi."

"Hi. New comic book?"

"Yep. *Batman.* It's all about aliens. Men from Mars."

"Sounds really cool to me," said the older A.C.

"Yep."

A.C. looked up at his mother. "Fine boy, you have here. And this is another son?" he said, turning to his older brother. A.C. quietly admired the tall, lean and fine-featured young man.

She smiled. "I have two wonderful boys. This is Patrick."

A.C. looked at Patrick and then shook his hand. "Glad to meet you."

"Patrick's going to be a doctor," said the younger son.

Patrick blushed. His eyes averted the direct gaze of the stranger. "We'll see," he said slowly, "that's a long way off in the future."

"Patrick, you will find the future has a way of arriving very fast. I'm sure you will make a great doctor."

"I hope so. But first, I have to get through college. I'm hoping for a scholarship to Tulane. I'm doing research now to build up my experience. I don't know."

A.C. looked at the boy. He was already carrying a load. He appeared delicate, unlike his younger brother, who was all piss and vinegar. "You know, Patrick, my mother always used to say that our Guardian Angel will protect and guide us. And believe me, I've been around awhile. My angel's always there. And so is yours," said Currant.

Patrick smiled and looked at his mother. "That's funny. That's what Mom always says."

Mary Currant beamed. "See, I told you so, Patrick. You'll make a fine doctor. Doctor Patrick MacAndrew Brennan. Don't worry." She washed her eyes over the older A.C., glanced at her two sons, then back. "I want to thank you, Mr. Crawford. Your comments are very affirming. You know, sometimes I worry about Patrick. He's a very intense boy. He takes life very seriously. Sometimes too seriously."

"Mom. Please." Patrick grimaced. "Nice meeting you. I have to go now."

A.C. locked onto Patrick's eyes. He held out his hand. They shook hands over the fence. "Never ever lose your dream, Patrick. Keep the faith. The future is all yours."

"Thanks. Mr. Crawford." He turned and headed into the house.

"Goodbye, Patrick."

"Well, I've taken up enough of your time, Mrs. Currant."

"Not a problem, Mr. Crawford," she said quietly.

He looked down on little A.C., studying the comic book cover. Currant pulled something out of his coat pocket. "Son, I'd like to show you something. Look at this." His open palm displayed the brightly polished silver miniature replica of a 2017 Mercedes Benz coupe. "What do you think of this? The doors open. The headlights glow, and if you shake, it makes a sound like an engine." He demonstrated all this for the boy.

"Wow," said Arthur, "that's cool. What is it?"

"It's a car of the future. I'd like you to have it, but we will have to do a trade."

"Trade what?"

"That *Batman* for this car. I'd really like to have something to read on the ride home tonight. Nothing like the Caped Crusader to wile away the hours."

Mary Currant looked puzzled but went along with the process. The boy looked at her for direction. "It's your decision, Arthur."

The kid thought for a moment and looked at the little car. He took it from A.C.'s hand and carefully studied it. I really like this. It's a deal." He handed over the comic book and kept the trinket. "I already read the *Batman.*"

A.C. smiled. "Well, then, it's a good deal for both of us."

Little A.C. nodded as he played with his new keepsake. He looked up at Currant. "Gee, Mister, this thing's really cool. Thanks."

Currant put both hands up as if to say it was nothing. "It was a good deal, Arthur. I love Batman too. A good, righteous man with duel personas. Not unlike myself, in a way." He laughed lightly. "We need more Batmen around to take care of the bad guys." He took one long, last look at his little self and his mother. Emotion rose again, and his heart beat like an old school-house clock. He wanted to say many things, but he knew he could not. He wished he could tell her he loved her. He wanted to tell her the truth, but he couldn't. He wanted to tell her not to worry. Her boys would be fine. Life would be good. He knew he had a mission ahead to make certain that Patrick's life would continue. He knew he could not fail in that goal. That thought was all that was necessary to pull him away from this moment and his family. "I have to go, Mrs. Currant. Give my best to the mister. Remember me, please. In a way, I left a little part of me here in your house."

Mary Currant nodded as if she understood completely. To A.C., she now looked like a mystical, soft, radiant, and loving vision. He knew he would always carry this image with him.

"You know. All things and all people are connected in so many strange and wonderful ways. And the little car...."

She looked at him, waiting for him to complete his

sentence. He was very intense. She seemed to understand this effort to create a bridge over time. The inventor and his mother stared deep into each other's souls, forging a moment that would remain forever.

A.C. continued, and she listened attentively. "The little car is a talisman as well as a toy. It has the power to bring you good luck. Look closely sometimes when you need something, and you will know what I mean. It's extraordinary. It's the car of the future...it's full of good fortune...and pleasant surprises. Goodbye, Mrs. Currant. Goodbye, A.C." He gave them a quick wave, turned, and walked away.

"Good memories, Mr. Crawford. Come back again," she said slowly. "God bless you."

He looked back. "Thanks, Mrs. Currant. I was a boy once too. Thank you for letting me go home again.

In the distance, he could hear Little A.C. say, "I really like this car, Mom. I really do."

Currant walked away down the street, knowing precisely what he had to do. His whole body tingled with anticipation of his work ahead.

O.A. LOG TTA2028-3

INVESTIGATOR: Joell Costas

DATE: November 14, 1963 (July 15, 2028)

PROJECT: JFK-11.02.63

REPORT OF PHYSICAL CONDITION:

Recently, I have been experiencing severe abdominal pain and other symptoms that might affect my ability to complete the assignment. I had no choice but to seek immediate medical attention. The condition worsened to the point where I needed to visit a local downtown Chicago hospital to have it evaluated. After running a series of tests and procedures, doctors here have informed me I have gastric cancer. While surgery can be performed to remove the tumor, there is no cure. Doctors were unable to determine whether the cancer had spread. In any event, their prognosis for this type of disease suggests it will usually result in incapacitation and death in a relatively short period of time. Considering the event timetable, I am convinced I can complete this assignment and maintain the continuity of the historical event tree. I will make no additional visits to medical practitioners.

Advise if this information will cause the *Office* to introduce other operatives or initiate any other changes related to this assignment as soon as possible.

TRANSMITTED VIA CODED TIME JUSTIFIER AT 17:27 CT 07/15/28.

-Chapter XVIII-

Saving PMB

Early evening, the cab dropped off A.C. Currant on Louisiana Parkway. He told the driver to wait. Standing at the curb, the darkness quickly enveloped him. The mock-Spanish-style residence was bathed in blackness. He slowly approached the two-story stucco edifice, wondering if the house was empty. Gingerly he looked through the door glass for a sign of life, but there was none. The place was a grim mausoleum heavy with the odors of mold and magnolia. The doorbell elicited a muted response from somewhere in the rear of the house. He waited. Again he rang and waited. The house was dead.

He pushed his face closer, now almost on the glass. Then abruptly, the piercing black eyes of another human stared at him for a moment like a mirror image. His "reflection" was a white-faced, bald-headed clown wearing arched eyebrows of crimson paint. Currant backed off. David Ferrie opened the door. He wore a mortician's grin.

"This is a pleasant surprise. A doctor who makes house calls. What brings you to my humble abode?"

Currant stumbled over his words, startled by the quickness of Ferrie's arrival and how he looked.

"I can see you are taken aback by my naked pate. Such is the fate of surprise guests," said Ferrie continuing to wear the smile.

"My apologies for the late hour. May I come in?"

Ferrie nodded and welcomed him into the foyer. They walked up the stairs to his apartment. Entering his parlor, he switched on a small Tiffany lamp that offered just enough light for Currant to locate an over-stuffed chair. Taking a seat, Currant briefly glanced at his reflection in an oval wall mirror which was surrounded by an assemblage of framed photos: Ferrie the young seminarian, Ferrie the gregarious Civil Air Patrol captain, Ferrie the neatly uniformed Eastern Airlines pilot, Ferrie the dedicated trainer of freedom fighters, and others all featuring men and boys doing manly things. David Ferrie sat nearby in the compact confines, sighing as he dropped his large frame into the chair. He crossed one leg over the other. His foot dangled inches from the physicist's knee. Currant straightened.

"I'd offer you a drink, Doctor. But after Thursday night's outing, I doubt either of us wants to test our limits again."

"No thanks. Had enough." Currant paused, gathering his words. "I wanted to talk to you alone."

Ferrie smiled. "I prefer this setting for conversation. More intimate." He looked directly into Currant's eyes and exhaled. "Our boys' night out was fun, but I'm afraid conversation with our friends, Guy and Jack, is, by the nature of their interests, rather limited. Particularly Jack...if you know what I mean. He does have a way of alienating almost everyone he touches."

"I noticed you, and he might have some issues."

Ferrie laughed. "Issues? It's like having issues with a household pest. Maybe a pesky little mouse or a giant palmetto bug." He chuckled again. "A palmetto bug is more like it. Banister puts up with him, and Banister's a good client. But I digress. Let's not dwell on him. What about you? You seem to be having fun. I did enjoy speaking with your young man Zak. He's quite a charmer. Quiet. But one look into his eyes, and I knew he was very intelligent. Should have brought him along, Doc'. He's nice to look at. You know I admire you. You seem to relate to your young charges well. It's good for men our age to be able to do so. Wouldn't you agree?"

"I do enjoy working with young people."

"Especially Zak?"

Currant squirmed in his chair. "I'm a teacher David. I enjoy working with youth. It keeps me young."

"I'll bet it does—youth has a way of its own." Ferrie paused and looked over to the photos on the wall. For a moment, he appeared lost in his own world. Then he turned back to Currant. He ran a hand back over his bare head. "Alopecia areata."

"Sorry..."

"My condition. Loss of body hair. It started a few years ago. Permanent. I'm afraid. Not a pleasant thing to be viewed as a freak. You might wonder why I don't invest in a Hollywood rug and some decent eyebrow makeup."

"Hadn't thought about it, David."

"Hard to believe that. Everybody thinks about it. That's why I wear that red shag carpet on my head and the grease paint eyebrows. People don't forget me, Doctor. They'll always remember David Ferrie. I'm like Popeye. I am...what I am. At my age, I don't give a damn about it. I take what I want out of life, and I give back what I can. It's a fair trade in an otherwise unfair world. Screw'em if they can't take a joke. So what's on your mind? You didn't come here to discuss my physical beauty."

Currant gazed across the room, recomposing, forgetting the presence of the clown-man for the moment, anchoring his thoughts and focusing. He churned inside but maintained control. "Mr. Ferrie..."

"Dave..."

"Dave. You have a young friend who is my nephew."

"Really. And who might that be?"

"Patrick Brennan."

"Yes, I see," said Ferrie, not missing a beat. "Patrick is your nephew. I didn't know that. What an outstanding coincidence that you and your students should come to me here in New Orleans. Hundreds of miles from your home. And to think that you are Patrick's uncle. Mother or father's side?"

Currant stared into Ferrie's black eyes. "His mother is my sister. She remarried after her first husband died. The late Mr. Brennan was his father. The family moved here from Massachusetts. Not really a coincidence, though, Dave."

Ferrie smiled. "I thought not." He twisted in his chair and moved closer to Currant. "Patrick is a fine boy.

Very smart. Very good looking. I don't know much about his home life. Never met his parents. He is a big help with my lab work. Wants to become a medical researcher. He wants to cure cancer. Did you know that?"

"Yes, he has told me that."

"You know I'm quite an expert on that subject. You could call me 'Doctor' too, but don't bother. Anyway, that's why he likes to work with me. He handles the mice. Quite well, I might add. I imagine he gets that scientific bent from you, Doctor Currant."

"Possibly," Currant looked into the man's eyes. "You like young men, don't you, Dave?"

Ferrie stopped smiling. "What are you trying to say, Doctor?"

"You know," said Currant.

"I know you're making me uncomfortable. You take advantage of my hospitality. You and your students pop into my life, blowing smoke up Guy Banister's ass. We do a little socializing. And now you seem to be going someplace else. What's your point? Are you concerned about my relationship with your nephew?"

Currant sat, silent.

"He was one of my Falcons, you know. My air patrol. Metairie Falcon Cadet Squadron. Patrick was a solid cadet. Understood the principles well. Very patriotic too."

"Is that you with your Falcons?" Currant pointed to the black and white photo of men dressed in army fatigues having a cookout with a group of young boys. Ferrie wore a combat helmet.

"That was a while back. Before the Falcons, I was a commander in the Civil Air Patrol. You know I'm a pilot. Flew with Eastern Airlines for several years. I love flying. It's very freeing to float above the world, A.C...may I call you that?"

"Right...yes," said Currant.

"See this?" The clown man pointed to a series of scars on his right arm. "I got that flying into Cuba. Not too long ago. I'm not just a cartoon character playing war with some kids. It's more complicated than that."

"Maybe that's so, Dave, but let's stick with kids for a moment."

"OK. I'll stay there. You know, many of my cadets moved on to join the Air Force...the Marines..the other services. They're the future, Doc. Those kids are the future. This country needs them. I love those kids."

Currant fired back. "You had to shut down the Falcons because you were caught with your fingers around the wrong *stick*. Didn't you?"

Ferrie smiled. "Excellent, Doctor. Very funny. Malicious rumors spread by my enemies. But those charges were dropped. Totally unsubstantiated. That's all behind us. Why bring that up now?"

"Because I am concerned about my nephew Patrick."

"He's a big boy now. You need not be concerned. I can't help it that he prefers to work with me rather than stay home with his stepfather. I don't think the two of them really get on. Maybe I'm a better father figure? The fact is he's a smart boy and a quick learner. He's a lucky young man. Working in cancer research at the age of sixteen. That will be a real feather in his cap when he applies at Tulane. Won't it?"

Currant looked at Ferrie, who seemed to be drifting annoyingly closer. He got up and moved over to the wall of framed photos. He studied them before speaking. "Well, Dave. I'll tell you what I'm up to...straight out. I'm here to put an end to your relationship with Patrick."

"What relationship? He's my lab assistant."

Currant's eyes locked into the two black orbs floating menacingly beneath the red-painted eyebrows. "Let's drop the pretense, Ferrie. You're a homosexual. You like young boys. You like Patrick. You want to become his special friend. Well, it's not going to happen."

"So you say, Doctor. Do you intend to take residence in our fair city?"

"No. We're leaving soon. But I am asking you to end it now."

Ferrie laughed lightly. "And if I don't?"

Currant moved in front of Ferrie. "You will. Because
I say, you will. I know all about you, Dave. I know your
friends, your enemies, your wants and desires. Your
weaknesses and your strengths. Vanity is your weakness.
Lack of self-respect is your weakness. Young boys are
your weakness. You lost your job as an airline pilot
because of it. And now you couldn't be ordained in a two-
pew church.You think you have friends in the
government, Cuban exiles, mobster buddies. These are
not your friends."

Ferrie stood up, and the two men faced each other.
"Listen. You don't want to test my friendship with those
people. They are not as forgiving as I am."

"I'm not afraid of them. They will never find me, but
I can always find you. And I will bring the wrath of hell
upon you if you don't do what I say. If you want to
continue your life, such as it is, you best accept the fact
that you can do without this one young man."

"Really," said Ferrie, "Really? Let's put our cards on
the table, Doctor A.C. Currant. While I enjoyed your dog
and pony show here in New Orleans, I'm afraid you've
played this 'high school high jinks' game in one city too
many."

Currant was puzzled. It was not the expected
response.

"I see. You're surprised. As I said, I have friends. I
even have friends in Chicago. My group of friends is
always talking. Conversation is the lifeblood of a good
organization. Wouldn't you agree? Anyway. You and your
junior reporters stirred up some dust around the
President's trip to Chicago. I guess everything worked out
OK. One of those no harm...no foul things. You just a
concerned citizen Doc' or what?"

"I'm only concerned about Patrick."

"And that's why you entered our crazy little world?"

"It is."

"Well. All right. I doubt I would get a straight answer
from you. And you may not get one out of me. But I'll offer
you a deal. Do you like to deal, Doc?"

"I'm not *dealing* with my nephew's life."

Ferrie's eyebrows raised into arches like two red-orange rainbows. "Yes, you will. Because you won't chase me away from young Patrick. Hell...it's a long ride back on that little red motor scooter across the causeway to Covington. Maybe he'll rest up and stay here overnight. I can take care of him. I can make him real comfortable." He smiled wickedly. "But I might leave him alone. If you and your entourage stay out of politics."

"I don't care about politics."

"What about Chicago?"

"That's done. What do you want?"

"What do I want? Well, I want you to move on to something else. I want you to stay out of other people's business, and then maybe I'll stay out of your business. Does that seem reasonable? And before you answer. Think about this." Ferrie rubbed his chin. "I don't like to be threatened, Doctor. And worse than that for you, my friends don't like threats."

"I really don't care what you like outside of my nephew. I want you to call him tomorrow and tell him that you no longer need his services. And that's that."

"Or?"

"Or I will have you killed before the end of the month."

Ferrie's incessant smile evaporated. He looked pained. His face tightened and turned red.

Currant continued, "Are you willing to bet your friends with the CIA, the Cubans, or your mobster buddies will save you? Those people use guys like you. No matter what you think, you are on the outside looking in."

Ferrie got into Currant's face. "What do you know about me? I'm working for great causes. People like me will be saving this country, while academics like you will be parsing passages of history books, wondering what happened to their basic freedoms. I'll trust my friends ahead of your Pollyannaish view of a democratic society. You're living in a world of illusion. You're naïve Doctor Currant. You're idealistic. You're an intelligent fool."

"You think killing JFK is a basic freedom?"

Ferrie laughed. "Do you think I'm out to kill Kennedy?"

"That thought has crossed my mind. I've seen evidence of your hatred. I know your friends."

"Who? Banister...Martin? I can blow smoke, too, Doc. Don't make any assumptions, my friend. I have a reputation to protect, and appearances can be deceiving. These are delicate and dangerous times. Caesar and his senators would play like a comic book compared to today's mix."

"You deny you want to eliminate him?"

"I don't need to confirm or deny anything for you. But I will present you with the idea that your interference might get JFK killed. His head is in the guillotine. They might let him pull it out...if changes are made."

"Like what?"

Ferrie contemplated. "Fair question. His head will remain on his shoulders if Castro's head is removed. Or if Castro is removed. Either way. Otherwise..." Ferrie made a slicing motion across his throat."

"And that would please you."

Ferrie chuckled. "That would please a whole lot of people who are about to be tossed out of the boat by JFK. Me...I like the man. He fills out a suit...he's a real leader... and he's a Catholic. The young people like him. His wife is pretty. Nice kids. I'm sure he and his brother are doing their best to resolve things. His brother's a prick. But JFK's a smart man. And he knows he's a marked man. He doesn't have much time. He has my sincere empathy. His balls are in a vice. But I can tell you, in all honesty, he would be better off if you stayed clear."

Ferrie's had moved closer and closer as he talked. Now the two men stood face to face. Currant smelled the onions from Ferrie's last meal. Tiny rivulets of sweat smeared the red eyebrow paint rippled across his forehead. Inches away, Ferrie swallowed hard, his Adam's apple rolled in his throat. He was a relatively big man, but Currant had no fear. He was as committed to Patrick as

Ferrie was committed to his cause.

Currant spoke softly in measured tones. "Obviously, I am serious about this matter. Possibly you don't care about your own life. You've made a mess of it. Maybe you don't care about the lives of the young men you touch. But I do. I'm only requesting your cooperation in this one case. I'll let the rest of the world take care of itself. Leave Patrick Brennan alone." He stopped and waited. "You will be saving his life and your own. Should you decide not to follow my instructions, he will still live, but you will not. Do I make myself clear, Mr. Ferrie?"

Ferrie looked like he was about to do something physical, but something turned inside him. His face relaxed. He dropped back, sat down in the armchair, and smiled a peaceful smile.

"Damn," he said. "I wish I had an uncle like you when I was young. Who knows? Maybe things would have turned out differently. Hell. I'll bet you would give it a shot. Not that I care. I'm a dead man, any way you look at it. But everyone has his dream. Everyone has an axe to grind. I'm a lone woodman trying to clear out the deadwood and vines choking the American dream. I don't want to build a cross for JFK...nor you...nor your nephew." He shrugged his shoulders. "It's simple, Doc'. You agree to stay out of politics, and I'll agree to stay away from your nephew. Agreed?"

Currant looked down at the man. He was a bag of broken promises and unfulfilled dreams. He almost felt a tinge of sympathy. "I'm going, David. Make your call tomorrow. And make it a permanent separation. I'll be watching."

Ferrie looked up. He shrugged his shoulders and nodded. "You got it, Doc. I'll get rid of him. But don't forget. I can always renew my acquaintance with young Patrick. You know he loves to be hypnotized. I'm sure he could be great fun. Remember...I'll be watching too. You should move on to something else. This is out of your hands and my hands." Ferrie stood and looked out the front window. He saw the waiting cab below. "Your chariot awaits, Don Quixote. *Pax Vobiscum*."

Later that evening in the hotel, at the predetermined time, Currant made the call to Tom Quinn.

"Quinn here."

"Tom. This is A.C. Currant"

"Well, you caught me just in time. I'm in Miami. I've got news. I followed JFK the entire day. There was another motorcade. In Tampa. And guess what?"

"What?"

"There was something going on in the background, just like Chicago. I spoke with an old friend of mine down here...Chief Mullins. He was a busy man today. That was one hell of a long caravan. Same kind of dangerous route as the one planned for Chicago. I got to hand it to the President. He was cool and calm the whole time. But he had to be on edge. He just didn't show it."

Currant sensed that Quinn was very excited. "Tom. Settle down. Did something happen?"

"No. He made it through OK. But something was going down. The Chief said three people made threats. They got one of the guys in a cell now. Trust me, Mullins and his crew had this thing locked down. All the underpasses were guarded by cops or military. They had all the rooftops cleared. He had Secret Service men standing on the back bumper the whole trip and motorcycle cops running with the limo at the four corners. Along the way, somebody tossed a candy bar that landed on the hood of the Secret Service follow-up car. They thought it was a stick of dynamite. Damn, Currant. This was an exciting day."

"Do you think the danger is over?"

There was a pause.

"I think the only reason nothing happened today is because they tightened the screws. He was lucky. But if they ever loosen security, I'm afraid they will move in for the kill."

"Who?"

"Who knows? Someone is going to get him. There

was another hard left turn on this route. Just like the
Chicago plan. This one was in front of a big hotel. 19
stories. Tallest in Florida. Motorcade had to slow to a
crawl there. I was crossing my fingers. That would have
been it. The place was loaded with windows. Anyone with
a decent rifle could have picked him off."

"So what about Miami?"

"Miami. Right. He had a dinner speech tonight, and
then he went home. He used a helicopter. They got smart.
No motorcade. So nothing happened here. Thank God.
But it's not over.

"But what?"

"But he's headed for Texas next. Thursday and
Friday. Five cities. You know that state is like a shooting
gallery. I think he's in real trouble."

Currant thought. "I agree. This is like he is running
the gauntlet. Somewhere, someplace someone is going to
slip up. Intentionally or otherwise. What cities?" He could
hear Quinn fumbling with his notes.

"He's going to San Antonio, Houston...uh...Fort
Worth, Dallas, and Austin. That's a lot of real estate to
cover. On the 21st and 22nd. You still in New Orleans?"

"We are."

"You going to Texas?"

"I have a purchase to make, but we'll make it. Texas
is only a long day's drive from here. We'll get some wheels
and then head out as soon as possible. Leave word at your
office how to reach you. I'll call you back and tell you
what's happening."

"Currant..."

"What?"

"How will you know where to go? You can't be
everywhere at once."

"I don't know, but we have to try. My friends would
be very disappointed if we gave up the fight."

"*Semper fi*, my friend. Give my best to your cub
reporters."

LOG of Zak Newman --- November 18, 1963: 10:58

(Day 21 of time travel)

A few days remain before we have to go back to the future. A.C. said 28 days maximum. Today is Day 21. Quinn's telephone call to A.C. put more pressure on the timeline. JFK is still in trouble. The man is like a cat, or so it seems. He survived Chicago, Tampa, and Miami. But his goose could be cooked in any one of five cities in the great state of Texas. We have no idea where. Why does he keep campaigning for votes? I wonder if he has a death wish. The people who want to kill him have more than a wish—they are determined.

We did find some info on "Oswald." Last August, a man named Oswald was arrested in New Orleans after a scuffle with some anti-Castro people. He passed out pamphlets promoting something called the "Fair Play For Cuba Committee." Turns out he's an ex-Marine, just like Vallee. He lived in Russia for a while. So he doesn't look like someone who would go drinking with Banister and his friends. But who knows? In their world, "black" is "white," and "left" is "right." Oswald's first name is "Lee." The person who tipped off the Feds about the Chicago attempt was named "Lee." Coincidence? Why would "the Rabbit Oswald," a good friend of Banister, be running a pro-Castro committee?

I'm convinced that whoever is behind this didn't draw it up on a napkin. The Chicago hit teams had long guns with scopes, four shooters, and a pliable patsy in Thomas Vallee. And I suspect it had local insiders like Richard Cain to grease the wheels. According to Quinn, the only thing that kept JFK alive in Tampa was the tight security provided by the local police. I wonder how good security will be in Texas? Lots of guns in the Lone Star state. The killers can use the Chicago scenario—long rifles and multiple shooters in several locations to get the job done. Firing simultaneous shots will reduce the number of apparent *shots making the* "lone nut" *theory more believable. In the end, one person will do it or will appear to do it. It will probably involve shooting from the adjacent buildings and may employ a difficult slowdown turn just like the one in Chicago. The trick will be to blame the whole thing on one* boobala*. Otherwise, it will smell like what it is, an organized effort to topple the Kennedys. That wouldn't work well for anyone. Let's see what happens in the next few days. Who knows? Maybe we can save him again.*

I can speculate on the "Why?" *Today Jack—tomorrow Bobby—the day after tomorrow Teddy—two days after tomorrow comes John-John. Looks like all Kennedys—all day—all night. So I guess it's now or never for* "them." *But who are they? Cain looks like the Outfit, the Mob, the Syndicate, what have you. Since Bobby, the Attorney General, has been JFK's legal pit bull, he's been attacking these guys. I imagine the* good fellows *are sick of the brothers Kennedy. Our quick research showed that in 1961 Bobby had the head mobster of New Orleans, Carlos Marcello, kidnapped. He was left for dead in the middle of some Latin American jungle. Currant thinks Ferrie piloted the plane that returned Marcello to the States. The crime boss was pissed, no doubt. Some say Kennedy's father, Joe, was wired into the Mob and asked for their help to elect his son. The Outfit helped squeeze out a victory in Illinois for JFK in the tight presidential race against Nixon. Afterward, the Kennedys turned their back on the Mob. So, in addition to losing its Cuban*

hangout to Castro, the guy they helped elect the President
and his brother were screwing them. Maybe 'Old Joe'
forgot to tell his boys that they owed the boys big time.

But the Kennedys just seem to go bump, bump, bump into
the night. The Cuban freedom fighters hate them for the
Bay of Pigs failure. And the CIA can't be too pleased
about that or the fact that the top guys in their
organization were fired. And Big Oil is always hot about
JFK. The potential of tampering with their holy law—the
Depletion Allowance—rankles them. The far Right Wing
people are confident JFK is soft on Commies and hate
him. Vice-President Johnson has his problems, too, with
the Billy Sol Estes/Bobby Baker situation. Newspapers
here say he's gone for the election in '64. Someone is
going to hang for all that criminal activity. Without a
change, LBJ is in line for a jail cell. And the aging head of
the American Federal Police, J. Edgar Hoover, will be
losing his job soon. His boss, Bobby Kennedy, wants to
get rid of him. I'm sure he'd love to say "goodbye" to the K
boys.

In the old History (before our involvement), everyone came
out smelling like a rose—everyone except JFK and the
man who was framed for the crime, Tom Vallee. Cuba
went back under the control of the big corporations and
the Mob. Marcello won his deportation case and
eventually retired to the Cayman Islands. Big Oil stayed
big, and the rugged Texan independent oilmen slept every
night under red, white, and blue American Flag sheets.
Johnson, of course, became President, and although he
had his troubles in Vietnam and was later impeached
and convicted for more corruption, he was never tried for
treason or anything nasty like that. Even Allen Dulles and
his cronies got their old jobs back at the CIA. And they

finally got their war with the Commies in Vietnam. That help helped the Military-Industrial Complex eliminate its feelings of inferiority. And Hoover remained on the job as the Director and slept comfortably the remainder of his life in his ladies' underwear. All these things happened because someone shot JFK in Chicago. Best of all, for the conspirators, nobody ever questioned anything about the assassination. It was a done deal—like so many other "lone nut" crimes. One man with a giant hard-on. Who can defend against that? Who could see it coming? Maybe the Secret Service? The FBI? Military Intelligence? Nope.

So now what's going to happen? Maybe JFK will be saved again, and then he'll kick butt. Or maybe he'll see the light and make peace with all these folks that hate him—I doubt it, but who knows? I guess the point is that this whole thing is a powder keg, which almost blew up with the Cuban Bay of Pigs—then the fuse was lit again and burned down to the nub in October of 1962 with the Cuban Missile Crisis—then last summer Bobby killed off the training of Cuban rebels ending their dream—and now JFK may be making nice-nice with Castro while still planning a Cuban coup. JFK is a marked man. Highly motivated, hate-filled people—mobsters—anti-Castro Cubans—pissed-off spooks—are all waiting in the wings to rush in and kill him. The people pulling the strings only have to invite these hotheads onto the stage. That proverbial short-fuse is definitely lit again. Close your eyes and hold your ears because something terrible is coming—the sum of all hopes and fears—a trip to Texas.

END: 11-18-63

-Chapter XIX-

A Rose by Any Other Name

The red and white '55 Chevrolet Bel Air convertible chased the sinking sun on a lonely two-lane highway. A foxtail tied its antenna, top-down, radio up, A.C. behind the wheel. Ethan rode shotgun. Emma and Zak sat in the back.

Dr. Currant shared the lead with Frankie Valli as the radio played *Walk Like a Man.* The old man can still hit the high notes, thought Ethan. He watched the wind twist Currant's hair into a madcap. "This is the life. No more trains. We've got our own wheels. You can't beat that, Dr. Currant."

A.C. jumped out of his falsetto, turned down the radio volume, glanced over to Ethan, and replied. "Best car ever made. Ever. It is a thing of beauty, and it's all mine."

"For now," replied Ethan.

"Forever," said Currant. "Forever."

Ethan shook his head. Earlier today, Currant bought this car in New Orleans. For a day and a half, the four adventurers had doggedly hunted from one car dealer to the next, from one classified ad seller to another, until A.C. found his dream car. A young man named Chuck from Metairie was about to enter the Army. He wanted to find a good home for his pride and joy. He and A.C. bonded in a second, and Chuck was left happily holding $550 cash, knowing he had found just the right person for his beautiful Bel Air. Ethan had to admit the car was a great choice for a road trip into the unknown. Riding comfortably nestled in the smooth, two-tone leather seat, his elbow hanging over the door, the warm wind beating on his face, Ethan felt something he had never felt before—the absolute freedom of youth. For the moment, he had no cares, no pain, no future, and no past. He was a seventeen-year-old in 1963. He glanced at this sister and Zak in the back seat. They also wore looks of wonderment.

Low on the dark horizon, the waning light of a rich orange sun ball caught his eye. Its rays reflected off the marshy swamp waters lining the road. Hordes of restless water bugs expanded upward *en masse* in a dance of death, feeding a squadron of darting bats circling above. Curious sounds filled the air. Night creatures slithered and skittered about, preparing for the evening's battle. A.C. drove the convertible at a leisurely pace. He seemed to be absorbing the entire scene. To Ethan, homeboy Currant looked at peace as the sights, sounds, and smells of the Louisiana backcountry washed over him. As Currant continued making music with the Valli from New Jersey, Ethan was reminded of the Vallee from Chicago. He wondered what had happened to him. There were no news stories about the Chicago attempt on JFK's life. It was as if it had never happened. What do you do with an unused patsy? Ethan's mind burped—if that Vallee takes up *singing* as a hobby, he'll be *walking like a man* very quickly—a dead man. But Vallee was gone now, soon to be a forgotten man from a long time ago in Chicago. He dropped that thought. Now they were headed for the home state of the 'favorite son,' Vice-President Lyndon Johnson. Off to save JFK again.

No other cars passed them in either direction. A swollen sun rolled over the horizon, and the world grew darker. Ethan checked his road map. They had traveled about two hours from New Orleans. Ahead was the small town of Eunice, Louisiana, just west of Baton Rouge, a pit stop on a meandering path leading to Texas.

"How far are we going tonight, A.C.?" asked Ethan.

"Not too far. I think we could use a good night's sleep. Maybe another half hour. Or maybe the next town. It's getting dark. We better look for a sure thing rather than find ourselves driving all night." The Chevy rolled along into the cover of trees. True darkness was now upon them. Ahead, just past a bend in the road, a stopped car came into view. It sat halfway on the shoulder, lights on. Two people emerged from either side and walked to the front of their vehicle. Something was wrong. In seconds, A.C. drove smoothly onto the shoulder and brought the convertible to a dead stop behind the parked car. The time travelers looked at each as if wondering what lay next. Night noise swam in the dark, moist air. The engine of the parked Ford still churned noisily. A.C. was the first out, followed by Ethan and the other two.

Ethan cautiously trailed Currant around the car. Like theater spots, its headlights illuminated the dramatic night scene in heavy contrast. Two people stood next to someone on the ground. One kneeled. As Ethan got closer, he saw that the prone body was that of a woman. She moaned.

"Hello," offered Currant. "Can we help?"

The man was probably not as old as Currant, but he looked twenty years older. He wore the clothes of a farmer—clean but worn. "She's hurt," he said.

Ethan looked again at the woman, then the old man. "Did you hit her?"

His wife, a small woman, nervously shook her head. "No. No. I should say not," she almost shouted.

"She was here. Right where she is now. Just layin' there. I think she's hurt. She's got some cuts. And she's out of it. Not makin' sense."

Ethan bent over the woman. She moaned again softly. She appeared about forty, although he found it very difficult to guess the age of people of this time. To him, they all looked older. She had a pie face set in a puffy horse collar of hair. Her eyes were wet and glassy. A bit of drool eased out of her mouth. She had a few cuts on her arms and face but no other visible damage. She may have internal injuries, he thought. "We shouldn't move her. Can you go for help? We're just traveling through." Ethan said these words quietly and calmly to the elderly couple. He could tell they were shaken.

"We can," said the man. "We're from Eunice, just up

the road. We'll call someone."

"Fine," said A.C. "You do that. We'll stay here with her until help arrives."

The older couple nodded dumbly and then slowly receded into their car. Carefully they reentered the highway and, once clear, moved off quickly.

Emma now stood over the woman along with the others. "How is she?"

"She looks OK," said Ethan. "But she's on something, or else she took a blow to the head." He knelt down and bent over the woman. "Miss. Can you hear me? Tell me your name." She wasn't a pretty woman, he thought. She looked worn out, old before her time. High forehead, big bad hair, a tired mouth, and eyes with a bold nose, she looked like someone who had been around the block more than a few times. He asked her name again.

This time she stirred as she tried to lift her head but gave up quickly. For about ten seconds, she appeared to be thinking. "Melba." The word came out slow and slurred. It sounded like 'Mayba' to Ethan.

"All right, Mayba." Her eyes offered only a blank stare. "Were you hit by a car?" The woman did not respond. "Emma. Can you get me something to put under her head?"

Zak peeled off his sweatshirt and handed it to Emma, who rolled it and passed it over to Ethan. Gently he lifted her head and slid it into place.

"Thanks," the woman said as if drugged. "Nobody hit me. They tossed me out of the bar...'Silver Slipper.'"

Currant moved in and kneeled next to her. "Who are *they*?"

She swallowed hard.

Ethan looked up. "Zak. Can you get that bottle of soda?"

Zak retrieved a bottle of Dr. Pepper and an opener for Ethan. He flipped the top off and lifted her head, pouring a shot into her mouth. This seemed to bring her back to the living.

"Who tossed you out?" pressed Currant.

She looked at him with cold eyes. "Those two bastards I came up here with. They said I was 'deadweight.' Deadweight. Those bastards."

"What happened?" Emma asked.

Melba checked out the source of the feminine voice. "Hi. Honey. Didn't see ya." She squinted at Emma. "Say you're a pretty one. So young..."

Ethan arose and spoke quietly to his friends. "I'd say she is...or was on drugs. All we can do is wait for the ambulance."

The woman on the ground spoke again. "I jus' walked over here and fell down. Nobody came by. 'Til you." She rolled her head to one side. "Say...anybody got a smoke?"

"No. Sorry," said Currant.

She lifted her head slightly. "Gonna' kill Kennedy," she mumbled almost imperceptibly.

The four time travelers looked at each other. Currant moved closer to her leaning his ear into the space above her head. "What's that?"

"Those guys are gonna' kill Kennedy." She dropped her head back and moaned.

"How do you know that?" demanded Ethan.

"I was with them in a car for a couple days. Comin' up from Florida. Bad guys. Don't let them find me." She began choking. Ethan offered her more soda. She sipped.

"Thanks, kid."

Emma leaned in and spoke softly, "There's nobody here, Mayba. Just us. You're safe. Help is coming."

Her lips mouthed a word..."Rose."

"What?"

"Call me Rose, honey. Rose Cheramie."

"OK. Rose." Currant took charge. He got right into her face. "Where are they going to kill Kennedy?"

"Dallas."

"Where in Dallas?"

The woman looked puzzled. She blinked. "Don't know. Don't..." Then she closed her eyes.

Currant grabbed her chin gently and waggled it back and forth. "She's out."

Ethan spotted the flashing lights of the ambulance in the distance. In a minute, a white '50s Cadillac ambulance pulled up alongside. The pulsating safety lights cut across the faces of the travelers. Red flashing lights, black night, croaking frogs, and a woman passed out on the ground, the two white-smocked attendants jumped out and quickly went to work. To Ethan, they didn't seem to care about her injuries. They rapidly got her onto the stretcher and slid her into the back. "She's going to Moosa Memorial. If you want to follow." They climbed back into the vehicle, made a quick three-point turn, and drove away quickly.

"Let's get out of here," said Currant. The others needed no invitation. They jumped in the convertible, put up the convertible top, and A.C. laid rubber in a getaway. They worked their way through the sleepy small town, respecting the speed limit and attracting no attention. But once outside the city limits, Currant pushed the car into the seventies traveling at least twenty miles before easing back. There was no mention of Rose Cheramie's proclamation until then.

"You believe her?" asked Ethan.

"I do. It's happening," said Currant excitedly.

"I guess we're going to Dallas," said Ethan. "It's not over."

Currant looked at him. His eyes danced in his head. "That's right, Ethan. We're part of history now."

"Wonder if that's good or bad," said Ethan.

Zak and Emma gazed into the bayou's blackness from the back seat. Emma looked at Zak with tears in her eyes. "I feel sorry for that woman. She looked a thousand years old...without hope or dreams."

Zak reached over and held her hand.

O.A. LOG TTA2028-4

INVESTIGATOR: Joell Costas

DATE: November 21, 1963 (July 23, 2028)

PROJECT: JFK-11.02.63

PROGRESS REPORT:

I entered Dallas yesterday. If the four time travelers can determine that Dallas is the location of the next attempt, they may also arrive here. If they do, my intention is to intercept them. Today, I surveyed the assassination site at Dealey Plaza. The local papers have printed reports and maps of the 45-minute motorcade route JFK will take from Love Field (airport for arrival from Fort Worth) to the Trade Mart building (a luncheon destination). The maps are rudimentary, but the related stories provide detailed descriptions indicating the exact route, including the problematic 120-degree left turn from Houston Street onto Elm Street in front of the Texas School Book Depository. The current *History* declares that at 12:30 p.m. CST, a single shooter, LEE HARVEY OSWALD, will inflict mortal wounds upon the PRESIDENT. Shortly after the assassination, OSWALD will be killed by an organized crime operative JACK RUBY/Rubenstein.

It should be noted that the six nearby buildings surrounding Dealey Plaza have multiple floors offering excellent shooting positions from windows, fire escapes, and roofs. Triangulation of gunfire is assured, given the many excellent shooting locations from the upper floors of adjacent buildings, from ground-level positions on either side of the plaza, and at the railroad overpass at the bottom of Elm Street. Frequent freight train movements across this overpass increase visual confusion and may provide a possible escape route. The entire site is shaped like a scoop. The motorcade will enter the trap heading southwest at the top of the hill at Houston and Elm streets traveling at a very slow speed due to the tight turn. After the turn, there is no reason why the President's car could not speed ahead. The parade will be finished. But as we know, the limo will move slowly through the shooting range to ensure the outcome. The Dealey Plaza location provides an excellent enfilade-killing zone. Some guns will have silencers, while others will not. All shooters will have spotter/radio men. Several assassins will be positioned in multiple locations. They will fire as one, on radio command, in sequence to create the illusion that only one man is shooting. Considering the adjacent parking lots, streets, and railroad tracks, the shooters' escape opportunity is excellent.

In summary, this is an exceptional location for Executive Action. I walked the entire area today and saw no sign of anyone fitting the description of the travelers. Nor did I see any suspicious activity. I watched people enter the Depository building this morning while I looked for LEE HARVEY OSWALD, the future designated assassin, with negative results.

THOMAS QUINN, the reporter for the *Chicago's American,* is in Dallas staying in a hotel frequented by newsmen. It is my intention to approach him today regarding the time travelers.

Per my most recent contact with the *Office*, I am preparing for the arrival of additional investigators, as required by the Director. They are due here at about 11:00 a.m. tomorrow, November 22, 1963. I have acquired time-appropriate communications equipment for our use during the event.

TRANSMITTED VIA CODED TIME JUSTIFIER AT 11:42 CT 07/21/28.

-Chapter XX-

Shooting Fish in a Barrel

Joell Costas entered the lobby of Quinn's downbeat downtown hotel. The room clerk, a thin, middle-aged white man with long stringy sideburns and bad teeth, spotted him coming. His lips pursed, and eyes narrowed. Costas knew the part he must play.

"Good morning, sir," said Costas as he assumed a deferential posture. "I'm here to meet with Mr. Thomas Quinn. He's staying here." The time-cop maintained a flat New York accent that seemed to perplex the man behind the counter.

The clerk turned down the volume on the small desktop television, and the voice of Don Pardo announcing a game show slipped into the background. The man's eyes tracked over Costas's body like a cow up for auction.

Costas waited.

"And who are you?" His drawl was laced with disdain.

"My name is Lucas. Art Lucas. I'm Mr. Quinn's photographer. He's a reporter for *Chicago's American.*" Costas showed the 35mm Nikon camera that hung on a strap around his neck as evidence.

"Photographer," said the man. "I see. Pretty fancy camera ya' have there."

"Yes, sir."

"Well, OK. Le/me check ta' see if he's in." The clerk dialed Quinn's room but received no response. "He's out. You'll have to leave."

Costas lowered his head in mock dejection. "Couldn't I wait here for a few minutes? Mr. Quinn is expecting me."

The man squished his mouth, apparently trying to

think. "OK. A few minutes. Sit over there." He motioned to a section of beat-up chairs. "But don't sit in the window."

"Yes, sir," said Costas. "Thank you." He took a seat in the corner, his presence obscured by an artificial palm tree.

The man watched him closely. Then nodding in satisfaction, he kicked up the TV volume and resumed viewing.

Costas attempted to relax into a nearby stuffed chair but soon stuck to its plastic membrane. He glanced at his bare arms. His bronze skin glistened with tiny drops of sweat, and the underarms of his shirt were water-stained. The lobby was not air-conditioned, and the temperature outside was rising. . The clerk kept a watchful eye on him. It was getting uncomfortable. He toyed with the camera for about twenty-five minutes and sat on the edge of his chair. He waited. In his wallet, Costas had a photo of Quinn that he had boldly stolen off the reporter's desk in the *American's* offices. But he didn't have to refresh his memory. The image was locked into his brain: Quinn, his wife, and two kids all smiling. A noise in the vestibule marked Quinn's entrance, and one look achieved identification. Costas rushed to greet him.

"Tom. Glad we could meet up like this," said Costas. Quinn pulled back first and then looked at the investigator and his camera. "You are?"

Costas smiled broadly. "Art Lucas...action photographer...and a friend of some friends. Can we talk?" Costas motioned toward the chairs. Quinn nodded in agreement.

The desk clerk lifted his head to check out the two. He lit a cigarette and studied them for a moment. Then apparently satisfied, he drifted back into the game show.

They sat next to each other. "So you're in town to cover the President," said Costas.

"Right. And who are these 'mutual' friends?"

"Your journalism students and their teacher. The people you met in Chicago. I spoke with Miss Kostik. She was most helpful." Costas studied Quinn carefully. Quinn appeared to connect to the words.

He paused, then spoke. "Yeah. I remember the kids. All big for their age, as I remember. Brother-Sister act and another young guy who said nothing. So?"

"Well, it appears that you all have a serious interest in JFK. Is that true?"

Quinn's face contorted into a scowl. "Listen, Art. It's my job to be interested in newsmakers. But I usually ask the questions. What's in it for me? Let's get beyond the 'action photographer' gig. Are you a cop or a babysitter? What do you care about those kids?"

Costas smiled and reached into his pants pocket, and retrieved his wallet. With some flair, he showed a badge and handed over a laminated identification card.

"*Arthur Lucas, Detective Investigator. New York Police Department: Division of Field Investigators,*" Quinn mumbled the words quietly to himself as he returned the I.D. "Fishing quite a way from home waters, aren't you?"

"Not fishing at all. In the sporting sense. Although we do have a net set across the country. I've just come from Chicago. I'm tracking the 'teacher,' Earl Teliphin."

"Never heard of him," said Quinn.

"You may know him by another name. But he's with the three kids that you met. He's got them convinced they can solve crimes. Change history. Be heroes. And those kids are just young enough and dumb enough to believe it. You remember them, right?"

"Yeah. I remember that crew. They stopped by my office. Said they were journalism students. I kinda' gave 'em the bum's rush. We don't have too much time to waste on aspiring reporters. Job's tough enough without trying to make it sound good."

"So, did they say where they were from?"

"Thought you would know that," replied Quinn. "You're trailing them. This guy Earl, is he some kind of pervert or something?"

"Let's put it this way. We consider it a possible kidnapping."

"Big kids for napping. Why not the FBI, then?"

Costas nodded. "They're on it too, but my Commissioner has a personal interest in this matter."

"Yeah. What's that?"

"Sorry, can't say," said Costas. "What about it? Did they mention where they were from?"

Beads of sweat showed on Quinn's forehead. Costas knew Quinn was either hot or feeling pressure. He hoped it was the latter.

"Out East someplace. I don't remember the name of their high school."

"What about this fellow Earl. Did you see him?"

"No. Just the kids," said Quinn.

"Did they ask about JFK? He was scheduled to be in town when they visited you wasn't he?"

"Maybe. I think they said they wanted to see him drive into town. But he never showed. Why are you in Dallas?"

Quinn stood up as if to end the conversation. Costas followed suit.

"We got a tip. As I said, Teliphin is moving them around. We think he convinced them that JFK is a possible target and that they can break the case."

"Is he?"

"What?"

"A target?"

Costas cleared his throat. "The President always is. That's why they have the Secret Service. But I doubt that Teliphin gives a damn about Kennedy. He has something funny in mind. We don't know what. But I'll tell you this. He's been busted before...molestation. You're right. He's a pervert and a con man. These kids need all the help they can get."

"Give me a card. If I see them or if anything pops up, I'll give you a call. Say, what's with the camera anyway?"

Costas pulled out a business card and wrote something on the back. He handed it to Quinn. "Down here in the Big D, they might be amused by a black man with a camera. But they won't be smiling at a black man with a gun. Better for me to work around the edges. This isn't exactly a bastion of tolerance if you know what I mean," he said quietly with a quick glance at the room clerk.

Quinn nodded. "Gotcha."

"I wrote my local number down. Call me if you see them."

Quinn got up, looked at Costas like he was taking mental notes, then turned away, saying nothing, and entered the elevator.

On his way out, the time-cop thanked the room clerk again and gave him a big smile. The man returned a "don't come back" look. Costas ignored it and walked outside onto the sidewalk to collect his thoughts. He was pleased to move out of the spotlight of hate. 1963 Texas race relations made everyday interaction between people of contrasting skin colors a painful experience. His thoughts swung to Quinn. The man was tight-lipped. And he suspected he was not revealing as much as he knew. But he could be a good tail if the travelers were in town. Costas figured they would connect with Quinn soon. When they did, he would have them.

The time travelers arrived in Dallas mid-afternoon on the 21st of November 1963. After buying a couple of newspapers, their second stop was a drive-in restaurant featuring carhops serving lunch on roller skates. Zak and Ethan enjoyed the girls in their silver and blue cheerleader outfits. Emma scoffed at the whole idea. A.C. Currant was preoccupied thumbing through the newspapers. After delivering the cheeseburgers, fries, and drinks, the roller-girls exchanged teenage giggle-banter with the two studs from the future. Zak was animated and enthusiastic but muted as usual. Currant brought the two romantics back to the present.

He held the first page of the *Dallas Times-Herald* and pointed to a map of the JFK motorcade route. "This is all we have to work on. We know from the Chicago attempt that this will be an ambush. Multiple shooters from different positions. This fellow Lee Oswald may be in on it. Here's a map of the parade route."

"Oswald was handing out pro-Castro leaflets in New Orleans when he was arrested," said Ethan. "Our friend Vallee was also a Castro supporter if you believe his famous last words: 'Long live Fidel.' And according to Zak's sensing devices, Oswald has a special place in Ferrie's love box. And Ferrie has a history of training Cuban rebels just like Vallee. Is there a pattern here?"

"We don't even know if this man Oswald is in Dallas," said Emma.

"That's true," said Currant. "But you remember someone named Lee blew the whistle to the FBI about the proposed Chicago hit. We've got dots here that have to be connected."

Zak munched on his burger and swallowed hard after making solid eye contact with a blonde waitress. She smiled at him, and he flashed a broad bright smile back.

Emma glanced at him. "Zak? You with us? You know we're working here."

Zak nodded and signed an apology.

Currant looked back at the newspaper. "I think we should drive the motorcade route today. Let's look for likely spots. According to the map, three or four hard, slow turns will have to be made. We'll look for a situation like Chicago. Remember, in the old history, the Lincoln came up the expressway exit ramp and stopped. Then it made a hard left turn into the firing range. My guess is that we'll find something like that here." He tossed the newspapers in Ethan's direction and checked his watch. "Getting late. Let's get out to the airport and work our way back in. Tomorrow it will be JFK's turn, but today it's ours. Ethan, you're the navigator. Just follow the map."

It was a short ride to the Love Field area. Mockingbird Lane connected to the airport's main exit in an area devoid of tall buildings or any buildings close to the road. They headed north, checking the route.

"This is the first hard turn ahead," Ethan's words

were lost in the sounds of an incoming four-engine jet blasting overhead.

Currant drove the convertible steadily along the divided lane four-lane highway. "Easy turn," he said as he negotiated the bend in the road from Mockingbird to Lemmon Avenue. He pushed the Chevy to the speed limit.

"There's no cover around here. They'd be traveling pretty fast, too,' said Emma.

Lemmon Avenue was a quiet, fast ten-minute ride to the next turn onto Turtle Creek Boulevard. Another soft turn led them to a road with wooded park areas on one side and suburban nothingness on the other. This road then changed its name to Cedar Springs Road, which offered more of the same.

"Nothing here," said Currant. "They'll be traveling safe and free as the wind."

The divided highway narrowed as they approached the heart of the city. When they reached North Harwood Street, they faced a 90-degree turn. Currant stopped at the light and then made the left turn. It was an open area of low warehouses and parking lots. "Not exactly a sniper's killing zone," commented Ethan to Currant.

They motored on through an area scattered with low office buildings and finally made a hard right turn on Main Street—the heart of downtown Dallas. Tomorrow, these sidewalks would be filled with people, thought Ethan. The roof of the municipal building could offer a firing position for a rifleman. Moreover, near this 90-degree turn onto Main Street, the other adjacent lots were vacant or filled with one-story buildings. The limo carrying JFK and his entourage might be vulnerable here. The roadways were narrow. "This might be it. He'd have to slow down here," Currant commented. He parked the car on Main Street but kept the engine running.

"So...?" he asked.

Emma jumped into the conversation. "Good sniper's nest possibilities on the roof of that old building."

"City Hall," said Currant.

"But that's it. Not enough positions," said Ethan.

"We're looking for a real shooting gallery. Lots of sniper's nest possibilities. One of them will be a spot for the 'designated chump.' Some guy like Vallee ready to expose a banner or something equally sinister."

"I agree. Let's move on," said Currant. He donned a pair of sunglasses to fight off the bright sun.

For the citizens of Dallas, Main Street would provide the best view of the young President. JFK was known to love to press the flesh, so the motorcade might stop at any time. But the assassins could not know when these moments would occur. Currant thought about the possibilities. Anyone could dash out of the crowd, run to the limo, toss a hand grenade, or fire a pistol at JFK. But this would mean almost certain death for the assassin since the Secret Service would shoot him as soon as they spotted him. Or they would throw themselves in front of the President following their training. There was no guarantee of success. The grenade may be the best method, he thought. But very messy with terrible public relations, so brutal a killing that the public would demand a full investigation. And this method would be no sure thing either. A wounded but surviving Kennedy would be the worst case for the conspirators. Dead yes; a martyr, yes, but not a surviving hero.

Currant speculated the most likely scenario would be a quick, clean kill that could be blamed on someone that fit the "lone nut" mold. Up to this point, the motorcade route did not provide a killing zone as suitable as Chicago's Jackson Boulevard had been. Perhaps the time travelers would be successful after all. Maybe the assassins would fail for lack of a proper shooting gallery. Right, he thought, and maybe pigs will fly. They continued through a canyon of tall buildings in the old downtown section. Then at Houston Street, everything opened up. Ahead Main Street continued into the triple underpass where Dealey Plaza welcomed them with outstretched grassy green arms, fountains, trees, and colonnades under a bright blue sky. Currant, dazzled by the scene before him, almost forgot to turn right onto

Houston Street. Then he saw the sign. The street was now one way going in the wrong direction. They were forced to stay on Main Street and continue down the hill into the dark abyss of the triple underpass. Lost for about fifteen minutes and doubling back, they eventually found themselves again approaching Dealey Plaza, this time from the north on Houston, going with traffic now. They parked the car adjacent to the massive red brick building on the corner of Elm and Houston and jumped out of the Bel Air, happy to stretch their legs.

Glancing up at the big building, they read the bold raised letters over the door: *Texas School Book Depository.* The travelers viewed the plaza and the nearby tall buildings that framed the corner. Across Houston, opposite the Depository, stood the seven-story Dal-Tex building. And the slightly taller Records building stood on the south side of Elm, catty-corner to the Depository. Three tall buildings looked down upon the 120-degree slow turn from Houston Street to Elm, a significant challenge for the President's security team. Standing at the corner curb waiting to cross, they looked west. A curved, white-painted concrete pergola stood on the grassy knoll to the right of Elm Street. Beyond that, a wooden fence framed the edges of a large open parking lot. The stoplight changed, and they crossed Elm to the plaza. Together they looked down the street of death that ended in the blackened underpass. The grassy knoll provided excellent forward concealed shooting positions with its shadowing assemblage of fences, walls, and bushes. Behind them, the tall buildings had their own ominous potential. Currant gathered his flock in a circle.

"Is this it?" Everyone nodded in agreement. The inventor shook his head up and down absentmindedly. "This is it," he mumbled to himself. "This will be the site of the ambush. This is where they will kill him. Like shooting a fish in a barrel."

LOG of Zak Newman --- November 22, 1963: 07:12

(Day 25 of time travel)

*Today is another day of terrifying possibility. I'm outside
our motel room, sitting in a rusty lawn chair beneath a
leaky canvas awning. It's drizzling, but the clouds seem
to be heading elsewhere, taking the rain with them.
That's good for the parade today. What a night for the
time travelers. We were lucky to find a room. The town is
booked. In fact, one room is all we had last night. To say
the least, it was an uncomfortable evening. Two beds and
a sofa for four people. I took the couch. Emma got one bed
for herself, and Ethan and A.C. Currant shared the other.
I'm happy this is the first and last time for us to become
even closer buddies—a little too cozy for my blood.*

*A young boy about ten or eleven came wandering by
carrying a pile of handbills just a minute ago. He was
shoving them under the doors of the motel units, but he
handed one to me.*

*"Last one," he said in a squeaky little cowboy voice, "
you're a lucky man."*

*He seemed a likable kid, but the small poster he handed
me was frightening. It had two photos of JFK, arranged
front and side profile, like a police wanted poster. In fact,
the headline read—WANTED FOR TREASON. Below the
photos were a list of his "crimes," which included
generally giving the Communists a pass and encouraging
them to create race riots, screwing up relations with other
countries, and lying about his personal life, including an
unreported previous marriage and divorce. Nice greeting
to the President. I wish him luck in Dallas. Also, the
morning newspaper has a full-page ad paid for by*

prominent citizens of Dallas. These people probably belong to the John Birch Society or the Minutemen (two of the more radical and powerful right-wing groups in 1963). The words are wrapped in a black border as if to mourn him. A banner welcomes "Mr. Kennedy" but then follows with more negative commentary about JFK being soft on Commies. In fact so soft that the head of the Communist Party of America praised the good work being done by his administration.

This town will be tough going for JFK. It is filled with nut-balls. Even The History *provided a little story about Adlai Stevenson, the Ambassador to the United Nations under JFK. He made a stop here last month in late October. A woman bopped him on the head with a protester placard because she didn't like his politics. Of course, if our thinking is correct, all of this local hate-mongering is but a background for the real thing—a plot to kill the President done by professionals.*

Last night before we drifted off to sleep, Emma made a suggestion. Even though yesterday's simulated motorcade trip leads us to believe that there is only one viable shooting location—the plaza at the end of Main Street. We should still inspect the Love Field airport and the Trade Mart (JFK's proposed entry and luncheon locations). It was agreed this should be done. Of course, what are we going to do anyway? We can't tell the police that something bad is going to happen. We might end up in jail. And Dr. Currant has lectured us not to take chances. He doesn't want any of us hurt. He's allowing Emma and me to go to the other two sites, and he and Ethan will head to the plaza. The good news is that I get to drive A.C.'s car. I really like that machine. Late last night, he let me test-drive it in the motel parking lot. I think I have the hang of it. At least, I hope so.

Emma and I will drive to the airport to check it out and make sure JFK gets on the road safely or—who knows? Assuming he does, we will head to the Trade Mart. Afterward, we will meet Ethan and Dr. Currant in Dealey Plaza to report our findings. A.C. has instructed us to act like detectives, keep our eyes open, mentally record what is happening, and yell for help if necessary.

That's the plan. I'm hoping nothing happens. Then we can leave the Dallas "nut house" and head back home. I've had enough. We've been lucky so far, but we are pressing each day we remain in 1963. These are dangerous times. We're running out of time to make it back to Mystic Heights and 2028.

END: 11-22-63

-Chapter XXI-

Lone Nuts in a Lone Star State of Mind

On the morning of the 22nd, A.C. called Quinn. He got the local number from the blonde at the *American's* offices. They didn't talk long. Quinn was surprised they were in town. He was in Dallas because his Chicago FBI contact told him of an urgent telex bulletin sent to all the Bureau offices five days earlier at 1:45 a.m. EST on November 17th. The telex identified a threat to assassinate Kennedy in Dallas on the 22nd or 23rd by a militant revolutionary group. Currant told him about Dealey Plaza, suggesting this site most resembled the Chicago attempt situation. The two men agreed they would meet later at Dealey Plaza. Almost as an afterthought, Quinn mentioned his meeting the day before with a New York cop named Arthur Lucas, who was looking for three high school kids in the company of an older man. He suggested there was something fishy about the cop. Currant agreed the man sounded bogus but offered no more. With that, they ended the conversation. Space was at a premium in the motel room, and Currant assembled the troops in a conversation circle. He sat on the bed, and the youths sat on the sofa. They spoke in hushed tones as if someone might be listening to their conversation.

"I just spoke with Quinn. He's in town. He gave me disturbing news. I think we have company from the future," said Currant.

"Who?" asked Ethan.

"A fellow who calls himself Arthur Lucas. He showed a New York City cop I.D. to Quinn. Says I kidnapped you three. I'm guessing he told Quinn that I was some kind of child molester."

The youths laughed.

"*Funny,*" signed Zak.

"Any description of this guy Lucas?"

"Quinn said he was a skinny, black man, about my height. Talked with a New York accent."

"If he's a time-cop, we better get moving. I'll bet he's watching Quinn's movements, and most likely, he's recording his phone calls, including your call today. Did you mention our location?"

Currant thought. "Just Dallas. He'll know we're in Dallas."

Ethan stood. "Let's get it together and get out of here. Emma, you and Zak are off to the airport. Dr. Currant and I will head downtown."

Fifteen minutes later, bags packed and bill paid, Zak drove the Chevy out of the motel parking lot. Currant, the driving instructor, sat next to him. Right away, Zak cut off a pickup truck featuring a full shotgun rack. Currant understood why it happened. The Bel Air's top was up. Its plastic rear window only offered a small view of the road behind and no view of the next lane. Currant looked back and gave the truck driver the double upturned palms *"We screwed up...sorry."* The pickup truck driver and his buddy glowered menacingly as they raced defiantly past the convertible.

"Sorry, boss," signed Zak as best he could while driving. Emma passed on his condolences.

"That will happen. Use your side mirrors," said Currant. "Let's face it, you only have about fifteen minutes of experience. Just be careful with my beauty. OK?"

It was just past eight a.m., and traffic was light. They drifted through downtown Dallas driving down Elm Street until Currant told Zak to pull over and park. Ethan and Currant left and walked toward Dealey Plaza, a few blocks distant. Emma moved to the front seat next to Zak. After reviewing a gas station city map, she directed him to move on. It was a six-mile ride to Love Field, and Emma proved an excellent navigator. For his part, Zak was a much more relaxed driver. Emma looked at him behind the wheel and was amazed at his learning speed. It's in the genes, she thought. They arrived at the airport and parked in an open lot. The terminal building was a modern glass and steel structure patterned in greens and earth-tone reds. As the two time travelers walked the long spike of a covered pedway into the building, Zak checked the wristwatch he had purchased in Chicago: *8:40*. JFK was due in two hours, and although they had successfully reached their destination, they didn't know which gate was reserved for Air Force One. They bumped along the American Airlines portion of the terminal. Passengers. Men in suits and ties and women in tidy outfits capped by the latest hats hurried in an organized frenzy of anticipation. Emma could see it in their eyes. Air travel was still an exciting novelty in 1963, and jet travel was the latest experience.

Emma stopped at a concession counter, reaching out to grab Zak's hand. "Hold up," she said. "I'm going to buy a camera. I don't want to have to rely on our memories."

Zak signed the words: *"Very dangerous. You'll be creating evidence of our trip."*

"Don't worry. You'll thank me for this." She had just enough money to buy a Kodak Instamatic and a couple rolls of film. She studied the camera instructions and loaded the film. To test the camera, she immediately took a photo of Zak standing in front of a tall bronze statue of a Texas Ranger, complete with a ten-gallon hat and gun drawn ready to duel. Zak appeared embarrassed. "Hold it," she said. "And smile..." Zak obeyed, and she clicked off a shot. "Looking good, Black Bart. He had his gun pointed directly at your head." As she walked up to him, she whispered quietly: "It's a good cover, Zak. Two high school kids...maybe two love-sick puppies...taking in the sights...creating a special keepsake photo album."

Zak quickly signed. *"You're weird. Let's get down to business."*

They continued down the concourse. Ahead there was a commotion at one of the counters. Emma watched as a small parade of very special-looking people moved quickly past her, not thirty feet from where she was standing.

"Zak," she said in an excited but hushed voice. "I know that man. That nose. It's like a Bob Hope. Yeah...that's Richard Nixon. He's going to be a president. He was Vice-President with Eisenhower. He lost the election to JFK in 1960." She thought he looked ordinary, not like "a man of the people," but just common, inconsequential, slightly nervous, and tense.

Zak followed her eyes, and he saw the assembled entourage. He looked closely and then nodded affirmatively.

"What the heck is he doing here in Dallas? I'm getting his photo." She grabbed her camera from her purse and quickly snapped a photo. "Got it," she said proudly.

Zak shrugged his shoulders. As fast as Nixon appeared, he and his group were given a pass by the gatekeepers and then pushed on. They marched away from the two travelers. It had all happened so quickly Emma was astounded. "Zak," she said. "We may get to see two presidents in one day." She smiled. "Remarkable. Simply remarkable."

Zak signed, *"Maybe three. If they get Kennedy, then Johnson would be President. Maybe we'll see him."*

Emma sighed. "Pleasant thought, Zak," she said. "Let's hope not."

A light drizzle laid a misty haze over the grassy green undulations of Dealey Plaza. A. C. Currant, and Ethan sat on a stone bench facing Houston Street under the cover of Currant's sizeable black umbrella. Currant checked his watch: *9:12.* Kennedy would not arrive at this location for another three hours. They had time. They waited for Quinn.

"What time did he say he'd be here?"

Currant rechecked his watch. "Between 9:00 and 9:30. He's still got a few minutes."

"What's our plan? What can we do? The only thing

we think we know is that this is the spot."

"Right," agreed Currant. "Unless they go after him at the airport...or the Trade Mart."

"Doubt that. I think they'll stick with their plan like Chicago. Open-top car. Slow him down to a crawl and kill him." Ethan dropped his voice as an old woman walked by. She glanced at the two as if they were creatures from outer space. Out of earshot, Ethan commented. "You know, Doctor. Is it my imagination, or do we attract a crowd? Is there something funny about the way we look or dress? I don't see it."

Currant looked Ethan up and down. "Maybe she figured you should be in school. You know that's a requirement in this time. School-age kids shouldn't be wandering about. That's what they called 'playing hooky.' They were very strict when I was a kid. In school every day of the week except Saturday and Sunday."

Ethan smiled. "That's one thing I wouldn't miss. Except for our required history classes with Mr. Dufour and those silly sex education classes, I haven't been in a classroom since I was seven. I finished my 'socializing' courses, and Emma and I went into the *Educapsules*. Dad would buy new ones every other year."

"Well, it was different when I was a kid. We went to school. We sat in a classroom. We were never loose on the street like you are now. We were solid, reliable, boys and girls."

"Well, good for you, 'Daddy-O.'" Ethan chuckled. "But you have a point. I keep forgetting I'm considered a schoolboy here. I'll try to play the part. Say," he said, looking up the street toward the Book Depository building "isn't that Quinn?"

"Right." Currant waved, and Quinn nodded in recognition.

The reporter looked tired. Currant gave him some bench. He looked as if he had been sleeping in his clothes. He ran his fingers through the remains of the hair on his head but didn't say anything. He just pulled out a pack of cigarettes and offered one to Currant, who waved him off. After lighting up and sucking in a voluminous drag, holding it, then exhaling loudly, he spoke. "Well, here we are...'The Three Stooges'—Larry, Moe, and Curly."

Currant smiled and glanced over to Ethan, who wore a quizzical look.

"Greetings, Tom. Happy to see you. Want a little of the umbrella?" offered Currant.

Quinn shook his head.

"Were you followed?"

With fatigued eyes, Quinn lifted his head and stared back at A.C. "By whom?"

"Does it make a difference? This guy Lucas for one?"

Quinn smiled. "You've got some strange things going on, don't you? Out to save the President...the kidnapper detective...or is it the joker of journalism? Before we go any further, Dr. Currant. Who the hell is that guy Lucas? He didn't look like any cop I've ever seen."

Currant asked Quinn for a description, and the reporter gave him a detailed description of the time-cop's physical features, mannerisms, and credentials.

"My guess is that he is on to us, Tom. I'll tell you this. I'm not a pervert, child molester, kidnapper, or whatever. I am an inventor. I am a scientist. But, it's true...I know nothing about journalism."

"Now we're getting someplace." Quinn looked over to Ethan sitting next to A.C. "What about you, junior? You vouch for the elder's statement here?"

Ethan smiled. "Dr. Currant is at times annoying, but he's no kidnapper. Heck, Zak and I could take him whenever we wanted. Anyway, let's focus on JFK. He really *is* in trouble."

Quinn nodded. "Gotta' point there, son. So what's the plan of attack?" He blew out a couple of smoke rings while waiting for their response.

Currant brought Quinn up to date on their meetings in New Orleans with Ferrie and Banister. Quinn said Banister was a dangerous right-wing activist and had heard Ferrie had CIA and Mob connections. Currant told him about their chance meeting with the prescient roadside victim named Melba or Rose and about the two nasty men who tossed her out of a car. "Assassins, she said, "headed for Dallas to kill JFK." He walked Quinn through the motorcade route and pointed out the ambush qualities of the surroundings. And he mentioned that a man named Lee Oswald might be involved.

Quinn laughed when they told him he was another former Marine like Vallee and himself. He agreed Oswald might be another designated fall guy. If so, he would work near Dealey Plaza just like Vallee worked at the Jackson Boulevard sniper's nest location. But where?

Ethan was tasked to go door to door at all nearby buildings that might offer a clear shot. He would make inquires whether Oswald worked in one of them. Maybe he could talk to the man and tell him he was being set up.

Currant repeated Jack Martin's words aloud, "Oswald the Rabbit...may he pop out of his hole and fire a shot heard around the world."

"Oswald the Rabbit," said Quinn. "This thing gets stranger by the minute. Maybe Bugs Bunny will show up next wearing six-shooters and a black hat. Anyway, I'm going to visit my newspaper friends here. They'll have a feel for things. It's not far from here."

"All right. I'm just going to set myself at the corner of Houston and Elm and keep my eyes open." Currant checked his watch: *10:06.* Let's meet back here at about noon. JFK's not due until about 12:25. OK?"

They agreed. The drizzle had stopped, and the sun was creeping around the remaining clouds. Currant folded his umbrella and walked toward the corner of Houston and Elm while the two others headed out in different directions. Quinn headed south to the newspaper offices, and Ethan walked across the street to the county buildings.

O.A. LOG TTA2028-5

INVESTIGATOR: Joell Costas

DATE: November 22, 1963 (July 23, 2028)

PROJECT: JFK-11.02.63

PROGRESS REPORT:

I am ready for the 11:00 AM arrival of the three ADDITIONAL INVESTIGATORS. I have prepared all required communication and mission-related equipment.

Yesterday, after I met with the reporter THOMAS QUINN, I monitored QUINN'S telephone conversations. This morning he was contacted by a man he called DOC. They agreed to meet at Dealey Plaza. QUINN also informed DOC that I was looking for him and the others. Based on this discussion, I must assume the time travelers are aware of my intention to stop them.

Earlier this morning, I observed QUINN, an older man (presumably DOC), and a young man meeting in the plaza. They talked for about 20 minutes and then departed in different directions. I did not see a young woman or another young man.

I will contact the man called DOC this morning after I conference with our incoming ADDITIONAL INVESTIGATORS. DOC appears to be the leader of the group of time travelers. I am not ruling out executive action concerning him or his associates. However, I will first attempt to confront DOC to reason with him to minimize the number of event disruptions.

I can assure *The Authority* that our team will preserve *The History*. Our primary goal is to provide back up, if necessary, to achieve the desired outcome. If the time-local participants fail in their efforts, we will assure temporal continuity. The secondary goals of the plotters, such as manipulation of evidence, elimination of witnesses, media coverage, political scheming, and other misdirection, are beyond our control. However, considering the known complexities of the upcoming event, it is doubtful that the time travelers will be able to interfere with any of these secondary intentions of the plotters.

Lastly, the previous diagnosis of cancer in my body by the Chicago doctors appears to have been totally incorrect. All negative health symptoms have disappeared. My health is now excellent. I can report that I am fit for duty. Therefore, I hereby withdraw my previous report (O.A. LOG TTA2028-3) regarding health limitations.

TRANSMITTED VIA CODED TIME JUSTIFIER AT 10:22 CT 07/23/28.

-Chapter XXII-

Matryoshki

Quinn quickly walked the four blocks to the offices of *The Dallas Morning News.* He entered the building seeking his reporter friend, Dwayne Tillis, and was directed to the City Room. He felt at home. *The News* had the same old shoe look as the *American* in Chicago. Large industrial windows with cast iron radiators below, round concrete columns, a high ceiling, school house hanging lights, and rows of reporters busy typing, talking, and telephoning at desks filled with scattered papers and files. Somehow amidst the din and disorder, Tillis spotted Quinn and rushed over to him.

"Tom Quinn. Thought you'd wash up on a beach by now. Welcome to Dallas."

"Good to see you, D.W. "

"Guess you're here for the festivities. Didn't think your boss would be too interested in our little burg."

"I'm working on my own," said Quinn. "Say...is there someplace we can grab a coffee if you got time?"

"Follow me, friend, but I don't have much time. Today's a big day."

Tillis guided them to the first-floor cafeteria. They sat in a quiet corner. Quinn chomped on his donut while he waltzed through the pleasantries. The banter was soon put to rest, and Quinn settled in and told Tillis about the Chicago JFK threats, the canceled Presidential visit, and his trek across the country following JFK. "What about it, D.W. You hear anything about an attempt here?"

"God no," said Tillis. "But I don't have a hot line to heaven. I work the police blotter. You know that, Tom."

Quinn leaned into Tillis and semi-whispered, "I got wind of an FBI bulletin a few days ago that warned that a militant group is going to try something. Here in Dallas."

"Shit." Tillis shook his head. "We heard nothing about that. But this is the place if something's going down. There's a whole lot of hate here. It's the Wild West, Tom. Wild West."

Just then, Quinn spotted a guy wolfing down a breakfast a couple of tables away, a heavy-set man with a widow's peak, dark hair, wearing a dark suit. He appeared to be studying their conversation. When their eyes met, the man removed the napkin tucked in this shirt, wiped his mouth clean, flipped the napkin back onto the table, and walked toward the two reporters. He stood over them.

"Hello, D.W.," he said casually. "Always a pleasure. Here to run an ad for the 'Carousel.' Just grabbed a breakfast while I'm at it."

"Jack." Tillis nodded.

The man looked at Quinn.

"This is a reporter friend of mine from Chicago. Tom Quinn."

"Chicago. My old hometown. Still miss it. Don't miss the winters, though. Nice to meet ya', Tom. Here." He pulled a card from his shirt pocket. "Jack Ruby. I own a club here. Stop by...anytime. It's a fun place. Lots of girls." Ruby smiled. "Have a drink on me."

Before Quinn could reply, the man flashed a quick smile, just as quickly removed it, and then walked away. He had a funny gait...like a duck crossing a busy street.

"Quite the glad-hander. Isn't he?"

Tillis nodded. "Jack's a piece of work. He's all over this town. Connected, they say."

"The world's full of connected people. Sometimes I wish I was," said Quinn. "You know, I got the feeling he was listening to our conversation about the FBI Telex. Seemed a little jumpy."

"That's the way he is, Tom. The man walks around like his ass is on fire."

They cut short the Ruby conversation and continued. Tillis suggested the FBI bulletin would increase security around the President. But then, he remembered something he had heard when he came to work in the morning. One of the night-beat reporters said that he got a tip that ten Secret Service agents were out drinking last night in a place called 'The Cellar' in Fort Worth.

"'Til five in the morning. That's what I heard," said Tillis.

Quinn slid his chin over to one side, thinking. "Well, it seems like it's all coming together. Bad guys on the loose. The guards are all drinking. I hope I'm wrong, but...."

The two men talked for another five minutes. Tillis provided Quinn with background on the city players, the cops, the politicians, and the route. Then he offered his opinion. "If somebody wanted to do him in, it wouldn't be too hard. Anyone could take a shot at him. But if you wanted him dead, for sure. That's another story."

"How's that?"

"Well...cops, the military, the Secret Service, the FBI. I'll bet they're all here today. That's a boatload of protection for someone to get through."

"It only takes one shot, D.W."

"Agreed, but it better be a good one. Kennedy's agents will get in front of him the moment something happens. They're trained to jump into action immediately. That's their job. And there's a bunch of them. It's not good that some of them have been out partying. But you remember how they saved Harry Truman's hide. They stopped two Puerto Rican nationalists out to get him. Armed to the teeth. Quite a gun battle. Maybe some of those same agents are on this detail. I'm not saying it can't be done, but it wouldn't be easy. I'd put my money on the Praetorian Guard," his words drifted for a moment, "unless the 'fix was in.' Then all bets are off."

"It happens," said Quinn.

Tillis thought. "A lot of dead emperors would agree with you."

"You think the 'fix is in'?"

"Sorry, Tom. I just read the blotter...not tea leaves,"

Tillis smiled and stood. "Gotta' go, my friend. See you tonight, Tom. We'll swap old war stories over drinks."

A.C. Currant strolled the Elm Street sidewalk toward the white concrete pergola that capped the north side of Dealey Plaza. To his right was an open parking lot; to the left, another walk followed Elm Street into the dark underbelly of the triple overpass. Straight ahead was a quiet place with overhanging trees, dappled sunlight on the ground, and empty of people. The motorcade was not due for at least an hour. He sat on a low concrete wall looking west across the plaza. His umbrella, now closed, lay next to him. No more rain today, except maybe raining bullets. His eyes took in the killing zone. He was fascinated by the consistency of the planned attack from place to place. Chicago, Tampa, and now Dallas were all the same. Bottle up the quarry and shoot at him from many directions. Chop him down. Allow for no escape. Be merciless. In some overarching way, this methodology of death was enlightened. Like the slaughter of an animal, a clean kill, so fast that there is no time for the victim to experience pain, be aware of his doom, or have the luxury of contemplation. Throwing the switch and turning out the light. That was the plan. No lingering, agonizing, or false hope, just a well-executed execution. Everyman dies, he thought. Everyman is erased from the ledger. Possibly history will remember him, but even this is little consolation to a dead man. Life is for the living. His brother Patrick is now living, at this moment, in that little town in Louisiana. This was the truth. And for Currant, that was the only thing that had any meaning to him. He wanted his brother to live. Patrick had a life ahead of him. He had the right to live. All else was irrelevant.

Currant thought about his confrontation with Ferrie in New Orleans. If somehow JFK survived, David Ferrie might assume that Currant and his gang of junior reporters broke up the scheme. He might risk resuming his relationship with Patrick. Currant knew he could not rely only on his attempted intimidation of Ferrie.

Therefore he had a couple of other plans in place. Neither plan involved killing Ferrie. Currant was not a killer and had chosen a more subtle resolution. While in New Orleans, he had hired a private detective. The man would watch Ferrie ensuring he had no additional contact with Patrick. If there was even one such contact, his mother would get an anonymous telephone call telling her that Ferrie was a dangerous pedophile and that she should keep Patrick away from him at all costs. Lastly, the same detective had provided him with photostats of Ferrie's earlier arrest records on morals charges. He mailed these to his mother without explanation or sender identification before leaving New Orleans. This was risky. He preferred not to interfere with his family's history any more than absolutely necessary. He knew the alteration of historical human events required a light touch. For some reason, he believed Ferrie would stick by their bargain. After today and JFK's demise, he assumed Ferrie would want to maintain a low profile without any arrests. Currant was comfortable that he had done everything that could be done for Patrick.

The sun beat down on A.C.'s head, slowly distilling his thoughts into an almost alcoholic brain brew. His mind drifted like a rudderless boat in choppy waters. He wondered about Emma, Ethan, and Zak. He wanted them safe too. He wished he could keep them away from the maelstrom soon to be upon this peaceful place. But that would not happen. They were dedicated to saving JFK, even at the risk of revealing the truth of their existence here in Dallas, Texas, U.S.A. 1963. He had drilled into their heads the dangers of being exposed, the issues of altering events, but even as he warned them, he had thoughts of his own need to save his brother. Changing history was a tempting proposition for young and old alike. Ethan wanted JFK alive. Emma wanted to make the world better, and Currant wanted his brother to live. They were time travelers for a reason, not just time tourists. They all wanted a better world. A universal desire and a noble quest, but each person's ideal world is different.

Each bets on his own horse in every race. Except in a dead heat, there could only be one winner. Even that was an unsatisfactory outcome. Nobody wanted to just run a good race. Every life was a one-time wager, and most people wanted to win. But there would be other races. Babies were born, lives lived, and lives expired. The human race continued.

A dark shadow fell upon him. Uneasy, Currant sensed someone near him. Death was in the air. He looked up to his left. The sun formed a bright halo around the head of a man. His face was dark and shaded. He wore eyeglasses. His black hair was tucked into a dark gray beret. He was tall and thin with large hands. His clothes, a light-colored jacket, baggy pants, white socks, and worn shoes, looked like they were purchased at a thrift store on another planet. He was an odd-looking fellow, thought Currant.

"May I?" the stranger asked, pointing to a vacant seat next to Currant. His voice was well-modulated, deep, and without a trace of regional accent.

"It's a free country," replied A.C, waving his hand with unconcern. "Fine with me."

When he sat, Currant took a good look at him, a light-skinned man of color in his early forties. His features were delicate except for a prominent nose. The new neighbor smiled. Currant just watched him like he would watch a coiled snake.

"Doc. Or should I say, Doctor?"

Currant reacted to the use of his name.

"Sorry. Didn't mean to startle you. But I have been waiting for you and your friends. I have a good idea who you are. If you know what I mean."

A.C. looked at the man without commenting. Then he turned his head away and gazed into the artificial valley of Dealey Plaza.

"Your reporter friend calls you 'Doc'"...what kind of doctor are you?" His easy tone had not changed.

"Physicist," said Currant.

"So you're the man behind the machine.

Congratulations. That's one significant accomplishment. We don't get many cases like yours anymore. It's always fun, isn't it?"

"What?"

"Time travel."

Currant's mind froze, then recovered. "I guess we're busted."

"That you are."

"What about the kids? They're just kids."

"Right. Journalism students on a holiday, I heard. Nice cover, Doc. Very imaginative. My name's Joell. You?"

"I go by A.C."

"Great, A.C. How would you like those initials to stand for 'all clear'?"

Currant gave him a look of bewilderment. "I'd like the kids to be in the clear. They really are just kids."

"Not to worry, A.C., I'm actually on your side. You and your friends did commit the cardinal sin of time travel. You altered *The History*. As you can guess, that's truly frowned upon by the folks in charge. But thankfully, maybe things can work themselves out...if there is no more warping of the fabric. For sure, you've changed *The History* with your Chicago shenanigans. But apparently, nothing really radical changes. That is, if everything goes as intended today. As I said...I get it."

"You know our original intention was strictly fact-finding...kind of a history super-lesson...but then things just got out of hand," said Currant.

"They always do," said Joell. "That's why the process is forbidden. Joy riding through time is too dangerous a game to play at home. Even trained professionals like us walk softly and carefully over these eggshell moments in time. But what's passed is past. Now you have to play ball". Joell smiled. "Or we take everything away. *The Office* will suck you and your little friends up like dirtballs on a carpet. You will be expunged." He shook his head and exhaled before speaking again. "Our people sent out three other time-cops today to make sure that everything goes smoothly.

It's not my idea. But after the big show, they will take you back with them, and you will spend the rest of your time in isolation chambers. Maybe they'll let you out to become test dummies, walking beta programs, zombies, whatever. Nothing nice."

"Look, Joell. I just want to return to the future and take my charges with me. This JFK thing is done now. I can see it's a waste of time to even think we could change the inevitable."

"You won't change anything today, A.C. This thing will happen. Do you see that intersection?" He pointed to Houston and Elm streets. "It will happen there at the turn. Or if it doesn't happen there, it will happen just down the hill near that sign. Or maybe that will fail. Then it will happen just before the underpass. And if the deed is not done by then, it will be done just on the other side of those tracks. The other end of the tunnel. Or if not there, then on the freeway. I hope not."

"Why not?"

"Bad, of course, for JFK, but that would also be very bad for America...very demoralizing. Each failure and each subsequent attempt ratchets up the action and the number of people who will be killed or injured in addition to our friend JFK. But make no mistake. It will be done."

"This is history, isn't it?" said Currant.

"Big time, Doc. And you are a part of it."

Currant thought for a moment. "Who? ...Who is behind this?"

Joell looked at Currant in amazement. "Who? Who's doing this? Better yet...who cares? The man made a mess of things. He was a political mistake who took himself too seriously. The whole family does, including his wife and her family. They're the kind of people who can really screw things up. A little bit of power is dangerous. We're not all floating around on some yacht off Hyannis Port. We're on this one planet packed with people, and everyone thinks he's smarter than his neighbor. There are rules, Doc. There are rules. His demise will be the result of mob action. Not the crime syndicate, but groups of

people...some good and some bad...some sophisticated
and some crude...but not a dissenter in the bunch. It's
time to do it and time for everyone to see it done. Even
JFK knows that. He's known it for months."

"Are you saying he has been told?"

"No." Joell chuckled. "But he's a smart guy. He
knows he's at the end of his rope. He's been on a political
binge trying to fix everything his way fast because he
knows he is history. Time has caught up with him today.
And you, my friend, will be a part of history. Now how
does that sound?" Joell said it as if he was closing the
deal on an automobile purchase.

A.C. twisted his head and considered. "I'm ready,"
he said. "We've done what we can do. Honestly, I get the
picture too. I'm an old guy. I've been around this block a
few times. We will go quietly. But can we go?" His eyes
pleaded with Joell.

"You mean leave this godforsaken cow pasture?"

"Yes."

"I think so. I have to keep my three friends occupied
after the deed is done. I think that's possible. But I warn
you...even if you do get away. Don't think that they won't
catch you. I don't want to know where you are from. I'm
not giving you advice. But I am giving you freedom."

"Why?"

"You ask too many questions, Doc. You should be
saying 'thanks.' But I'll give you a quick answer that
probably won't be very satisfying. Something you
did...somebody you talked to...something changed
history for the better. It made the world a better place for
a whole lot of people, including me. Probably just a stroke
of luck. But it happened. So now we, you and me, don't
want to change another thing. I just want to go back to
the future and stay there, and so should you. No more
questions. OK?"

"OK. I'm with you. Thanks." A.C. looked around.
The plaza area was filling in with people waiting to see the
President. "He'll be coming soon. What should I do?"

Joell smiled. "Just grab your umbrella and follow

me. You're about to become part of history. And I know
that's what you want. Right?"

"Yes," said Currant quietly. "Why not?"

The airport speakers announced: "*President John F.
Kennedy and First Lady, Mrs. Kennedy, are now arriving.*"
As Zak and Emma rushed out of the terminal building,
she cursed under her breath. Zak had demanded they eat
breakfast. Then they searched the terminal for ambush
locations and wasted too much time trying to get their
bearings. Finally, they decided nothing good or bad would
happen inside the building. Unless the gunmen were on
the roof or willing to shoot through the thick window
glass, the only real opportunities for ambush were
outside. Now, as Zak and Emma ran towards airport
runways, they saw the assembled crowds. The largest
congregation of people was directly in front of the Air
Force One taxi area. The white, blue, and silver four-
engine jet was low in the sky, wheels almost touching the
tarmac. They watched from a distance. The plane landed,
and the crowd cheered. People surged forward. Some ran
frenzied toward the taxiing aircraft. Fire trucks trailed the
plane into its final position. Emma surveyed the area for
options. She saw policemen on the rooftop of the airport
terminal building. She saw the sunglass-wearing Secret
Service men forming a security barrier between the people
and the plane. Every thing looked secure.

Movable stairs were rolled into place, and the door
of Air Force One opened. Soon Mrs. Kennedy made her
appearance. The crowd cheered. Her pink designer outfit
included a cute little matching hat. She looked like a doll.
JFK came out next. He was all teeth, suntan, and
muscles, thought Emma—a stunning man—a radiant
being straight out of the Camelot story. He did look the
part. The royal couple quickly moved through mobs of
people who reached out to touch the blessed. Emma
glanced to her right and saw the waiting motorcade cars
in the distance. She grabbed Zak and tugged him in that
direction. Halfway along the parked line of cars, she

spotted an area where the crowd thinned. She ran to it.
She was part of the event now. In seconds, JFK
approached. A seasoned politician, he knew how to shake
hands and continue moving reasonably rapidly,
hesitating, but never really stopping. Then he stood about
ten feet from Emma. He looked like one of her Hollywood
movie stars, impeccably dressed, tall, and handsome.

"Mr. President!" she shouted. "Mr. President!"

JFK heard her call, found her, and smiled broadly.
He took a few quick steps in her direction. The crowd
surged against Emma. Many hands sought to make a
connection. She strained and reached over the fence as
far as she could, her fingers beckoning him to come
closer. He leaned into her and grabbed her hand with
both of his. Strong hands, as she looked into his eyes.
They danced magically.

"Thanks for coming. You're a lovely young lady," he
said in a soft voice that could be heard over the crowd. It
seemed like he held her hand too long to maintain his
momentum as if he didn't want to say goodbye. Emma
didn't hear the crowd sounds anymore. She was lost in
the moment. She had met the king. Then, as quickly as
he had arrived, he was gone. Jackie Kennedy caught up
to her husband, and Emma looked into her eyes. They
focused coldly on her, black and empty, disturbing. Then,
in a second, Jackie's total appearance changed back to
the smiling angel image. Tiny hairs on the back of Emma's
neck screamed with primitive recognition. Something was
very wrong with this picture. She experienced a
tremendous, overwhelming psychic disconnect, an
instantaneous nightmare that pounced on her like a
vicious hyena.

Zak caught up with Emma and tapped her shoulder
from behind. She looked at him with glazed eyes. "This is
all wrong. I know it. It's all terribly wrong. I hate this."

"Bad vibes," he signed. Then he pointed to the
motorcade cars. With no more time to think, the time
travelers ran ahead, twisting through people to get a
better view. The king and queen were positioned in the

back seat of the big Lincoln. Slowly the limo rolled away. A Secret Service agent-filled Cadillac followed close behind. Kennedy looked back in their direction. Emma watched sadly.

"Zak. Did you see that?" She realized the Secret Service agents running next to the car at the back didn't get onto the rear bumper. They appeared to be called off by someone in the Cadillac. One of these two agents, who had been told to stay off the rear bumper, now stood blank-faced as the Presidential Lincoln drew away. He threw out his outstretched palms as if to say, 'What's happening?' His face quickly contorted into concern, frustration, and possibly resignation as he recognized the security team's disorganized and dangerously inept behavior.

"Zak. They're leaving him unprotected. Damn it. They're dumping him." She retrieved her camera and took a photo.

The Lincoln drove toward downtown Dallas. The President was unaware he had no protection from the rear, with no agents on the bumper. Emma and Zak watched the cars go.

"Let's go," said Emma. "We have to get ahead of him." They quickly returned to their parked Chevy. Zak put the top down and climbed behind the wheel. He started the engine and looked up. "One second.... smile," demanded Emma again. She backed up to capture the entire car and driver. "There you go," she said as she snapped the shutter. "I'm getting good at this."

Quinn walked toward the intersection of Houston and Elm along the County buildings lining this side of the street. He checked his watch, *12:12,* and realized he had plenty of time. The motorcade was not due for another 15 minutes. He stopped walking when he reached the middle of the block. The stone and brick of the Criminal Courts building rose to his right. He thought this was a good spot, maybe not a safe spot, but one that offered a great view. Looking catty-corner across the road and beyond, he thought he saw Currant standing on the north side of Elm Street. He couldn't be sure, and he wasn't going to move from his spot. A young couple in front shared the view with him. Nearby, from a motorcycle cop's radio, a voice said that the motorcade had reached Cedar Springs Road.

"Look!" said the man to the young woman near him. "See that. Must be Secret Service."

The woman looked up, as did Quinn. "Where?"

"There in the Depository building. On the far left. Next to the round windows," answered the man.

Quinn scanned the building and found the location on the west side of the Depository structure. He saw someone through the windows. Quite clearly, the man was holding a rifle in front of him. There was another man at his side. This is it. Maybe they're Secret Service, or perhaps they're killers. The men moved back out of view. Quinn looked at the entire façade. The Depository building offered an excellent view of the oncoming motorcade as it approached on Houston heading north, an easy shot, dead on. He waited with a rising sense of fear. The crowd had grown appreciably in the few minutes since he arrived. They were three deep along the curb. The people were jubilant.

Ethan Callan-Wright crossed Houston Street. He hadn't seen either Quinn or Currant. He moved quickly now. In his mind, he had spent too much time in the two County buildings trying in vain to determine if Lee Oswald worked in one of them. The last building was the Dal-Tex building. The guard there had little to offer. He didn't know all the people who worked in the building by name, and hundreds worked there. He seemed surprised that JFK was coming.

On the other side of Houston Street, Ethan looked back and studied the Dal-Tex building. Fire escapes ran up the side of the building facing Dealey Plaza. Windows were open and populated with onlookers. Plenty of windows to shoot from, and the hanging fire escapes provided good cover. He turned and focused on the last building, the big, red-brick Texas Book Depository. He jogged toward the plaza, clearing the building corner and skillfully dodging spectators lining the street. When he reached the top of the entrance stairs, he glanced back toward the plaza and Houston Street. The crowd was growing. A noisy nervousness gripped the air. A young woman stood nearby. Assuming she was an employee, he inquired whether she knew Lee Oswald. She shook her head and ignored him. She turned back to the action. He saw another woman who was obviously pregnant. Taking a deep breath to calm himself, he asked her if she knew Lee Oswald. Surprisingly, she said she did. In fact, she had just seen him in the adjacent lobby. Ethan thanked her and entered the building. Inside, the masonry structure was dark, cool, and quiet. Straight ahead was a set of double doors. He pushed through and found himself in a large warehouse room full of boxes piled high. He saw nobody.

"Oswald," he shouted without response. The word bounced around the concrete surfaces.

Everything was dead quiet. He checked his watch: *12:16*. Impulsively, he backtracked to the stairs in the front lobby. He bounded up the stairway two steps at a time. His footfalls echoed off the walls. As he turned on the first landing, he looked up and saw a man standing on the second-floor landing. The man's empty hands rested on the railing. His view from the second story was of Houston Street. He looked like someone waiting for the motorcade to arrive, a young man, thin, with light brown hair and a receding hairline. Ethan's abrupt entry did not startle him. He was calm.

"Lee Oswald?" The words coughed out of his mouth.

"That's right," said the man. "Who wants to know?"

Ethan paused and breathed deeply. He was amazed. Somehow he had found the man Oswald. Slowly, he climbed the few remaining stairs and spoke when he reached the landing. "I'm Ethan Callan-Wright. I don't have much time. So I'll be quick. Do you know a man named David Ferrie?"

Oswald turned to face Ethan. He put his hands on his hips. "I don't know why you would ask me that. Who are you? Who do you represent?"

Ethan opened his hands in front of him and tried to find the words. "I don't represent anybody. I met Ferrie in New Orleans. I know you know him. I know he's part of something. I know you think you are part of something. There's not much time. I believe you're being set up."

"Set up. For what?"

"Look. JFK will be riding right by this building in a few minutes. You've got something going today. Something strange. Are you hanging a banner out? Something about Cuba? Do you work for the government?"

"I don't know what you are talking about," said Oswald. He looked intense. He didn't say anything for the next few seconds. "Who are you?"

Ethan paused, not knowing what to say. "I'm a guy who saw a guy just like you get set up in Chicago. A guy named Thomas Vallee. Another motorcade. You know about Chicago, right? I'm sure you do. You're here. This can't be a coincidence. Your life is in danger. So is the President's."

Oswald responded. "Listen. I don't know who you are. I don't know where you got your information. And I don't have time to find out. If you're trying to be a hero...forget it. I appreciate the effort. But the deck is stacked against you. Believe me...heroes are out of fashion. Clear out while you have a chance. You're right about the danger. You've entered a minefield. This is my business. This is the stuff of professionals. Don't get involved. Why don't you go watch the parade? You stay here, and you'll have more trouble than you can handle."

Ethan stood. "But..."

"But nothing. Go!" Oswald waved his hand toward the stairs. "Let it be. Go. Now. Enjoy your life."

Ethan could hear the rising voices of the crowd outside. JFK was coming. Slowly he turned away from the man. He didn't know what else to do. Obviously, Oswald was unarmed and apparently disinterested in the main attraction outside. Something was missing. There was nothing or nobody to stop here. He knew he had to get outside. He scrambled down the stairs. When he reached the lower landing, he looked back. Oswald had moved to the entry door leading to the second-floor offices. As he held the door open, their eyes met one more time. Oswald shook his head and pursed his lips. He glanced at Houston Street one more time and then stared into space. He appeared deep in thought, wearing a look of sadness and resignation.

"We're not going to make it," announced Emma. "Forget about the Trade Mart. We've got to get to Dealey Plaza. Can't you go faster?"

Zak looked over and made a face. He pointed ahead to the traffic jam. After looping south around downtown to avoid the motorcade traffic, the Chevy convertible was stuck on the Stemmons Freeway heading north.

"They must have stopped all traffic because of the motorcade." Emma looked ahead. The next crossing was Commerce Street. She checked the dashboard clock: *12:22.* "Zak, I have to go. I can't wait here, or I'll miss the whole thing. Move the car over to the curb. I'm getting out."

Since traffic was not moving, there was no way Zak could move from the center lane to the right lane. Zak expressed his frustration with his hands. He told her they were stuck. Emma struggled with her emotions. "I'll meet you at the plaza later. I'm out of here. Be careful," she said.

Zak signed, "*OK,*" and warned her, "*bullets may be flying.*"

Emma grabbed her new camera, opened the door, and jumped out into traffic. Horns honked at her, and people shouted. She ignored the uproar she was causing and focused on getting to Dealey Plaza. She ran ahead, cutting between cars, and finally reached the road shoulder. Then she scrambled up the sloping grade. She guessed she was heading in the right direction. At the top lay a small parking lot. She rested on her hands on her knees, breathing hard while gathering her senses, and then climbed the next obstacle, a railroad embankment. Once on the tracks, she looked left. A scattering of people walked about the triple overpass, but a policeman directed them away. Security, she thought, that's good. She negotiated five sets of railroad tracks, climbed a small fence, and found herself in another parking lot. Out of breath, she paused at the south pergola.

Standing in the shade, she surveyed the view. All traffic was stopped on the roads and freeway ramps, and people dotted the green hills of the plaza. Emma could orient herself since she had memorized the motorcade route map. She knew she was close. The big clock on the roof of the Depository building showed *12:25*. The home stretch, she thought as she ran across the lawn through the cars on the ramp, across more lawn, through the cars and trucks stopped on Main Street, then onto Dealey Plaza Park. It was *12:26* now, and she was in position. The crowd noise was increasing. Looking to her right, she saw the motorcade's lead motorcycles approaching Main Street. He was coming. She stood dead opposite the north pergola and the grassy knoll across Elm Street. She rested her hands on her knees again and tried to catch her breath. The run had done her in, but she knew she would be in a perfect position to see everything. JFK was coming.

Quinn had moved up the street and positioned himself at the curb at Elm and Houston in front of the Records building. The two men in the upper windows were not visible now. He looked toward the Depository building. A few minutes ago, there was some kind of disturbance going on. People gathered around one man who was lying on the ground. After a couple of minutes, an ambulance arrived. They loaded the man into their vehicle and took off. Now, at the top of the Depository entry steps, a crowd of watchers had gathered. One of them could be Ethan, he thought. He rescanned the Depository façade. This time he spotted a gun barrel hanging out of an open window on the right side of the building. He couldn't see the man holding the rifle, just his elbow resting on the sill. Another man was visible, standing next to the gunman. Are these the same two he had seen a few minutes earlier at the other end of the building? He couldn't say. He looked across Houston Street. People were filling the corner. Quinn noticed a stocky man on the sidewalk across the street talking into a small walkie-talkie as he looked toward Main Street. The crowd noise increased. The Kennedy entourage approached, activating an unseen, moving energy field.

Ethan had given up on Oswald and positioned himself on the front entrance steps of the Depository. His conversation with Oswald had gone nowhere. That the *rabbit man* was at this location at this time was a calcifying event, which seemed to lock into place with his New Orleans information. But Oswald had shown little interest. Ethan knew now that man was not the assassin. History rolled on. There was nothing more he could do. The pilot car of the motorcade had made the right turn onto Houston Street. Then a white car followed by the big blue Lincoln with more motorcycles leading the way. The crowds of people on either side of the street screamed wildly. People jumped up and down to get a better view. Ethan steeled himself against the possibility that there was a shooter in the building behind him at this moment. If so, he would have the JFK target moving toward him in bright sunlight on level ground. A perfect shot. This could be the moment, but no shots were fired. The vehicles kept coming. Before the cars reached the turn, one of the three lead motorcycles left the motorcade and headed straight ahead on Houston. The others made the turn and headed down Elm. The lead white car made the difficult 120-degree turn.

The Lincoln followed, making the turn wide and

slow. Ethan saw the occupants now. The driver and another Secret Service man sat in the front seat. Governor and Mrs. Connally occupied the back jump seats. Behind them, in the rear bench seat, sat Mrs. Kennedy and JFK. The car almost stopped in that difficult turn. Another opportunity for a shot thought Ethan, but no shots were fired. Maybe he would live. Maybe there were no shooters. JFK looked to his right, waving gently, smiling brightly; Ethan's eyes met his for an instant. Then the car slid down the hill toward the underpass, followed by another car full of Secret Service agents. A sharp noise from above. Ethan looked up. Startled pigeons on roofs flew skyward. He refocused on the blue Lincoln. Everything looked normal. Was this a shot?

A.C. Currant stood on the grass near the sidewalk uphill from the large green traffic sign. He squinted in the bright sunshine. But his black umbrella was open, and he held it above his head. This was his opportunity to be a part of history. He knew that cameras would be recording the moment. He wanted attention and proof that he was the man there at that moment—a man of destiny—the 'Umbrella Man.' He knew it was all vanity. He also knew JFK would not survive this little downhill run. To his right, Joell Costas stood almost on the curb. A.C. heard the first report, almost like a firecracker, not very loud. JFK stopped waving and leaned forward slightly. Then, he reacted to something else. His arms flew up as if to fend off an on-rushing football opponent. But this was no game. In the excitement, Currant raised and lowered his open umbrella. It was his way of defining this moment. It was happening. Below, Joell also reacted to the shots. He threw up his right arm almost in a salute. Then made a fist. Currant had no idea what this meant, but he guessed he was providing a signal to someone that the President was hit. Seconds later, the limo slowed to a crawl and almost stopped. Currant watched in awe. Everything seemed to stop.

Across the street, Emma watched the procession. She stood on the lawn, empty of people but for an isolated few. She had taken another photo as the limo struggled through the hard left turn, which was utterly ridiculous from a security standpoint. He was a sitting duck. This was the end of the road, the motorcade, and the end of JFK. As the limo approached, two women in front of her stepped off the curb onto the street. One of them held a camera. A second ago, Emma spotted A.C. Currant standing across the street, his black umbrella elevated, a symbol of impending doom. He's nuts, she thought. Then she looked back at the limo. JFK was smiling, just like when he had taken her hand. He looked fabulous one moment, then hurt. His arms rose as he defended against attack—forearms against bullets. How pitiful, she thought. The car moved on. Connally was a smiling cowboy one moment and a grimacing victim the next. Then he fell out of view. The crossfire, bullet-ballet continued. JFK's head drifted downward as if he was falling asleep. Calmly Jackie moved closer to him with one arm around his back and the other gently touching his raised arm. It's a shooting gallery! Pull him down, Jackie! Emma screamed silently. What was she thinking?

The limo slowed to almost a stop. Time seemed to stop. The Secret Service driver looked back at the wounded President. Why? Why do that? Didn't you hear the damn shots? Drive you fool. Go. Now. Instinctively, she took another photo. Then more shots—bang-boom—two noises as one. The first a distant rifle shot—the second nearby and muffled. The top of JFK's head opened like a can of beans. Stuff flew upward—a pink rainbow of brain matter. At the same instant, above his head in the darkness beyond the car, up on the hill, above the wooden fence, a yellow-red ball of flame erupted through the dense green foliage. Scorched live leaves produced white smoke that billowed through the trees above the picket fence.

Only after a good portion of JFK's head disappeared did the driver return to his duty. The car that had momentarily stopped raced ahead. Jackie immediately raised her arm as if to rid herself of the bloody corpse at her side. With her left hand, she used her lifeless husband's body for leverage as she appeared to escape onto the trunk of the death-car. One of the Secret Service agents from the follow-up car leaped onto the limo and pushed her back. Then he flipped onto the pile of bloody bodies as they rushed away. It all happened in seconds. Emma was stunned. So quick, she thought. So efficient. So brutal. Her new friend JFK was dead.

People screamed. Sirens wailed. While all others ran amok, Joell Costas carefully took one step off the curb and sat down. A.C. Currant closed his umbrella and joined Costas on the curb like two spectators resting. The time-cop had a little closing business. He pulled a walkie-talkie from his back pocket and said something. Currant heard the same word twice. It sounded like "86". Costas set the radio on the ground and looked back at Currant. For a few moments, neither man said anything. A line of motorcade cars kicked up dust as they rumbled past, chasing the dead Kennedy. In seconds, the last of these slid down Elm Street, swallowed by the underpass and disappearing into the darkness. Motorcycle policemen braked hard and laid down their bikes, scurrying about, guns drawn. Concerned parents shielded their children from bullets on the fly. Angry throngs cried out and rushed up the grassy knoll chasing the killers. No one paid any attention to the two curbside time travelers. They were invisible.

"Well, Doc. There's your history. All nice and tidy. And we didn't have to do a thing. All I did was raise my arm to say hello to JFK," he smiled. "Everything else was done right here, right now, in this year. The actors played their parts perfectly. Very nice. And no interference from any of your people." Joell looked at Currant with intensity. "For your sake, I'm going to give my three boys up. However, that won't last long. They have the finest phony identification available. The cops won't hold them long. You better get your friends, and go back to where you came from. You may have a couple of hours or a day or two lead, but I wouldn't chance it. Get out of town now." He stood up, and Currant stood next to him.

"We will. But why? Why are you letting us go?"

Joell smiled. "Part of history, Doc. You solved your problem, and that solved mine."

"You know about my problem?"

"I have an idea. I know you went to New Orleans. Trying to go home to fix something, weren't you?" He paused and looked up the hill toward the pergola and the wooden fence. Then he focused on the one person walking away from the grassy knoll.

Currant followed his eyes and saw a man walking deliberately along the sidewalk in front of the white concrete structure. He wore a hat, carried a small case, and walked quickly amidst the chaos. Joell spotted him too. "Shooter," he said.

"Oh. Right," acknowledged Currant as if it was obvious. He looked across Elm Street and spotted Emma with a camera in her hand. She had one knee on the ground. She looked dazed but unharmed.

Joell spoke his final words capturing Currant's attention again. "Assume we know everything. We probably do. Goodbye, Doc. Have a good trip back. Don't do anything foolish." He turned and walked past the grassy knoll toward the triple underpass.

Currant watched the man disappear into history. Then his eyes panned the scene. He knew this was his last chance to survey the conspiratorial carnage and its aftermath. All was sadly and devastatingly quiet. Only fears, tears, and pain remained. He turned and strolled slowly in the other direction, up the hill, tapping the tip of his folded umbrella on the concrete walk. The horror of what he had just witnessed rattled about his brain like a steel marble in a glass jar. Enough, he thought.

Ethan stood frozen at the top of the Depository stairs. Now, just seconds after the killing, the scene before him was still full of sound and fury. A motorcycle policeman drove up, dropped his vehicle, and jumped off. He ran up the steps, gun in hand, past Ethan and entered the building, followed by another man. Ethan stumbled down the stairs in a state of shock. His foreknowledge of the possibility did not shield him from the horrible reality of the crime. He leaned against one of the entrance columns and collected his thoughts. He saw A.C. Currant sitting on a curb down the hill along Elm Street. Moments passed. Then he looked back at the building entrance. To his surprise, his quarry, Lee Oswald, calmly exited the front door, casually walked down the steps, and worked his way through the crowd heading toward downtown along Elm Street. He watched him until he disappeared from view. Ethan looked back at Currant. The physicist walked up the hill toward him, and Ethan walked down to meet him.

"It's over," said Currant. "I saw the whole thing. He's dead for sure."

"For sure?"

"Yes. His head was completely destroyed. It was hideous."

"We were too little...too late," said Ethan. "I tried my best. I actually found Oswald. But that was a waste. He didn't seem to even know what was going on. I just saw him take off out the front door. No big hurry. Pretty nonchalant. I think he was a red herring...." Just then, Ethan looked away from Currant. Something caught his eye. A man ran down the slope leading to Elm Street. "It's Oswald...look!"

Currant looked back at the man who reached a light-colored station wagon car parked on Elm by this time. The man quickly jumped in the passenger side, and in seconds it was gone. "I thought you said he was walking down Elm Street the other way."

"I did. But that was Oswald," said Ethan. "This is crazy. A man can't be in two places at once. Can he?"

"Not unless he's got a twin. Oswalds are popping up everywhere...like rabbits." Currant reached up and grabbed Ethan's shoulders with both hands. "We need to round up our troops and get out of town. We have company now."

"Company?"

"Time-police."

Emma tried to stand, but she was dizzy. The adrenaline subsided, her knees knocked, and tears filled her eyes. She crouched, transfixed, holding her camera weakly in her right hand. Then, abruptly, she felt someone grab it. "Hey!"

A big man in a dark gray suit, white shirt, and tie flashed his credentials at her: *Secret Service*. "I'll take that, Miss. You'll get it back in a few days." Sirens wailed painfully in the distance as downed people began to rise off the turf like zombies in a horror movie; chaos still reigned.

"But," Emma moaned. She was too beaten to say anything more.

"What's your name? Where do you live? We'll get it back to you." The tone of his voice was too 'matter of fact' under the circumstances.

Emma came to her senses. "Forget it. It's too horrible. I don't want to ever see that again."

"Smart thinking, young lady." Then with her camera in his grip, he headed back up the hill away from the devastation.

Emma dropped into a crouch again and cried softly. "Bastards," she mumbled.

(Day 25 of time travel)

Well, the deed is done. And so are the time travelers. We've left town, and we're back on the road. It's hard to say whether our trip was a success or failure. After all, it was supposed to be a history lesson—not a mission to save the Camelot king. It certainly was an education. We've learned a lot about life in the '60s. It's a rough time and place. Ask JFK. We may have bought him twenty additional days on this planet, but in the end, he's still out of the picture. His top is down, and so is ours. The wind is whistling through my hair. Soon the sun will set on this horrible day. In the darkness that follows, a nation will cry itself to sleep.

According to the radio news, the mystery man Oswald is in police custody and charged with killing the President and a cop. Jackie Kennedy continues to wear her bloodstained and brain-speckled pink outfit. What's left of JFK is in a box on Air Force One. And the U.S.A. is now under the command of the new President, Lyndon Baines Johnson. That was quick. Thank our lucky stars for the rules of succession. So everything is going smoothly for some people. Not so for Emma. She is next to me—very quiet, still sniffling. Apparently, she grew very attached to the handsome young prince in their brief moments together before his demise. I guess she reflects most of the people of the United States. As we drive from town to town, escaping the nastiness that is Dallas, we see tear-streaked, red faces everywhere. The people have been crushed. This is the day the grand illusion died—the day the sweet sauce of faithful patriotism was overwhelmed by the stench of the rotten fish of reality. The one-of-kind tasty dish of democracy, now almost two hundred years old, will no longer be palatable or even edible to those with sensitive taste buds. Of course, hungry people will continue to eat no matter how fishy it smells—because they are hungry. I suspect those that can't stomach it will die off because this is now the new American diet.

Essentially, these thoughts have filled Ethan's conversation since the assassination. He's become a cynic's cynic. And Dr. Currant has been very quiet. He's offered no explanation for his behavior except to say that we owe our lives to a time-cop named Joell. He seems to have little interest in the death of JFK. It's almost as if he has forgotten the grand panorama of history. He is totally focused on the essence of living. He keeps saying that everyone still has his life regardless of JFK losing his. Great leaders and evil forces come and go. But, all that is beyond us. History is just a backdrop for our own lives, nothing more and nothing less. Like the night storm that roars through the forest of life, ripping down trees and frightening children with its thunder and lightning, this too shall pass, and the sun shall rise again. "Our lives go on. Our lives go on." This is something he continues to mumble while he drives. Otherwise, he is not talking.

With my great genetic "gift," I can feel my friends' pain. They are crushed by their memories of the day. Although I did not witness the assassination, I did interview someone who saw "the man behind the curtain" or, more correctly, the fence. After Emma dashed away and left me stuck in traffic on the freeway, I had nothing to do but wait. Nearby, shortly after that, bullets filled the air. But I only endured the nasty atmosphere of automobile exhaust. Eventually, it was over, the President had been

*exterminated, and traffic flowed again. I put the Chevy in
Drive and motored on. Things appeared pretty normal.*

*I was focused on getting back to Dealey. But not too far
ahead, just past the Elm Street on-ramp, I saw a man on
the left side of the road waving frantically. I stopped the
Chevy and jumped out to see what was wrong.
Surprise—this guy was mute just like me—a serious-
looking fellow, maybe late twenties; he wore glasses, his
ears were prominent, and his jaw was square. He was
also deaf. By the time I reached his side, he was
hyperventilating. He was signing vigorously but
erratically. It was all gibberish. I knew why no other cars
had stopped. The drivers could make no sense of the
situation. However, I could. I tested my signing with him,
and he immediately appeared relieved. He calmed. I
asked him to lean against the car to catch his breath.
After a few moments, he told me his name was Ed and
said he had seen something terrible happen. He walked
me back to his vantage point. A few minutes earlier, he
had watched history unfold from this place. Now, the two
of us looked across the expressway. In the distance, the
red brick Book Depository was visible. You could see the
parking lot on the west side of the building, the backsides
of the grassy knoll pergola and wooden fence, and the
railroad tracks in the foreground. I asked Ed to sign
slowly so I could understand, and he told me his story.*

*He had stopped on the freeway side to watch the
Presidential motorcade. While waiting for it to arrive, he
had a view of all activity in the entire area to the west of
the Depository and north of Elm Street starting about
11:50 am. He saw a light-colored station wagon enter the
open parking area and circle the lot; eventually, it parked
near the switching tower. Later, he saw a man in a plaid*

shirt walk around the end of the L-shaped wooden fence and talk to another man wearing a business suit. There was also a uniformed policeman nearby. Both the plaid-shirted man and the policeman walked out of view along the Depository side of the fence. Another man dressed like a worker stood near the railroad tracks.

The business suit man met with this train worker briefly and then walked back to the fence. In time he bent over, straightened up, and looked over the wooden fence toward Elm Street. Soon there was a puff of smoke. The man then turned, and Ed saw that he had a rifle in his hands. He ran to the train worker and tossed the rifle. The worker caught the rifle, broke it down, placed it into a bag, and then walked away along the tracks.

Meanwhile, the businessman casually walked back through the parking lot. A policeman (not the same one who Ed saw earlier) with a pistol in hand confronted him. This must have been just after the assassination. The businessman showed the cop some identification. The policeman accepted the credentials and moved on. The businessman then casually walked to the station wagon parked near the switching tower, and the car drove away. Following all this, Ed saw the big blue limo drive up the nearby expressway ramp—the death car racing to Parkland Hospital. The wounded players were knotted into a bloody ball in the back. JFK was slumped down, his head resting on the seat. His head had a fist-sized hole behind his right ear. It was an awful sight.

This silent horror movie was his story, and he was relieved to be able to tell it to someone who could understand him. I said goodbye to Ed, and he drove away. Shortly after, I met up with our group at the corner of Houston and Elm. Tom Quinn was there too. At our powwow, Quinn told us of his sightings of men with guns on the book depository's sixth floor. Everyone agreed that shots came from many directions. Ethan told of his ambiguous meeting with Oswald. Emma spoke of the shooter on the knoll. People ran toward the hill in great numbers in the aftermath, trying to find the shooters. She also mentioned the Secret Service man who confiscated her camera. I told the story of the mute man. Only Dr. Currant was without a story. He said it was too horrible to discuss. We were all tremendously excited. Emma cried. It was time to go. We left Tom Quinn standing in front of the Depository. It was sad to leave him. He had been a good comrade for us. But he did say that he would continue to work on the story no matter where it leads him or how long it takes.

We only had a few days left to get back to the TimeTravelle. Tomorrow will be day twenty-six. Dr. Currant said he couldn't guarantee our safe return to 2028 if our trip exceeded twenty-eight days. We still had over 1,400 miles to go to reach Mystic Heights. I hope the Chevy makes it. We suggested taking a train or plane, but A.C. would have none of those thoughts. He loves this car, and he will drive it home.

END: 11-22-63

-Chapter XXIII-

Ruby—Don't Take Your Love to Town

The reporter, Quinn, stayed on in Dallas and kept his secrets to himself after the assassination, including his own knowledge of the men on the sixth floor, Zak's story about the men behind the fence, Emma's detailed description of the destruction of JFK, and Ethan's run-in with Oswald. Now Oswald was the police prime suspect. Quinn stayed with the other reporters sorting out what had happened. About midnight on the evening of the assassination, he was in the basement of the police headquarters. A news conference was scheduled to present the alleged assassin Lee Harvey Oswald, as he was now known.

This Oswald was a man who didn't waste time. In eighty-one minutes, Oswald shot the President, left the book depository, traveled home by bus and cab, picked up a handgun, left home, walked a few minutes, met with a police officer and shot him dead, and then walked to a movie theater, sat down to watch a movie until surrounded and captured by police. Now he was in custody. Others were brought in for questioning as part of a leaky dragnet set up after the shooting. These included three "tramps" hiding in a railroad boxcar next to the Depository parking lot. Quinn saw these men that afternoon being taken into custody by two shotgun-wielding Dallas cops. He got a good look at them. They really didn't look the part. They were clean, smooth-faced, with decent haircuts. However, they did look like people who were uncertain of how to dress. One wore a sport coat and jeans and maintained his golf shirt collar entirely up *a la* European style. The tallest of the three had messy hair and wore a sport coat and a sick smile. The last tramp looked older, and he wore a funny little hat. Their shoes were serviceable but not stylish. While Quinn realized they could be tramps, he had met enough real vagabonds to know these men were not hoboes. Later he heard that they had been released. Other men, some quite unsavory and suspicious but unseen by Quinn, had also been arrested and released. But by late evening, the table had been set by the purveyors of justice. Oswald was their man.

Quinn was present when Oswald was moved from room to room through the tight corridors of the police building. They were jammed with cameramen, reporters, police, and others. Security was terrible. Strangely, the man Quinn had met that morning in the lunchroom of the *Dallas Morning News* was wandering about. Quinn looked in his coat pocket for his business card: *Jack Ruby, Proprietor*. He was a nightclub owner. Quinn wondered what he was doing here at the police station. Oswald answered *ad hoc* questions fired at him by reporters. He was questioned by one of the reporters about whether he had killed the President. "They are taking me in because of the fact that I lived in the Soviet Union. I am just a patsy." Later under the same circumstances, he said, "I did not shoot anybody." Quinn wondered about this man. He was a composed assassin who did not cry: "Sic Semper Tyrannus", and never claimed he killed the President or the policeman. Oswald did not appear naïve. When facing reporters, he seemed to be fencing with them, buying time and remaining non-committal. He was waiting for something to happen—but what?

Midnight arrived, and the basement was hot, smoke-filled, and crowded with reporters. Oswald was again paraded before the newsmen and photographers about ten hours after his arrest. He made a brief statement. He denied involvement with any killings, and he requested legal assistance. Later in a question-answer period, District Attorney Henry Wade announced that Oswald was a member of the "Free Cuba Movement." Immediately, a man standing on a table in the back of the room corrected him. He told Wade it was the "Fair Play for Cuba Committee," not the "Free Cuba Movement." Quinn looked back at the man. It was that Ruby character again. This time he was dressed in a reporter costume wearing dark-framed glasses and holding a clipboard and pen in his hand. One expected him to don a fedora with a *PRESS* card tucked in the front band. Quinn found something very wrong with this situation. Jack Ruby, strip-joint owner, and a junior reporter, was covering the "story of the century"? Is that guy packin'? What's that bulge in his pocket? How the hell does he get in here? And how the hell does he know the name of some obscure pro-Cuba organization? How did he have the balls to make his correction part of this history-making press conference when he has nothing to do with the press? Quinn smelled a pattern here—too much Ruby—and Ruby too knowledgeable to just be a *meshuggah* bystander. Later that night, in another crowded corridor, Ruby snuggled up to him and grabbed his hand for a shake.

"What about it, Mac? Any news on that scum being transferred to County?"

"Name's Quinn. And I don't know shit, Jack. What are you doing here?"

Ruby was steady. "Me. I'm a buff. I'm always here. These guys all know me."

"Just want to be part of history, huh?"

"Doesn't everyone?" answered Ruby, and he waddled off to buttonhole another reporter.

At first, Quinn figured him for a gadfly. Later, when he spoke with other reporters about the man, they had a new name for him. They called him "The Creep." He was part of whatever was happening here in Dallas. Quinn needed help. The following Saturday, he called his office in Chicago and spoke with Jack Montana, who was pleased that the *American* had somebody on the spot, even if it wasn't him. Quinn asked Montana to check out Ruby's local history. Later that day, they reconnected again by phone.

"Ruby's wired," said Montana

"How so?"

"He bumped around here in Chicago doing odds and ends for the Outfit and then settled in with the Scrap Iron Union in the '30s. Started out as low-level hired help, but he moved up. They used to call him "Sparky." Guess he has quite a temper."

"Scrap Iron. Paul Dorfman's operation."

"Right. Looks like he was the number two guy before the Teamsters took over."

"What else?"

"He was Jack Rubenstein here...not Ruby. Small fish. Not "made," but definitely wired. He was arrested for the murder of a guy named Cooke, who apparently got in the way of the union. He beat that charge, though. That was in 1940. The Outfit sent him down to Texas in '47. Opening up a new territory. His ties are here in Chicago, Tom."

"I'm still wondering why this greasy guy is playing reporter and sticking so close to Oswald. Better yet. Why are the police allowing this guy anywhere near their operations? For Cri' sake, he runs a strip club. He's wired, huh? You know anything about the Dallas cops?"

"I would imagine they're like our boys in blue. Most straight and some very crooked."

"Right. Thanks, Jack. Gotta' go now. I'll get back to you," said Quinn.

He would return the call to Jack Montana after Oswald was dead. Quinn was in the basement of police headquarters when Oswald was being moved to the County jail. Ruby was there also. Handcuffed to police guards on either side of him, Oswald was walking a few feet to the waiting transfer car—reporters—cops everywhere—amidst a rush of noise and excitement. Quinn watched Oswald, who was squinting under the bright lights. As he entered the garage basement, a car horn sounded two times. The alleged Presidential assassin took a few steps toward oblivion before Ruby, dressed like a B-movie hitman, popped out of the crowd and rushed forward, his arm extended. Revolver in hand,

Ruby fired one shot into Oswald's gut. Oswald crumpled down. Then a plain-clothes detective mounted the recumbent Oswald and started heart massage. Quinn knew about gut wounds from his Marine days. He knew artificial respiration for a gut gunshot victim would not save his life but would ensure his death.

Why would Ruby pretend to be a reporter—stalk Oswald for two days—wait for the ideal moment—and then kill him on live television? In retrospect, it seemed totally premeditated. Later, Ruby would say he shot Oswald to save Mrs. Kennedy the pain of testifying at an Oswald trial. Bring on the love thought Quinn; bring on the love.

Quinn tracked the ambulance carrying the moribund assassin to the hospital and waited. A short time later, at 1:07 p.m. Sunday, November 24, 1963, Lee Harvey Oswald died. America cheered, thought Quinn, swift justice. But Quinn wasn't biting. Afterward, there was a news conference at Parkland Hospital. Oswald's emergency room doctors participated. When it was over, one of them ducked out, took off in his car, and Quinn followed him home. There was a crowd gathered when they arrived. The doctor cut a quick swath into his driveway, exited his vehicle, dodged reporters, and rushed to his house. Quinn fired out a question.

"Doctor. You were there. Did Oswald confess before he died?"

The doctor looked back and said cryptically, "Why don't you ask LBJ? He's the man in charge now." With that, he found his key, opened the lock, entered, and shut the door behind him.

Quinn stood in place long after the others had left, unable to move. "LBJ?" He was puzzled by the doctor's response. A persistent, dull, sucker-punch pain churned in Quinn's gut. He felt manipulated. The bizarre events of the past few days overwhelmed him. Slowly he regained his composure and returned to his car. He sat quietly, alone, listening to his breathing. His eyes watered. What was happening? His gut tried to tell him, but his raging emotions drowned out the subtle thoughts of the muse that warned of the unspeakable.

O.A. LOG TTA2028-6

INVESTIGATOR: Joell Costas

DATE: November 25, 1963 (July 26, 2028)

PROJECT: JFK-11.02.63

PROGRESS REPORT

President JOHN FITZGERALD KENNEDY was pronounced dead on November 22, 1963, at 1:00 P.M. CST. The mechanism of his death was created and implemented by the people of 1963, and *The Authority* only monitored the event. It did not instigate, aid, or enforce his demise.

LEE HARVEY OSWALD was arrested as the President's assassin on November 22, 1963, at 1:51 P.M., CST

The three ADDITIONAL INVESTIGATORS were concealed in a railroad boxcar and taken into custody immediately after the assassination at approximately 2:00 P.M. CST. After providing suitable cover stories, they were not charged and were subsequently released.

LYNDON BAINES JOHNSON was sworn in as the 36th President of the United States on November 22, 1963, at 2:39 P.M., CST

OSWALD was pronounced dead on November 24, 1963, at 1:07 P.M. CST after being shot by JACK RUBY, a nightclub operator.

The TIME TRAVELERS have now been identified as three youths (two boys and a girl) and one older man. They are posing as high school journalism students and their teacher. We have the name DOC for the older man but no other names. We do not know if they remain in the area, but we are confident their presence here in Dallas has had little effect on *The History.* Since I have no idea their current whereabouts, I have decided to return home today to minimize the possibility of my contamination affecting future events. As of this moment, the events of *The History* are intact. It is my opinion that our team has accomplished our goal. However, against my recommendation, the ADDITIONAL INVESTIGATORS have determined to exploit their credentials to contact local and federal authorities regarding the TIME TRAVELERS whereabouts. It is their intent to track and apprehend them. I disagree with this action, as I believe it may result in unwanted temporal deviations. They will report directly to *The Authority* regarding their progress if any.

THOMAS QUINN, the reporter, remains in Dallas. I have had no additional contact with him. Although he might be able to provide further information, I have strongly suggested to the ADDITIONAL INVESTIGATORS that this approach be avoided. QUINN is of this time, and by profession, is highly cautious and inquisitive.

Subject to debriefing and analysis, this concludes my activities related to JFK-11.02.63. I shall return home ASAP.

TRANSMITTED VIA CODED TIME JUSTIFIER AT 1:17 P.M. CT 07/26/28.

-Chapter XXIV-

Return to the Rabbit Hole

Late afternoon on the 22nd of November, 1963, the Chevy convertible cut northeast across the Texas plains. The road was a straight, black line connecting an unbroken dark red sea of soil to the clear blue sky. Currant maintained a steady pace, about three to five miles over the posted speed limit. He didn't want to attract the attention of any police, local or time-cops. Ethan rode shotgun and seemed fixated on the wildly waving foxtail tied to the radio antenna. Currant glanced over his shoulder and saw that Zak was writing his log. Emma wore the face of a widow. She hadn't said much since they left Dallas. Currant was pleased to notice that Zak would take hold of Emma's hand and give it a gentle squeeze to comfort her every so often.

"How are you doing back there?"

Zak nodded.

"Emma?"

She stirred. "OK, Doctor, but I could use something to eat." Her voice crackled.

He was pleased she had broken out of her funk. "Not a bad idea. I could use a bite myself," said Currant. "How 'bout you, brother, Ethan?"

Ethan broke away from the captivating rhythm of the fluttering foxtail. "That's an idea with merit. Come to think of it. I haven't eaten anything since breakfast. Let's do it."

Stretching, Ethan leaned back in his seat and looked up at the sky. Something caught his attention. "Hey. Look at that." He pointed to a small black and white airplane sliding across the sky, maybe 3000 feet in the air on the right side of the car.

Currant glanced up. "Think it's following us?"

For the first time since Dallas, Emma laughed. Then Zak and Ethan. "Relax 'Dr. Paranoid'. It's a big country. Anyway. How would anyone know who or where we are?"

The physicist gripped the wheel tighter. A minute later, the engine noise above continued, but it was diminishing. He took another quick look at the sky and spotted the black and white dot. This time more distant. It seemed to be heading away. Another minute and it was no longer in sight. Satisfied that Emma was correct, he refocused on the highway ahead. Not more than a mile down the road, they spied an eatery. He pulled the Chevy off the pavement and dustily bounced the car through a rutted parking lot, sliding into a spot in front of the weatherworn diner. It was dead quiet now. They were in the middle of nowhere with nothing but miles of dirt, scrub grass, fence posts, and barbed wire.

Ethan sniffed the air like a dog in heat. "Ribs," he declared. "Damn, they do smell good."

They removed themselves from the car, slowly unpacking their bodies and minds. It had been a terrible day, thought Currant. A good meal would help turn things around. He checked the sign above the door and chuckled: *Rib-A-Rama—Best Grub East of the Pecos.* "This is the place to chow down," he announced. "Come and get it."

Entering the diner, they found three patrons and the owner watching a tiny television that hung off the wall. The regulars hardly noticed the newcomers.

Two seasoned cowboys book-ended a fat redheaded lady who sat on a stool between them. "Son of a bitch got what was comin' to him. What's all the fuss about? He won't be missed. We got Lyndon now. He'll straighten things out," said the taller of the two Levi's-clad ranchers.

"They should give that guy a medal," said the other.

The woman behind the counter leaned into the seated diners. "We've got company, friends." She turned to the time travelers. "What can we do for you?"

They ordered ribs, chicken, and seasoned fries with

mayonnaise.

After shouting the order to a backroom cook, the woman twisted the TV dial to improve reception and got a Dallas station. The black-and-white TV delivered the latest news and speculation regarding the assassination: *"Police have arrested the killer of JFK... a man named Oswald...a rifle was found in his workplace...Oswald was probably a Communist sympathizer since he had lived in Russia and his wife was a Russian...a man named Zapruder said he shot a home movie of the whole thing."* The reporter then talked about the wound to Kennedy's head.

Hearing this, Emma, who was distraught, asked if they could eat outside. They found a picnic table around the side of the building and spread out the food and drink. The comfort food did its job. They ate quietly and said little. The heat of the late afternoon sun was tempered by a light breeze.

Thought Currant at another time, it could have been a pleasant late lunch. Zak appeared to carry a heavy load. "Zak. You OK? You must be worn down with all the emotion in the air."

Zak nodded balefully. He ate his ribs without conviction.

"Ethan?"

The tall twin traveler smiled at Currant. "Don't worry about me. We did what we could. Maybe some good will come out of this. I hope so."

"Emma. What are you thinking?"

Emma sipped on her lemonade. She shrugged her shoulders. "He was a nice man. He didn't have to die. I was better off before I met him." She shook her head. "He was betrayed. Butchered. Why?"

The table talk went dead. Tears welled up in the girl's eyes. Zak offered her a paper napkin that she used to stem the flow.

"I'll tell you what I think. If you want," said Currant. "Maybe we should all say something. Clear the air. Lighten our load."

Zak looked very despondent. He signed that the emotional weight was heavy. The combined pain of hundreds of millions of mourners worldwide was almost unbearable. He asked if he could take a walk while they talked. Currant agreed, and Zak wandered away, seeking solace in the emptiness of the surrounding country.

"What did the time-cop Joell say?" Ethan asked. "Did he know who was behind this? It's the same setup as Chicago and Tampa. That strange woman in Eunice sure knew it was coming to Dallas. The FBI issued a warning bulletin. Then we saw the twin 'Oswalds.' Remember what Banister said in New Orleans. He said there were multiple 'Oswalds.' an army of little rabbits ready to fight."

"What about *Harvey*?" asked Emma in a quiet voice.

The others looked at her blankly.

"The pooka—an Irish legend—a benevolent shape-shifting six-foot three-inch tall invisible rabbit. Guys—the movie *Harvey*. 1950. James Stewart. Seriously, do you not know anything? You are cinematically challenged." She was regaining her strength. She looked up at the sky for divine guidance to help her relate to these lesser minds.

Ethan looked puzzled. "So..."

"So. It's Lee 'Harvey' Oswald. The invisible rabbit. Maybe that name is simply a code. A cover for a type of programmed assassin created by someone in power. Maybe somewhere, a big guy named 'Harvey' is pulling all the strings—the rabbit puppeteer. There are too many bunny references here to be ignored. Doctor Currant, you said that Banister talked of 'Oswald' bunnies hopping all the way to Cuba."

A.C. looked at Emma with sympathy. "We drank quite a bit that night in New Orleans, Emma. I wouldn't put too much into that rabbit discussion, except that we accidentally found out about Lee Oswald."

Emma smiled. "Hey, I was the last one to get on this conspiracy bandwagon. You can't fault me for using my imagination."

"A thousand robotic rabbits charging up San Juan Hill...at this point, I'll believe anything. We've gone down into the rabbit hole of time, and it is a '*Wonderland,*'" said Currant.

"No doubt it's a conspiracy," Ethan declared. "Zak's mute friend. That guy named Ed. He saw one of the shooters. But who?"

Currant shook his head. "He wasn't that helpful. I have to believe we will never know who pulled the levers to activate the machine. The plotters are no doubt unknown to people at the bottom. Oswald, his 'twin,' Ferrie, that cop that was killed, all the rest of the bit players, the shooters, the spotters, the radiomen. They're all stovepiped. I'm sure. You could beat them bloody in a torture chamber, and you'll never find a way to the top."

"What about an investigation?"

"There will be some kind of investigation and formal cover-up report. But in the past, those have offered minimal disclosure...or none. Someone will take the fall. Maybe one person...maybe several. Expendables. They'll bury the file in time until nobody is left who cares."

"Somebody has to take the fall," said Emma absentmindedly. "That's what Bogart said."

Ethan perked up at the mention of Humphrey Bogart's name. "What's that?"

"Oh. Nothing. Just a line from the *Maltese Falcon.* It's a movie about a metal bird encrusted with jewels lost in time. Many people want it and end up killing each other in the process."

"I like Bogey. Anyway, it sounds like the American Eagle to me," said Ethan. "Somebody wanted *that* bird also, and they grabbed it in '63. But who's the fall-guy here?"

"Gotta' be Oswald. It's the same setup as Vallee in Chicago," said Currant.

Emma jumped in. "I keep thinking maybe we could have stopped it. Maybe we could have done something."

"Emma. Give it up. Remember, we were guessing about everything. We couldn't expose ourselves. What could we do? Run out in the street waving our arms, shouting 'Hey JFK! Duck'."

"I wish I had," she said.

"You would be in jail right now instead of enjoying these dustbowl delights for lunch. No, we didn't fail. This had to happen...and it did. It was destiny," said Ethan. "No one is more frustrated than me."

"It was a public execution," said Currant. "Very messy. Very ugly. This was a warning put out by people who feared they were losing control. I think everyone got the message."

"No changes wanted. No outsider agitators allowed. Stay out. The U.S.A. is our game, and we own the ball, the players, and all the spectators," said Emma.

"That's right. So now we know more about the real history...not just *The History*. And, we just have to let it be," said Currant.

At that moment, Zak rounded the corner of the building on the run. He was breathing heavily. He made grunting sounds.

"Sign Zak...sign," said Emma.

Zak took a deep breath and then signed hectically.

Currant knew it was trouble. He looked to Emma for answers. "What?"

"The plane is coming. It's landing on the highway," signed Zak.

They jumped up and ran around to the front of the building. Up the road, the black and white monoplane shot toward them, shuttling along the empty blacktop highway as if it were a winged car. It turned in gently at the parking lot entrance kicking up a cloud of dust. About a hundred feet from them, the pilot revved the engine and spun it around to face the road. A blast of dirty prop wash kicked up. In defense, they hid their faces. The pilot cut the engine, and the prop spun to rest in silence, releasing a final cough. Their world was empty and quiet, except for a soft humming sound that came and went as the wind rustled the plane's taut antenna wire. High above, two black buzzards silently scanned the ground for dead meat. Miniature dust devils scooted about the parking lot. Currant brushed his forehead with the back of his hand, squinted, and read the insignia on one of the side doors: *Texas Highway Patrol*. "Damn," he muttered under his breath. "Stay cool, kids. Don't move. And don't say anything."

Four men exited the plane. The pilot, a tall, skinny, rangy sort, was dressed in a well-pressed uniform of the Highway Patrol. The other three wore plain clothes: one tall, one old, and one scrawny with a mean, stern face. The latter wore a strange outfit—a heavy tweed sport coat with fat lapels—a pink short-sleeved golf shirt buttoned to the neck—too-tight blue jeans—and scuffed shoes with pointed toes. His shirt collar stood straight up and out as if it had a mind of its own. He looked like a wayward Frenchman, someone not quite able to fit into the "1963 Dress Code Americana". Currant knew immediately that they were time-cops.

As they approached the four time travelers, Currant's mind spun into a "fight or flight" mode, then locked down into a "screw it"' state of mind. The uniform cop glanced at them as he passed on his way to the restaurant entrance. He gave a little tip of his cap to Emma. She smiled weakly. The other three drifted behind in a single file. 'Frenchy' stayed glum and kept walking. Nearing them, the tall one slowed down, and he and the old one stood together facing them. It was like a budget version of one of Emma's spaghetti Westerns, thought Currant. He could almost hear the music from *The Good, Bad, and the Ugly* playing in the background.

"Howdy, buckaroos," said the old guy as if he meant it.

Currant smiled. "Nice day, pilgrim," said Currant as if he meant it.

The tall one looked over to the Chevy and back. "Nice car. Mind if I take a look?" Without waiting for a response, he drifted over toward the car.

"No problem. Knock yourself out," said Currant.

The old man moved closer. "Say, you're a mighty

good-looking batch of buckaroos. You remind me of my youth." He looked into Currant's eyes. "Captain Bobby R. Sykes, Texas Rangers...didn't catch your name, friend."

Currant stayed with his eyes. "Didn't throw it...but you can call me Doc."

The old guy smiled broadly, took off his hat, and beat it into his knee, creating a puff of dust. OK, Doc. Nice knowing 'ya. How's the food in this cantina?"

Currant played along. "Best food East of the Pecos."

"So they say." He summoned up a silly grin. "Would you all mind if I took a quick snapshot? Something for the wife to see, so she doesn't get the idea that me and my boys are just out eating and drinking all day. She'd be mighty pleased to know I've been talkin' to a pretty little cowgirl like you, Miss."

"I suppose that would be OK. My students are used to the attention. Here in Texas, the four of us stand out like a peg-legged man at a hoedown. We're not from these parts...we're from Chicago. How 'bout you, pilgrim?"

"Coming from Big D...lookin' for bad guys. You seen any?"

"Nope."

The old guy smiled. "Thought not. Say, what about that picture?" He pulled an Instamatic camera from his jacket.

Currant nodded, and they assembled four abreast—Ethan, Emma, Zak, and A.C. He glanced over and watched the tall guy rising up from the other side of the car as if he had been checking the tire. Then the man circled the Chevy, nodding and smiling as if he was going to buy it.

"Smile..." said the old guy as he took their picture. "Very nice. Mabel will like that one. Happy trails to you." He stretched out a parting look for each of them. Then for Emma, he gripped the brim of his beat-up "pork pie" hat..."Ma'am," he drawled. He tossed out a toothy smile and gave them all a jaunty wave, then walked away. He and the tall guy mozied along into the restaurant, talking and laughing.

"Happy trails, pardner," Currant muttered to himself. Quickly he huddled with the team. "Let's go now," he said. "Zak, you drive, and Ethan, you get my valise out of the trunk."

Zak and Ethan nodded in agreement. Emma looked puzzled.

"What's up?" She asked as they walked rapidly to the car.

"They're time-cops," said Currant. "They know who we are. We're getting out of here as fast as possible."

They popped into the convertible. Zak took the wheel—Emma, shotgun—Ethan and Currant in the back seat. Pebbles and dust blew out behind the Chevy as it chewed its way onto the road.

"Take it up to sixty-five, Zak. No more," said Currant as he searched the paisley valise on the seat next to him.

Emma turned back. Her arm hung over the edge of the front seat. Her hair flew wildly, and her eyes danced with excitement. "What about the photo? His camera looked just like my camera. The one they took from me in Dallas. I wonder if they developed our shots?"

"Sure they did. Did you take one of the Chevy?"

She nodded.

"That's how they found us. Sorry about the photo he took. It couldn't be helped. But don't worry, it won't matter," said Currant flatly.

"What do you mean?"

"They'll be on to us again soon enough. They probably hid a transmitter in the car. They want to follow us to our 'rabbit hole.' They don't want to make a fuss here in 1963. They just want to track us to Mystic Heights. Then they'll relay our location to 'the future. We'll be grabbed as soon as we pop our heads out of the ground in 2028."

"What can we do?"

"Wait...I'll take care of it." For forty minutes, Currant sat quietly with his arms outstretched on the seatback. The wind blew his hair about. The sun-baked his face. He was at peace. Red soil was giving way to grassland. Texas was getting prettier until they heard the sound of the plane again.

"There it is," shouted Emma. Her face wore a desperate look.

A.C. looked up and spotted the plane. "Right on time. A sandwich and a beer, and they're right back on us. Now we'll never shake them off," said Currant without emotion. "Zak. Keep a steady pace, son. Ethan...you squeeze over in the corner." Currant reached into his paisley bag and withdrew a tubular, dull metal object. He looked again into the sky. They were pacing them on his side of the car. No pretending anymore, the old 'Texas Ranger' knew his quarry was running out of time—no deviations—no delay—the time travelers had to head straight home. The plane followed them mile-for-mile as they neared the Arkansas border. Since the Chevy traveled slower, the pilot compensated by running figure-eight patterns in the sky. Currant figured they were locking in on the location transmitter they had planted on their car.

"What's that?" asked Emma looking back.

"Pulsed energy weapon. Hand-held. 2500-yard range. Causes no physical damage except for a little extra heat and sound. But it plays havoc with the human nervous system." He twisted and extended the front of the tube, doubling its length. The device had handles on either side, a flat perforated metal box hung beneath, and a thick polished black disk was fixed to its back. "Zak. Maintain a straight, steady pace." Currant rolled up the rear window a couple of inches to use as a brace. He then pulled out a rod from the center of the device and attached its base to the window. He could now pivot the device with control in any direction. "Steady Zak. We'll probably have only one chance at this."

Zak didn't look back. He was a rock.

"Are you going to shoot at them with that?" asked Emma.

"Right," said Current. "Remember, this is my

business. You have nothing to do with this decision. Duck your head now, Emma." He made sure she followed his order. "Good." He verified Ethan was clear.

He was ready. He armed the weapon by placing his index finger on the disk's sensor location. In a second, the glow of a green light indicator twinkled in his eyes. Currant looked through the weapon's viewport. The device came alive, emitting a low-pitched whine. Rapidly, both the volume and pitch rose. The plane began another crossing pattern in front of the car. Currant brought the tube around and aimed the weapon at the plane's cockpit. The device screamed. He gently squeezed the trigger buttons of both handles simultaneously. In seconds it locked onto the target. There was a loud popping sound, and an almost sensuous dazzling ball of red-orange plasma rolled out of the device and expanded into a colorful fuzzy funnel. Currant held his position and watched the mystery unfold. "So long, pilgrim..." muttered Currant.

Emma lifted her head to see. "Nothing happened," she said with a hint of relief. The plane continued on.

"Wait," said Currant. Seconds passed. Then, almost imperceptibly, the nose of the plane began to drop—a little—then lower and lower—finally, it pointed straight down. As it crossed in front of them, it went into a screaming dive.

Emma covered her eyes as it hit the ground and burst into flames a few hundred yards to the left side of the road. She screamed. "You killed them all."

Zak looked in the rearview mirror. For a second, Currant's eyes caught his. Zak tossed his head back and gripped the wheel tightly. Then he relaxed. He exhaled a lung full of tension and reached over to hold Emma's hand. She looked at him for a moment, then turned back, dropped her shoulders, rested her head on the seatback, and stared blankly into the sky.

Currant disarmed and repacked the weapon tossing it on the seat next to him. He leaned forward so everyone could hear him clearly. "I did it. Remember, I did it. Not you. This is the risk we took. This is the fate of time travelers and time-cops. Something had to give."

Emma sat stoically. Zak drove in silence, still holding her hand. Ethan pulled himself out of the corner, tapped Currant on the shoulder, and extended his hand. A.C. accepted his gesture. They shook hands. "Thanks, Doctor," he said quietly. "Thanks for everything."

-Chapter XXV-

2028 Redux

On the twenty-eighth day of time travel in the early morning, just outside New York City, Currant wheeled the Chevy into a post office parking lot. They were in the "home stretch." He knew the time-cops were out of the picture. Joell was back in 2028, and "Captain Bobby Sykes" and his friends were now only an unsolvable mystery for the medical examiner. In Little Rock, the time travelers had electronically scanned the car. Their search revealed a single location transmitter inside the rear bumper, a gift from the tall tramp. Ethan tossed it into the back of a passing semi-truck headed west to throw off any remaining hounds. But Currant was now unconcerned about time-cops. He had taken care of them. He wanted to return to Mystic Heights and the *TimeTravelle* as quickly as possible.

But first things first, thought Currant, time to settle up with Quinn. To be on the safe side, he bought five first-class stamps for 25 cents. He licked and applied them to the envelope one by one, just like he had done 65 years ago in his home in Covington. The taste of the stamps brought back a flood of memories—of his youth, his mother and father, and the house they shared so briefly with his brother Patrick. Currant floated ahead through the decades that followed. What was it all about, he wondered—a whirlwind of people, places, and things. He invented the time machine for one reason. He hoped that when he returned, all his efforts would be rewarded. He addressed the little square envelope to the reporter, Tom Quinn, and then planted it in the mailbox. It landed quietly atop the other written invitations, notices, bills, complaints, fears, threats, rewards, hopes, dreams, and all the other important human concerns of that day in

1963, piled letter-upon-letter in the box. Maybe there were even some children's letters to Santa. In a few days, back from the horrors of Dallas, Quinn might look upon the one he received from Santa Currant, the master of time travel, as an early Christmas gift. Quinn was a good man and a great friend. He deserved nothing but the best. Currant smiled and returned to the car.

Three more hours of steady driving brought the time travelers back to Mystic Heights. They cruised through town in their nifty car, gathering looks of appreciation from the town folk.

Currant exhaled loudly. "It's good to be home. Isn't it?"

"You're so right, Doctor. It's been a long trip," said Ethan stretching his arms out, his hands pushing into the fabric top.

"Don't stretch it, Ethan. It's a classic," said A.C., not smiling.

"Sorry, boss," he replied as he carefully withdrew his hands.

Emma's voice floated up to Currant and Ethan from the back. She had been sleeping with her head on Zak's shoulder, but now she returned to life. "You won't believe this. But I'm actually looking forward to going home. I want to sleep in my own bed and be at peace in my own house. This trip has been very stressful. And Zak." She looked at her seatmate. "Zak, you will be able to talk again. I'll bet you are excited about that."

Zak nodded and signed to affirm her speculation.

"What are you going to do with this car?" Ethan asked. "You can't take it with you."

"You'll be surprised," replied the inventor as he patted his hand on the dashboard.

They drove up the winding road that led away from the heart of Mystic Heights and toward the war memorial. Currant scanned the ocean to his left. It was a beautiful clear, nippy day with sun reflecting brightly off the blue water. A few die-hard sailors skirted about in small boats, denying the change of seasons. It was late November

1963, and winter was coming. As Currant glanced at the boats, he contemplated the seasons of his own life. For some lucky people, it was human nature to live in the *now* and ignore the future. The aging time machine magician vowed to himself that, except when riding the *TimeTravelle*, he would become such a person. Then he saw a dirt road to the right, and he quickly cut the Chevy into the turn.

"Where are we headed?" Ethan asked.

"You'll see."

A few minutes of bouncy driving brought them to an old farm. A.C. smiled as he drove into an entry drive and parked in front of a run-down barn building. A short distance away, an old stone foundation was all that remained of a long-ago farmhouse. He got out, and the others joined him.

Ethan stretched. "Days of cross-country driving are enough for me. I'm beat. What's happening?"

Currant smiled. "I own this place. Or at least I will own it in about fifteen years. Belonged to my mother's grandfather originally."

"Lucky you," said Emma with a smirk.

"It doesn't look like much, but it will serve my purpose." Currant pulled a heavy lock and chain from the trunk of the car. "Follow me," he said, walking toward the silo. They stood at the base of the tall structure. A rectangular one-story windowless stone box of a building was attached to the deteriorating round stone silo. He pulled open a pair of large doors, revealing a spacious workroom. It was large enough to accommodate an automobile. In a matter of minutes, the Chevy was tucked into the building. Currant enlisted the help of Zak and Ethan to place four large stones under the axles at the wheels. Then one by one, he released the air in the tires so that the car now rested on the boulders. He grabbed a large tarpaulin from the trunk, and they carefully covered the car from bumper to bumper.

"Thank you, fellows. This will be mine in a few years. I just hope she starts then." Currant grabbed the paisley cloth valise that contained their tools, the weapon, and the remaining money. He left the other bags in the trunk. The doors swung closed, the chain was engaged, and the lock buckled. "So long, my friend," said Currant.

"You better hope that no one discovers your Bel Air beauty," said Emma.

Currant smiled. "Got that figured out." He pulled a couple of metal signs from his bag. They each read: *QUARANTINED. Dangerous Toxic Waste. Do Not Enter.* For added measure, they included a skull and bones graphic and the address of the county health office. He nailed the two signs to trees at either side of the entrance. "Let's go home, guys. We've done enough," he said. He checked his watch. "We have exactly sixteen minutes to take our positions."

Fourteen minutes later, they were all in position facing the chessboard, wearing goggles, breathing heavily from their fast walk from the farm. Emma east, Ethan west, Currant south, and Zak north had their spot in front of a paired column.

Sea birds soared overhead, floating on the invisible. A.C. took one last look at the town of Mystic Heights in 1963. Then, he looked at his charges and shouted, "Do not move!" Randall Tower's clock hands pointed to the heavens, and it chimed melodically. The bell rang: seven, eight, nine, ten, eleven—twelve was lost in time. The crackling sounds commenced. Colors danced before them. Then the background removed itself—a crazy waterfall of noise—they were going back to the future. Images appeared to fly by all around him. His stomach rebelled. He was getting sick. I'm too old for this, he thought. Then the blinding white light, and they were back. Currant was buckled over. He looked up and stared at his three friends. They all laughed almost hysterically. From someplace, Currant heard a distant voice. Slowly, he removed his goggles. His ears rang.

"Doctor Currant. You made it back. You're alive," shouted Jacques Dufour. He ran to Currant and threw his arms around him. *"Mon ami. Mon ami. Tu retournes."*

Currant shook his head to clear it. He looked at his old friend. "*Qui. Dufour. Je retourne. Je suis ici.*" He looked around. The others seemed groggy, also. For some reason, the return trip in time was far more taxing on the human body than their travel to 1963, kind of a 'jumbo-jetlag,' thought Currant.

Warren Wright rolled up in his *gyromobe* and greeted his two children giving each a bear hug. "Did you have to wait until the twenty-eighth day? You had me worried."

"Come on, Dad," said Ethan. "We got wrapped up in our case."

"Forget the case," said Emma. "I'm happy to be back." She smiled and hugged her father again. "Love you, Dad."

Mr. Wright kissed her on the forehead. And then he did something astounding. He stepped out of the *gyromobe* and stood straight and tall in front of the Twins.

"Dad. You can walk," said Ethan and Emma together. Tears rushed down Emma's cheeks.

Wright smiled broadly. "That I can. Thanks to the good doctor. His baseball skills and the 'butterfly' effect."

Currant walked up to Mr. Wright and hugged him. "Damn. So this is what it was all about. I stop a little red ball from going into the street in Chicago in 1963...."

"And the toddler doesn't run out into traffic. And the car doesn't swerve to dodge him. And it doesn't smash into another car killing two people. Those people were the parents of the cop who accidentally shot me. So that man can continue his schooling. And he graduates from law school instead of joining the police force. Therefore he was not there to shoot me in the back five years ago. And it doesn't happen. And as you can see, I am here walking around enjoying this reunion."

"I take back everything I said about you, Warren. Even if it was in jest. You are a great detective," declared Currant.

"Elementary my Dear Currant...elementary," said Wright. "And thanks again...from my heart." He did a mock bow in front of the inventor with a flourish. "I bequeath you, my *gyromobe*," said Wright.

"Thanks, Warren. I may be getting a little older, but I'm not there yet. I've got a few good miles left in me." Then spontaneously, Currant danced a little jig around the Twins, Mr. Wright and Jacques Dufour. "See," he said. "You can walk. And I can dance. Isn't it great?"

Dufour broke away from the group and grabbed something from a nearby table. Quickly, he walked over to Zak, who had been sitting quietly in the corner. "Here. I'll bet you'll be happy to have this back."

Zak smiled and took the *Voicenator,* quickly affixing it to his neck. He activated it and approached his friends. "Hey," he said in a loud and clear voice. "It's my turn to talk. In fact, for the next month, I'm going to do all the talking. Man, this is wonderful. I felt like a lion without teeth in 1963. It's good to be back."

Emma interjected. 'I'm sure you have a lot to say, but that will have to wait. I want to talk...." Emma smiled. "Just kidding, Zak. Talk away. Talk to yourself. Talk to the moon. Talk to the animals. Talk. Talk. Talk. Enjoy." She gave him a big hug.

"Well, I will say one thing more," said Zak. "This was the most exciting time of my life. Thanks, Dr. Currant."

They all nodded. "You're the best. We had some tough times, but you kept it going, and without the *TimeTravelle,* nothing would have happened," said Ethan.

"OK. Enough. Remember, you're just journalism students. Show some respect for your teacher." Currant tapped his hand on his vest pocket to make the point. Then he seemed mystified for a moment. He reached into his pocket and pulled out a tiny toy-sized silver 2017 Mercedes Benz coupe. He held it up to the light, checking it out from all angles. "I wonder where my *Batman* comic is...?"

The others did not understand. He gave the toy a tiny kiss as if it was an old friend and gently placed it back into his pocket. "I got this when I was a little boy from a friend in 1963...a very nice man." He laughed softly.

"Dr. Currant," said Dufour. "I have another surprise for you. Someone has come a long way to be here." He pointed to an area off the platform in a dark recess of the lab. On cue, someone walked into the bright lights. An older man approached. He looked old—someone who, unlike Currant, couldn't benefit from the miracle anti-aging cures that came on the market too late for him.

Current, still recovering from the effects of the return to 2028, squinted his eyes, searching his mental recesses for recognition. As the man neared, he looked familiar to A.C., but he could not say for sure. Then it came to him.

"Patrick?" he asked delicately.

"Yes, A.C.," said the man smiling gently.

Currant legs became shaky, and he wavered for a moment. Then he reached out, and the two men shook hands. He looked into his brother's eyes, and his own eyes filled with tears. He grabbed him and hugged him. After a long time, they separated. Currant reached into his pocket and pulled out the little car. "Remember this?"

Dr. Patrick MacAndrew Brennan held the toy and studied it. "I do remember. One day back in the mid-Sixties, Mom found five large cut diamonds hidden right here under the hood. They were worth quite a bundle in those days. Hey, you didn't have anything to do with that, did you?"

Currant smiled. "Just an 'anonymous' donor providing for the higher education of two poor kids from Louisiana who wanted to make a difference."

"You always said this was your lucky charm. So it is. Thanks, little brother."

"A world-famous cancer researcher." Currant smiled broadly.

The old man nodded. "Some say."

Dufour interjected. "He's being too modest, A.C. He wiped that scourge off the face of the planet."

"My brother. My brother Patrick. You saved the life of a time-cop named Joell. I'm very grateful for that. It's so good to be with you."

Patrick nodded without understanding.

The Twins and Zak smiled knowingly as the two brothers reached out and hugged each other again on the bridge of time.

"One more thing, Patrick," said Currant releasing his grip. He looked into his long-lost sibling's eyes with a twinkle in his own. "Did you ever want to drive a red and white '55 Chevy Bel Air convertible?"

Patrick Brennan smiled broadly. "Do you have one?"

"I do now, brother. Let's do it."

"*Hijole!*" said Zak. "A big hand for the Chevy boys."

Everyone laughed and applauded.

Zak reached into his shirt pocket and pulled out a small envelope. Inside, neatly folded in half, was the strip of photos they had taken in Chicago. A.C. Currant, Ethan, Emma, and Zak stacked one atop the other in a timeless montage. "Check it out," said Zak. "These beauties are 65 years old."

Ethan snapped them from Zak's hand and took a quick look. He smiled and nodded. "Everyone looks great. Thankfully your feet wouldn't fit into the booth, Emma."

"What?"

"Just kidding."

Emma looked down at her feet. "My feet aren't too big. Are they?"

"Enormous," said Ethan laughing. "Ask anyone in 1963. Enormous, Sis. But I'll bet they'll look great in the year 2058."

"Warm up the *TimeTravelle,* Dr. Currant," said Emma. "Let's send my dinosaur-brained brother back to the Stone Age."

LOG of Zak Newman --- January 1, 2029

Today is New Year's Day, 2029. Good and bad people around the world are recalling the past and setting goals for the future. For better or worse, the Time Travel Twins, Dr. Currant, and I did manage to modify The History. *Somewhere, there is a time-cop named Joell who owes his life to Patrick Brennan's efforts to eliminate cancer. Brennan, the man who conquered cancer for all mankind, owes his life to his little brother, A.C. Currant. And thanks to Dr. Currant, Mr. Wright can walk again. That's all good.*

JFK is still dead. In the decades that have passed, his bones have been thoroughly worked over by his enemies—they say he was a philanderer—a drug user—a dangerous incompetent—easy on Communists—etc. etc. In time, the media seemed to ease up a little, presenting him as more humanized. They showed a man with obvious weaknesses but also someone with the strength to attempt to build bridges to boogeymen enemies like the U.S.S.R. He was also a leader with a strong sense of human decency, able to sanction and breathe life into the Civil Rights movement. Camelot was a public relations exercise, but President John F. Kennedy was not. He was a man who tried to make a difference.

While not a total bust, the whole continuing assassination cover-up is now only an oft-told fairy tale called The Warren Commission Report. *When the Chicago attempt to kill JFK failed, it opened the doors to Dallas, and while the power structure did manage to kill the President, it was a mess. The whole JFK assassination package made no sense, no matter how it was massaged by the media, the politicians, and the spooks. Over the years, hundreds of books have been written exposing almost every detail and player in the conspiracy. Still, those authors have been consistently ignored by the major media or written off as kooks or fools. The JFK assassination has become our nation's "elephant in the living room"—very obvious, painfully ignored, and the cause of great damage to the country. The American people suffer from attention deficit disorder, and as Emma says, "they can't handle the truth." Maybe they could, but the corporate-owned media will never provide that opportunity. Emma also recommends the old movie* Network—*done in the 1970s— for those who* "are as mad as hell and can't take it anymore." *I've seen it. The depressing thing is that it is still very relevant in 2029. The more things change...*

Our reporter friend Quinn helped straighten out The History. *He doggedly pursued the case for the rest of his life and won the Pulitzer Prize for his efforts. His investigative work led to a Congressional Investigation in 1978—it spawned many additional 'shut-them-up' witness murders—and Congress ultimately declared the JFK killing "to be the result of a conspiracy"—of course, the Justice Department and FBI publicly ignored this revelation, but quietly, over time, they did lock up some of the bottom-of-the-pyramid conspirators—mostly mobsters. The politicians, military, governmental agents, and influential private citizens were left untouched. Quinn ended his career as a consultant to Oliver Stone for his* JFK *movie. The "Umbrella Man" lives on in that movie and as an iconic mystery. Over time, several men have claimed to be the 'bombastic Bumbershoot,' but we know the real "Umbrella Man." Of course, Dr. Currant's plan to make himself part of history failed because his ever-present fear of time-police keeps his eyes wide open and his mouth shut. Once and a while, people notice the resemblance. Currant can only chuckle and deny it.*

What else? Johnson didn't get impeached. Even though he was a big crook and the most likely candidate for puppet master of the "Crime of the Century." On November 22, 1963, some of his more apparent crimes caught up with him. The big, bossy Texan had one foot in a jail cell that day, but LBJ was in control of the country after JFK was conveniently eliminated. Once in power, he quickly terminated all investigations that would expose his criminal alliance with Billy Sol Estes, mobsters, and killers. He dreamed of becoming a great President who would implement far-reaching, pork-filled social programs and conquer the inferior North Vietnamese by winning the war in a blaze of Presidential glory. To do this, he mortgaged the financial and moral future of the country. Eventually, the Vietnam War shrunk his giant genitals and ego. He scurried off the pages of history like a frightened rat.

And Richard Cain, our man in Chicago, died like JFK in 1973; they blew his head off. Two masked men entered a Chicago diner, told all the patrons, including Cain, to line up against the wall, and then one of them fired a shotgun into Cain's head. He fell to the floor, and the other gave him a second head blast. His secrets died with him.

Another nasty dude, J. Edgar Hoover, the head of the FBI, died in bed. The funeral was closed-casket. Rumor has it he was buried in his favorite simple black sheath with a single string of pearls around his neck. Considering his treasonous actions, it should have been a rope.

Fidel Castro retained his little Caribbean Commie beachhead until he died of natural causes in 2015. Cuba is now a fine place to vacation—golfing, fishing, gambling, and entertainment—just like in the 1950s. The Chinese run Cuba's offshore oil production, and the little island is now one of the richest per capita places in the world. Others didn't fare so well—thousands of dead soldiers in Vietnam and millions of American military muscle victims. Jack's brothers Bobby and Teddy, Martin Luther King, Richard Nixon, Malcolm X, George Wallace, John Lennon, and Ronald Reagan got in the way of "progress." They ignored the message of the ritual killing of JFK in 1963, and they paid the price. However, after Reagan, "the powers that be" ended domestic political "Executive Action." Assassination is now an archaic and obsolete tool. There are no remaining political leaders to be killed. There's no need to kill a corporate president; you just fire him and provide a golden parachute. Corporate America and the rest of the corporate political world rolls on, well-organized, in control, and feeding on its own greed and power. The days of individual, charismatic world leaders are over.

I hope Quinn enjoyed his life. I liked that man. He exemplified the best of his generation—no BS, do your job, and stay true to your values. Before we returned to the future, we sent him that 'Voice-O-Graph' test recording we made on State Street in Chicago sixty-five years ago. I think he always suspected we were different, but he trusted us, and we trusted him. Dr. Currant included a note with the record telling Quinn to watch for the Microsoft IPO in 1986—buy as much stock as possible, even if he had to borrow the funds. We're sure he followed our retirement investment advice. He died peacefully in his Key West oceanfront mansion—very nice indeed. Goodbye, Mr. Quinn. Thanks.

Our time traveling is over for now. But as far as we know, by luck or design, we four travelers somehow *accomplished much of what we set out to do. Maybe in the future, we'll go back to the past again. I can only hope. I'm getting a little bored again. I want to feel alive. Like I did in 1963. I ache for the rush of reality—the unpredictable wildness of an ocean of possibilities—the thrill of anticipating the unknown tomorrow. I crave all this and those delicious five-cent candy bars.*

END LOG

-THE END-

BOOKS BY OTHERS RELATED TO THE EVENTS DESCRIBED IN SAVING JFK

Crossfire: The Plot that Killed Kennedy by Jim Marrs
Published by Basic Books. 1993

Say Goodbye to America by Matthew Smith
Mainstream Publishing. 2001

A Farewell to Justice by Joan Mellen
Published by Potomac Books, Inc. 2005

Ultimate Sacrifice by Waldron and Hartman
Published by Carroll & Graf. 2005

Legacy of Secrecy by Waldron and Hartman
Published by Counterpoint Press. 2008

JFK and the Unspeakable by James W. Douglass
Published by Orbis Books. 2008

The Echo from Dealey Plaza by Abraham Bolden
Published by Harmony Books. 2008

Last Word by Mark Lane.
Skyhorse Publishing. 2011

LBJ: The Mastermind of the JFK Assassination
by Philip F. Nelson. Skyhorse Publishing 2011

Patriotism Unhinged 1963-2024 by James Manning
2025

TIME TRAVEL TWINS

By W. Green

SAVING JFK
Volume 1
The Twins want to stop the Chicago assassination of JFK in November 1963 and create a better future for their world of 2028.

X-OOMING FDR
Volumes 2, 3, 4
Determined to redesign history and the life of a man who is only a footnote in the history books of the 21st century, the Twins travel into danger and intrigue.

SAVING TRUMP
Volume 5
The year is 2016, and the Twins and Zak team up with their descendants, Samantha and Jason Keene, during the presidential election. Donald Trump is in...but does he continue?

Thanks for Reading *Saving JFK*

Did you like the book? Reviews help the author get the word out. Please create an on-line review. And check out the other books in this series. Thanks.
---W. Green